THE BROKEN DEAD

THE BROKEN DEAD

OTHERWORLDLY ANARCHIST

BOOK FOUR

Dreamer's Riot

Podium

Cover design by Mika Hiyashiro

ISBN: 979-8-3470-2860-3

Published in 2026 by Podium Publishing
www.podiumentertainment.com

Podium

THE BROKEN DEAD

CHAPTER ONE

The Past

The water is everywhere, violent and sharp. It batters and bloats me like a forgotten corpse. I fight to break free, but I can't swim. I feel whole, but as I struggle against the waves, only one hand exists to push the currents back. The sharpest waves carry the past with them, cutting into me and carrying my blood into the rapids around me. A thousand mistakes tear at me, a little at a time, taking just a little skin as each collides with me. I can't stop it; I can't even breathe.

Some of them are easy, their stings tolerable and familiar. An argument with Ed. Waiting too long to tell them about Annie. Realizing my father would hate me in this life as much as the last. Learning both of my parents hated me the first time. Then I am slapped in the face as I open my door, and I know it's coming. But not yet. First, I have other mistakes to remember. They grow more painful. Mary, the child hoping for a brighter future. The girl I couldn't protect. The other house of penance, burned to the ground. These eat at me far more. Then I am in a room with Autumn, yelling at her, treating her like a woman far older than she was. I try to turn away, but I am on a rooftop with her, fighting to want to save her. A rooftop I put her on. And I know it is coming.

Darian's spell forms over the city because I was too slow. Grief like an avalanche tries to drown me. I use it to fight back, but I can't save them all. I can't. People are dying in the hundreds because I wasn't careful enough, wasn't fast enough, strong enough. And their deaths were painful, sudden. How must it have felt for their loved ones, to have a life and a family and to see them gone in a moment? How must it have hurt?

I felt it. Every single one. I want to turn away, but I can't. I'm still being beaten and drowned by the furious waves. And then I am there, in that old, abandoned building, joking with my brother, making light of my own misery as he retrieves the jewelry from my missing arm. I feel sick. I want to stop it, to change it. I can feel the mistake—when I break my promise to my mother. I can't watch it happen again. I can't.

I have no choice.

I turn, and I leave. I leave him there, after he helped to save my life. After he helped to keep me stable and sane. I leave him there. "Stay safe." These were the last words I would ever say to my brother. "Stay safe." What a fucking joke. What does that even mean, in a city that is about to burn? "Stay safe." Stay fucking safe. I left him with a platitude, and he died.

This doesn't just cut into me—it tears through me. It carves a hole in my chest and tears at the flesh around my heart. It hurts. It hurts too much to bear, and suddenly, I am back on that rooftop, not stopping Autumn from jumping but pushing her myself. Then I am there again, but I fall instead. One more day. That is what I'd said to her: One more day. I can face one more day. One. More. Day.

My eyes are weary as I open them to a blurry world. There is something . . . red in my face. My body is sore, revealing the poor quality of my sleep. Thick, crusty rheum cakes my eyes as I struggle to focus.

"Annie, are you all right?" Sara asks. I blink a couple times, and the red blur resolves into her auburn hair, hanging over me as she jostles my shoulders. "You were . . . whimpering in your sleep again." I bite my lip in embarrassment at this. As I regain consciousness, I become disgustingly aware that I've sweat through my nightshirt again. This does not help banish the feeling of vulnerability.

"Sorry, I didn't mean to wake you," I apologize. Sarafyna has been through so much more than me, and yet, every single morning for two weeks, I have woken her up with my nightmares of leaving Henry behind. "We do have a spare tent. You don't have to deal with me every morning. I know you must be tired," I offer. I don't know how I want her to respond. Her warmth has been what allows me to sleep every night, but the burden of putting that on her is unfair, and it is getting to me.

"I want to be here with you. I like being here with you. And I could never leave you trapped in a dream like that," she dismisses. Her hand runs along my arm as she says this, and I feel that familiar spark of warmth. It's small, but it radiates through me and helps thaw the ice in my blood. "Come on, let's get cleaned up and make breakfast. It's not long until sunrise."

I sniff then nod as she stands. Even at night, shrouded in darkness, she is beautiful. I don't know if I could keep doing this without her. But I can. "One more day," I whisper.

"One more day," she agrees, looking down at me one more time with a gentle smile. Her scars are more prominent than ever now; the scars not just of her past but of what she did to survive it. I haven't seen them fade or disappear since we took her back from the Kingdom of Endings. This too is beautiful.

I finally stand as well and put up a sheet so both of us can get dressed. This act carries enough tension to collapse a lung, but neither of us knows how to move past it. We do this every day because, well, life is strange. If we weren't dating, it wouldn't feel strange to change in front of each other. If we had started sleeping together, it would also be normal.

But with everything that has happened . . . it's weird. We are both ready to move forward, but we're both emotionally petrified by our recent history. So we live together. Share a tent while traveling. Sleep in the same bed—or bedroll, as the case may be. But we both feel an ever-building tension we are both too broken to address. Which leaves us with this sheet.

God, I am so useless with this shit now.

As usual, the tension fades a bit as we both emerge from our tent into our quiet campsite. We have been traveling for about a week now, finally fulfilling my promise to Ember. There are no roads on the route we have to take, as close as Sara could get us to this supposed border with the Republic, so we have had to travel on foot. Around us are three more tents for Autumn, August, and Ember, respectively.

As usual, I first look to Autumn's tent, still closed. I lift up my goggles to get a look inside and see her still sleeping, or at least in bed. She hasn't had any more luck with consistent sleep than I have. Ember too remains in her tent, but August's . . . August's tent is empty. Immediately, my hackles rise and my muscles tense.

"Shit, where's August?" I curse. Sara raises an eyebrow and starts looking around while adrenaline floods my body and my breathing shortens.

"August? AUGUST!" I scream. Where did he go? I can't see him anywhere. We don't know what is out here; we've never been this far before. Shit. Shit shit shit. "August, where are you?" I yell again. Sara's hand rests on my shoulder as Autumn bursts out of her tent in her nightgown and a panic, while Ember blearily emerges from hers.

"August is missing?" Autumn immediately interrogates while Ember wrinkles her nose. I keep scanning the mundane evergreen trees all around us, but he fails to present himself.

"Relax, he's taking a piss," Ember dismisses. Almost immediately, the man himself emerges, the colors appearing on my goggles a moment later. I pull them off and see my friend—messy hair and baggy pajama pants—looking at me sheepishly.

"Sorry, sorry. I was only gone a moment!" he apologizes before he sees my face and his own pales. "Are you, uh, all right, Lil?"

I shudder and try to shake it off, forcing my face into a neutral expression. "N-no, I'm sorry. I don't know why I . . . I'm sorry," I apologize.

What was that? Since when have I failed to keep calm over something so small? We haven't run into a single enemy this entire trip, and I'd actually expected some of Ember's old friends to show up at some point. But it has been safe. There is no reason to react so strongly to an empty tent. I must have seen and missed him with my radar spell, if he was that close. But I was panicking. Over nothing.

Fuck, this could get dangerous. I can't be like this. People are counting on me to be better than this. I can see the same thought in Ember's eyes. "One more day," I whisper again. Autumn catches my eye and gives me a hesitant nod.

After bringing down every king of Potestia, I had promised to help Ember. Or at least see what her country was like; meet the sages. But she needs the woman who fought for Potestia, not this puddle of sweat and anxiety. How does Sara manage like she does all the time? How has she gone into the Radiant Woods so many times? I feel like I am the one shackled now. Once loss has struck once, it's like it lurks around every corner, waiting for an opportunity to strike again.

No one says anything to me. Autumn and Sara understand. August does a little. And Ember . . . is Ember. She is at her best when she is quiet. It is awkward as we put breakfast together and pack up the tents. No one speaks, really. But we have to get going. Another day on the road.

We are quiet for hours. Ember is always too annoyed to talk to anyone, Autumn hardly ever speaks at all, and the awkward exchange this morning has silenced the rest of us. I spend the time reflecting on the state of my family when we left. My mother's artificial warmth. Gilbert's pleading that I stay. And Ed's . . . I don't know how to describe Ed. He seems to have disconnected from reality entirely. One look at Sara reveals she is thinking of her own family, Sam and Peter.

It's a somber march toward Republic land.

That is, until we emerge from the woods and a black dot finally appears on the horizon. Ember's actual hackles rise.

"There it is. The barrier. I hope you are ready, Sarafyna. New sages often struggle to pass through this," Ember advises. I squint, but I can't make it out.

"That's maintained by Nexus energy?" I ask. "Any idea how that works?"

"How the fuck should I know," Ember retorts. "I just know you can't pass through without a Nexus sage, and it protects us from the Nexus itself." I roll my eyes at her.

"My apologies," I intone. "I will stop asking questions. I'll communicate exclusively with meaningless hand signals and make a plan to kill the sages based on whatever information that provides." I don't expect her to be sunshine and rainbows, but for fuck's sake, is she going to make me regret every damn thing I don't know shit about?

"Just don't waste my time with questions I obviously would have told you about before, all right?" she grumbles, and I roll my eyes again.

"You know, I'd say you talk like someone who has never had their ass kicked, but I know for a fact that you have. Don't make me sic my girl-friend on you," I quip back. I say that, but I feel slightly grateful at the same time. For how insufferable she is, bickering with her makes me feel a little normal again. It allows me to think of, well, something that isn't my brother.

"It's . . . It's wrong," Sara interjects, and I'm immediately covered in gooseflesh.

"What do you mean?" I ask as she shudders.

"It's like the Radiant Woods but . . . sturdier? I don't know. I don't know . . ." She trails off while I nod, moving closer to her and running my left hand against her back. Or, my real hand. I am still unused to my right; it feels real but . . . *not*, at the same time. I can't tell if it actually itches or if that is a phantom feeling from the real limb I lost. In any case, we keep walking, and the speck in the distance gradually grows into, well, not a speck.

A massive obsidian stone hovers in the sky. Even I can feel it now—the air around it, trying to reject us. To push us back. Every moment, I think it is too large to exist; then, a moment later, I learn I was not as close as I thought, and it is even larger. Hours pass, partially due to distance and partially due to the slowing effect proximity to it seems to have.

Everyone is exhausted by the time we stand beneath it, but eventually, it is nearly directly above us, and Ember holds out a hand, making contact with an invisible wall.

"This is it," she says. "We won't be safe once we pass through. There will be monsters. There will be bandits. And worst of all, there will be the Guardians of Stone. We cannot let our guards down, and if we run into anyone sapient, let me speak first," she warns. "You will reveal your ignorance too quickly if any of you do."

"If only there had been a friendly resident of this country to answer our questions over the week it took us to get here." I scoff while she glares at me. "Yeah, I get it. We appoint you public relations manager, the job you were clearly born for. Come on, we need to get through. This stone in the sky is giving me the creeps."

"I agree; we gotta get out of here," August chimes in.

"That would be up to our local sage here," Ember responds, looking at Sara, who is biting her lip and rubbing her arms as if she is cold.

"You all right, Sara?" I ask, suddenly less focused on shit talking Ember and far more focused on the woman next to me. I need to pay more attention to her. If I have been struggling with the loss of Henry, how much must she have been fighting with her own trauma this entire time?

"I'm . . . fine," she replies. "Just . . . It's just not right. It feels like sickness. Like if sickness left my body and filled the air around me, but I can still feel it. You're right, we need to get far away from here." With that, she holds up one hand, and I can feel the pressure in the air lessen. Ember actually stumbles as the wall she is pressing her hand to seems to turn to liquid.

I nod, wasting no more of our time or Sara's effort than necessary. Taking a deep breath, I walk forward into a brand-new world.

CHAPTER TWO

Across the Border

Moving through the border feels like fighting my body in a dream. Like I don't quite exist in reality and the signals from my brain to my body aren't translating correctly.

Well, most of my body feels like this; stubborn, slow, and pained. Or perhaps it would be more accurate to say all my body feels this way. My right arm, leg, and left foot don't struggle at all; my new . . . pieces. The bits I haven't accepted yet, and the pieces that run entirely off mana.

With this in mind, I send mana through my entire body, almost like I'm making a modification. Instead of altering my DNA, however, I simply move the rest of my body, like I am using a remote control on myself. The experience is . . . bizarre, but it works. I move much more quickly and freely, emerging into freedom in a matter of minutes.

Looking back, I see the rest of the group continuing to struggle. Ember has a look of intense focus, but she sort of always has that. Nevertheless, she moves quite slowly. Autumn has her arm around August's shoulders, and he carries the both of them through, lagging well behind Ember. Sara stands directly in the middle, her hands to either side as if she is holding the sides of a doorframe. Her face is remarkably peaceful, even bringing a slight blush to my cheeks as I watch her. She doesn't struggle to control herself at all. Her efforts go entirely toward helping us through. As always.

How does she do it? After everything she has lived through, after what the Nexus did to her, how does she make herself vulnerable to it again?

My panic at August's absence earlier in the morning haunts me. It's not the first time I have overreacted since Henry's death. Even leaving my family behind, in a safe place, was hard for me. After leaving Henry behind and . . . I know I can't protect my friends all the time. I know I can't protect my family all the time. I have to trust them to fight on their own while I am not around. I know this. I have always known this. But the concept of the cost and the cost itself . . .

Henry was smiling when I left him. He trusted me, and he paid for it. And I can never apologize for my failure. How can I take friends to hostile territory and turn my back on them again? How can I face my pain like Sarafyna does? I don't know. But I need to figure it out.

As I run in this little hamster wheel in my mind, Ember emerges, irritated as ever. Well, almost. She is irritated, but something is . . . missing. It's almost like meeting an identical twin. That feeling of recognition colliding with an indescribable understanding that you are looking at a different person. It's not exactly the same; I do recognize her as Ember, but . . . I feel more comfortable around her, despite her scowl. Like some weight between us has been lifted for some reason.

In fact, now that I am distracted from . . . Now that I am distracted, I realize it's not just Ember. I feel like I've just removed weights from my arms and legs. I am no stronger, but I feel lighter than I have for as long as I can remember. Like seeing the night sky from the desert instead of the city for the first time.

"What is taking them so long? That was a far easier trip across the border than the last. Your girlfriend there is a remarkably powerful sage. Those twins should already be here," Ember complains. Whatever has changed about her, it isn't her winning personality.

"Well, they haven't crossed it before; you have. Cut them some slack," I rebuke.

"It didn't seem to bother you much," she challenges, and I sigh.

"Yes, well. I lost a lot of weight recently," I explain, flexing the mesh-covered fingers of my artificial hand. "Made it easier."

Ember grunts in irritation. "I don't know why you asked those two to join us. They aren't strong enough; they'll only be a liability. You had far better options," she says, and I take a deep breath through my nose. I want to answer her, but I can't. I don't know why I wanted the twins. Not . . . exactly. I certainly can't articulate it, so I change the subject.

"I need to get stronger myself. A lot stronger. If these sages are as bad as you say, I'm no more prepared to fight them than they are," I respond.

"Especially here, on this side of the border," Ember agrees.

"What does that mean?" I ask. Why would it matter which side of the border we are on?

"You can't feel it? You really are off your game. No matter, you'll see what I mean soon. But you're right; you need to get stronger. Do you have a plan for that?" It's her turn to avoid a question, I see. I'll have time to ask about that tonight. For the time being, I can simply answer her.

I look at my new arm, allowing the royal aura to reveal itself for a moment. It's far weaker than it was in Visenar, but there are fewer people around, and we are farther from the Radiant Woods. Not nearly as much grief to support it. Nevertheless, it looks like defiance of reality itself, cracking and distorting the air around it with colorless mana.

"I need to learn to use this better. If I am going to have these stuck to me, I need to make use of the boost they give me. And, well, now that the cancer is . . . I mean, it isn't gone, but it is under control . . . In any case, I can start altering my body again. A lot of dead bad guys who wouldn't be dead without my crimes against the Collector on that front," I answer honestly.

Ember physically recoils at the final suggestion but seems to regain her composure fairly quickly. She apparently has not moved past her revulsion at altering the body. I really need to ask her about that at some point. It is not unique, exactly. People fear change and loss of control in every world I've lived in. But there is something pervasive about this particular idea that smells of more than just the usual flavor of rotten.

"Well, whatever it is, do it quickly. Now that we've crossed the border, you'll need as many tricks as you can get. You're not in your playpen anymore," she condescends. Again, something in the back of my mind prickles at her words, but nothing feels normal right now. Instead of answering her, I simply examine the mana around my arm. I need to get stronger. I need better, faster spells, and perhaps, I need to consider leaving humanity behind entirely. If anyone can recognize a hot girl after she grows claws, it's my girlfriend. I suppose it depends on how discreet I can remain in this new country.

On the one hand, I am apparently the great evil prophecy of death and destruction come to life. On the other, that's the stupidest fucking thing

I have ever heard in two lives. I will acknowledge that I, apparently, have been reincarnated. I am living an entire second life. I cannot dismiss the idea that there is a goddess somewhere who is responsible for this; I certainly lack a biological explanation for it. But this does not mean I accept that some bullshit prophecy holds water. I'm almost certainly not the only one either. I have seen other women with similar physical traits as well. Even my red eyes, while not extremely common, show up in other people.

I'll talk with Sara about it when she is done. As that thought crosses my mind, Autumn and August emerge at last, exhausted but on the other side. I rush to their side immediately as both gasp for breath. Sara strolls out easily and joins us before I can even speak, putting her hand on Autumn's shoulder and presumably offering her a little divine strength. It works, as the color returns to the weary girl's face.

"Are you all right, Autumn?" I ask quietly.

"That was impressive, Sarafyna. The sage who brought me over last time didn't make it half so easy," Ember calls from behind me. I growl but don't respond. Sara is wrong; I am not the most tone-deaf woman in the world. Or she is intentionally mocking the twins for struggling, in which case, I may need to leave a rotten fish in her tent tonight. Either way, that doesn't matter right now.

"She's . . . She's just tired," August explains, giving me a worried look his sister can't see. "It's been a . . . long week." Autumn looks up at me with the fatigue of the nearly apathetic.

"One more day," I say. Only her eyes move, meeting mine.

"One more day," she agrees half-heartedly. It'll have to do. I'll let August comfort her for now. She is more comfortable around him anyway, and more so since . . .

"I think that's enough for today. Is there an inn or something anywhere nearby, Ember?" I ask.

"Why would there be an inn? We are hardly in the city," August inquires.

"Potestia is, or was, weird as fuck," I answer honestly. "Nothing made sense there. I imagine smaller settlements and traveling traders are more common over here. Inns outside of major cities are considerably more likely, even if they are only in little farming towns. So, Ember?" I ask again.

"Not this close to the border," she dismisses. "Only the Guardians of Stone come anywhere near here, and they live in something of a company town. We'll have to camp again."

"Ugh," I spit. "Mortified to hear the concept of company towns exists here. But I suppose we didn't come all this way for no reason. All right. Sorry, Autumn, August. I don't think hanging around here to meet these 'Guardians of Stone' is a top-ten idea of all time. We need to find a place to camp as soon as possible."

"This way," Ember says with little fanfare before turning and walking away from the invisible wall behind us. A bit rude, but no time to complain. I am enjoying the extended break from murdering people, especially after watching Godfrey die. I don't want to break the streak because I got in a fight with a pissy ailur and let the border patrol find us.

I sigh and look back at the twins. August nods and Autumn looks down. It's confirmation enough, so I follow Ember. There are more woods a few hundred yards away, almost like they had been cleared for this wall. If we move quickly, we will have concealment in no time at all.

Sara catches up to me in short order despite the quick pace everyone is keeping. "Are you doing all right, Annie? You look tired," she speaks as soon as she is beside me. I look up with a tight smile.

"Not even fucking close. But . . . yeah," I answer as honestly as I can. She seems to understand. "You?" I follow. I should have been asking her that every day for years. I don't intend to let it go unsaid ever again.

"No. Not even a little. But . . . yeah," she answers in kind. As we make it to the safety of the trees and pass inside, I offer her my hand. She accepts it quietly and happily as we slow to a walk. "So, what were you talking about with Ember while you waited?"

I look down at my free arm, my steel arm, before responding. "Getting stronger," I answer. "Now that the cancer is under control thanks to . . . these, I am first trying to decide how I can improve myself to get stronger. I want to explore the new way I gather mana as well, and what I can do with these new limbs, but . . . I'm not sure. They don't feel like mine. Like, I didn't choose or design them. So I want to start with something I did choose first," I explain. Sara squeezes my organic hand gently, sending another burst of aimless warmth through me.

"I can understand that. I do think . . ." Her scars actually intensify as she speaks. "I do think they will feel like you eventually. But I understand. So, what is the problem?"

"Well, I have always made changes based on how visible they were before. I am wondering if something like claws to deliver poison would be better. Or hell, horns. Carapace. Scales. Real, visible changes. Things to give me a more obvious leg up in a fight . . . Or equal amount of legs, I guess," I explain.

"But giving horns to the famous demon queen of legend might be a little conspicuous?" she guesses, and I nod.

"Something like that. But I already match the description they have of me. I figure that ship has maybe sailed already."

"Perhaps, but you still look human if you cover your arm. Looking a bit like a character from a famous story isn't quite so obvious as scales."

"You'd think. But believe me, a passing resemblance to a woman people are scared of and a sharp tongue? There are people back on Earth who'd have me burning as a witch before I ever cast a spell," I quip.

"You could always change your hair and eyes," she suggests. I shake my head.

"That would be a waste of time I could spend getting stronger, unless we invent contacts and hair dye. Besides, the scar refuses to go away no matter what I do. That's going to be a big tell," I dismiss.

"Well, I suppose we can reach a town and see if anyone ties you to a stake," she jokes.

"I mean, if you think that's a good idea, you can tie me to whatever—" I stop myself mid-joke, then blush. "Uh, yeah that's what we'll have to do. I can make a decision after I see how other people respond. Probably wise; it really does seem likely I'll be fine like this." Ugh. Get it together, Annie. That was close to crossing a line, and the blush reflected on Sara's face reveals it.

She leans in close to my ear and whispers, "Well, for what it's worth, I think you would look great with scales." My blush deepens and electricity runs down my spine. I try to respond, but another voice loudly interrupts our conversation.

"HALT!" a man yells from behind us.

Well. Fuck.

CHAPTER THREE

Seeing Red

"Sara, comms," I whisper, and she nods in affirmation. She knows exactly how to respond, but I was hoping we wouldn't need it so early. I don't feel anything different, but Sara squeezes my hand as she increases her concentration. I take a deep breath as I wait for another command from the intrusive voice.

"All you, halt and put your hands over your heads!" the voice calls again. I put my hands in the air as instructed, hesitating to let go of Sara for only a moment. I want to turn and look for the twins, but I am familiar enough with this situation to avoid sudden or unasked for movements, at least until I know I can get away with them.

Unfortunately, I don't know what we are dealing with here; what sort of weapons, magic, and procedures I might need to respond to. Still, I itch to check on the twins. It's like a hook in my cheek wants me to turn around, but I know it's not safe to do so. I should have had my goggles on; I would have seen this coming and hidden in time. I'd be able to see the twins now, at least.

It occurs to me the goggles are a convenience and I can still cast all the necessary light magic directly. Unfortunately, I barely summon a spark of the mana necessary before the man shouts at me again. "If you try and cast a single spell, I'll kill you where you stand. Hold still, and do not cast!"

I curse internally. Of course. It's been so long since I've been this far from the Radiant Woods, I forgot what other mages have to deal with. My mana is visible here. Even with Autumn and I, there is not enough grief to completely erase the visibility of my mana to other mages. And so, I am stuck blind to everything behind me. This knowledge digs into the back of my head like a slow drill, but I have to be smart. I have to wait.

"We aren't attacking!" Ember assures our assailant. Good, she is finally fucking speaking. "Have you cut off his whisper sphere?" she adds under her breath.

"I think so," Sara quietly confirms. "It doesn't feel exactly the same, but it's similar. It shouldn't be working right now."

"You think so, or you know? This isn't a fucking game!" Embers hisses.

"She thinks, that's what she fucking said. Just talk to this guy and try to get us out of this; you'll have to gamble a little. That's how this shit works," I defend while Ember scoffs. Just then, we hear swearing behind us.

"Piece of shit," the man challenging us complains, and I smile.

"Sounds like she has it cut off," I whisper.

"All you, turn toward the sound of my voice!" the man commands. I comply, sighing in relief the moment I turn and see the twins doing the same. It is sickening, the amount of weight that simultaneously lifts and falls on my shoulders as I see them. I still carry a lot of anger for Autumn. I still rely on her continued survival. I never left that tower where I hoped she would jump as I tried to talk her down.

I choke the complex well of emotions down and examine the man threatening us.

The first thing I notice is his humanity. He is neither an ailur nor volu, so the two new cultures Ember has described to me aren't the only ones involved in border patrol. He has a bow pointed at us, one of the first I've actually seen in this world. With magic spells and no need to really hunt, the tools existed but were not widespread in Potestia. Interestingly, it is a compound bow. I am no historian, but I don't believe Earth had those before the twentieth century. He also lacks a quiver or any other way to store arrows, although he has one drawn. He is, notably, struggling to hold the weapon steady. This may be the first time he has ever actually had to do his job, which means he may be especially ready to let that arrow fly.

"We're so sorry. You're a Guardian of Stone, right?" Ember calls to him. I suppress a scoff. I guess she doesn't always have thorns on her tongue, just with her allies. "We don't mean any harm! We got lost while camping, then when we saw the stone from a distance, well, we've always wanted to see it!"

This lie does seem to calm him a bit, but not enough. He is still trembling far more than someone with a drawn bow pointed at other people should. I'm fairly certain I could put up force mana in time to block an arrow if he does loose one, but I'd rather not risk it. And it seems like any too sudden movement will put that to the test.

Hell, I feel like I'm back home already.

"You willingly approached the border with the Nexus, in a restricted area, just to see a stone?" he asks incredulously. "Do you think I'm an idiot?"

"No, of course not!" Ember assures him. "Truth be told, if anyone is an idiot, it's me. It's just—" Ember starts, but the arrow points directly at me as the assailant interrupts her.

"Your friend there. Red eyes. A scar over the left. Black hair. Sounds awfully familiar to the Celestial Sage's revelation about the demon queen. And you brought her this close to the Nexus?" he interrogates.

I police my expression as best I can. That's one tick in favor of starting new body modifications now. If I am going to have to obscure my face and body either way, I might as well have the extra advantage in a fight. But perhaps he only made the connection because of our proximity to the border. Ember laughs as I contemplate how quickly I was identified, and it only takes me a breath to join her. It's immediately obvious what angle she is hoping to take here.

"Oh, shit, you had me going for a second there. It's not funny, comparing people to the actual demon queen! But I guess that is our fault. It's something of a . . . game. We're enthusiasts of a sort. The scar is just makeup and her hair is dyed. We are so sorry; we meant to be in and out. We don't want any trouble," Ember insists. The man seems to relax and tense at the same time as his anxiety shifts to clear annoyance.

"Oh, you're some of . . . those perverts," he groans. All right, rude. You do not need to be a pervert to dress up like me. I'm cool as shit! Although it is a relief to hear there are methods of hair dye available. Maybe I'll be able to disguise my identity after all. "I don't care what sort of sick interests you have. This is a restricted area. I'm going to have to take you all into custody. All you, slowly lower yourselves onto your left knees, and your left knees only!"

Ember groans as the man instructs us one movement at a time to a more easily controlled position. "Don't let him see your arm, or any of your prosthetics," she hisses under her breath. "If he sees those, he will try to kill us." I suppose these are probably not widespread in this new culture. Although they could be, if they aren't being held back somehow like Potestia was. It didn't exactly take us decades to figure them out; mana makes advancement much easier to pursue. Still, immediately trying to kill us seems like an extreme reaction.

"Kill us? Don't tell me these are part of this fucking prophecy? If there was a prophecy about my missing limbs and you didn't say shit, I swear to God, Ember . . ." I whisper back as I lower to my second knee.

"Don't be absurd, of course there isn't. He will still try to kill us if he sees them, however. Hide them, whatever it takes," she insists.

"Why didn't you say something about that before we tried to fucking sneak past them?" I counter quietly. Meanwhile, I am forced to take a prone position at our enemy's command.

"I—" she starts then stops, like the answer gets caught in her throat. "I—" Again, she can't answer. It doesn't sound like she is struggling to explain herself; not in the way I would expect. Her voice is confident until something plugs it like a cork.

"He's approaching," Sara warns, and we all quiet down. I'll have to get an explanation later.

"Shit . . ." the man whispers as he approaches. There is a moment of silence as his footfalls stop and nothing happens. Then, he approaches me. He must have passed the twins, which seems unwise, until an unfamiliar woman addresses him.

"Is your sphere working? I can't contact Guardian One," she inquires.

"No, something must be affecting all them," he answers with irritation. "And I only have one set of shackles. Toss me yours; we can at least restrain two of them for now. Fucking insane tourists."

"It would be pretty strange for tourists to show up at the exact time our whisper spheres failed. Are you sure they don't have a sage?" the woman questions. Meanwhile, I hear shuffling as she provides her partner with a spare set of shackles while, presumably, keeping her distance as his overwatch.

"No way a sage would just let us arrest them. I thought so too, especially with this one . . . I'll admit I got a little spooked. But if she or any of the others were who they looked like . . . well, they would have just killed us both," the man dismissed. He's not entirely wrong.

We could kill him, I suppose. But there are a few details that make this less than an ideal solution. I don't actually know fuck all about this new country, or why these people are guarding the border like this. Since I am not actually an evil demon queen, I can't just kill someone without at least some sense of the situation. Not even border patrol. For all I know, they are here for the supposed monsters in the Radiant Woods. Even if I could, people investigate when their guards die or disappear. I would much rather be caught and released than avoid a manhunt on the road for the next few weeks, provided that is an option, which Ember seems to think it is.

I guess this could be a long con from Ember, but I don't think so. Especially if she is worried about my limbs being discovered. In any case, I don't mind leaning into the understanding. If we can get back on the road without being chased, I'm happy to let them briefly believe that Demon Queen Lillith is a mindless murder machine.

I feel the man's presence as he hovers over me, and I sigh as I am of course one of the lucky two to be restrained. His knee rests on my back as he grabs my left hand and secures a shackle around it. I immediately feel the mana in most of my body dissipate, feeling pained and faint as my tumors breathe in the freedom my missing mana gives them. So this is what these feel like without my circle.

Of course, that is the mana in most of my body. My . . . *unique* appendages continue to gather mana from all around me, even pulling some from the overloaded cancer cells throughout my body. My mouth fills with the taste of copper, but I am able to flood my veins with mana from my arm and legs.

It's only as the magic returns and fights against this dissipation cuff that I realize blackness had started to edge at my vision, and blood had begun to run down my nose. Yet, I am fine. It is both a relieving and terrifying revelation. What would disable most mages would kill me, if not for these tools. These tools partially designed by Ember. Ember, who . . . Fuck. Ember, who told me not to let this shithead discover them.

Just as this thought finally makes it through the dizziness, I feel him grasping my right arm to cuff it as well. I can read the future in the moment of hesitation that follows, but it's too late. He is forcing my sleeve up. "She's a cultist!" he cries. I can't see him. I can't see anything but the dirt, mud, and leaves. But I can feel it, like the moment before a car crash or that breath before diving into the water. Ember was right. He is about to kill me.

I erect a wall of force behind my back and hear the strain of the arrow as inertia pushes it into a greater opposing force. It was maybe an inch from my skull when I stopped it. Well, that just about answers how careful I have to be with this man's life. His knee is still lodged in my back, indicating he rapidly drew and released an arrow from extremely close range. But he is not strong enough to hold me down. Especially not after he just tried to fucking murder me.

I tear both my arms away from him, noticing greater resistance with my right than left. It is considerably feebler, which will take some getting used to.

I stand as if there was no weight on my back at all, and my would-be murderer stumbles to the ground, a look of pure terror on his face. My boot lands on his neck, reinforced by force mana, and I hold him down as I scan the area for his friend. I don't find her immediately, and anxiety wraps its hands around my throat. I look toward Sara, then the twins, and finally Ember. Sara and Ember have already regained their feet, whereas August and Autumn struggle. Where is the other one? Where is she?

I finally remember my goggles, rushing to put them on. There is a strangled howl of pain that sends chills through my spine. Who is it? Who's hurt this time? Who did I let die this time? The world is color. The goggles let me see everyone, but I can't make out what state they are in. Someone is trying to scream . . . gurgling, choking on blood. I shouldn't have bothered with the fucking goggles; she took advantage of my guard being down! I failed again. I was right here, but I failed again!

Except, something isn't right. They are all still standing. On alert. Using their own mana. No one is—The gurgling cries cut off, and I almost slip in the blood beneath my foot. Fuck. I'd forgotten him. But where—There she is. I catch a flicker of color behind me, putting up a force barrier, but I am too slow. Her arrow flies past me toward Henry.

I scream and charge her. I want to save him. I have to stop her from hurting him again. I think she is one of the bird people? I can't remember what they are called. I can't remember anything. The color takes over and fills my vision and my consciousness alike. I am still screaming and hitting and hitting. I am on the ground, my fists colliding with the bird woman. The world is blue and red and black.

I keep swinging. I keep screaming. I keep sobbing. I am still hitting her. Beating her. Making her pay. I can't stop myself. My right hand holds her throat as my left swings again and again. Hands try to catch it, but I refuse to slow down. Another set of hands grabs my right shoulder and tries to pull me off. I can't remember what I am doing here. I have to save Henry.

"Annie!" Sara screams into my ear. "Annie we are all right! We are all okay! You can stop now! Please, stop now!" I feel dizzy as her voice finally breaks through to me. I pause and pant, my fist protesting in agonized pain.

Someone pulls the goggles I used to find my opponent off. Below me is the volu woman who tried to kill one of us. What is left of her. She is no longer recognizable as a previously sapient creature. Sara is trying to heal me, and as I look at my remaining human hand, I see why. My fingers are mangled and broken, unable to take the strength I'd put behind each blow. They are open and bleeding, with fragments of beak lodged into them. I hadn't even noticed.

"Is he—Is August all right?" I finally ask. "Is everyone all right? Did I save them?" I plead. Sara looks at me with sorrow like I haven't seen since she thought her father had fled from her.

CHAPTER FOUR

Cowardice

We run. Because of me, we run. Autumn is exhausted. Ember is annoyed, as usual. Sara and August are both terrified on behalf of someone they love. And my fucking hand still hurts. Sara did her best to heal it for me, but we didn't have a moment to spare. I'd killed two guards, and I'd done it loudly. Even now, I shudder under the burden of Sara's concern.

I can't do that again. We were lucky that time. Sara protected August from the arrow that missed me, and there was no one else around. But this won't be the last time we are in danger. This won't be the last time the people I care about are in danger.

I have always trusted my friends and family to take risks. I have always known those risks wouldn't play out in my favor forever. But there is knowing, and then there is feeling the pound of flesh torn from you as you hear someone who counted on you is dead. In an instant. With no warning. I wasn't even there to witness it. I didn't even know to grieve for hours after his death. And it hurts. It fucking hurts.

So my trust is wavering. My ability to let the people around me manage their own risks is decaying—or maybe my entire mind is decaying. In either case, there is a fear that lives in my chest now, beating like my heart won't. A fear I haven't got the courage to face. When that courage is necessary, I spiral. I panic. I see colors and splinter the bones in my hand against an already dead enemy.

It's going to become a self-fulfilling prophecy; I can feel it. I am going to panic again, and another arrow will miss. Another enemy will slip away from me. And because I was too afraid, someone I love is going to die again. I know this. I know this down to my marrow.

Which is why Ember isn't the only one who is furious at me. I am too. If it were a simple choice, I could change. If I were deciding to put everyone's safety entirely on my own back, I could recognize the flaw and stop. But it's not. I'm not consciously choosing to forgo wisdom to protect them at all costs. At least then I could do it competently. It's something far, far worse. It's cowardice. I have become a coward. I am too afraid of turning my head and returning to find another corpse. I am too afraid of the rough hands of fate digging through my heart like a vulture picking away pieces of rotten meat.

And now we run. And run. And run. We can't hesitate. We can't rest. Because the Guardians of Stone are going to go looking for their missing people. They will find little, thanks to Sarafyna; the bodies now live in her scars, providing her with extra mana she can hardly use. This is likely the only reason we have a chance of escaping. Because missing guards could be drunk, but corpses mean enemies. Regardless, we can no longer risk finding a quiet place to camp. We have to get away from the border now.

As we run, I notice Autumn clutching her side. The sun sinks in the sky as I hold up a fist, indicating we need to stop.

"Not yet," Ember hisses. "Thanks to you, we need to get farther from the border before they start looking for invaders rather than deserters." I nod. It's somewhat debatable whose fault it is entirely, considering the details about my arm she failed to inform me of until after we were caught. But I own that it was at least partially my fault. If anyone heard my screaming, we may have less time than we think.

"I know that, Ember. But pushing past what everyone can do will slow us down, not speed us up. We need to stop and let Autumn rest, or at least figure out a way to move forward without putting more strain on her," I explain.

"I can keep going. It's fine," Autumn chimes in.

"No, it's not. You're exhausted, and so am I. Lily is right," August insists, reprimanding his sister.

"He's right, Autumn. Trust me. Pushing yourself further than your body is capable of will only cause problems. It's why it took me so long to get . . ." I trail off and take a deep breath. "I have let people down because of it in the past."

"Then why did you bring deadweight?" Ember snarls.

"Because I need her!" I growl back. "Look, we just need a new plan. Autumn, I can carry you. I have plenty of energy left." Ember scoffs at this and crosses her arms as she looks away. Whatever clarity I felt from her when we first crossed the border has vanished; I don't know when. She is back to the familiar woman who saved my life in the most insufferable way possible.

"I don't want to be a burden," Autumn protests while I shake my head.

"I'm the burden. Come on, we don't have time to debate this," I insist. She looks away guiltily, but sniffs before nodding. As I kneel down to give her the chance to climb on my back, I notice Sara modifying herself. The sick, fleshy, liquid sound of it is a little unsettling, even after all these years. At the same time, it is familiar, and I have a strange positive emotional reaction to it. New muscles tighten her sleeves as her pants tear to make way for an extra set of legs.

"August, you look tired too. The rest of us have advantages you don't. I'll carry you as Annie carries Autumn," she offers. August blushes.

"Oh no, I really couldn't let a woman—" he starts before I cut him off.

"Oh, shut up. She already tore her clothes. And she's a badass; let her carry you. You need the rest just as much as Autumn," I reprimand. He looks like he wants to argue, but . . . August is August. He sighs and nods, only blushing a little as he climbs onto my girlfriend's back.

"Collector, I feel like a child," he grumbles, but he complies anyway.

"Are you all done? Can we get going, or do we need to go around the circle and express our feelings a little more? I'm fine either way. If I have to be executed for treason and the occult, I'll be glad to know you thoroughly discussed who was the biggest burden first," Ember taunts.

"Shut the fuck up; we are going," I challenge, too emotionally exhausted to quip back. And, as soon as I promise, I follow through. We are running again. Despite the extra weight, we do move faster this way. Ember literally bounds on all fours while I am easily able to increase my pace without having to match the twin's top speed. And Sara? Sarafyna is artistry in motion, and not just in the way all women are. No, she moves like a spider with fewer legs. She responds to every bump and obstacle like water, flowing over, around, and through them with an easy glide. It must feel like flying to August.

Or, considering her long hair flying in his face, maybe he is reconsidering his willingness to travel this way. Either way, we move quickly. Incredibly quickly. We run for hours, and even I have to start drawing more heavily on mana to stay awake. It is Ember who first tires and slows as the wooded path transitions to open field, and finally, what is clearly a well-traveled road. She slows to a jog, then a walk, then finally stops to catch her breath as we move from grass to dirt.

I am a sweaty mess. Autumn and August are both asleep, Sara is a goddess, and Ember's fur is matted with dirt. All us are ready to take a break.

"Autumn," I whisper. "Autumn, I need to take my bag off." She stirs quickly, sleep being a gift of exhaustion rather than comfort.

"Are you all right?" she asks before she even takes in our surroundings.

"I'm fine, you are just covering the strap. Sara needs a change of clothes before we run into anyone. We all do, really. It's been a long day. Well, night, now. We don't need to be answering any questions about our current state," I explain.

Ember looks back at me, literally panting in exhaustion. She quickly tries to compose herself, but like the rest of us, she hardly has the strength to do so properly. I gently let Autumn down as I approach Ember to find out what she wants to say. My left arm is stiff as sin, but my right is comfortable. Small favors of dismemberment, I suppose. Regardless, I take the bag, hanging irritatingly from my chest, and start digging for new clothes.

The group arranges itself in a familiar pattern, with a dreary August temporarily taking point as everyone changes and he tries to focus entirely too hard on the road in front of us.

"This—" Ember takes a deep breath. "This should be enough. I know where we are now. Provided you keep your . . . alterations hidden, we should be no more suspicious than anyone else passing by. A few more miles, and there is an inn as well," she says, much to the relief of all involved.

"An inn, in the middle of nowhere? Still seems weird to me," August calls back, his head rigidly looking forward. I chuckle a little as Autumn, the slowest to change, pulls a new shirt on.

"Relax, August, we're all dressed. And this is not the middle of nowhere.

Based on the state of this road, I'd say it's well traveled, maybe even a major trade route," I answer.

"What for?" he presses, finally turning around and rejoining us.

"Trade. What the fuck else would it be for?" Ember rolls her eyes in exasperation.

"Oh, no need to be so catty," I quip, feeling considerably better than I had earlier. For all the exhaustion of an hours-long run with a woman on your back, it certainly is good at banishing other worries from your mind. And we are safe now, which helps more than a little. "He didn't grow up in a world that needed trade routes. Or . . . anything, really. In fact, I'd just love it if you could explain why things are so different this side of Radiance . . ." I trail off before a thought occurs to me.

"Wait, 'catty' isn't like a slur or anything, is it?" Ember grunts in irritation before speeding a little to walk in front of us. "That's extremely unhelpful!" I call to no response but added tension in her shoulders. Well. She didn't act like it was a slur. I'll just avoid cat jokes in the future, maybe.

"Anyway, most cities lack all the things they want or need, and have to trade with other cities. Not unlike our communities, but without an insanely hot eldritch girl to expedite delivery."

"Hot?" August asks.

"She means attractive," Sara chimes in. "She calls me that at least fifteen times a day."

"Why would that mean attractive?" August presses while I just gesture at her.

"'Cause look how hot she is," I explain like it should be obvious.

"I don't understand anything," he complains, and Sara laughs.

"No one understands Annie. I just try to believe the compliment." She chuckles, rubbing the back of her neck awkwardly and blushing.

"All right, whatever. I still don't understand all this 'Annie' nonsense anyway. I guess I can write the trade thing off as another mystery." August sighs. It's now my turn to laugh. We tried explaining my otherworldly origins to him, but he never quite got a handle on it.

"I'll give you this, August," I respond. "You are very good at being all right with things you don't understand. That's a surprisingly rare skill."

"Thanks!" he cheerfully agrees. "I get a lot of practice!" This transforms a brewing chuckle of my own to a full-blown laugh, and even Autumn smiles alongside him. It is a moment sweeter than fresh figs. It is also interrupted by evidence of the greater frequency of travel in this country. I hear it before I see it, but a wagon presents itself around the bend, and my breath catches. We should be safe, but I can't help the anxiety that wells up at the idea of our group's first real contact with a new society.

"Looks like it's time to meet some new people," I whisper, tension rippling through the group. "Hey, maybe they'll give us a ride. If I still had feet, I swear they would be killing me."

CHAPTER FIVE

Do I Look Pretty?

Well, aren't you all far too pretty to be walking out here all alone, this late at night?"

I groan as the driver slows his horses and the wagon comes to a stop. There is a smarmy confidence in his wide smile, like a man expecting my clothes to fall off with a wink. He is classically handsome in a generic Hollywood star kind of way, and he exudes self-satisfaction. I hate him instantly. But I would really like a ride.

"We're too pretty for a lot of unpleasant things, but here we are," I intone. "You happen to have room in the wagon for five? Just to the nearest inn," I ask, badly suppressing a grimace. His eyes crawl down my body like a centipede before finding their way back up Autumn's. His brazen ogling would be enough to make an eternal enemy of me on its own, but the way he wrinkles his nose in disgust as he makes it to Sarafyna's scars cements his place on my shit list. Finally, August retrieves his water skin from his bag, and the stranger finally notices him. He spends little time examining either August or Ember.

"We've got room for three. I'm sure the strongest of you can make it on foot, and the rest of us can get to know each other in the meantime," he smiles greedily. Well, the first one is a bust, but we were only on the road for a few minutes before we spotted this wagon. There is a good chance another will be along shortly. I look back at the group for confirmation.

"We're all right," Autumn says, although her face betrays her fatigue. I asked her to come with me. I'm still not certain why myself, but I asked her to. And she has exhausted herself because of my mistake. Even worse, there is some spark deep in the darkest corner of my soul that feels satisfaction at that. The part that still wants to hold her exclusively accountable for my brother's death. I will not be a woman who indulges in that. I won't. So I grimace but push forward.

"So, if we remove one driver, that's room for at least four, isn't it?" I suggest. Perhaps not the most effective method of getting a ride, but just because I'm willing to suffer this man's presence to help my friend doesn't mean I have to suffer it in silence.

"I was just thinking the same thing," a new voice says as another man appears from the back of the wagon. He looks a few years older than the slimy driver. His mostly smooth, brown skin is etched with smile lines whose depth exceeds all other indicators of age. He wears a gentle grin that contrasts with his driver's like water and smoke.

As my other human companions examine him with mild surprise, I am again reminded of the differences between this country and Potestia. Potestia had a conspicuous lack of diversity, but I was the only one there to notice every damn person was pale as a ghost. It's less strange to them than a woman with fur and cat ears, however, so they adjust quickly.

"You are a guest yourself, Turner. If you are going to try and turn away other travelers, maybe you are the one I should leave behind, no?" the new man suggests.

Turner, apparently, scoffs. "Hardly the same. I am replacing your lost escort *and* driver. You need me more than I need you. These vagrants are just looking for a free ride."

"Oh, I don't think we are the ones looking for a free ride," I joke. "And I get the feeling we aren't the ones with no hope of getting one. If this isn't your wagon, calm your stiffy down and let the grown-ups talk," I dismiss, much to the amusement of the other stranger.

"We really could use a little help," Sara chimes in. "We can drive too."

"We aren't going far, just the inn down the way. A few hours by cart," Ember adds, almost apathetically.

"That shouldn't be too difficult. I'd love to help," the wagon's owner responds. "Problem is, Turner is correct, if only a little. We can squeeze four more in for a short trip, but five would be too many, especially with an ailur. Unless one of you can turn into an extra horse or magically take up less space, we really will run out of space," he apologizes.

Funny he should mention that. Sara very much can do those things, but . . . I can't exactly tell them that. I get the feeling transforming anyone's body is going to be met with distrust and physical protests. I'll need a plausible excuse to "leave Sara behind."

"Like I said, the strongest should stay behind. He will have the easiest time making it to the inn on his own," Turner repeats.

"Didn't you say you were an escort? Like . . . in case of attack, right?" August asks. "If we are worried about that, wouldn't it be better to have more strength available?"

"And leave one of these little slips of women alone to face the same possible attacks? What sort of man are you?" Turner sneers, and I see my in.

"No, August, this overly excitable stain of a person is right. Through no fault of his own, of course. Yes, he's just going to an extremely dry well hoping to get wet, but he stumbled across a good point on the way to embarrassing himself," I say.

"What did you say, cunt?" Turner snarls at me, but I fail to acknowledge him.

"Someone at least as powerful as the wagon's escort should be the one walking back on their own. That's the best way to keep everyone safe, right?"

"I guess that makes sense, but you don't have to—" August starts, but I hold a finger up to his lips.

"No use protesting. It's what's best for everyone," I cut him off.

"You heard her; you're walking. Don't worry, I'll keep an eye on them for you." Turner winks at August. "Maybe even help teach this one a few things. Like how a woman's mouth looks better smiling than spewing shit." I raise an eyebrow at him.

"I smile all the time; I'm sure you'll see it when something warrants it," I respond.

"Well, hold on now," the older man says. "Are you all sure about this? These roads can be dangerous at night. I'd feel awful if something happened to you. And for how unpleasant Turner can be, he is very capable. I'd be happy to camp here with you until another wagon comes along?"

Whereas Turner is speedrunning a meeting between my boot and his undersized testicles, this man is quickly ingratiating himself to me. "No, no, that's all right; thank you for your kindness. We can handle ourselves, I promise. A couple of us really need the rest."

"Even so . . ." he protests as I snap my fingers.

"Tell you what. Turner here keeps suggesting we leave the most capable behind, so let's have a little spar. If any of us can hold our own against him, will you be more comfortable taking the rest to the inn?" I ask. The amiable traveler looks at me skeptically.

"I'd really rather just wait with you. There is a reason we had to pick up a replacement escort, after all. But . . ." He glances back at his wagon then rubs the back of his neck. "Well, I suppose that would be all right."

"And why should I? If I win, that just means I have to wait here for longer. What reason could I possibly have to spar with your little friend?" he complains.

"Humans are such cowards," Ember grumbles.

"Yeah, don't be a little bitch boy," I agree. "Or maybe you don't make such a fearsome escort after all?"

"You know what? Fine. I'll spar. But don't complain when I break your little boyfriend," he scoffs, finally climbing down from the driver's seat. He marches up to August with his nose high enough in the air I'm worried something will fly in.

"The fuck you want with him?" I ask in amusement. "You're supposed to fight the strongest of us, right?"

He looks back at me in irritation. "Ailur don't count; it's not a fair comparison," he dismisses.

"Ember isn't our best, except at giving me a rash when she speaks. No. You are fighting me," I announce. He laughs at me.

"I've known a few girls like you. The men you think you beat? They went easy on you because they wanted to fuck you. Don't let it get to your head," he sneers.

I cross my arms. "Well, shit. They were committed to the bit; I'll give them that much. Some real convincing performances over the years. Take note, Sarafyna," I joke, gesturing toward my own body. "To die for, apparently."

"You really want to do this? I will fight a woman if I have to," Turner insists.

"You have to," I respond.

He shrugs, crossing his own arms as brilliant gold mana erupts from him, sparkling in the night and lighting him up like a beacon to any mages in the area. It rolls and swirls around itself in a pretty but clearly directed way before it coalesces into a number of gold coins with sharp edges. Constantly feeding them mana, he is able to turn and spin them with flawless timing as they appear in waves around him. A flick of his mana and that could tear someone to shreds. Well, someone with no defenses. Gold is an . . . odd choice for this, but I suppose it may have its advantages if he really understands it. I mean, I've seen *Land of the Lustrous*, and it worked out pretty well there.

Still. His posturing is less than effective. I can feel the mana pulling from my tumors and accumulating in my synthetic arm. I am going to have to hold back. Lightning would be too easy and do too much damage, but I think I can toy with him a bit with my other aspects.

"Are you sure? I won't hold back. Surrender now, or you'll look like that bitch with the melted face," he threatens. My amusement vanishes.

Technically, my mana is perfectly visible. Far more visible than it has been since I was a little girl, actually. Enough that I am surprised as it builds in a reality-warping aura around my right arm. The blue is vibrant beyond belief, even brighter than the brilliant gold of my opponent's mana. Despite this, he doesn't see it. I don't think anyone does. The high-pressure water forms so quickly around my arm and fires with such force that my arm jerks back in the other direction. I feel the flesh that has started to grow into and heal around the new arm tear and bleed. I'd barely considered the spell I wanted to cast, but it formed with little to no effort.

It is not the most powerful spell I have cast, lacking the raw force of much of my magic in the past, but it is quick and concentrated. By the time I regain control of my arm, all the threatening coins have collapsed into a gold-and-red puddle on what used to be an arrogant prick. *Oh shit. I could have held back more.* I hit him too hard for a spar.

"Sara, help," I call, but there is no need. She is already on her way to him. Orange force mana erupts from me and pushes the sharp coins to the side so Sara can put her hand on the wounded, soaked man.

"He's fine, just badly bruised," she assures. "The blood is from his own coins landing on him. He's alive."

I try not to laugh, but it is difficult, and a giggle escapes. I don't know how I did that, but if I can figure it out, I may have an answer to Ember's question. I may have a way to get stronger. And in the meantime, this little shit fucked his own face up in a dick-measuring contest with someone who lacks one.

I can't help it—I let the laugh out as I offer him a wide grin. He struggles to focus for a moment before his eyes finally lock onto my pearly white teeth.

"Hey there, buddy. Told you I'd smile when it made sense. So? Do I look pretty?"

CHAPTER SIX

Grin and Bear It

Are you sure it's safe to leave her and not stay behind yourself?" the wagon's owner asks, and I nod. We are loaded up into the back of the wagon now, with Ember sitting up front with dickweed. Or, uh, Turner, I think his name was. I can see now why one person needed to stay behind. With the twins, me, and the three original occupants of the back, we are all rubbing elbows behind the cargo.

"Oh, definitely. If there is anyone here with a chance of knocking my ass flat, it's Sarafyna. Don't worry; if I am safe, she is," I assure. I even mostly believe it. The truth is, I don't plan on parting ways with Sara anytime soon, but only the horses will notice that as she clings to the bottom of the wagon in a form I can only describe as soupy. Of course, if I wasn't a coward—too afraid of leaving a loved one and never seeing them again—she would be perfectly capable on her own.

"Well, if you say so," he reluctantly agrees. "We can get going, then, uh . . ." He trails off before looking at me a bit sheepishly and speaking more quietly. "What was the ailur's name? Actually, I didn't get anyone's name, sorry. That silliness with the duel distracted me. I'm Quinn, by the way." Ember got the message despite the interruption, and I feel the wagon start to move as I answer.

"She is Ember," I answer easily. "And I am Annie. Pleasure to meet you, Quinn." Quinn gives me a slightly surprised look, but it fades as August introduces himself.

"August, and this is my sister, Autumn. She's, uh, not feeling particularly chatty. But we are pleased to meet you as well," August chimes in as cheerfully as he can. Quinn gives Autumn a confused look before smiling back at me and gesturing at the two remaining passengers.

"This is my husband, Kobe, and our daughter, Gia," Quinn introduces. I note that Gia actually shares a lot of features with Quinn, and idly wonder if they used a surrogate or some other process.

"Nice to meet you!" Kobe, the shorter Mediterranean man says as he cradles his baby daughter. "Is your name really Annie? That's wild; is the scar real or are you just leaning into the whole thing?" I want to raise an eyebrow at him but do my best to suppress it. I have an unpleasant feeling that Ember left out yet another important detail.

"Kobe, I'm certain our guest doesn't want to talk about her scars," Quinn reprimands, but I shake my head.

"No, please, I don't mind in the slightest," I assure. "The scar is, unfortunately, real. As you can imagine, I was less than pleased when I got it." *That should be vague enough.* It's an honest response that doesn't let on that I am confused. Kobe clearly expects me to know what he means, and honestly, I'm a little afraid I do.

"That's an insane coincidence! But hey, at least your name isn't Lillith. The eyes, the scar, and even the name 'Annie'? You're right out of every kid's nightmares!" Kobe laughs as Quinn blushes.

"I'm sorry, my husband lacks a filter. Look, we don't believe in any of that nonsense, but you know how it is. What with the election coming up, sages always come up with new ways to get attention. Kobe just pays a little too much attention to that stuff," Quinn apologizes.

"Yeah, sorry, sorry," Kobe agrees. "Honestly, even if we did believe in prophecies, you can't just add on to one whenever you want, right? I'm sure it's been a headache for you ever since the 'Annie' thing came out. My condolences. Good on you for sticking to it, though."

That is equal parts irritating and interesting. *So much for having a safe backup name.* I will apparently also be immediately identified by appearance alone. Although Turner said nothing, so it's not obvious enough to always be worth commenting on. I suppose a few women probably get looks for the black hair and red eye combo, assuming the eye color isn't unique to Potestia. Which, obviously, it is not.

It is interesting, if I am reading the implication right, to learn the name

"Annie" is a recent addition to this so-called *prophecy*. I wonder if it's the only part that has been added recently. I'll have to wait until I get to the nearest city to know for sure. Hopefully, they have invented the fucking printing press and newspapers in the Republic. If the warning of my impending horrors are a recent addition, it should be easy to parse which bits are actually about me and, maybe, where the information is coming from. And of course, if this prophecy is part of an active political campaign, I can be sure of two things: the average person will be largely unaware of it, and it will be so in my face I will hardly be able to avoid it.

"Yes, well, I have been known to be stubborn. I promise I am not a demon queen; I don't think," I respond, injecting a dry humor into my voice.

"Even so, I would have expected you to choose something else to go by, just to avoid the headache," Kobe countered.

"To quote a great, endlessly wise man: Why should I change? She's the one who sucks, right?"

Kobe laughs openly at this, and Quinn cracks a smile. August chokes back a laugh as well, considering I technically insulted myself. That's his only response, however. He is staying mostly quiet, focusing on his sister instead of the conversation. We discussed this ahead of time, deciding too many people who clearly knew nothing about the country would be suspicious. And August is honestly just a terrible liar.

"I'll drink to that!" Kobe chuckles as Quinn gently raps his shoulder with a few knuckles.

"No drinking with Gia in the room—you know that!"

"I know, I know; it's just an expression!" Kobe assures to a curt nod from his husband. I decide to take this opportunity to change the subject.

"So, how did the three of you end up with short dick, long jacket up there as an escort?"

Quinn sighs. "Ah, highwaymen. We were a larger convoy with hired guards, but we were attacked on the road. Turner up there showed up out of nowhere and fought them off, but most of us had already been killed. In exchange for the fees we were supposed to pay our actual guards, he offered to escort us the rest of the way. Considering how easily he scared off those damn bandits, we figured it was worth it."

"A real shock to meet two women who can knock him on his ass like that on the road, after all that," Kobe adds. "Turns out everyone makes a better guard than my brother ever did. So much for all his boasting." As he says this, something turns in my stomach, and I wonder if our rations are keeping poorly.

"Seriously. The way he told it, he could fight a sage, but turns out most random travelers are more impressive than him," Quinn agrees. I start to feel a little more queasy at this.

"Well, give your brother some credit," I respond. "Maybe if he'd been there, he'd have done just as well," I offer, feeling a little bad for the abused sibling and starting to wonder if I'll need to make a restroom stop soon.

"Oh, he was." Kobe sighs. "Charged in like an idiot and was one of the first to die." I'd been settling in, letting the bumps in the road become familiar, but this forces me fully awake, a nameless dread settling over me as my eyes widen. That sickness starts to tighten inside me.

"I'm sorry, did you say your brother died on this trip?" I ask, just to be clear.

"Yeah, I'm afraid so. His timing could have been better too; Mom is going to be furious at the loss of income," he groans. I am cold and quiet. Autumn is finally paying full attention, horror clear on her face. Quinn and Kobe notice this, and Kobe rushes to reassure us. "Oh, don't worry. It's just an inconvenience, more than anything. We aren't in financial trouble or anything!"

What is going on? I don't understand this couple. "How long ago was this?" I ask, and both men shrug, Kobe putting more nervous energy into rocking his silent daughter than before.

"A week or so," Quinn answers.

"And you don't care at all?" Autumn interjects, pain clear in her voice. "He's dead, and you don't care at all? You lost someone—someone who tried to protect you, to protect your daughter—and you don't even have a tear to shed?" Her voice speeds up as anger and grief pour out of her.

The couple before us looks confused more than anything. A tear runs down Kobe's face, but this only confuses him further. I can feel grief. I can feel my own, cold and hard. Autumn's grief overflows like a poison well. And from these men, I feel . . . nothing. Do they both have ASPD? What is . . . ?

Something occurs to me, and I hold up a hand to stop Autumn.

"What, is this normal to you? Lily, they don't care at all!"

"Autumn, I know. Just . . . give me a moment," I say as calmly as I can. "Let me think."

"Did she just call you *Lily*?" Quinn asks. "I thought your name was Annie, but . . . Lily, as in—"

I shake my head, thinking of a lie so I can get to the important bit.

"I do sex work. The demon queen Lillith is popular right now, and I look the part. It pays the bills. She has gotten used to calling me by my working name, that's all," I answer, and he visibly relaxes.

"Right, that makes sense," he responds as I fix him with a cold stare. I glance back at Gia. She really does look like him.

"Your daughter, is she adopted?" I ask, and he rubs the back of his neck nervously but shakes his head.

"No," Kobe answers. "Quinn had Gia before we met, from a past marriage. Why does it matter? Why do you two seem so agitated?" I let out a deep breath as August frantically tries to calm his angry sister.

"What happened to her mother? Divorce?" I press, and this time, it's Quinn's eyes that quiver a little despite his confusion.

"My wife died, if you really need to know," Quinn responds in irritation. I still feel nothing from him, despite a growing sickness. Not like food poisoning, I realize. More like sick hunger; the kind that makes all food sound unappetizing until you eat it. Gia doesn't even look a year old yet, despite her eerie calm. His wife must have been alive as recently as six months ago, and he's already remarried?

"You ended up with Kobe pretty quickly, didn't you?"

Quinn shrugs. "It was a bit of a whirlwind romance. Why does that matter?" he asks, mildly offended.

They don't feel it. They aren't feeling any grief at all. Everyone is grieving—everyone. But these two men—by all accounts, kind men—don't care that their loved ones are dead. Fuck, even the child feels no grief. Her silence begins to disturb me on a new level. She fights fatigue like any child, but she doesn't cry. She is frustrated, but not even a little sad.

"What is wrong with you people?" Autumn asks. "What the fuck is wrong with you? How can you breathe? How can you even breathe? I don't . . . I don't understand. What is wrong with you?"

"I don't think it's their fault," I whisper. August and Autumn both look at me with near disgust, while the men in front of me seem irritated. "I think . . . I think, in a way, it's mine . . ."

I say "I think" because I haven't confirmed it. But I know. I know the truth. It wasn't anything I did, but they are like this because of me. Or because of people who are afraid of me. A lot of things about Ember are suddenly clicking into place. I can't be certain, but I can test it. And I'll know for sure when we get to the city.

I stomp on the floor once before raising my voice. "Their minds are being controlled. Ember's too, I think. Their minds, or maybe their hearts. They don't have a choice. I don't think they *can* grieve," I announce. The wagon is silent for a moment as everyone processes what I've said in their own way. But Sara gets the message. That sickness twists inside me, coiling like a string, tension building with each twist. Sara is doing something. She is fighting something. And then, in a moment, it snaps.

It's less than a second before I am drowning in fresh grief and Quinn's vomit at the same time.

CHAPTER SEVEN

The Weight of Ignorance

Gilbert

I was so happy.

When I was younger, I was happy too. Until my thirteen-year-old sister forced my eyes open and made me look at my reflection. At the bruises and blood my joy left behind. I was a selfish man when I was younger. A blind man. I took what I wanted and turned my head, and people suffered for it. Women I cared about suffered for it. But I changed. I opened my eyes, and I worked to be a better man.

And I was happy again after my brother was returned to me. When we moved to Visenar. Then again when we left. Every change in the world around me made the world a brighter place, a world where I could love—genuinely love—without hurting anyone. Where I could be honest and accepted and keep my eyes open to any pain I was causing. I met Mali. I met Julie. Even Jeremy, who did not like being called *Jack*. Leaving Potestia and living with them was so . . . kind. So simple. So easy.

Before I knew it, I was blind again. I knew what my sister was doing. I knew she'd never stopped fighting, and I knew Edward and Henry were helping. And they didn't need me. Not me. I'd done my part, everything an older brother should; I'd helped bring Henry home safe. Even without me, Lily was making everything better, kinder, and I loved her for it. But I was still me. Still oblivious, unable to see anything that wasn't shoved in front of me. Still too fucking comfortable. I ignored the danger; it was so easy to do. Everything had always worked out before, right? Everything. Lily had stopped Baldwin. She had saved Leo. She had escaped her own execution.

It'd all started when we first went looking for Henry. When she fought the Manticorps. Her alone, as a child. She was . . . unstoppable. A force of nature. Brilliant, fierce, kind, and brutal.

I feared her for a while. What she would do. But somehow, that fear settled into admiration; idolization, even. She was a hero—a brilliant hero who would always, always win, and anyone who stood in her way would pay the price. Yeah, she would make speeches, warn us of the dangers of the new lifestyle we were choosing. Of learning magic when the nobility didn't want us to have it. But it wasn't real danger because she was there. And she wouldn't let that risk be realized. We had the Mage of Mourning on our side, and anyone who wanted to take our joy away had to go through her.

This became a certainty. Risk became the senseless panic of the overly anxious. We were safe, and we would always be safe. Our new lives had been won, and there was an immovable object between them and any-one who wanted to take them away. And I let Lily do this for us. Edward wanted to help. Henry wanted to help. And I respected them for it. But Lily didn't need them, not really. They just owed her, by way of thanks or apology. But she didn't need them. And she didn't need me.

Everything would always work out.

Whatever Lily faced, whatever any of us faced, and whoever wanted to take the old, cruel world back . . . everything would always work out. I trusted Lily. I trust Lillith.

Henry is dead.

I will never be happy again. I will never be safe again. No one will. I have always been described as oblivious, uncaring. Lily says I keep my head in the clouds. I thought it was lovable, but it wasn't. It was cruelty. Cruelty to everyone who needed Lily's help. Cruelty to Henry and Ed. Cruelty to Lily. Just because my sister is strong, just because she can take the pres-sure of the world and fail to collapse, that doesn't mean she doesn't need support.

If I had learned combat magic and gone with them, would Henry still be alive? I can barely use magic at all. I never understood the *recipe* or *equation* thing Lillith always tried to explain to me. I just wanted to live in peace, and I let my kind little sister crumple under the weight of my peace.

I'm told she's not younger than me at all. Ed says she is some other woman from some other world, but I don't understand any of that. She is still Lily to me. And she could have used my help. Henry deserved to have my help, my protection. They both deserved an older brother with his eyes open.

"Are you all right?" a voice asks, and I take a sharp breath through my nose. I have moved to the towers the rest of my family live in. I haven't been answering my whisper sphere. I can't even think of Mali, Julie, or Jeremy. I like them, but they aren't a support system, not really. We were all just having fun together.

Mom knows I'm no more okay than she is. Ed knows too, and he's in Visenar again, like every day. I realize no one has actually asked me that since I came here. I continue to look out over the horizon at the Radiant Woods in the distance. I am sitting on the balcony of an unused public area on the tenth floor of the tower. No one comes this high, usually, although our population is expanding every day with Potestia free.

It's a surprise to meet anyone up here at all, much less anyone who cares how I am doing. I don't answer, instead looking back at the intruder with weary eyes. He's a tall man, with a square jaw and a missing right arm. I recognize him pretty quickly. He saved Edward's life, after all. He could have a prosthetic, like Lily does, but he had it removed after a few days; I'm not sure why. This man is Dominic, the last remaining royal, here to protect us in Lillith's absence. *What does he want with me?*

"Yeah, me neither," he says, sitting down a few paces away from me. I suppose he wouldn't be. His entire family is dead. I don't know the entire story, but apparently, he played a part in his own grandfather's death. I don't know what he wants with me, really, so I just grunt and continue looking out over the world I have ignored for too long. "But . . . I'm trying to do better."

I don't understand what he means at first. We all want to feel better, but we can't just make that happen. I am prepared to ignore him when it clicks into place. Even now, I am considering how pointless it would be *for me* without considering that he might be the one who needs someone to talk to.

"What do you mean?" I ask, choking back the anxiety of my own grief. Maybe, for once, I can help him. Even if I can't, I need to start trying. It might be the only way out of this pit I live in now. To be a better man, I need my eyes open. Even if I am a husk myself, I can be different than I was in the past. I just need to stop being oblivious, and if all I can do is listen, that's what I'll do.

"I spent a long time thinking I was a good man, but I wasn't. I was blind to everything around me. To my loved ones. To the people I was supposed to rule. To myself. I mean I am trying to be better than the man I am," he answers matter-of-factly. A stone sinks through my chest, and I bite my lip.

"Yeah," I say. That's the only answer I have for him. *Yeah*. But it's enough. It carries my entire story with it. I can't help him, but I can understand him. Not exactly, since I am no ruler; I don't know what he went through. But I know what it means to look the other way for too long, until it is too late.

"Yeah," he agrees. We sit in silence for a while after that, I don't know how long, but the balcony feels slightly less lonely. And I feel slightly less empty. I wonder if he came here for the same thing. Just for the comfort of someone else who'd made the same mistake.

Finally, I decide to ask, "How did you know?" looking him in the face for the first time. He has weary eyes and a half smile.

"I'm not much help to Ed, I'm afraid. What he's going through is . . . different. But he is worried about you. And he said you would understand," he answers. I nod. Of course. Of course he did; meanwhile, I have barely thought of Ed. All I know about him is he has been volunteering in Visenar every day. I haven't even asked. I haven't spoken much to Mom either, but Ed was paying attention to me. Fuck, when did I become the asshole brother?

"Maybe. I don't know. But . . . I can talk if you want," I offer. Dominic sighs.

"I think something is going to happen soon, and I don't want to be alone when it does," he responds in what feels like an odd change of subject.

"Happen? Like what?"

He lets the question hang in the air for a moment before answering.

"I don't know. But something has changed. Something is going to change. I don't think we are safe," he replies. His words ring true in a way I can't understand, like the way a bell resonates with your bones. "But, and this may sound selfish, but you and I—we have a chance to finally pay attention. We have a chance to do the right thing. It's not much, but it's a chance."

Water runs down my face at this. I wish it didn't. I don't want to feel hope because of something like that. But he's right. I can't live my life knowing I sat out the fight when I was really needed. I can't look back and only see oblivious Gil while my family was fighting and dying.

"How will we know?" I say, but as I ask the question, I realize he is right. There is something wrong, something not quite right, like closing a door after the wood has warped. There is fear in the air, an anxiety that should be healing but is only getting worse. Maybe it's because Lily is gone. Maybe it's because so many people don't know how to move forward now. But that doesn't feel right. It's not right. There is danger on the horizon, and everyone can feel it.

There are shadows in the distance, spreading over the cold mountains, too soon for the sunset. I can barely make them out, but something is moving.

"I don't know," Dominic admits. "But, if it's all right, I'd like to watch for it with you." I nod. The shadows are gone, as quickly as they came. But with the conversation I am having, as surreal as it is, I feel like it must be something. Or I am just trying to see something because Dominic gave me hope that I would. I squint, but everything remains calm.

"We should call my sister," I suggest, and Dominic puts his hand on my shoulder.

"What is it?" he asks.

"I don't know. Nothing. But . . . we should call my sister," I repeat, looking up at him as I do. He looks concerned but searches his body for a whisper sphere, a once coveted relic only priests and nobles used. I suppose he's always had one, but long-distance spheres were uncommon even for nobles. It's strange to see the person next to me idly searching for one.

"All right," he agrees. "Guess I am calling the killer who terrified all my friends for years." I almost crack a smile at that, but I let him channel his mana and intent to contact Lily. His sphere lights up, but . . . nothing happens.

The vague sense of dread in the air fills my lungs like smoke as the sphere goes dark again, failing to find the intended target of the call.

CHAPTER EIGHT

Where We All Go

Charlotte

They are all moving in the same direction," Leo insists. He's right, as usual. I was supposed to be the mentor, but . . . I'm no mentor. The evidence of that sits around the fire with Leo and I as we discuss the movements of the residents of the Radiant Woods. The evidence lives in my skin and my blood. In the soft curve of my hips I had always known were mine. In the angle to Leo's jaw and the hair that grows from it.

It took a week or two after Leo's new abilities awakened, but I am who I have always been now, through and through. So is he. A man and his mother. We are who we have always been, and we fit in the bodies we have now because Leo refused to accept a reality defined by the control of other people. The same way I did, once. The same way I always cried out to do.

Even more than that, evidence of Leo's bravery lives in the man and woman who join us; "monsters" we encountered as we tried to find our way home. People who had been left here for who knows how long.

But not just any people—both of them are like us, framed as monsters, as something to be feared, avoided, and discarded. Both of them given their humanity back. Both shocked and sobbing when they finally woke up as who they really were and not the distortion that had been chosen for them by these woods. Not just human but . . . Like us, they'd had a lie chosen for them the moment they were born.

Vance, the older of the two, had been beaten and given to the church of the Collector when he refused to be a mother. Ryanna, who looks no older than Leo, had been abandoned here when she told her parents her name. And yet, Vance has the body of a man and Ryanna the body of a woman. A change both new and welcomed by both.

I have a great deal of pride whenever I look at Leo now. Pride and shame. Because he was right. I'd wanted to save everyone; I didn't want to lose anyone else ever again, and I didn't want Leo to lose anyone like I had. I thought I was saving Lillith and Sarafyna and Leo. I thought I was saving everyone. But . . . both of these people are just like us.

Lillith told me about the houses of penance. She told me what eventually happened to its residents. I have always understood that people like me must have been among the undesirables abandoned in this way. But we have found and saved two people. And both of them are like me. That is no coincidence. How many of us . . . How many of us have been disposed of like this? Why? Why? Why do this to us? What have we ever done to anyone? What have we ever done but try to live and breathe and look at the light?

This was always where I was heading. The Radiant Woods. I alone had been spared for so long because of my position, because of my mana. But once the struggle for the throne was over? Once there was no one left to challenge whoever was left on the throne? Once they didn't need me to secure their own power? This is where I was heading. This is where *Leo* was heading. This is where all us end up, eventually. That much is clear now. This is where we have *always* ended up. Which means this . . . this is where Amelia is.

That is the thought that has been running through my head since we found Ryanna. This is where I would have sent Leo. This is where Amelia is. This is where Leo was going. This is where Amelia is. I spent my entire life thinking my childhood friend was dead, thinking she had been killed. But she disappeared. And this is where they put all us.

I was willing to give up everything—the body I'd always wanted, only half finished; my joy, my future—because I had seen so many people fail. I had lost so many friends to a fight we never, ever won. I was willing to live in misery to give my son a chance at the joy I would never find. But it was a lie. A false dichotomy. There was never a choice, never a compromise. There never would *be* a compromise. We are all left here. It was only a matter of when. It was never a real choice.

I don't know what happened to Lillith, but if she is dead, it's my fault. Everyone who died because of the deal I thought I struck is on my shoulders. I don't know how to live with that.

I could have lived with a return to normal, a return to misery. A world where everyone got their lives back. It would have even been an improvement. Former slaves would have been allowed to return to freedom.

But that was a lie. I can feel it when I look at Vance, when I look at Ryanna. I had bought a desperate lie because I could at least dream of a future for Leo. Because I thought I had found a way to survive with chains around my ankles. I can't even see how much damage I caused. All I can see are three people who didn't break where I did. I would be beyond miserable, except . . . this is where Amelia is. She could be alive. I can see her again. I can see her as she actually looks, if I can get Leo to her.

"Mom, are you listening?" Leo asks. He still calls me *Mom*, even more now. He was the only friend I managed to keep alive, to keep safe. And I'd kept him that way for so long I started to think I could play the game well enough to keep him alive forever. I am such a fool. I don't deserve that title. I almost took everything from him.

"Mom?" he asks again, and a hand gently lands on my shoulder, forcing me to jump. Oh. Right. Again, everyone but me is looking forward, where I am only lamenting my past.

It's Vance's hand on my shoulder, and I look up into his glass eyes. Vance and Ryanna don't speak much. Not yet. Vance hardly speaks at all, if he doesn't have to. But their eyes tell years of stories. I wince.

"Yes, Leo? Sorry, I was lost in thought," I respond.

"That's all right," he says. "What do you think? About where they are going?" I look at Leo and bite my lip.

"You said they seem to be heading in the same direction?"

He nods. "It's hard to tell, since the Radiant Woods recede when I approach them, but tracks are left behind, and for the last few days, they have all started to point the same way."

"Um, do either of you remember any patterns like that?" I ask, looking toward our new friends. Vance simply shakes his head, while Ryanna puts a finger to her chin in thought.

"I don't think I was stuck here as long as he was," she answers hesitantly, "but I don't remember ever being pushed in one direction over another. I was never even allowed near anyone else. Sorry." I shake my head.

"You have nothing to be sorry for," I insist, and she blushes before apologizing again.

"Right, sorry, I just—"

"I get it," I interrupt her. "I think we are all forced to apologize a little too often. But I think . . ." I trail off, worried to make another guess. I was so wrong last time I tried to gamble on the future. But Leo wasn't.

"I think this is a good thing," Leo says, echoing the thought I was too afraid to share. "If all the monsters go to the same place, we can save all them at once, right?" I nod gently as Ryanna seems to get jittery at the thought.

"Do you think they'll be like us?" she asks excitedly.

I smile gently. She's right to be excited—excited to no longer be alone, especially after what she has been through. Excited to actually change people's lives. I understand it. I am excited at the feeble hope of saving Amelia, if there is anything left of her after all this time. If she is even still alive at all.

Ryanna deserves this joy. Even after Leo found her, life hasn't exactly been easy. We eat when the Radiant Woods dissolves and we find edible fruits and vegetables in the real flora left behind. They only have clothes because I spent time aspecting cloth mana, and I am no seamstress able to put it together sensibly. She should be miserable, but whenever we find new tracks, she is so hopeful.

"Yes," I answer. "In one way or another. Maybe they won't be exactly like us, although I think quite a few will. But yes, I think in some sense, they will be."

"Why do you think they suddenly changed course?" Vance asks. He is less optimistic, always so weary. He doesn't speak much, but he always asks the questions we don't want to.

"I don't know, but . . ." I pause, picturing the claws. The teeth. The carapace. Monsters meant for war. To kill and destroy. "But I think it will be best if we find them first."

"We have nowhere else to go," Leo adds. "They are going either to where the Radiant Woods wants them or they are helping us. And . . . And I think I know where they are going."

"Oh, to this Lillith girl?" Ryanna asks. "You seem to think about her a lot. I don't know why they would be going to her though."

Leo shakes his head.

"I don't know if they are going to her specifically, but I'm betting she has something to do with it. When the world shifts beneath your feet, she usually does it," he answers.

"Except when it's you shifting the world beneath mine," Ryanna counters. "So, is she a sweetheart or something?" Leo shakes his head, unembarrassed.

"No, nothing like that. I'm not really interested in women that way. She's just . . . someone kind," he answers. Vance seems to understand this, and I do too.

"I hope you are right," I say. And I do. I hope Lillith is alive to face whatever is coming. Because that would mean I didn't get her killed. "If anyone could face them without hurting them, it would be her. If anyone knows to even try, it's her. I hope you are right."

"So. What do we do? Do we just . . . follow?" Vance asks.

My skin itches to take action, and I can feel it in everyone around me too. We all have our reasons. We all have our pasts and futures to fight for. Ryanna wants to meet more of us. Leo wants to see the rest of his family and rejoin the fight. Vance . . . I don't know what he wants, but he is moving forward.

And me? I want everything to be all right. I want to know that despite me, everyone survived. I want to see with my own eyes that I was wrong, that a better world could be won. Because even now, I have a hard time really believing it. Even now, something burrows into my ear and taunts me, tells me that the little comfort I had was the best I could ever have. But Leo rejected that, and these two people have lives again because of that rejection. But me? I need to really see it to genuinely believe it is possible on a wide scale.

"Yes," I respond. "Yes, and we do it quickly; as quickly as we can. We move whenever we have the energy. We don't let a single person suffer in those woods for a single day longer than we have to. We follow them, and we find a home."

"You heard her," Leo says. "We follow."

CHAPTER NINE

Lose-Lose

Lillith

I haven't had a cold bath since I aspected both heat and water mana. The hot showers I am able to create with these have been one of my favorite tastes of Earth that I missed for so many years. Whether I am covered in sweat, blood, or in today's case, vomit, a hot shower is usually the best feeling in the world. Even washing these things from the mesh skin on my artificial limbs usually carries its own sense of satisfaction.

It's cold today. It's so cold. I try adding more heat mana.

We'd finally made it to the inn. And it was nice to see an inn for travelers. It was nice to see any signs of regular travel, truth be told. After all those years in Potestia, any sign of free movement should feel refreshing, but Quinn and Kobe are not all right, and I don't know how to help. I'm struggling to imagine what it must be like to hover just above tragedy, unable to acknowledge it until whatever was holding you up vanished and left you drowning. And that's just what happened. I drowned them; Sara and I both did. It wasn't even the wrong thing to do—but it didn't feel right either.

Why is the damn water so cold? Again, I increase the heat mana I am supplying to the water.

I barely noticed the smell of sickness on me on the rest of the ride to this inn. I almost wished Sara had never pushed through whatever divine magic or Nexus energy or whatever you want to call it that was stealing their grief from them. Having the weight of their lives crash down around them like that . . . that could be deadly.

At the same time, what was done to them is beyond disgusting. How could we have left them in that state? Even as they unraveled before me, all I could do was cling on to a faint hope—a desperate hope—that they were unique. But I am at an inn now, a place of rest for the weary, a congregation point for travelers. It's not exactly busy, but it's busy enough.

No one is grieving. Not a soul anywhere near me feels a shred of grief. Just me, Sarafyna, and the twins. If the sages are doing this, then Ember is right: They need to die. If the people of this country aren't even allowed to grieve? They cannot continue to exist in this world. I owe their death to every one of their subjects—or citizens, I suppose. I doubt the sages know the difference.

But I don't know what to do. Freeing Potestians from mind control was one thing. They were robbed of trust for each other, of self-sufficiency. But grief? The grief of every tragedy every person has ever lived through? All at once and without warning? If killing the sages drops all that at once, I will be killing more than a few of their victims with them.

Why is the water still so cold? Again, I increase the intensity of my heat mana.

"Annie, are you all right?" Sara asks through the room's folding screen. This inn doesn't exactly have showers installed, so I am creating water behind it and evaporating it as it collects in a force basin at my feet. I close my eyes before answering.

"This is because of me," I say. "It's not my fault—I know it's not my fault. I know. The responsibility for abuse is owned by the abuser. But they did it because of me, and I can't shake that feeling. I can't shake that guilt. It's frost in my blood, and it is an effective leash on me. You know that. Grief can't empower me, and I can't kill the people doing it, or the built pressure of all that anxiety will crush the people in this country. In this world. They are holding their own people hostage. What am I going to do, Sara? I can barely handle my own grief right now. How can I ask an entire world to stomach theirs when they don't even understand what that means?"

Sara is quiet for a long time. "I don't know, my love. I don't know. But I do know you are spiraling. I know the feeling well. That desperate powerlessness, that aimlessness. I understand," she says. She's right. Of course she understands. But that doesn't actually help me. "You need to take a step back. Ever since Henry—Ever since your last big fight, you haven't been yourself. You aren't asking the questions you would usually ask."

"Like what?" I snap, but she fails to react.

"Like, if this is because of you, how long have they been doing it?"

I grunt before shivering a bit in the cold water. "I don't know. They have their prophecy, so maybe thousands of . . ." I trail off because I see her point. I'm not thinking about it enough. "How much of that prophecy is actually about me? How much was recently added? If they only discovered things like the name *Annie* recently . . . maybe they only discovered my grief mana recently."

Sara doesn't respond to this, recognizing a little bit of the normal Lillith emerging. This is a good start. She's right; I was spiraling. But it's not hopeless. If it's recent enough, these people may understand what's been done to them, which could be good and bad. Some may not want their grief back. That could create active opposition to removing the people who lobotomized their soul like this.

Shit, I'm spiraling again.

"We need to do something," I finally speak. "I can't conceive of a counter for this. Not yet. I need to do something in my power. Find answers. Plan." I stop creating water, pulling a towel off the screen to wrap around myself. It stings for some reason, but I can't think about it. I'm too focused. And too cold. "How is everyone back home? Have you had a chance to look for Leo today?" She is quiet in response to this, and I feel the tension in the air.

"I want to talk about that, actually. But not until you are in the right state of mind," she responds.

"Please, just tell me," I say. There is another moment of silence and then a sigh, just as I am tying my hair up in another towel.

"The whisper sphere isn't working. Neither is the hat." I freeze. "This was my first chance to check, but it's the border; those stones in the sky. I can feel it. They are cutting off my contact with the other side."

"The hat shop?" I ask immediately. If her hat shop collapses, the people we left behind are dead. Anyone inside will be left in the Radiant Woods. The rest won't be able to travel anymore. I feel my breath shorten until she speaks again.

"No, that is all right. I can still feel it," she hurriedly assures. "But I can't connect with it directly. This hat is just a pretty hat now. I can't look for Leo, and we can't talk to anyone back home. We're alone out here, Annie."

Shit. Shit shit shit.

"And they are alone back there," I whisper. I emerge from the screen to get dressed as Sara gasps.

"Annie, are you all right?" she asks again, and I wince.

"No. I don't know what to do. What are we going to do, Sara?" I respond, but she shakes her head.

"No, physically. Annie, look at yourself!" she insists. I turn to the old, battered mirror and flinch. My entire body is bright red, and my eyes look dazed. "How much did you heat the water?"

I bite my lip. It felt so cold. So unbearably cold. "I was just distracted," I answer. It's even almost true. Sara looks at me with concern, looking like she has something else to say, and I am terrified I know what. We are across the border now. Leo is still trapped in the Radiant Woods. We can't risk her hat shop losing against the Radiant Woods. They need her back home.

You should go back. The words won't come out. I can't lose her again. I need to protect her. *You should go back.* I can't do this without her. *You should go back.* Leo needs her. My family needs her. I can handle myself, for now. She can come in and check on us when we actually have a plan that makes it safe for her to free everyone's grief for them. She should go back.

I open my mouth to force the words out, and I can see she knows what they are.

"I need to bring Ember back here," I say instead. "We need to push through whatever is stopping her from telling us everything. I'll need your help." She closes her mouth and eyes at the same time.

"Do you want me to go with you?" she asks. She wants me to tell her to stay with me. I can feel it. And I want to. I shouldn't. It's selfish, but I want to. I can't say yes. That would be abandoning my family like I abandoned Henry. I can't say no, or I will be abandoning Sara.

I look up at her and see . . . fear. Is she as afraid of leaving me behind as I am to see her go? Or is it something else? I do still rely on her to effectively keep the cancer under control, but it doesn't grow like it used to. Not since my circle broke. Not since my new limbs started handling excess mana. So I should be safe, even with the border between us. But she is as afraid as I am, terrified of leaving me. I can feel it, so I make a selfish choice. I take a risk for my own benefit, and for Sara's. I will wait. One more day. I'll say the words I need to say after one more day. They can't begrudge me one more day. They will be safe for one more day.

I pretend to misunderstand her. "No, that's all right. We don't want anyone asking questions about how you made it here so quickly. I'll go get her and bring her back," I respond. She lets out a sigh and nods. As I gather my clothes and disappear behind the screen again, she whispers.

"I need you too, Annie. Just as much as you need me."

I swallow her words like sweet hemlock. One more day. I can face the reality of the situation tomorrow. Today, I need her help. I put on a simple tunic and pants with a pair of boots and gloves, enough to cover all my less fleshy limbs, which will apparently mean instant execution.

As I walk to the door, I look back at Sara. "Thanks for talking me off that ledge. I love you. Be back in a minute." I can still feel the fear of the choice we are going to have to make in the air. But she smiles at me anyway.

"I love you too."

Ember isn't in her room when I knock, so I make my way to the tavern on the first floor. It is a bit odd, seeing the three different sapient species mingling. I'd spent most of my life in this world thinking humans were the only ones here. In fact, in Potestia, I'd only met *white* humans. This inn is a large change of pace in both respects.

Which brings up a lot of questions about Potestia. It doesn't make a lot of sense. Those borders can't have been around forever, and people like to travel. This sort of thing usually doesn't happen unless it's intentional. Then again, until I found a house of penance, I'd never met anyone with a disability either. That could be the answer itself, I suppose. I'll have to add it to my list of questions for Ember.

I spot her at the counter with a drink, likely recovering from her own emotional block being cleared. I move to meet up with her when Quinn stops me.

"Miss Annie," he greets, a sheepish look on his face. His eyes are still red from crying, and he moves like he is sore, but he wears a smile now. "I wanted to apologize for earlier. I don't know what came over me. I—I lost myself. So did Kobe. We are mortified. Please, is there anything we can do to make it up to you? One of us can go back and get your friend?"

I examine him for a moment. He feels just as he did when I met him. Sara is a few floors up, and her influence has already been washed away. There isn't a shred of grief emanating from him.

So even Sarafyna doesn't have a long-term solution. Shit. I need her here just as much as she is needed back home.

"Don't worry about it; she'll be all right. I'm glad you are feeling better," I dismiss. A man scoffs to the side.

"I wouldn't count on that," Turner says. I turn to see him smirking. "You may be strong enough to sucker punch me, but a woman walking all alone like that? Well, she'll be the one being ambushed."

"Sucker punch? I fought you face-to-face in an open challenge. I even let you cast first. What did you want me to do? Shout out my spell like a ninja of the hidden leaf? What would I have to do for you to expect an attack if none of that counted?"

He laughs.

"I'm just warning you. You abandoned her, and I wouldn't be surprised if you never saw her again," he sneers. There is an air of certainty in his voice I don't like. His entire story of meeting Quinn and his family is suspicious, actually. I'll have to investigate before their party leaves.

"Well, you do seem like an expert on losing contact with women. I'll take it under advisement. Now, if you don't mind, I have business elsewhere."

"I do mind, actually. I overheard your conversation earlier. I hear you like to play demon queen for men who can pay for the privilege. I can believe that. You certainly have the look for it. But then . . . why are you so practiced with magic? Why were you traveling on foot? Something stinks about your story, and I don't like it much. Care to explain?"

"To you? Not really. But I'm generous. We can have a conversation about shady stories all you want when I'm done with my business," I promise. "Who knows, maybe you'll even get a chance to see me 'playing demon queen.'" I inject as much promise into my words as I can, although the actual promise behind them is likely different than he is picturing. He thinks he has something on me, which I suppose he's not wrong. But I think we have different ideas about how a demon would behave. He just wants to feel in control again, and I want to stop him from leaving with Quinn before I can confirm my suspicions about him.

He grins at this. "Well, hurry along, then. I wouldn't want to keep you; not with such an important conversation in our future. I'll be in room four when you are ready to explain yourself."

"Be still my heart," I intone to a toothy grin. If nothing else, I'll get the chance to kick his ass again. I could certainly use such a chance. But he's right. I have more important business to deal with. I finally make it to Ember and put my hand on her arm. "We need to talk."

Malice and Praise

What the fuck do you want?" Ember demands as soon as I get her back to my room. "I am every bit as tired as you are, and I was sort of ambushed earlier when you—when you—" She stops, a look of confusion clouding her face as the words fail to come. "The point is you blindsided me, and I'm simply not in the mood for more shit tonight. Let me rest." When she says this, I do feel a bit guilty. She may have been listening, but she wouldn't have known she was about to get hit with that all at once.

"Sorry, I didn't realize exactly what would happen," Sara says. "I could feel something was wrong, but I didn't know what it would be like to have it all removed at once." I hadn't actually witnessed or heard any response from Ember at all, but that doesn't mean she wasn't hit every bit as hard as the others in the wagon.

"Well, now you do," Ember snaps. "So can we get this over with so I can enjoy one fucking day of peace before everything goes back to the third plane?" Her near-constant attitude is as grating as ever, but I am growing to have more empathy for it. Grief serves a purpose, after all, and hers was ripped away from her. Now, maybe talking to her has always been like a game of whac-a-mole from the wrong end, but it does hit differently knowing she has an excuse for it. I sigh.

"I understand. I do. But what happened earlier is why we need to talk. Ember, you left some pretty important shit out when you were prepping us to come here. To come here *specifically* at your request. We all almost got murdered because of the artificial limbs *you* helped design. Yes, you have responded poorly to the idea of body modifications, but that is not the same as a decent warning. If prosthetics result in a shoot-on-sight order, I could have used that information earlier."

She rolls her eyes. "I don't know what to tell you," she complains. "I can't brief you on an entire culture before bringing you here. I brought back the demon queen of fucking legend; maybe I just had higher expectations of you."

"Yeah, that's not really the same thing, sport. And I have a feeling I know why. For a long time now, simple proximity to my lovely girlfriend here has been enough to clear out any . . . mental influence. But we have mostly been up against priests and the Radiant Woods, which have their own brand of fucked up. In any case, we incorrectly assumed the same would happen to you if there was any emotional or mind control on you," I say.

"Sorry," Sara interjects. "I can often tell if Nexus energy is actively being used, but I don't always notice lasting effects if I'm not looking for them. I should have checked. I should have helped sooner." Ember gives her an irritated glance, but I continue before she has a chance to protest.

"Right. Today revealed you have been under the effects of Nexus energy for a long time. I think Sara's proximity helped loosen it a little, hence the turn from attempting to kill me to asking for my help with killing your bosses. But not entirely. You haven't been given your grief back, and if I am right, you actively work against yourself, trying to sabotage us. Not in serious ways, but with these omissions of details. Everything you know about this so-called *prophecy*: Why I was labeled a cultist and nearly killed. The shit you have been holding back despite clearly not wanting me dead, at least yet. I think the sages have buried their claws deep in your soul, and you can't fight back as hard as you need to."

Ember gives me a cold stare but doesn't respond. I am about to continue when I notice a slight tremor all around her body. She wants to respond to me. She wants to remain silent. It all translates to a cold glare. Shit.

"Ember, I want to try again. It didn't last long earlier, but I want to try and free you again. I know, it was horrible. But we need to talk, and we need to talk without your lips sewn shut. Let me free you, if only for a while. Please," Sara pleads, her gentler voice cutting deep where mine cannot.

Ember remains silent, continuing to tremble. I look her in the eye and she nearly snarls, baring the sharp teeth of a carnivore at me. At the same time, water runs through the fur of her face, and she gives a quick nod.

"I'm sorry. This is my fault. We should have tried looking at this before we left, when we could do it more gently. I missed it. But you can trust Sara, more than you can trust me," I promise. Then Sara reaches a hand out and touches Ember. I reach my left hand out as well, offering what little comfort I can to a woman who clearly holds me in low esteem.

Keeping this in mind, I am slow, allowing her the opportunity to decline the offer, but she doesn't. The trembling calms a little as both hands make contact and Sarafyna gets to work. I can almost feel it. Not physically, exactly, but in the way you can feel an argument about to break out or a fallen child ready to scream. Sara pushes against the foreign influence on Ember's soul, and the aura of the fight saturates the air around us.

Ember's breathing shortens and speeds at a rate I have rarely seen outside of animals. A deep purr escapes her, which startles me despite her other feline qualities. It is not the purr of contentment or happiness Suzume often offers me. It is, instead, a desperate attempt at self-comfort from a terrified woman. It hurts. She knows how painful it is, facing all her grief at once. She is doing it anyway, and my evaluation of her character is starting to shift.

It's hard to really know her motivations. I don't even know what she has to grieve for, but it's something. Since Sara brought her back, I have felt deep grief from her many times. In fact, the first time I didn't was when we crossed the border, before Sara rejoined us. I'd thought it was some kind of extra peace, but it wasn't. She is in pain, and for a moment, neither of us could feel it, even a little.

But even what Sara had let Ember feel wasn't all it. The flood that had come from her on the wagon had nearly drowned out the man who'd vomited as he remembered to grieve for his dead wife. When Sarafyna really pushed, that's when we really met Ember. I can feel it again now. The increasing grief. The agony. And I see the red anger on Ember's face. She isn't going to vomit. She isn't going to weep. She is more ready than she has ever been to draw blood. She grieves a lot like me.

"Are you all right?" Sara asks while Ember grits her teeth.

"Just cut the shit and get it over with," Ember growls. I grimace, bracing myself alongside the ailur woman. And Sarafyna does as she's told.

She pushes, and she pushes hard. The membrane protecting Ember from whatever hurt her starts to tear, and I feel the grief as it escapes; I suffocate in it, while Ember's scowl only deepens. And then it breaks. Whatever control was strangling her snaps, and her rage crescendos. I feel the sickness of oil in water, and my mana grows more powerful by magnitudes in an instant.

"Ask your fucking questions," Ember says, and I nod. I don't hesitate as Sara focuses on keeping Ember free.

"Why did they try to kill me when they saw my arm?" I ask immediately.

"Citizens who excessively alter the natural state of their body are all called cultists. The sages hate them. All them," she explains through gritted teeth.

"Natural? It's a fucking prosthetic! I barely altered shit! The fuck do they even mean by *natural*?" I exclaim.

"I don't know. They have a long list. Anyone who uses alchemical concoctions to focus; anyone who replaces a lost or missing limb; even unnaturally colored hair could get you labeled a cultist, a worshipper of the ancient demon queen. You two . . . You two will definitely piss them off," Ember answers.

"Why do they care?" Sara asks, her eyes closed in focus but her brow furrowing at Ember's explanation.

"Control. And malice," I answer immediately. "That's all it is. It's like an itch to them. An itch they can never scratch. They must own everyone, must dictate everyone's lives. Being unhealthy is a moral failing. Failing to bend the knee is a moral failing. Living outside the box they build for you is a fucking moral failing. They loathe us. They want to control us. And every inch of us is subject to their malice."

Ember nods.

"Yes. And they will die for it. But that's not all it is, Lillith. They are afraid. Not just the fear you are describing; I've seen that too. But they are fucking terrified. They live like gods but act like they fear a real one when they encounter too many cultists. You are all to be killed on sight, if you are found. More so than anyone else they hate. I don't know why," Ember says, hot tears running through her fur now.

I clench my own fists. All right. I'll take her word for it. It makes sense she won't have answers for everything. This means any changes I make will definitely be noticed, but . . . my limbs are going to give me away anyway.

I'm going to have to mostly hide my body regardless. And to be honest, I want to make them fear me more.

I'm going to start again. I'm going to show them exactly how much I can warp my body from their ideal design. How far I can stray from their control. But I can dwell on that later.

"This prophecy about me—how much of it is old, and how much new?" I ask.

"I don't pay much attention to that shit. Few people took it more seriously than they would a child's story until one of the sages started pushing it out everywhere a few years ago. That was when the name 'Annie' was first introduced. I think the chimera pet is a revelation from the same sage.

"It was startling, how fast the fairy tale of you became a major concern all around two countries. I don't know why, but I know they are afraid of you, and that means you can help me kill them," Ember answers. "They shut down half their own playgrounds because of you. Tried to shut down yours, even. But they are too afraid to pass through the Nexus, and yours is surrounded by it."

This answer introduces a large number of new questions, but for some reason, one word seems more important to me than the others. "Playgrounds?" I ask.

"That's what they call all the countries on the third plane," she explains. "All them are playgrounds."

"The third plane, as in hell," I say. "That's Potestia?" I think she has referred to it similarly before, but I had been distracted and sick.

"Potestia and all the countries like it. The Republic and Council Lands are the first plane, the Nexus the second, and the countries like the one you lived in the third," she confirms.

That's . . . interesting. How did the country I live in become the mythical version of hell everyone always referenced? I guess I can see a sick way in which a griefless country might look like heaven, but why do the people growing up in the third plane still refer to it as a terrible place where they might be sent? There must be a long story behind that.

"And why do they call them playgrounds?" I press. Ember is trembling now, her claws drawing blood from her hands. This will have to be the last question for the night.

"Because that is what they are," she replies through gritted teeth.

"The Nexus is pushing back harder," Sara interjects. "Someone really doesn't want her answering this."

"No shit," Ember spits. "This is the first question you've asked that anyone at the bar out there couldn't have answered, were it safe to ask them." She takes a deep breath, and I brace myself. "How many gods do you think can live side by side, trading and sharing power and praise?" My face pales as the realization settles onto me. "How much praise do these mewling idiots even deserve in a world that has already met dozens of them?"

Fuck.

"It's a game. They build them. They send whatever groups they want to live around there. Sometimes people they hate. Sometimes groups they prefer. Then, one at a time, they go and live in one themselves. They spend a couple years there, or a couple decades, basking in a world where they are the special ones, where they have all the advantages. That's what the third plane is. It's where the sages make sure they are the only god to worship.

The soap. The goddamn soap only the nobles could use. The restricted knowledge and advancement. The thousand stagnant years. Every oddity of a country that could only have been sustained by the goddamn Radiant Woods interfering directly. Their desire to help Godfrey reset it. It was all starting to make sense.

Playgrounds. Not countries. Places to receive unearned praise, to show up and "invent" ideas the country should have worked its way to itself. Because that's always how it goes, isn't it? Deny, deny, deny. Hoard, hoard, hoard. Then show off the ideas you stole from someone else. Someone who works for you or lives in another fucking world, and demand praise for it. But because they are so small, so petty, so drunk on themselves, they can't even think of anything useful, so they starve people of basic necessities and easy ideas. Because they are easier to remember. Easier to understand. Easier to pretend they came up with it when they sell it to the people they intentionally stole it from.

But I still have questions. "What happens when they are done there? What about the fucking Collector? If the sages are meant to be the special ones, why does the church serve the fucking Nexus? How did Potestia get completely sealed off by the Radiant Woods? Why do the sages fear it so much?" She answers none of these. The flood of grief coming from her snaps away like an overstressed rubber band. The trembling stops.

"I'm sorry," Sara says. "It started fighting back, and . . . I couldn't. I couldn't hold on longer."

"Is that all? Can I get some fucking rest now?" Ember insists, and I nod. She marches out of the room like nothing happened, but my blood is on fire.

"Ember was right. We need to kill every single sage."

Just Enough Rope

I didn't get every question answered, not even close. But I know enough now to make a few decisions. Whatever my feelings toward Ember as a person are, she is right. This country, both of these countries, need liberation. Quite a few places do, if they are herding us like sheep to play hapless townsfolk for their fantasy fulfilment. I need names. I need details. I need to know every single person I need to kill to free this world from the vise grip of pathetic authority.

I also need to get stronger. The kings I sacrificed so much to kill were the mages they successfully suppressed and controlled for a thousand years. Well, maybe. I know their control was still effective in ways. At the same time, it's possible the royal family's power grew to exceed expectations as the Radiant Woods cut us off from direct access. But that only begs the question of how they maintained control. My head hurts. I'm tired, angry, and scared.

"What's the plan?" Sara asks. "Do we just . . . do the same thing as last time?" I shake my head before I answer, using steel mana to summon the new jewelry I want to use to aid my growth. Little weapons I can use to bridge the gap. I speak as the rings form.

"It won't work. In a sick way, we got lucky in Potestia. They controlled their entire population with divine magic; anyone would lash out against that kind of direct, forceful manipulation once they had room to breathe.

It gave the kings of Potestia more obvious control, but it was also erasable. Freeing Potestia was like unlocking a literal chain. But this is a republic. I don't know about the Council Lands, but this is going to be much more difficult."

"But they are being controlled here too, aren't they?" Sara asks.

"Well, yes," I concede. "But it's not the same. It may be with people like Ember—agents they actually expected to encounter me—but the average citizen? Stealing people's grief is an entirely different can of worms. First of all, it's not safe to rip that Band-Aid off right away. Grief wasn't meant to build up and hit like a truck all at once. You are supposed to feel and process through it over time. If we just tear that wall down without a plan, it will break people.

"Besides, some people may actually feel grateful to not feel grief. I don't know if they have therapists here—they didn't in Potestia—but . . . many people won't realize the damage its absence has done to them. All that pain at once? They won't join hands with the person who handed it to them. They will hate me. Hell, they have already been conditioned to."

"But we can't leave them this way either," Sara protests. I nod in agreement.

"We can't, but we need to figure out a way to do it safely. I just . . . don't know how. How could I? We need time. But that's not the only problem. Like I said, it's a republic, which means the culture probably isn't built with the commoners fighting against the nobility—it's citizens fighting against each other over which rich asshole they want to rule them. Thousands of ideas. Thousands of tribes.

"And while a lot of people will hate individual sages, they will offer their loyalty to others instead. A republic is a country run on a popularity contest rather than lineage like a monarchy. Everyone will live in ideological wars with each other while their oppressors treat their competition like a colleague they are going against for a promotion," I explain.

Sara furrows her brow. "So we are unlikely to easily build communities out of regular people this time. That makes sense. I am a good sage though. Maybe some of the leaders here are as well. Couldn't we start with them and the people loyal to them?"

I am not excessively hopeful about that. "Well, we can check. We need to learn as much as we can about all them anyway. There will probably already be groups who are benevolent and want the same things we do, especially if stealing grief is a more recent act. Shit, I should have asked Ember about that earlier.

"I doubt we'll find any supporters of any sage we can work with, however. If they are participating in the culture, they are probably complicit in it to some degree. Authority structures are usually set up so you can't advance in them without accepting their abuses on some level. And in my experience with elections . . . well, the most popular groups usually either actively want to kill people like us, or they want us to be quiet about being killed.

"In any case, there is no way to simply start hunting the rich. Rather than mind control, they will likely have used manipulation. Otherwise, they wouldn't need elections at all. The wealthy will have fans among their victims. This doesn't mean we shouldn't kill abusers all the same, but it does mean we will usually make as many enemies among the common people as allies when we do. That's how they work. They give people teams to root for so they can feel like they are winning a competition. When they get exploited, the losers believe they can stop it by winning next time. And the winners? Well, sure, they are still getting exploited, but at least their team is winning and they can gloat over the losers."

"So it's not mind control but a type of control that looks like agency." Sara scowls. "I am familiar with that, at least." I can see memories of her time in the Radiant Woods flash across her face. The way it kept her there after she had learned to escape on her own. The way it sent the "monsters" to kill me when I was there. She understands even better than I do.

"Just enough rope to hang themselves with," I confirm.

"So, no plan yet, then," she guesses.

"No plan yet," I agree with a nod. "First, we learn. Then, maybe we organize. But we need a shit ton more information. And I need more power."

As I say this, I finish the last of the rings. There's one for my nose, lip, eyebrow, and other similar ideas; I've even created new earrings. My limbs don't have to be the only things that store power; a few more trinkets like these, and I'll have a real advantage. "It has been an absolutely shitty day. I need to go blow off some steam," I say.

"Do you need any help?" Sara offers. I pause for a moment before nodding.

"Yeah, actually. I promised to meet up with our new friend, Turner.

I suspect he has made some poor decisions recently and needs a friendly neighborhood feminist to show him the error of his ways."

Sarafyna, my kind, gentle, slightly shy girlfriend gives me a grin too wide for the human face, displaying entirely too many teeth. She has enjoyed this part a little too much ever since escaping the Radiant Woods. I can hardly blame her.

"And what can I do to help?" she asks.

"Nothing much, just stay hidden and keep an eye on me," I reply. "This creep already knows I can beat him in a contest of magic. He may pretend he thinks I was lucky or cheated or some bullshit, but he knows. I think he is planning to blackmail me, as my hastily built excuse does carry some contradictions. But if he's not a complete moron, he'll expect a violent response instead of compliance. Things could get a little dicey if he has a riot spike or something similar unless, of course, I have a great, powerful, sexy, hat-obsessed sage backing me up."

Sara blushes a little but nods.

"I'll keep myself scarce. Lead the way," she agrees.

Turner opens his door with a smirk and invites me in. "I invited some friends to discuss the issue at hand," he says as I walk in to find a large, gruff, human man and a volu woman in leather armor. Interesting. I'd thought he was just a creep looking for a roll in the hay with a demon queen lookalike. For free, of course. But this doesn't look like a particularly horny group, so what does he want, then?

"A pleasure," I intone, flicking my eyes back and forth as Turner locks the door behind him. They say nothing, and I casually take a seat on a chaise to the side. "So. Let's talk."

"Yes," Turner agrees. "You were going to explain why a whore has so much mana, and why you were traveling on foot."

"I prefer 'sex worker,' actually," I dismiss, beginning to pick at one fingernail as if bored. "And I'd be more interested in your story. Showing up out of nowhere. Traveling on foot, which you seem to find strange, to rescue a caravan just as it's attacked. And you just happen to have 'friends' waiting for you at the first inn we stop at. What are the odds of that?"

"I don't care what you prefer or what you want to talk about. We both know you're not some common whore," he says. "We have you outnumbered, and in case you are thinking you are strong enough to fight all us, we already have your friend. Because you are right, I wasn't there by coincidence. I was there on something of a . . . recruitment mission. And the woman you left, the ugly one, she's been recruited by now. The rest of my crew would have picked her up shortly after we left; I let them know about your high appraisal of her combat abilities via whisper. If you ever want to see her again, you'll do as I say."

I hold my hand to my chest and put on an obviously mocking expression of shock.

"Well. That's quite the pickle, isn't it?" I respond. "I suppose since you've got me by the balls here, you might as well tell me what you want me, and my very attractive friend, for."

"Still relaxed, are you? You still think you can beat us? Or maybe you didn't care much for the other woman. All right. Nadine, go ahead and activate it." Turner smirks.

As expected, the volu woman pulls a familiar-looking spike out of her bag. It probably doesn't work exactly like mine, but that is a riot spike. She activates it with her mana, and I am immediately glad I took a seat. All my artificial limbs go limp in an instant, and I start to feel sick. "It cost me quite a bit to acquire this, military grade and all. But I think you'll find it's quite effective. You may have stood a chance with magic, but now? You belong to us. You may as well accept it."

"And what do you plan to do with me? Sell me? To whom?"

He smiles. Behind him, a fleshy ooze slowly pours from the ceiling, creating something of a meaty web behind both of Turner's henchmen. As two massive spider legs extend from opposite sides of the room, I smile pleasantly at Turner.

"You'll see when you get there. Let's just say you are a far more lucrative catch than the mercs on the caravan were. The Lillith bit may even make you more valuable. They can sell that," he says.

In unison, two sharp black legs impale two throats, quick and nearly silent. *Fuck, my girlfriend is cool.* Flesh surrounds the bodies, dissolving them and adding their mana to Sarafyna's aura.

As meaty talons descend from above, I cross my human leg over my limp steel one. The foot hangs a bit awkwardly, but that's all right. He looks like he is about to speak again when the talons grab his shoulders and flesh wraps around his mouth, suffocating and gagging him. His eyes widen in horror as I rest my chin in my human hand.

"Huh. I guess my friend made it here safely after all. How nice. So, Turner. You want to answer my question now? What was the plan? And I'd prefer if you didn't scream, although I don't think it will do much. My friend—the *ugly one*, as you rudely called her—is likely blocking sound with her Nexus energy. You know how sages are." His eyes widen further and his struggling stops almost immediately. I nod, and Sara releases his mouth.

"I didn't know, I'm sorry. I never would have—" he immediately starts begging but I cut him off.

"What was the plan, Turner?"

"I—The arena. We recruit gladiators, usually from mercenaries and the like, but once you beat me and bragged about your—about Her Honor, we thought you would be valuable," he explains. I raise an eyebrow.

"Arena? Where is that?" I ask.

"You . . . You haven't heard of it? How is that possible?"

I sigh. "Oh, so it's common knowledge, then. I guess that is all I need to know. Well, that and where the rest of your friends are," I respond.

"Th-they went ahead. To the arena. Or they were supposed to. Last I heard, they were still looking for the—Her Honor. We didn't know she was a sage—we didn't know you were a sage!" he pleads. "And you, who are you?" His eyes fix desperately on mine, and I give him a wide grin.

"Well, who the fuck do I look like?" I ask. It takes him a moment before he realizes what I mean, and a minute is all he has left. Just as his mouth is opening in horror, Sara snaps his neck and absorbs him.

As she begins collecting her body back into one place and deactivating the riot spike, I grit my teeth. An arena, is it? That's problematic. Republics are already harder to start revolutions in, but if they openly have fucking gladiators? Well, the Overton window is already far, far wider than it should be.

Sages and their games. People's lives, games, and entertainment.

I have work to do.

CHAPTER TWELVE

Hurting to Heal

Are you sure you don't want to wait another day? We really don't mind! You must have been walking all night!" Quinn offers, but Sara shakes her head.

"I'm all right, really. We'd like to get to town quickly, so I don't mind resting on the way," she replies. Quinn looks to me with concern, but I just nod.

"She's made of sturdy stuff," I insist. "You don't need to worry about us, although we are grateful you do." Quinn shrugs and shakes his head.

"Well, I suppose if you don't mind. We do appreciate the escort; it makes us feel safer to have you traveling with us, what with Turner up and vanishing in the middle of the night. Didn't even bother to check out, and we haven't paid him in full yet. I wonder where he went," Quinn responds as I shrug.

"Maybe one of the sages ate him for being such a dipshit. It doesn't matter; we got you," I reply. Sara smiles innocently while Quinn simply sighs, turning to go find his husband and daughter.

We've decided to go the rest of the way with this group rather than hire another wagon. No point in cooking up fresh bullshit for someone new when these two have already bought our first serving. I also don't want to leave them alone. Travel between cities is more common and therefore more dangerous than it ever was in Potestia. He is safer without Turner than he ever was with him, but I still want to offer the family what safety I can.

August approaches as Sara and I are reloading our bags into the packed wagon. Autumn climbs onto the seat up front next to Ember, which concerns me a bit. Ember is not known for her kindness.

"Looks like it's us three today," he says. "Autumn is looking for some fresh air." I glance at his sister again as she rests her head against the frame of the wagon's cover. Her eyes are closed, and she is taking deep breaths of the open air. Her grief feels like an icy breeze, empowering and hurting me at the same time.

"Do you want me to talk to Ember? Make sure she doesn't say anything stupid?" I ask, but August shakes his head.

"No, but do you have a moment, uh, alone?" he asks. I glance at Sara, who nods.

"I'll go finish packing up the room," she agrees before leaving me and August to talk.

"What's up?" I ask. August barely glances up in confusion before dismissing my odd manner of speech, well used to it by now.

"It's Autumn. Lily, she's not doing well. I don't know how much longer asking for 'one more day' will help. I have to ask, will she ever feel better?" I bite my lip. August has been a really good sport. Without him, I don't know if I could keep Autumn going. But that very weight must be wearing on him.

"Define *better*." I sigh. "I don't know. Henry . . . my brother's death had a permanent effect on her. Everyone's death—" I pause. "How much did she tell you about her role in that last fight in Visenar?"

August hangs his head. "She told me everything, I think. I know why she blames herself, at least," he answers. I nod and continue.

"Right. The guilt of that, and everyone it affected . . . We can put the blame where it really belongs—with the man I killed. But her and I, we both made mistakes that made it possible for him to do so. That's not something you can just take off like a dirty shirt. Neither is the absence of someone you loved. It lives with you until you die, and you can never entirely be who you were before you lost them, before you made that mistake. Before you were hurt. But . . . it does get better. You learn ways to confront it and live with it. Autumn will heal, but she'll heal with a scar," I say. August's lips tighten.

"What about with . . . a shortcut?" he asks. I pause, still trying to Tetris all the bags to fit while leaving room for everyone riding inside.

"What do you mean?"

He looks at his feet when he replies. "I don't understand a lot of what's going on, but I understand enough. The people here, in the Republic—they don't have to feel all that grief, right? The only reason *we* can is because Sarafyna protects us from the influence of the sages, or whoever is doing it. Quinn and Kobe, they seem so happy without it. Couldn't we let Autumn feel the same?" His eyes are desperate, with water building up in the corners. I have to close my own for a moment, grieving the question on its own.

"That would surely kill her," I answer.

"W-what?" he asks. "Why? It isn't killing anyone else!"

"Is it not?" I counter. "Are you sure? Grief . . . Grief doesn't exist on its own like some kind of cancer to be scraped away. It's not a disease to be fought off. It's not the reason she is hurting—it's the reason she has a chance at working through it. People are complex and scary and confusing. We can't pick and choose which emotions to feel. Without grief, we still feel pain and loss and guilt. Grief is how we process trauma. Without it, whatever is hurting us doesn't go away. It festers like an infected wound. We can cover her eyes and plug her ears, but that will only make it impossible for her to go anywhere. No. People need to grieve. Without grief, there is no chance at healing."

"Quinn and Kobe don't seem to be in pain, Lily. Except when they had their grief back. The rest of the time, they seem happier than you or me," August complains.

"That's not because they don't feel that pain, August. That's because they lack the tools they need to express it! But just like physical agony hurts more if you can't scream, loss hurts more if you can't grieve. Mark my words: Quinn is no happier than your sister. He's just suffocating on emptiness he can't express.

"Think about it, August. He wasn't witnessing his wife die when he got his grief back. He was in a comfortable wagon among friends, with a new family. So why did he react so strongly? Why did they all collapse under grief the moment it was an option? Because the pain behind it never left, it just built and built and built. Never being processed. Never healing. Think of how many things there have been to grieve for in your life: every rejection, death, breakup. Imagine if you had never been able to move on, to shed a single tear over them, just living with each and every one like a fresh wound every day, all your life. Living in this country must be agony," I say.

August sets his jaw. "You don't know that, Lily. How can you know that? Autumn is hurting now, and all we have to do is let the pain stop! She can be herself again! I get what you're saying, but it's all just guessing! You don't really know how these people feel! Sara just has to let Autumn get better! That's all she has to do! Stop!" he insists. I sigh.

"What Sarafyna is doing for us is protecting us from outside influence. From force. From some other sage digging their fingers through our hearts and heads and setting things as they see fit. Even in a world where what these sages are doing is harmless, they don't get to rule our fucking minds! If Sara stops protecting your sister from that, who is to say it'll stop at grief? What if they change who she is as a person to fit their whims?

"Look at Ember! She is tearing herself apart trying to be who she is and who she was designed to be at the same time! And August, Sara can't fix it. She can give Ember moments of clarity, but that's it. Moments. Once they worm their way under Autumn's skin, they are there. We can't undo it. People who love control don't settle for compromises. They will take your sister from you entirely, and she will never really be happy again."

August balls his fists and punches the frame of the wagon. "Dammit, Lily. This is your fault! You did this to her! We would have been fine—we all would have been fine if we had never fucking met you. And now you won't even try to help her! I thought that was the whole point of you! To prevent grief like this! She is hurting so much, and it is your fucking fault!"

I wince.

"August, I want to help her. I do. I just can't do it the way you are asking me to. And I don't think Autumn wants that. She saw Quinn yesterday too, saw the option of grief being taken away. She is a grown woman, fully capable of asking for the same herself, but didn't you hear her? She was angry! She was furious that they weren't grieving like she was! She was disgusted by the thought. I won't do that to her, especially if she doesn't explicitly ask for it," I insist. There is no point arguing over blame. He's right. What Autumn is going through is my fault. Henry's death is my fault. And I can't even tell him I would undo everything I have done if I could. Too many people needed it to be done.

"Well, then let's ask her!" August insists, gently pounding his fist against the frame again, less in anger and more in frustration.

"I can't stop you from doing that," I respond. "But we're going to go to a larger city first. We're going to have a chance to see how this control affects the people there on a wide scale. Can you at least wait until you have actually seen it before you try to push this on her? Just let her grieve until then, and we can talk again if you still think it's a good idea." August glares at me.

"Fine. But we *will* be talking about this again," he agrees.

As he turns, his angry demeanor melts away, revealing the amiable man I have grown accustomed to. I'm a little taken aback, but I understand. August is a good man. A kind man. And he doesn't like disagreeing with me much. I don't think his crush ever faded entirely, despite his lack of pursuit once he learned why I was uninterested. But he loves his sister more than anything.

I understand. I do. Wanting that pain to just . . . go away. It would be hard not to feel like he does. But the solution he is suggesting is, well, abuse. Well intentioned, but abuse nonetheless. I wish we could help like he wants, but we can't. If Autumn can no longer process Henry's loss, she will undoubtedly die.

I am left to finish packing the wagon while trying to ignore the hollow aching in my chest.

The rest of the trip is quiet. Ember doesn't turn out to be a problem. She may say stupid shit about the twins when we get slowed down, but she is perfectly happy to remain silent the rest of the time. Those riding up front don't speak the entire way, which I suspect is what Autumn was looking for. August is fairly quiet as well, leaving Sara and I to make polite conversation with the owners of the wagon.

This is how we learn this arena is in Circoba, the city we are approaching. I suppose this makes sense, as Turner would likely have been looking to bring gladiators there relatively quickly.

I want to get a good look at it when I can, meet whoever runs it. And by *meet* I mean negotiate a speedy and clean divorce between their head and the rest of their body. But first, I want to visit the library. And the church.

The temple apparently exists in a similar capacity to the Potestian version, although some language has been changed. Some worship the sages, and others the Nexus directly, which if my guess is correct, means they technically worship the Collector.

In a way, they are kind of like different denominations, or even different religions which share a deity, although I am uncertain to what degree they are aware of each other. Then again, even after the sages were cut off from Potestia, they still managed to limit advancement somehow. A shared deity would certainly aid this, especially considering the level of mind control commoners were under. As for the nobles . . . well, you don't really need to control someone's mind to stop them from pursuing change when they are benefitting from the status quo.

Still. The library is first; an institution I am delighted to learn exists extensively in every city. I could have used one growing up in Potestia. I can certainly use one now. We are going to learn everything we can about these fucking sages, this country, and about the Council too. And when we do, we will do what we do best. Nothing ever burns down by itself, as they say.

As the wagon arrives in the city—the first I have seen without literal walls around it—I am again struck by the complete lack of grief around me. In a way, it's a relief. The feeling has always made me want to vomit. I've grown used to it over the years, but it's never been pleasant. On a surface level, it feels good to be around people without my stomach churning so much, but it's a bit like poison: If you are going to be served any at all, it's better to get the one you can taste.

"Are you all right, Annie?" Sara asks. I give her a half smile.

"I'm okay for now. It's just . . . too quiet, I guess," I respond awkwardly. There is plenty of noise outside the wagon to contest this. Enough that, although we haven't actually looked at our surroundings outside the comfortable cover, it's obvious we've entered a large, bustling place.

Quinn and Kobe look at me with confusion, but Sara understands. She wraps an arm around my waist, and I rest my head on her shoulder.

She whispers in my ear as the wagon slows. "We'll fix it, Annie. We'll fix everything."

Actual Lives

Oakley

Mr. Myer?" my assistant asks for the third time, finally forcing me to look away from the window and give her my attention. I don't have time for whatever it is she is bothering me with, but it's impossible to find anyone with any sense for the position.

"What is it?" I ask with irritation. I can't quite recall her name; Susan or Selena or something. It doesn't matter. I just need her to spit out whatever it is and leave me alone.

"Um, you have a meeting, sir. About the internships. It, um, started about twenty minutes ago," she informs me. I roll my eyes. This is what she is bothering me for? A bunch of journalism students working for credit?

"And what was it they wanted?" I groan. I am under too much stress for this. Hasn't she been watching the fucking news? Does she really think I have time for useless shit like this?

"Um, their internships are up, sir; we had promised them permanent positions based on performance, but none of the qualifying participants have received their offer letter yet. They are speaking to Aaron, the department head, but you said you wanted to sign off on any new positions. The meeting is with him," she explains. What a waste of my time.

"They're journalists, right? Have him open up a tip jar for them on the website," I answer before looking back out the window. "If they are any good, people will pay them to keep working." I can't think about that right now. It's not safe to think about that right now. Doesn't she know people have died? My friends have died, and she is here talking about interns?

"Sir?" I snap my eyes back to her. "I don't think that will bridge the—"

I slam my hand on the desk.

"If that and what we have already done for them isn't enough, tell him to fire them. We are a family here; we don't need entitled scum like that trying to leech off us. We can always get more interns. I'm done talking about this. Get out," I order. I am done with this. Does she not know what "chief executive officer" means? My life is at stake, and she wants me to worry about nobodies.

Once they catch that psycho bitch, it might be time to look into replacing her as well. If I could risk letting anyone new near me right now, she would already be gone.

"Yes, sir," she agrees before turning to leave.

"Wait." I stop her, one thought coming to mind. She pauses and turns back to me. "That one intern, James or something. Keep an eye on him and let me know where he ends up. I like his stuff; I'd like to keep reading it."

". . . Yes, sir," she agrees. That pause seals her fate. Once it is safe, I am definitely replacing her. It disgusts me that I have to even wait this long, but . . . I do. Once it's safe.

And it will be safe again. I'll make sure of it.

I am not prey—I am the predator. I will not be hunted. I will not be the latest name on the news, the latest casualty the uninformed masses cheer for. No. I will make a fucking example out of this woman, whoever she is, who thinks she can make *me* fear *her*. Interns. Who has time for a meeting about intern pay? People's actual lives are on the line here. Fuck her interns.

CHAPTER THIRTEEN

The Best of Us

Edward

I sit in front of the pillar of glass as I do every day. Visenar is taking a long time to clean up after all the destruction Darian left in his wake. I am here to help with that, but I always take some time here. No one has gotten around to this part yet. It's not in the way of anything, no homes or businesses destroyed nearby. It's on its way to the palace, a path few people tread anymore. Someone will want to remove it once everything else is done. I wonder if anyone will know who he was. If anyone will ask.

I killed him. That much is clear. I've never met another mage with glass mana, and by now, most people know I fought in the palace on Insurrection Day. It's obvious I killed him, and I did so in an instant. He was slowing me down, and I couldn't afford to be delayed. I couldn't. I barely remember the moment I realized I had to kill him, the panic that made me do it without hesitation. He looks afraid, now. Shocked. Like he didn't realize the danger until a moment before his death.

I wanted to be him so badly, so desperately. He has always been a pillar in my life to scale, a peak beyond my reach. Until the end. Until I needed to stop someone and he was in my way. I killed him so quickly it feels wrong, like he should have had some long speech, some final words. A goodbye of sorts. Instead, he was just an obstacle to get past.

Why does death have to be so fast? So permanent? I can't help but wonder, if I could have had a chance to really talk to him, if he could have been saved. If he could have let go of all the perceived slights to his pride like I did.

"Henry is dead," I say. I tell him this every day, and like every day, he fails to respond. "When he was taken the first time, it was my fault. He was there to get me, to save me from myself. From spiraling like . . . He was there for me. And he wanted to work with me to escape. I agreed, then . . . sacrificed him to escape myself. It was my fault he was taken."

Again, my—the man I killed just stares back, face still contorted in horror. Eyes still empty.

"I always thought I would make up for it someday. You know, after Lily saved him, after she fixed my mistake . . . He never told anyone what I did, kept it secret. Never threatened me with the information either. He didn't go looking for any justice for my cowardice. Never even brought it up privately. He just didn't trust me anymore, which was deserved. But somehow, it hurt so much more than everyone knowing what a coward I am. How weak I am. How much suffering my brother went through because of my cowardice.

"He still called me his brother, was still kind. Never once did he utter a single sharp word in my direction. The Collector knows Lily would have. She would have beat me into the ground with one of her lectures. I would have preferred that. Instead, I lived with my little brother constantly on the other side of thick glass. Smiling. Waving. But never within reach."

The man I killed doesn't condemn me for this. He never does. And it never feels better to confess to him. I continue anyway.

"I thought, if I kept fighting, kept making up for my past, someday that glass wall would come down. He wouldn't just forgive me but maybe even trust me again. I was going to prove that I wasn't the coward who abandoned him. And you know what? When I got the spikes back, I thought maybe I had gotten there. I fought Prince Kallon, one of the most powerful mages in the country. I faced him head-on and won. I didn't run away. I didn't hide. And I thought surely, this time, I will face my brother and he will know I'm not a fucking coward anymore. He will know that, next time, I will protect him. From now on, he can feel safe and at ease, knowing that I won't abandon him ever again."

I take a deep breath as my voice starts to tremor. "But I'd already seen him for the last time. I just didn't know it yet. One last awkward goodbye from a brother who never trusted me again. He is in another pillar, like you, but his is stone instead of glass. His death was also too quick. No final words or goodbyes. I guess one of us did grow up to be like you after all, in a way."

There is no humor in the joke, only bitterness. I am the only child anything like our father, and I will die ashamed of it, someday. "He was the best of us. Better than me, than Gil, than Lily. He deserved to be the happiest. And he is gone. And I don't know what to do. I am cleaning up the city, helping rebuild after all that destruction, but I'm lost. Aimless. What do I do now? How do I move forward?"

"E-Edward Endings?"

I tense up, turning to see a wiry man with his hat in his hand. He is jittery and carries a wild look in his eyes. He is in a full-on panic, but everything is calm; I can't understand it.

"Yes?" I offer. A wave of anxiety flows off him all at once as he realizes he's found me.

"Please, they need help. There was an attack. No one knows what to do; none of us are used to fighting. We still can't contact the Mage of Mourning, and we don't know who else to ask," he begs. My hackles raise. An attack? By whom? Why? And why am I the person they came looking for?

"Show me," I answer, and the wiry man nods, nearly breaking into a sprint toward the center of the city. There is a tremor in the air, like the sound of steel bending. It's just a feeling, but it runs down my spine and hastens my step. The city is ash and rubble as I run past. In all directions, there are pillars of stone. The closer we get to one, the more carnage we see. The further we get, the cleaner the city becomes. But we aren't heading for any of these. No, we are growing closer and closer to the massive tree in the city, where the gallows used to be.

We are headed toward the Radiant Woods.

I brace myself as we finally make it to our destination. Even so, I am unprepared.

The taste of iron in the air is thick, and it's clear to see why. My stomach churns. I'm not ready for this; I'm not who they needed. They need Lily, not me. Anyone but me.

Whatever fighting there is to do is over. Half a dozen volunteers lie dead at the base of the tree, surrounding the broken, mangled body of what can only be described as a monster. Its arms end in jagged, twisted blades. Its legs are the same, extending so far up that each step must have dug blades into its haunches. Its head has been crushed by a massive stone, while smaller rocks surround its bruised, bloody body. There are maybe ten remaining bystanders, exhausted and bloodied. Two are bandaging a third, while the rest catch their breath.

"W-what happened here?" I ask, horror washing over me. The terrified man who came to get me shakes his head, looking toward the wounded woman.

"Monsters aren't supposed to escape from the Woods," she grumbles. "I don't know why. But this one did." She spits in its direction, much to the chagrin of the woman in charge of bandaging her.

"Please, tell me everything," I ask, trying to suppress the shaking in my voice.

Gilbert

Dom watches the tree line as I draw. He's been keeping me company every day as I watch. Neither of us intend to miss suffering again. Neither of us intend to be too late to stop tragedy. We will not let anyone else die while we enjoy ourselves.

"Any luck?" I ask as he shakes his head, dropping the hand with the whisper sphere to his side.

"Still no contact," he answers. Shit. She is traveling on foot; she shouldn't be too far for these to work. As far as I know, with Sarafyna's whisper spheres, there is no such thing as *too far* to work, and yet, we haven't been able to contact any of them for days. They haven't stopped by the hat shop either. They are completely cut off from us. Which means, if something does happen, we are on our own.

This was always a possibility, but it wasn't considered likely so soon and is pretty close to the worst-case scenario. I pause while drawing Dom's nose.

"What do we do if we never get in contact with them?" I ask. He pauses.

"I . . . don't know. I'd like to believe I'll be able to protect everyone, but"—he sighs—"I've believed that before." I still haven't asked him for his entire story, but I heard about the last battle he was in, when Tumult was destroyed. He should have been stronger than his opposition, but he lost, and a lot of people died. He may understand what I'm going through even better than I do.

"We will," I say. "Whatever comes, we'll be ready."

He looks forward at the Radiant Woods again. "I hope so," he whispers.

I take a deep breath. I don't know how to comfort him, but he is helping me, and I want to do the same. I open my mouth to try, but a gentle buzzing goes off in my jacket, and I reach in to find my sphere is active.

"Hey," I greet. "Everything all right over there?" Only one person ever calls me on this sphere. My . . . friends back in the other community don't contact me as much. They can't really connect with me right now. I don't blame them. They are sympathetic, but they just don't get it. The grief they understand, but not the guilt. No, the only person who calls me now is Edward.

"No, Gil," Ed says, fear apparent in his voice. Dom's face shifts in an instant from melancholy to steel. "Something has changed. There was some kind of attack. Gil, the monsters in the Woods can leave now!" My blood runs cold for a moment. Dom clenches his fists.

"Wait. Wait, wait, wait. No, Lily said they are just people; that should be fine, right? She wished they would come out on their own so they'd be easier for Sara to find and help. But they aren't supposed to be able to survive outside the control of the Woods; not without a divine mage, right?" I ask.

"I don't know. But this one came out in Visenar, Gil. It killed six people! One of them killed six people! What if it's not the last?" Ed pleads, and my heart quickens.

"Gilbert, this isn't good," Dom whispers, taking the sphere from me. "Ed, this is important. This monster, did they attack first? Or did the people they killed make the first move?"

Ed is silent for a long moment, leaving Dom and I a chance to talk.

"Gilbert, if what Lily says is true and these monsters are innocent people . . . what's going to happen if they start showing up everywhere at once?"

"I—I don't know, but Sara won't be able to help them. But why would it attack the volunteers?" I ask.

"We don't know that they did. They could have escaped the Woods, looking like a monster, and incited what felt like self-defense. That's why I asked who attacked first. This is what I'm worried about, Gil. Is this a single instance, or is this going to happen all over? And what will people do if it does? People will die!"

My face pales.

"And if it did attack first?" I ask. Dom pauses, his eyes returning to the trees.

"If they did attack first . . . a lot more people will die," he responds. Just as he does, Ed's voice returns.

"I—I can't tell. No one is sure. What are we going to do, Gil?" he begs.

I look at Dominic, whose eyes are widening.

"I don't know," Dom replies. "But we need to figure something out quickly. It just happened here too."

CHAPTER FOURTEEN

Joy and Uncertainty

Charlotte

Someday, no one will be able to tell us what to do or who to be," Amelia promised. Her hand held mine as my heart pounded in my chest, not at the rush of her presence but out of fear. Of that ominous cloud of ever-present eyes. Of the shocked horror of my father, like he could appear from around any corner at any time.

The possibility terrified me almost enough for me to pull my hand back. Almost. I continued to hold my friend's hand. It was worth being caught. She saw me through everything. Through my name, my clothes, my father's watchful eye, she saw who I really was. Serenity.

"You think so?" I whispered. She gave me the confident smile only a child knows how to wear properly.

"Oh, definitely," she promised. "You'll be Serenity to everyone, and I'll be Amelia. And our kids will be whoever they want to be."

"How?" I asked. "How can we ever live like that, Amy? Dad will never allow it. He'll never let us go." Amelia's face failed to falter.

"He can't stop us, not forever! Someday, you and I can both go far away from here, where he'll never be able to reach us. And we'll let anyone else who wants to come with us. Mom says the world is bigger than your dad imagines, with more people in it than he's ever met. And when we are bigger and have our own money, we can see it all, until we find somewhere that no one else goes to. Somewhere where no one is in charge of us, and no one gets to choose our names for us!" she responded. But she was wrong. She didn't understand. Even what we were doing was dangerous.

"There is nowhere he can't reach," I whispered as she pouted.

"Oh, come on, Sera, sure there is! If he could control everything, he would have already stopped us from seeing each other!" she insisted.

The very suggestion forced me to look over my shoulder again. Our own little corner of the world remained untouched. It was a quiet spot under the stairs in a rarely used wing of the mansion. It should have felt like a refuge, but it always seemed to increase my sense of shame, like I was doing something wrong by hiding, by meeting up with a friend where we could be alone. Maybe it was just fear rather than shame, but after a lifetime with my father, I can't tell the difference anymore. Always feel one with the other; that was the message of every beating.

"If you say so," I agreed half-heartedly. It was a beautiful dream. I wished I could fully believe in it. A few months later, Amelia took the first step toward it, trusting her mother with it, the woman who'd made her believe. Not long after that, she was gone forever. I stopped hoping to see her again years ago. Decades. But . . . something has changed.

"Hey, Char-Char!" Ryanna greets, forcing my eyes to slowly open. "You awake yet?" I groan as the blur of the younger woman comes into focus. I'd been with Amelia again. I didn't want to wake up yet. "Leo found another one! Come see!" This wakes me up the rest of the way.

"Really? We weren't even traveling. How did he find someone?" I ask while she shrugs.

"I guess they just sort of stumbled into the clearing and started to heal," she answers, and I furrow my brow. That's odd. We have caught up to a few people already while following them. Our numbers have increased to seven or eight now. This is the first person to literally come to us.

"Aren't they all heading in the same direction? Why would someone come back this way?"

"Beats me. Maybe this time they'll remember why they were going that way in the first place," she answers. I suppose she is right; the best way to get answers is to ask our new friend. Part of me wonders if we will finally find someone who is simply injured or sick, like Lillith said we would. So far, everyone we have found has, well, shared our struggle.

Back in Potestia, I'd had to actively search for allies in this fight. Now, every single person we find and save is one of us, to the point that it is growing suspicious. The houses of penance were full but with few people like me. There must be a reason we are finding only people like us here.

At the same time, I can't help but hope. What if? What if this time, we find Amelia? What if there is hope after all?

My heart speeds up again as I follow Ryanna. Vance sits by the fire, content to wait for us to return as our newest members continue to sleep. We catch up to Leo, who wears a wide grin, something I am gradually becoming more familiar with. This is who he was born to be. Out here, with scraps for clothes and scraping for food—a fate that would leave most miserable and which I tried to save him from—he is so, so alive. At his feet sits another "monster," another victim. This one has finished transforming, and Leo has already given them his blanket.

"Well, this is new," our new member greets. No fear. No relief. Just curiosity. I am obviously entering in the middle of a conversation, but this person's unbothered demeanor still feels odd. But one thing is clear: This is not Amelia. Part of me is disappointed. Part of me accepts it immediately, almost with a sense of relief. I deserve the disappointment. And Amelia deserves better than me.

"Right? It takes some getting used to, but it feels . . ." Leo responds, trailing off at the end.

"Amazing," I finish under my breath. Leo nods enthusiastically. Not out of pride; not exactly. He is definitely proud to help people like this, but his joy is so much more pure than that. The joy of community. Of acceptance. Of change that no cruel god can deny. Leo bathes in the reality he has freed, and he overflows with the joy of genuine kindness. Every day, it becomes more pronounced. Every day, it tries to infect me. But I don't deserve it. He earned this joy despite me, not because of me. So I deny the tug at the corners of my mouth.

"Right, amazing! This is my mom, by the way. Her name is Charlotte. Mom, this is Frey! Frey is like us too, but not quite. How did you describe it, Frey?" Leo asks, addressing the person still sitting on the ground.

"Oh, I'm not like anyone but me," Frey responds. Ironically, the phrase immediately reminds me of another friend I had once. A friend I'd lost not to the Radiant Woods but to regular, everyday cruelty.

Again, my traitorous lips try to flick into a gentle smile. I distract myself with my worries instead of responding right away, looking around the clearing we stand in. It's similar to everywhere we have been, what the world looked like before the Radiant Woods grew over it. It's healing, like us. The oppressive reality dominating it has been removed, and the radius of healing seems to be growing as well. Leo is getting stronger, which only inspires fear for him. He is so happy, but we know so little.

I am happy for him. For myself, even, whether I deserve it or not. But what I have done is done. And we still don't know how things worked out back in Potestia. I should have fought with Lillith, should have given everything I had; I know that now. It doesn't mean I was wrong that it was hopeless, just that I was wrong not to fight anyway.

Everyone he loves, except for me, is probably dead because of my mistakes. And what will Leo's newfound joy look like when he returns and finds no one left? What about when the remaining mages of Potestia come after the rest of us? The more he has, the more it will hurt to lose. Above all else, that is what terrifies me. Before, he was miserable, and I hated that I couldn't help him. Now he is overjoyed, and I'm terrified of the whiplash when he loses all that at once.

"Mom, you all right?" Leo asks, and I focus back on his face, his sparkling smile. It makes me want to believe the world can never come crashing down around him. But it can. And I can't protect him. The last time I tried . . . I will never overcome the shame of trying to protect him, so I can only watch.

"I'm all right," I lie. Frey is standing now, and I realize I have been tuning out their conversation. "Just . . . Frey, I'm told you came toward us. Do you remember why?" I ask. I have little hope that they do. No one has remembered much so far. But . . . they were going the wrong way. Maybe, just maybe, this time will be different.

Frey shrugs. "What do you mean?"

"Apparently, most of us were heading in the same direction this whole time. You're the first to come toward us instead of us catching up," Ryanna answers. Frey tilts their head.

"Oh, I remember," they say. "The Nexus wanted me to go the other way real fuckin' bad. Kept telling me they'd turn me back to the way I was, let me go back home." They chuckle and let a sharp breath out their nose. "But you know what? Fuck the Nexus. I didn't want to go back anywhere, and if it wanted me to do something, I was going to do the opposite."

This only makes Leo grin more, and his infectious joy paints the same on Ryanna's face. I remain concerned.

"Wait, you remember before you got here?" I ask again, almost disbelieving.

"Yep, I remember every forsaken day in that shit."

???

I tap my foot impatiently. Sarafyna refuses to let that girl be dead, which is going to be a problem. She could be so powerful without the deadweight. Enough to kill the rest of the sages on her own. It would be better if she were the one to kill each as well. Alone, she is the exact sage I've been looking for for centuries. This world has grown stale, and I have grown weary of it, but the other sages are persistent. They have learned tricks for avoiding my little collector; they are so careful now. I haven't gotten a new one of any quality in so long. It needs to eat all them, and Sarafyna is how I make that happen.

Just as soon as the corpse she brought here with her is dealt with. She is spending so much of her energy keeping that woman alive. I need to arrange for their separation again, and this time, I'll have to handle the obstacle myself, so thoroughly there is no body left to force life back into. Sarafyna may be powerful, even more so than me at the moment, but even she lacks the power to create an entirely new body for her girlfriend's soul to inhabit. Only one person will ever have that power, and that is me, when all is said and done.

Then there is the damn negative mage. He'll need to be dealt with, once he is done with his current task. He could cause some serious hiccups in the plan. But I can work with all these moving pieces. I can use the negative mage to draw Sarafyna back, and once they are separated, I will destroy that walking corpse, and Sarafyna's rage will handle the rest of the sages for me. Her rage and her newfound power, once she's not spending so much of it defying death itself.

All the moving pieces give me a headache, but I grin anyway. Victory is so close I can taste it. It runs down my chin like drool. Just a few more weeks. A few more weeks, and it will all finally be over. I will finally, finally, transcend this hellhole.

CHAPTER FIFTEEN

Top of the Murder List

Lillith

It's good to be in a library again. Not a little bookshop but an actual, honest library. It's a little hint of the life I left behind a long time ago, the hallways of books, the smell of paper, and the hum of respectful silence.

The gooseflesh I've been wearing for weeks seems to calm for a moment as I sit at one of many quiet tables in quiet corners. Across from me, Sarafyna flips through a book, gently brushing her auburn hair behind her ear as it gets in the way. It is a gentle moment, the kind of no significance that I know will live with me until I die. She is beautiful, and the world is calm for a moment.

For a few hours, I don't have to think about the fact that I need to ask her to go back and check on the Potestians. About Leo, who we still haven't found. About letting her leave my sight, my protection. About the risk of waking up happy and hearing, secondhand, that someone I love has been dead for days. A moment where I can live in the radiant warmth of Sarafyna's presence.

I do need to ask her to go back, if only for a little while. I do. I've needed to for days. But . . . I can't bring myself to. It's funny. I can sacrifice myself again and again, risk my own death, lose my limbs and my fucking heartbeat, but once I realize I have to be separated from Sarafyna again, risk losing contact with her again, I am still so, so selfish. I am still not strong enough to really risk what I care about the most. I have to tell her to go back. I have to.

She purses her lips as something in the book she is looking through irritates her. It's adorable. I love her. I have to tell her. I have to ask her to do this. I am too selfish to get the words out.

"All righty, I got a few more of the books you were looking for!" an enthusiastic man exclaims, somehow sounding loud even while whispering. Orangish mana, not unlike mine, drops several dozen tomes next to our table. I grimace as I look up at the librarian, an apparently enthusiastic fan of the sages.

"Right, thanks," I respond. "If you don't mind, you can bring half them to the other table, for my friends."

"Oh, I already did that! This is half. Sorry about that, but you did ask for everything we have on the sages, after all!" Sara and I both glance at the mountain of literature and wrinkle our noses.

"That's . . . a lot," Sara laments while I bite my lip. On the one hand, it looks exhausting. On the other, it is an excuse to keep spending a moment of calm with Sara. I don't know whether to feel relieved or weary. I suppose both.

"What do you need all this for anyway?" the librarian asks. I pick a book from the top and blow a very thin layer of dust off it.

"Fanfiction," I intone without looking up. Somehow, I still feel the man light up with joy.

"You too?" he asks eagerly. Oh. Perhaps an ill-advised lie. I venture a glance up to see his eyes wide open and sparkling. I actually think it would be charming, if his enthusiasm wasn't for some of the slimiest creeps to ever bury their shit on this planet.

". . . Yep," I confirm, forcing a smile. "Me too."

"Oh, tell me when you're done! I'd love to exchange stories; I can even give you feedback as you work on yours, if you want. Do you want to read mine now?" he practically pleads. I am about to turn him down, but I shrug after a moment's consideration.

"We'd love to," I agree, and he practically jumps out of his boots with joy.

"Oh, I'll be back in a while. Will you still be here in an hour? Oh, why am I asking; look at these books, of course you will! I'll be back; I have to run home to get it! You can ask the other librarian if you need anything while I'm gone! In the meantime, I recommend the autobiography of Nathan, the Fortress Sage. *Great* revenge story. Good luck!" he gushes, turning on his heel and practically skipping away before I can answer.

"Is fanfiction what it sounds like?" Sara asks in confusion. I scratch the back of my head.

"Uh, basically. His own stories he made up about the sages," I answer.

"And you agreed to read his because . . . ?" she pushes. I sniff.

"Well, we aren't going to make it through all these this year, but if you want detailed and thoroughly researched information about something, there is no one better to go to than a fanfiction writer. And there is no one who will answer such questions so passionately. Honestly, the guy could end up being incredibly helpful," I respond.

"Oh, that makes sense. Kind of makes me feel bad for him though," Sara says. I scoff.

"When the sages are gone, I'll introduce him to *Pokémon*. Put his enthusiasm into something more positive."

"Is that something from your world?"

"*Pokémon* transcends worlds."

"I'm sure. I guess you'll just stroll back to Earth and grab it for him, then?"

"Yeah, got a problem?"

"No, not at all. Grab me something while you're there."

"Maybe I will. Get you one of those translucent sun visors."

"If you keep joking about those, I'm going to make one and force you to wear it."

"If you made me one, I would wear it with goddamn pride, and you know that."

Sara fails to hold back a laugh at this, and a volu woman a few tables away gives us a sharp look before shushing us. I choke on a laugh of my own.

"I know you would, Annie. Come on, let's actually get something done," Sara says. I sigh as reality calls me. Right. We are looking for weaknesses in the most powerful people in the country so we can murder them one by one. I offer a melancholy nod of assent before opening the book in my hands and beginning to skim.

Hours pass by like this. The librarian does, in fact, drop off his fanfic, which I agree to read. I spend most of the time learning about the sages and Nexus energy, with brief breaks to chat with Sarafyna.

I do learn a lot. Nexus magic is actually highly specialized. Each sage can do a little bit of everything, but most have one specific thing they kick ass at that the others don't; at least the major ones do. There are actually a large number of sages in the history books that amounted to very little. Some Nexus talents are more common than others, and they tend to have similar weaknesses. For instance, mind control. Apparently common among sages, but often fails when the subject of the control is touched. That's an almost nostalgic thought, in a macabre way.

"Oh, Jesus, get a load of this fucking guy," I practically spit. Sara looks up from her own book with weary eyes and raises an eyebrow, inviting me to explain. I'm flipping through the autobiography of Nathan, the Fortress Hero; the book the librarian had suggested. One of the more important ones, as he is currently in a prominent position in the Republic government, which takes priority over Council sages or already dead ones, who I am reading about last.

"All right, so the sage shows up from his own world, fully in his body rather than reincarnated like me. Most of these losers seem to be, actually. I'm growing more and more curious about my own reincarnation the more I read . . ." I trail off, getting a little distracted.

"What makes him special?" Sara asks, refocusing me on what I had been saying.

"Oh, right, sorry. All right, so, as you may have guessed from his title, his talent in Nexus magic is focused almost entirely on defense. Big old walls, force fields, shields, that kind of thing. He's one of the least susceptible to other sages' influence as well as mana. Anyway, I'm getting sidetracked again. The point is, he is good at protecting a lot of people at once from any kind of damage. Gonna be a real pain in the ass, truth be told. But the way he tells his story is just . . . the most obvious bullshit I've ever heard in my life.

"This guy shows up in this world, during a time when the sages are already widely revered, with the specific ability to protect people. The safest sage to be around, provided he is as kind as he would have us believe. This takes place in one of the playgrounds, I think, if I am reading this right. Anyway, he has this entire story about being betrayed, slandered, 'forced' to buy slaves who end up enjoying slavery. All sorts of justifications for some pretty gross behavior. There also seems to be some confusing implications about ailur and his relationship with them? I don't really understand it," I explain. Sara gives me a look of disgust before I offer her the book and she peruses the page I have open.

"What kind of implications? Wait, never mind. I don't think I want to know. How much of the story do you think is true?"

I hold one hand flat and wobble it back and forth. "Eh, some, probably. It's either made up entirely or this fucker is guilty as sin. I'm calling it now. Story doesn't really hold water, in any case. No one really gained anything out of 'smearing' him, but—and if it is a playground, this makes sense—he would get something out of the story. Flimsy justification for buying slaves too, I guess. Either way, it's all just one big power fantasy. I feel like I need a shower after just reading his smarmy-ass book."

Sara wrinkles her nose. "Not as lovable a character as our librarian friend implied, huh?" she guesses.

"Well, it's not really the librarian's fault. Taken at face value, I can see why he would be a fan of this story. This man, actually. It's not that different from my own story in a lot of ways. If you don't know about countries like Potestia, if you haven't witnessed them, most of it isn't so bad. Except, you know, the slave bit. That's fucked regardless. But knowing he arranged for all this? It just feels like a fantasy about putting lessers in their place.

"So yeah, this fuckin' guy is going to the top of the murder list. What a slimy little creep. He goes right after your friend, Rune. The Scholar Sage, you said? The one whose stories are much older than fifteen years, by the way. Can't wait to find out why he looked like a child to you. I bet I'll like that story just as much."

"Works for me. I'm happy to go after both of them, if you like," Sara agrees. I am about to look back at my book when she reaches one hand out to touch mine. "Annie, I think we have read enough for the day. We should get back to the inn . . . We need to talk."

My still heart sinks. I was a coward for too long. I am terrified. I am relieved. I read the entire conversation in her eyes. She isn't going to make me ask. She is just as smart as I am. She knows she needs to go back too.

But I don't want her to go. I don't want her to go.

CHAPTER SIXTEEN

Fear

I nervously shake my leg as I sit on my bed in the inn, feeling like a child in trouble. Sara sits on her bed across from me, biting her lip. Neither of us want to speak, and the tension in the air coils around us like a snake.

We both know what has to be said. We both know what has to be done. But neither of us wants to bring it up. Despite my confidence in all other things, Sarafyna has always carried the majority of the courage. However I may like to think of myself, however gentle and quiet she usually is, she remains bolder than me, and always will.

True to pattern, she speaks first.

"I'll come back," she promises, skipping the actual discussion about leaving. And she is right to. We already know why she has to go back; we can't delay anymore. We have known since we crossed the border and our original plan proved impossible. So she is promising to come back. "You know I'll be back before you've even managed to murder anyone. Probably."

This forces a laugh out of me before I even realize it's coming. "You underestimate me," I joke. "I'm going to need something to distract me, and I doubt they have any *Zelda* games here."

"Are those the options?" She chuckles. "Games and murder?"

"I'm a simple woman." I shrug, giving her a poorly hung smile. The brief reprieve of the conversation hangs in the air before reality grows too heavy for it to bear. The briefly pleasant mood rises like heat until it's no longer in reach. I hang my head.

Sara stands and moves to my bed, sitting quietly next to me. This is all she does. She has said a thousand things in the simple promise to come back, and she knows she doesn't need to elaborate. I let out a heavy sigh, and all the bravado I carry for the twins' sake is dragged out with it. Water runs quietly down my cheeks.

"I'm scared, Sara," I whisper. She lets out a quiet breath. Without looking, I know she is biting her lip again. I can see that expression with my eyes closed. It doesn't help. "I'm so scared. And it's stupid, so fucking stupid, because we have done worse than this before. You'll be gone what, a week? Far less time than we have been separated before. But . . . it always felt so certain that I would see you again. That no matter how far you went or what happened, you'd always come back, or I'd come to you. But . . . that doesn't feel so certain anymore. I know it never was, but—"

Sara puts her hand on my shoulder.

"I'm scared too," she whispers, barely audible. "Annie, I only ever feel safe when I'm with you. Even when we finally found my father, I—Well, I only ever feel safe when I'm with you, Annie. I am terrified to leave, even for a week. Even for a day. But because of that, I have spent a lot of time around you, to the point where, however terrified I am, I know I have to move forward. Over and over again, I have fallen for you as you do the impossible for everyone but yourself. It's how I learned to break reality myself.

"When I first fell for you, I didn't realize I was attracted to you. I thought I wanted to be you. *Then* I thought I was attracted to you. Now, I know it's both. I want to be what you are. What you have been for so many people, even when I am afraid.

"And I know. I know that being you is hard, and it's been harder lately. But you are still you. Which means I have to go to save you from asking me to. To save you from failing to ask me to. Because you are afraid for me, and you are afraid for the people we left behind. For your family. Your community. Leo. And I love you because there are so many of them and only one of me, and you still wanted to keep me by your side, even as you live in terror for all your other loved ones.

"I love you because you couldn't bring yourself to ask me to risk myself again after what happened last time. I love you because you were going to anyway, and because you would never forgive yourself if you didn't." Her hand moves from my shoulder to the side of my head, running her fingers through my hair.

"I love you too, Sara. You make everything feel normal again. Like I don't have to constantly wear a mask. Around you, I can be Annie and not the Mage of Mourning or whatever other title people have stapled to me. I feel love like an open wound. It hurts. And love isn't going to keep us alive to see each other again," I respond.

"I wonder about that," Sara muses, and a strange warmth washes over me with her words. "Well, it will help us trust each other to stay alive. And it will let us enjoy the time we do have together," she counters. She is right. I need to trust her. I *do* trust her. I trusted Henry too.

No. That isn't right. I know that isn't right.

I look up at my girlfriend while wearing a face of porcelain.

"Can we try the hat one more time?" I ask.

"It won't work," she answers. "I can feel that it won't work." I glance over at her bag and sigh. She is, of course, right. We have tried over and over again. As long as that barrier stands, it won't work.

"Yeah," I admit. "You're right. We need to take advantage of tonight. You need to go tomorrow to make sure everyone is safe, and stay safe yourself. Indulging in my cowardice would be a waste of tonight." It hurts. I am so afraid, but somehow, I still feel warm. I want to be myself again. I want to trust Sara again. I still feel like I am not me, but tonight, around Sarafyna, maybe I don't have to be. Maybe I can just be her girlfriend. We can feel warm and safe and sure of the future for one night.

"I was thinking the same thing," Sarafyna agrees.

Usually, in the evenings, we trade stories or read a book together. I look toward my bag, hanging off my headboard. "We can try that librarian's story. Worst-case scenario, it's funny; best case, it's actually good. I could use the distraction."

She smiles and nods, and we work our way through it, pausing to tell different stories and provide our own commentaries. Sara laughs at my Earth anecdotes, and I help her draw the different hats she insists each character should wear. It feels so achingly normal in a way that is almost a good pain, like the removal of a thorn or massaging an anxious knot. It is a beautiful, if melancholy, evening.

Sitting on a bed, Sarafyna's this time, I rest my head on her shoulder.

"Thanks, Sara. I'm still terrified, but at least right now . . . it's more numb. A normal evening was the perfect goodbye."

"A-almost, perfect," she stutters. "There is just one more thing I don't want to regret."

As she says this, she adjusts, prompting me to lift my head. She turns on the bed so she is facing me, and I hesitantly do the same. One of her hands gently runs up my rib cage; I can feel a nervous tremor in it as she does. The other lands on my cheek, then travels to the back of my head and pulls me into a deep kiss.

Her lips are soft and warm, and her teeth brush against my lower lip in a tentative way. The hand on my side continues to travel, barely missing my chest, hesitating as it does, before continuing and landing again on my shoulder. My entire body shivers as she pushes me, slowly and deliberately, until I am lying on my back. She breaks the kiss and looks down at me with almost cloudy eyes.

"Are you sure?" I plead, afraid she'll say no while still wanting to give her an out.

"Desperately," she promises, her lips meeting mine again, growing more confident with each kiss.

Lot, the enthusiastic librarian, is actually a pretty good writer. His version of the sages is actually much more complimentary than their own. Or at least, his version seems to subconsciously edit out all the parts that inspired my desire to commit violence. His story is something of an alternate history. I suspect the sages' versions are too, but I can respect the characters in his version. It's not the most amazing thing I've ever read, but it's not terrible. I may have enjoyed it more than usual because it was a distraction, and I was with Sarafyna.

It is also tied to a kind memory, one of the kindest of this life, however bittersweet it made the goodbye. I still feel like an idiot for making such a big deal about it. It's a week, if that. She'll be back with me soon. But this morning hurt nonetheless, and the endorphins released by last night's goodbye could only last so long, so I needed the distraction, and that's what Lot is.

He is . . . helping me with ideas for my story, so to speak.

"Do you have any theories about why the sages won't go near the Nexus?" I ask. Lot adjusts his round glasses.

"Oh, a million. But my leading one right now? I think it's a portal back to wherever they came from. See, they all stay far away from it unless they absolutely can't. They have the Guardians of Stone on the border, and a thick wall of Nexus energy making sure no one else approaches too!

"I think they must come from somewhere horrible; a desolate wasteland where normal people can't survive anymore. They don't want to get sucked back in. I think the border is to stop any citizens from wandering in too. Wherever they are from must be really dangerous," Lot guesses. "If you ask me? They are from the far future, here to stop the world from ending. That's why they all try to take leadership roles and prevent us from making the same mistakes of their past."

I can't decide how far off he is. The future thing doesn't make sense to me, considering I have been to Earth, but I suppose my story is different in a lot of ways. Maybe I am from a different world than the rest. The Radiant Woods feel more like a particularly colorful hell than a portal, but there is certainly some space fuckery going on with it. And there is no way it's uninvolved with how sages travel between worlds. I don't think going back is what they are afraid of though, and I know they don't want to keep all their citizens from ending up there. Just the ones they want to keep ruling.

"Oh, that makes perfect sense," I enthusiastically lie. "What kind of mistakes do you think led to that future?" I ask. He looks over his shoulder and leans in conspiratorially.

"Biological experimentation," he whispers. "We all know how body modification is illegal, and how cultists do it anyway, right?"

". . . Right," I agree. I do know this now, although I suspect I have come to different conclusions.

"Well, most people don't think too much about that—unless they are cultists, I guess. But I go to every public appearance of the Centurion Sage. I don't enjoy the arena, but I go whenever he addresses the public. And whenever they find cultists, he looks worried. Scared. And why would an all-powerful sage feel afraid . . . if not for his people? Something about what the cultists do scares him about the future. The reason he fears Demon Queen Lillith. I love the costume, by the way. Anyway, it all makes sense if he is trying to avoid the mistakes that led to our downfall the first time."

I rub my chin in thought.

Genuine fear. Sure, people often fear change and try to control people to avoid it, but it doesn't sound like that kind of fear. Lot is describing fear like a dark night and shadowy figures. Terror, like I feel being apart from my family. Lot is a fan of the sages, so the real answer didn't occur to him. What does an all-powerful sage have to fear if not on behalf of his people? Well, the answer to that is obvious, if you don't start from an assumption of benevolence.

"I'm from out of town," I say. "Can you tell me more about this arena?"

I am going to go find out for sure. I am going to look this sage in the eyes and find out what, exactly, he is afraid of.

CHAPTER SEVENTEEN

The Arena

I am practically suffocating in my hooded cloak, long-sleeve shirt, heavy pants, boots, gloves, and tinted spectacles. I look up at Ember with my lips in a perfect line. "I can't do this shit anymore. It's gotta be ninety degrees out!" I complain. She scoffs.

"I assume that means 'hot'? Well, it's better than being killed as a cultist on sight. Your tattoos and new, gaudy piercings alone will draw too much attention. A face in a thousand children's books and propaganda posters along with limbs of steel are going to be a bridge too far. Walk around in weather-appropriate clothes and you'll be dead in a week. Deal with it," Ember dismisses.

I turn to where I expect Sara to complain, only to be reminded that she is gone. This puts my complaints about the weather in perspective a bit, but I am legitimately growing concerned that this will eventually be just as obvious.

"If I walked into a bank dressed like this, they would set off a silent alarm."

"What does that even mean?" August asks. I glance at him on the other side of the room. We are all prepping for the day together as usual, getting our complaints out before we are in public and it's no longer safe to speak freely. Or we are discussing the day's plans, and I'm complaining while I still can. But no one else has to cook themselves alive all day, every day; I'm justified in a little whining.

"Just another reference to whatever reality she grew up in. Ignore it," Autumn drawls. Her tone conveys annoyance, but it makes me smile anyway. She has been engaging in more conversation lately, and generally just feeling more alive. I'm not a therapist, and as familiar with grief as I am, I don't know more than the basic stages of it. I know she is still in the depths of it, but she is moving forward, processing. And she can, at least, interact with everyone now. She is far less amiable than she once was, but I have been there myself. I'm just happy to hear her voice every day.

"Autumn's right," I agree. "Just off in my own little world. I suppose I'll survive another day of this torture."

"Just one more day," Autumn jokes with a smirk but little humor. Christ, that's a dark reference to make. I guess I'm not one to complain about gallows humor, but maybe, with Sara gone, I should start sharing a room with Autumn again. Moving forward doesn't mean being safe, after all. I'll bring it up later. For now, we have more important things to do.

"Right," I agree. "You know, you two don't have to come to this. It's not going to be pretty."

"Yes, we do," Autumn answers. "We need to be there." She makes eye contact with me, and her face is iron. I get the message and nod.

"Well, off we go, I suppose."

"About time," Ember grumbles. I stick my tongue out at her as she rolls her eyes. "Seriously? You pierced that too? The lip, nose, and eyebrow weren't enough? Are you trying to get the sages' attention with all this? They will kill you for even a suspicion, you moron."

I shrug.

"I wonder about that. I think my fate would probably be something entirely different than death if the sages themselves confront me. But that's beside the point. The more enchanted mana sources I have, the less sick I get, the quicker my cancer heals, and the more power I will have. Especially if my last fight is anything to go by. Besides, I suspect I won't be able to hide what I am much longer, even if I weren't planning a few extra modifications to help in the days to come."

"You aren't just saying that so you won't have to dress like that anymore, are you?" Ember asks. "Our lives are at stake here."

"No. No, I have no intention of risking any of you more than I have to," I answer seriously. I can try to joke my way through a lot, but putting my loved ones in danger without a second thought is too raw a subject for me to joke about. The shift in my tone is clear, and the room descends into an awkward silence. I sigh. "Come on. Today is going to be shitty; might as well get it over with."

We leave the inn and hire a carriage, no longer relying on Ember's money as much as Turner's. I shudder as we ride through the city. Despite all the sounds of a bustling community, it carries an uncanny quiet. No matter where we go or how far we travel, I can only feel grief from Autumn and August. Even the trickle Ember is allowed when Sara is near is missing. We are almost to the arena, a place where human lives are spent for an afternoon's entertainment, and I don't feel any grief from anyone. It's sickening.

I examine Autumn as she watches the town pass through the window.

"How are you feeling?" I ask for the thousandth time. I can feel it. I know how she is feeling, but I have to check.

"I still feel horrible, thanks for asking again," she responds. Which is fair. Since Sara left, I've been checking on her almost religiously. I don't know how the sages rob people of their grief here, if they have to see them first, or if a person's presence in the country is enough. I do know that once it affects someone, Sara struggles to remove it permanently. If we could have risked everyone else by keeping Sara here, it would have been much safer for Autumn, but we couldn't, and even Autumn understood that. I am relieved that she still seems safe from outside interference. For now.

I don't have time to press any further as we finally arrive, pay the coachman, and make our way to the entrance of the arena. It is clearly modeled after the Colosseum, which supports my theory that at least some of the sages are from my world. Probably. I guess a big round arena with theater-style seating isn't too complex to be recreated in multiple realities.

I shiver again at the complete lack of grief as Ember pays our entrance fees. I'll make sure to steal that back later. We don't really need it, but I don't much feel like giving some asshole money for the miserable day we are about to have.

The roar of the crowd is deafening as we make our way in, scaling the stairs to find the closest unoccupied seats we can. Despite showing up early, the fights started before we got here, and the front rows are already full. I almost stumble as a massive wave of mana washes over me. A man near the front has released his aura and is throwing his magic at the arena below. Massive stones disappear as soon as they pass the spectator wall.

Not dissolving. Not getting knocked back. They simply cease to exist well before they reach the fighters below.

"She cheated! She fucking cheated! I won't stand for this! Do you have any idea who I am?" the mage yells, trying to shove off the guards who come to collect him. Unfortunately for him, they flare their own mana and have mana-suppression cuffs around him in an instant.

He has enough mana to be a prominent noble in Potestia, but not nearly enough to stand up to security here, apparently. Well, that's just great. Over the fighting area, the two combatants are projected using light mana, so even from the upper seating they can be clearly observed. It's not unlike the illusion I used when I killed Darian.

Just as the man's aura disappears, I see what upset him so much, assuming he bet on the large man currently on his knees below. A massive woman, maybe six and a half feet tall and clad in red with a horned helmet, holds a single-edged blade to the side of his neck. She looks up toward the stands, and the illusion changes to show a man with olive skin and sharp, angry cheekbones. Markus, the Gladiator Sage. He holds his hand up with his thumb to the side before lifting it and pointing it toward his throat. Yeah, this guy has got to be from Earth.

The illusion returns to the two below, and the woman spins, decapitating her opponent. The twins tense beside me as I clench my fists and the crowd begins cheering. I feel sick as the now bloodied woman bows her head and turns to walk toward her entrance. She has metal cuffs around each wrist and her neck.

"Are those for mana suppression or general slavery?" I ask. Ember grunts.

"The former. Most fights in the arena use no magic, as most combatants don't have combat magic. Only special fights allow it at all," she explains. I bite my thumbnail, considering that, as a loud voice interrupts us to address the crowd.

"Things looked pretty shaky for a while there, especially when Gargoyle nearly took her leg, but as usual, the Demon is an unshakeable iron wall! A woman with the strength of three men and the ferocity of a dozen, ladies and gentlemen, allow me to present the victor, Bahamut the Demon!" it shouts, sound mana enhancing it. The illusion focuses on the woman's face as she rolls her eyes before disappearing without acknowledging the cheering crowd. The announcer moves on to the next bout as we find our seats, each of us feeling varying levels of sickness.

"This is disgusting," August whispers. I nod, glaring across the stadium to the prominently featured box where the sage sits. He'll be my first target. I turn to Ember.

"The mana suppression, does it work like regular cuffs or like riot spikes?"

Ember looks at me with suspicious eyes.

"Why?" she asks with a flat tone.

"You know damn well why. Which is it?" I respond as she sighs.

"Normal cuffs, I suspect. No reason to go through the extra effort for something like this. This is a terrible idea," she groans.

"What is?" August asks.

"Lily, I don't like this idea," Autumn says, barely audible. It's softer than her voice has been in a while. "Especially with Sara gone. It's not safe." This surprises me, considering Autumn's recent irritation with me, but perhaps it shouldn't. She is still Autumn. She is still my friend. She has redirected some of the anger at herself toward me, which was always coming, but that doesn't erase everything else. That doesn't erase whose sister I am.

"Look at them," I say as the new warriors come out. One man wears what appear to be tiger pelts and a helmet with a tiger's face, his eyes visible through the fangs in its mouth. The other wears little, a cloth and a giant axe. "The fighters here are themed."

"I'm sorry, what are we talking about?" August pushes.

"It's way too dangerous. You'll be visible to the whole world," Ember hisses at me. I shrug.

"There is a whole fucking culture here. Even without grief, there must be movements dedicated to fighting back, right? I can't hide forever, especially as I continue to . . ." I trail off, looking around and surrounding us in a sound barrier. It's annoyingly visible with no other grief sources, but who cares. People have private chats all the time. "If I continue to alter my body. This getup is also going to attract just as much attention eventually; it's obvious I'm trying to cover something up. And they have themes, Ember."

"I know they have fucking themes. But you can't really be considering this," she complains.

"I agree, Lily. We'll figure something else out," Autumn whispers, her previous annoyance replaced with worry.

"There is no better way to get close to that sage," I counter. "And it will be really convenient for all our future moves if there is someone in the city who famously looks exactly like Demon Queen Lillith. I can't keep telling people it's a sex work gimmick." August's eyes widen as he realizes what my plan is.

"You want to fight? Don't you have to be someone's slave for that?" he asks, his face paling.

"No," Ember grumbles. "For a chance at wealth and glory, free combatants are allowed to register and compete as well. But almost nobody is stupid enough to actually do it."

"Almost," I agree with a grin. This will make a great distraction. I just have to figure out a way to avoid killing my opponents. "Let's see about putting a Lillith costume together."

CHAPTER EIGHTEEN

Demon Queen

With mana and money, all things are possible. Or at least quickly creating decent armor that leans into my demon queen identity is possible. In any case, these clothes are more comfortable, sort of. I have a shirt and chain mail covering my upper torso and right arm. I also have bandages and a sleeve over that arm to ensure there are no accidental glimpses at the steel beneath. If there are, it will probably look like more armor, but you can't be too careful. I also wear gloves on both hands, with a gauntlet fastened to the right sporting claws for each fingertip. The left has to grip my weapon, so that glove is simple, textured fabric.

I also wear sturdy pants, a split chain mail skirt, and boots. All the chain mail has a slight red stain to the steel. I wanted to enchant it with a circle to gather mana like my limbs and piercings, but I can't figure out how to suppress the gathering mana if it is not actually connected to my body in some way. Instead, it is enchanted like the bracelet Ember first made me to simply gather the excess mana from my still-present cancer cells. It will help prevent any negative side effects of having my mana suppressed, at least.

To top off the effect, I wear a crown with a single horn protruding from the right side, my hair making it look like it grows directly from my head. My left arm and midriff are entirely visible, the now-useless circle covered with new scars and art. The black-and-purple bird of dawn tattoos on my arm and the multicolored tree on my stomach both contribute to the effect I'm going for, as does the new navel piercing.

I have more and higher quality protection than most of the gladiators, but not too much, and the work I have put into making my magic circle harder to break over the years makes what skin is visible a deceptively tempting target. They are going to need a lot more force than they realize to leave more than a nasty cut on my stomach. As for my arm, well, I will teach them to fear proximity to that.

All in all, I look like a proper barbarian demon queen. I look like Lillith. And I can finally breathe a little, although the chain mail still produces boob sweat at rates scientists previously thought impossible. But as a free competitor, I can go in public dressed like this without the mail. I can't avoid attracting attention for long, but I can make the attention I do attract expected and normal. I can even use a little light mana to change the color of the tattoos and pretend they wipe off if needed. It'll be tricky, but it'll work.

In any case, this should solve quite a few of our problems. I can even get to work on my new body modification ideas without causing too much of a fuss. People will simply think I am expanding my costume.

Hiding in plain sight. Nothing can go wrong.

All right, yeah, a lot of things can go wrong, but out of my terrible options, I think this offers the most freedom of movement and provides an opportunity to get close to a sage. Once I register, at least. As soon as my face is that of a known gladiator simply cosplaying the extremely smart, pretty, and talented Lillith of Endings, I can finally show my face outside of the inn and the library. For now, however, I wear my cloak over the entire getup.

I follow Ember as the twins find seats. Apparently, volunteers for the arena are rare. Who could have guessed that? In any case, it is something of a treat for the bloodthirsty audience, and even the hypothetically nonlethal test to let me participate is broadcast to the crowd. I guess it's a bit like *American Idol* but for public murder. So . . . a bit like *American Idol*. In any case, they get to watch to see if my plan comes together or comes crashing down around us all.

We finally arrive at a closed door, and Ember knocks far more aggressively than I would have thought was necessary. The prim woman who opens it doesn't seem to notice at all, however, looking first at Ember and then me. "What is it?" she asks, adjusting her thin glasses.

"My friend here wants to try for fame and fortune," Ember intones as the woman raises an eyebrow at me.

"No, she doesn't," she determines. She's right, actually, but wrong at the same time.

"I do," I insist. "I want to fight."

"Kid, you're a full head and shoulders shorter than just about all the gladiators in this arena. The only people you look capable of fighting are the fodder used in group combat, and you aren't winning any prizes joining their ranks, trust me. Go home. No one who isn't forced to should fight here, much less someone who might need a stool to reach the top shelf," she dismisses.

"First fight's supposed to be nonlethal anyway, right? Let me try," I respond immediately.

"Emphasis on *supposed*. The sage won't order your death, and your opponent will be instructed to use nonlethal force to encourage surrender, yes. But no one will be punished if you die in an accident, and many of the people here will enjoy putting you in your place. If I had to bet on you surviving, I wouldn't put money on it."

"You're not convincing this idiot of anything. Just wasting our time," Ember cuts in. The woman gives her a sharp look but refocuses on me quickly. As I nod in confirmation, she closes her eyes and begins to rub her temples in exasperation.

"Fine. Come in," she orders, standing to the side and allowing us to enter. We walk into a comfortable but humble office, where she sits behind a desk and pulls out a blank sheet of paper. "What's your name?" she asks.

"Call me Cordelia," I answer cheerfully. She sighs.

"Call you? Is that your name or not?"

"It's my name," I lie.

"All right, Cordelia. As I'm sure you know, our gladiators always have an alias and persona, sometimes based on past sages, sometimes on past criminals, other times on legends or fairy tales. These are usually assigned after a few fights, but free gladiators are allowed to choose their own. I'd make a recommendation, but we don't have any famous bean sprouts in fact or fiction, I'm afraid," she drawls. I lower the hood of my cloak, giving her a decent look at me for the first time.

"Lillith." I smile. "Demon Queen Lillith." She gives me a blank look for a moment before her lack of amusement weighs her lips down and adds ten years to her face.

"Sage's grace," she whispers, writing a few notes on the paper. "Well, if you survive, you'll certainly make a name for yourself quickly. And if not, well. At least the sage will find it amusing to watch you lose. All right. I'll see if we can't make room for you today. Usually, a few fights end more quickly than we'd like. There will be room in a bit. When you head out there, wait for the announcer to mark the beginning of your match. You can surrender at any time, even before the fight starts. I strongly advise you to do so when you see your opponent. If you feel fear, that's for a reason. Your mind is telling you that you are in over your head."

I nod. "Thanks, you've been a huge help," I answer. I could quip back at her, but honestly, she was genuinely trying to help me. I look like I am eighteen or nineteen, and I am in fact almost a full foot shorter than the other woman I saw competing. Even without grief, she was putting effort into sparing my life, and I'm not getting persnickety over that. Now, over her choice of job? I have some comments, but those would look pretty suspicious in my current position.

It's maybe an hour before they have a moment for me, and the weary woman leads me through the gate inside, past the other gladiators' cells, and to the waiting area just outside of the arena. I left my cloak and, regrettably, my hammer in her office. Apparently, giant war hammers aren't allowed in supposedly nonlethal fights. She didn't seem to believe I could use it effectively, anyway, considering its size.

I get a few whistles and crude comments from the rowdier gladiators I pass, but most can't be bothered to even look. I ignore them for now, and my escort secures mana-suppression cuffs around my wrists and neck. I feel immediately sick, and my artificial limbs almost collapse from under me, but as I suspected, these work like regular cuffs, and as such, mana quickly flows back into them, the sickness recedes, and I am able to stand.

"Sure you're up to this? If you are feeling woozy, follow that instinct," the woman tries one final time. I nod anyway.

"Oh, I am ready," I insist.

"Fine." She sighs. "The announcer is getting the crowd excited for the fight now; when that stone by the entrance lights up and the gate begins to open, walk out so he can introduce you. Good luck. Try to surrender before there is nothing we can do."

I nod again, and she shakes her head, turning and beginning the trip back to her office.

Well, that was easy. It's pretty gross how easy, actually. The only real barrier was the woman who walked me here trying to talk me out of it. Well, whatever. This arena won't be around when I'm done with this place anyway.

I can't make out the announcer's voice, although I am closer than many of the audience members. It must be intentionally muffled here, in case they want the crowd to be excited about something the gladiators are unaware of. I wait for a few moments in the eerie quiet until the stone lights up with red mana, creating a flickering red path for me to walk on. The gate slowly slides open, and I walk forward as instructed. The sounds collapse on me all at once: cheering, laughter, and the announcer's voice. I feel so cold.

"*Aaand* here she is! Our first volunteer in nearly six months, and with a chosen persona straight from the third plane! Competing against the Rogue in her debut match, hoping to qualify to fight her way up the ranks, we have a contestant wearing a name you have all heard! A name whispered by your children as you check beneath their beds, and a name shouted from podiums and plastered on posters across the Republic! As prophecy foretold, today we will witness the fearsome, the evil . . ." The announcer pauses as the sun touches my skin and the illusion in the air reveals my face. My black hair and ruby eyes. My colorful body art. My angry glare. "Demon Queen Lillith!"

The crowd erupts into cheers, laughter, gasps, and every other flavor of reaction. I look at the man waiting for me in the center of the arena. He is larger than me, but smaller than most other gladiators. He wears a mask and hood but no shirt, and there are scabbards for various missing knives strapped to his body in multiple places. His eyes carry hate.

"You shouldn't have come here," he shouts, his voice amplified for the crowd. "I will make certain you regret it." I raise my hand to the back of my neck, cracking it instead of responding before lifting my fists and spreading my feet, getting ready for combat.

"Looks like our demon queen is ready to go!" the announcer says. "Now, remember, this is a nonlethal fight, but that doesn't mean it's non-violent! Anything your opponent can survive is allowed, but nothing with the clear intent to kill. As both combatants are ready . . . Begin!"

The moment the final word is said, my opponent is moving. "The Rogue" is fast, considerably faster than I expected. The gap between us closes in the blink of an eye, and his boot is soon colliding with my chest, knocking me off my feet. My head bounces painfully off the dirt and stone, but I let the momentum carry me, lifting my legs and rolling backward and onto my feet again.

He clicks his tongue at me as I ready myself. Again, he charges, this time swinging an angry fist into my cheekbone. I breathe in the pain. He clearly expected me to fall to the ground, pausing for a brief moment as my sharp eyes cut to his. It is only a moment, however, and he swings his other fist into my solar plexus.

My thicker skin takes a huge amount of the impact, but he isn't a gladiator for nothing, and he knocks the air out of me easily. When I stand through that as well, he grabs my shoulders and drives his knee directly into the same spot before moving his hands to my head and forcing my face into the same knee. I feel my nose crack, tasting blood as he grips my hair in both hands.

He yanks once, then twice, then three times, trying to throw me to the ground, each time failing to move me. I continue to glare daggers at him as he widens baffled eyes. Finally, he grabs both sides of my head and rams his own into my already aching nose. He does this two more times to daze me before picking me up by the throat and throwing me onto the ground. The world blurs around me. I drink in the pain. I own it completely. He kicks me. Stomps on me. Screams at me. Every blow takes me back to the past. To the moment when I earned each one.

I don't know how long this goes on. He must kick me dozens of times as I lie on the bloody stone. He keeps going until blood fills my mouth and bruises decorate my body and face. Eventually, he must come to the conclusion I am unconscious because he stops, turns, and begins to walk away.

The announcer is saying something, but I don't care. That was enough. That was enough for today. I'm not cold anymore. I'm slow. I'm deliberate. Each movement hurts, but I climb to my feet. The Rogue and the announcer pause at the same time, and the former turns to look at me.

"Just give up so I don't have to kill you," he orders. "It would be a waste, oh demon queen, of what might be a pretty face under that hideous costume."

I spit into the dirt, leaving a new spatter of blood next to the others. He sighs. Again, he closes in on me in an instant. Again, he swings at my face. This time, however, I catch his arm with my right hand and swing my left once, hitting him in the head. I don't use all my strength, but I use enough. As I hold the unconscious man up by his arm, I look toward the crowd. For a brief moment, the arena is completely silent.

CHAPTER NINETEEN

Bread and Circuses

Just about everything hurts. My nose is definitely broken, and my entire body is littered with bruises, welts, and cuts. By all accounts, I should be struggling for days after a beating like that, but I'm not going to.

After the upset in my qualification match, the prim woman from earlier brought me to some kind of mass sleeping quarters under the arena, removing the mana-suppression cuffs and collar. A dozen beds line either side of the stone walls, and a few other gladiators occupy beds of their own, including the Rogue, the man I gently introduced to unconsciousness.

There isn't much else in this room, but there doesn't need to be. I can feel its effects the moment I walk in. It feels the same as when Sara helps me heal. It's slow, and my body fights it as it always does, but my wounds are correcting themselves. I'll have a few new scars, and my nose will probably be a bit crooked for the rest of my life, but I'll be in fighting shape again shortly.

This is definitely divine magic, or Nexus energy—whatever they want to call it. I suppose it makes sense, what with a sage running this place. No matter how many people are attacked and enslaved on the road, they can't actually have multiple fights every day where half the combatants die and the others are too badly injured to fight the next day. I suppose they must save the executions for either prominent matches or disposable slaves who can't fight well. The rest of us need to be healed quickly so we can go on to entertain the masses.

This is convenient for me, but also sickening. I wonder how many hospitals and clinics have the same effect applied to them, or if healing is more of a convenience to keep entertainment steady.

As a gash on my face closes, the woman I watched yesterday is escorted to her own bed, two rows away from mine. Bahamut the Demon. Not a terribly different persona from mine, really. A fairly different presentation though. I also note that, unlike me, she still has her cuffs and collar on. She seems to notice this as well, based on the nasty look she gives me.

"Moron," she grunts, shaking her head like I'm a disobedient child. This is all she says before lying back on her bed and closing her eyes.

"I get that a lot," I agree. Her jaw tenses before she opens her eyes and turns her head toward me.

"Do you think this is some kind of game? You're lucky to be alive. If you don't have to be here, then get the fuck out of here," she orders.

"I *do* have to be here. Maybe not for the same reason you do, but I have to be here," I reply.

"I don't care what debt you think this will fix. I don't care what trouble you are in. I don't even care if you think it's worth dying for. It's not worth it. Stay until you are fully healed, then never come back here," she demands. I tilt my head, eyeing the collar around her neck.

"How did you end up here?" I ask. She releases a deep, beleaguered sigh before sitting up again and glaring at me. Goddamn, she is tall. Pretty too, in a "prepared to commit violence" kind of way. She's clearly angry at me, and I'm a loyal woman, but if we met under different circumstances, I might blush. These are not those circumstances.

"Look. Risking your life isn't the hard part, all right? Obviously, that didn't shake you much anyway. But facing death is easy. Feels like just about everyone does it these days. Shit, maybe that's even why you are here. To have the most interesting suicide. But risking your life isn't admirable or brave or difficult. The hard part is winning. You've clearly managed that once, or you wouldn't be here, but eventually, it's going to mean killing an innocent person. You're proud of facing down death? Wait until it's someone else losing their life because of you," she lectures.

I feel like I've been punched in the stomach, and she has no idea exactly how perfectly she has me pegged. She is absolutely right. I could die a thousand times over. Hell, I've even done it once. Twice, actually.

But Henry.

Yeah, I understand what she means. But I refuse to let the nerve she struck show on my face.

"If death is easier to face than killing, why haven't you chosen it yet?" I ask. I actually agree with everything she has said, but watching her decapitate a man yesterday does make it hard to take it seriously coming from her. At the same time, I have decapitated more than a few people myself, so I understand the necessity sometimes. But she is speaking like killing innocent people is unavoidable as a gladiator, which means she must have made the choice to do so at some point.

"There is no choice. Not for me. You can leave any time you want, but I am going back out there every day whether I want to or not. Do you really think they are going to leave sparing people as an option? No. If you let a person live, the sage himself will kill them, he'll do it in front of you, and he'll make it so much worse. The choice is how quick their death will be, not if they die. That's the choice you have in front of you, if someone doesn't kill you first," she answers bitterly.

That . . . is not what I was expecting, but I suppose it should have been. "When you say *in front of you*, do you mean he comes down into the arena and tortures them then and there?"

She nods. "You don't look like you'd have the stomach to face that choice, however you present yourself. And you don't have to. So get out, now, before they decide you are too entertaining to remain free."

"You're right," I agree. "I don't. But I still can't leave." Her eyes lock on mine as she searches them. Finally, she shakes her head again and lies back down.

"Fine. I won't ask more. I won't push. And if I end up fighting you, I'll make sure you don't have to face the sage directly," she promises.

"Maybe that's what I'm looking for," I suggest, and she laughs humorlessly.

"Trust me, you don't want to meet the sage directly," she answers, her eyes closed now. I am about to answer, but the woman who brought me here appears in the entrance to the room.

"Cordelia," she calls. "Markus, the sage, has requested to meet you."

August

The fight after Lillith is far more violent, in a way. I can barely look at it. I just want to go back to the inn, but my sister wanted to be here. She's obviously not enjoying the fight any more than I am; I don't know how everyone else is. I have to close my eyes as the man with the horned helmet drives a knife into his opponent's shoulder. Based on the screaming and the cheering, that's not the end of it. I feel like vomiting, but when I open my eyes and look at Autumn, she has her eyes fixed on it.

"How can you watch this?" I ask.

She answers without even looking at me. "I have to." That's all she says. I don't understand it.

"Why? Why do you have to? Autumn, we can just leave, meet up with the others later. We don't have to sit through . . . this," I insist. She doesn't answer. I give her a moment, but it becomes clear she doesn't intend to. "When is she going to be back, anyway?" I finally ask.

"It will take a while, I imagine. She's probably not in any shape to head straight here after that beating," Autumn replies.

"I guess that's true," I admit. "But . . . why did she? It was like she wasn't even fighting back! She just stood there and took it, when she could have beat that guy at any moment! Was she trying to act like the fight was harder than it was? Was she distracted? Was it just to get more attention quickly? They hardly seem worth it. That hurt to watch, much less experience."

"That's not why," Autumn answers, but fails to elaborate.

"Why, then?" I push, but again, she doesn't respond. I dig my nails into my palms in frustration. I miss my sister. I'm worried for her. But she barely talks anymore, and when she does, it's like talking to a corpse. The liveliest she gets is angry, and even that is an improvement. She was clearly upset by Lillith's fight, but she won't say anything. She won't talk to me. She is like the shell of my best friend; alive but not living. Why did Lillith want her here? I don't understand. I want my sister back.

"Did I hear you right?" a man seated to my left asks. "You know the woman who fought under the demon queen's name?"

I shrug.

"Does it matter?" I answer with a question of my own.

"She was amazing! We haven't seen a new volunteer actually win in a couple of years now, and the way she did it was amazing! The Rogue is a quick one; tough too. Catching him like that, then knocking him out in a single hit? Especially after she proved she could take so many hits from him! That, and she pulls the demon queen look off perfectly. Shit, consider me a new fan of your friend. Will you introduce me?"

I'm a little taken aback, unable to answer at first.

"That's not why she did it," Autumn repeats. "And she's taken, I'm afraid."

"Ah well. That figures. I'd hate to make a man who could land *that* angry. Still, I'd love to meet her," the man laments.

"I don't think she's going to want to meet any new fans," I respond with an awkward smile. "But I'll pass your praise on to her!"

The smile fades as the announcer calls everyone's attention to the middle arena again. Both of the combatants look more like the meat at a butcher's shop than actual people. The volu man holds the human man's head by his hair and a dagger to his throat. Much like yesterday, an illusion of the sage appears in place of the gladiators. Again, he holds a thumb out to the side, but this time turns it down. His illusion fades, and the gladiators are visible again. The volu drops his opponent with a grunt and begins a limp back to his gate.

"I'm glad they don't always die," I say as the man next to me laughs.

"Not a fan of gore, huh? You may not have the stomach for the arena, then. I take it you aren't your gladiator woman's partner?" he teases.

"I do not, and I am not," I confirm. "I can handle gore if I have to. But this . . . this is something different."

He shrugs. "Where else would you even see it? It's all right, buddy; the arena isn't for everyone. Some men are more . . . faint than others. No shame if you don't want to come back; I'll cheer your friend on. And keep your sister here company, if she likes," he suggests.

Autumn doesn't bother responding, and I don't much feel the need to either. Instead, my attention goes to a man approaching the short wall separating the seating from the arena below. I'm not sure what about him catches my eye. He looks perfectly comfortable. Perfectly confident. But I feel anxious watching him for some reason. He turns back for a moment, waving cheerfully and saying something inaudible to someone else in the stands before climbing up on the wall.

"What in the third plane is he doing?" I ask, and the irritating man next to me follows my gaze.

"Oh, another one of those. Yeah, we get them here all the time. I guess they think the sage's barrier will hurt less," he answers.

"Hurt less than what?" I ask. Before I get an answer, the man on the wall casually steps off the wall, disappearing from view entirely. I jolt as

Autumn's hand catches my arm. She looks at the wall the man jumped from with wide, horrified eyes. No one else reacts even a little. Even the announcer simply continues to introduce a new set of fighters.

My skin feels like it's too tight as my heart pounds in my chest. What is happening here?

CHAPTER TWENTY

A Deal with the Devil

Lillith

Markus apparently lives here, at the arena, as I wasn't escorted to anything resembling an office or throne room or whatever sages rule from but an eerily familiar living room inside the colosseum walls. It didn't look *exactly* like any particular room I had been in as much as it carried a design similar to a thousand rooms I had seen before.

Or, rather, a thousand rooms *Annie* had seen before. It felt like the average middle-class home in the US, minus any technology. It is, truth be told, completely unexpected. I kind of figured I'd find myself in a decadent Roman estate, waiting around until Joaquin Phoenix showed up and commanded me to approach.

Instead, I feel like I'm visiting suburbia. There are curtains drawn on the other side of the room, which piques my curiosity. Based on the width of the arena walls and the location of the door, there shouldn't be much to look at behind them. Just another room, maybe, but certainly nothing worth looking at, at least not in the way you'd expect from a living room window. Maybe it's just to complete the general vibe of the space; it would feel a bit weird without one, even if this one is unlikely to let any sunlight in.

The sage isn't here, despite summoning me. At least he gave me enough time to heal up before calling for me. I wasn't expecting to encounter him so quickly, before I really made a name for myself or openly defied his order to kill.

I know how to stop sages from using their Nexus energy, and him getting close to me on his own is actually ideal, but I was planning on taking advantage of the demon queen persona to make some . . . changes without arousing suspicion. I already have a couple ways to deliver the necessary poison, but I'd hoped to add some easier delivery methods before actually using it. I was going to start just as soon as my debut was over. Go figure.

I don't know if I should try to kill him today. I'll try to avoid it, even if he is rudely late. I would have preferred to bring my cloak and cover up so he didn't get too close a look at any, uh, cultish things about me. I've covered up my false limbs pretty well, but I definitely don't want to be too closely examined by a sage if I can avoid it.

Well, I'll play it by ear. I'll try not to antagonize him and just probe for information in this meeting, and if things go south, I'll sink my fangs into him. While I wait, I might as well get a look around. Those weird curtains are calling to me.

I walk across the carpeted living room, wondering where he managed to get modern carpet and why, until I am close enough to touch the window. Just as I am reaching for the heavy fabric in front of it, a voice interrupts me.

"So, Cordelia, was it?" a man asks. I turn my head back, arm still extended to the curtain. And there he is, Markus the Gladiator Sage.

"That's me," I agree. He tilts his head.

"Interesting. You don't look much like a Cordelia. Not at all, truth be told," he notes.

All right, I don't want to fight a sage when I haven't prepared for it. An impromptu fight with one is a terrible idea, so I need to avoid antagonizing him right now. "Know a lot of Cordelias, do you?" I ask. Welp.

Markus laughs, indicating I haven't fucked up too badly yet. "I suppose I don't. Fair enough. Still, your persona's name seems to fit you better, don't you think?" he pushes. I shrug.

"It's the outfit, I suspect. I was going for demon queen, and that's what I got. I looked much more like a Cordelia before," I explain. I'm not sure what a Cordelia looks like, but I have a feeling Markus pictures her with fewer piercings and tattoos.

"So you did," he acknowledges. "May I ask why?"

"You may," I agree. The room is quiet for a moment before he realizes I am only going to answer the question he asked, not the one he implied. This could be dangerous, but after his first response, I want to feel him out a little. I need to know what sort of person he is, and where the borders of his patience are. If he is the right kind of asshole, this approach may actually end up being better.

Almost confirming my suspicion, he chuckles.

"Why Lillith? It's a pretty bold choice, considering the Void Sage's recent campaign against her, don't you think?" he asks. Yeah, I figured he'd be curious. Maybe not curious enough to call me over here immediately, but I forgot rich men always rush to the end of all interactions, so to speak.

"Exactly. What better way to get attention quickly, right? Besides, you already had a demon woman; I had to make it clear I was the next step up. Why, not a fan?" I ask.

He shakes his head. "Nah, I like it. Rowan is just making a big deal over nothing, if you ask me. Just trying to win the election with a big, scary, foreign enemy. Someone tries it every now and then, but it won't go anywhere. No, I feel the same way about it that you do: it's just good marketing. That combined with our first qualifying volunteer in forever, I think you'll attract a much larger audience, provided you survive. Do you think you can survive? You did take quite the beating today."

"I'll be fine. I can take a hit," I answer.

"That's an understatement." He laughs. "So tell me, what do you hope to get out of competing? Why are you here, my sweet little demon queen?"

I lean my neck over a bit to crack it before I answer. "Is fame and fortune not enough?"

"They are enough to try. Not enough to keep you here after a beating like that," he replies. Fair enough. I hadn't considered that when I was getting hit. I look at him in thought and remain quiet for a moment.

"I want to be feared," I finally answer, completely honestly. "I want the entire Republic to know who I am, and what I can do." This is true. In fact, I need the country to know who I am, and I need them to know I can kill sages. That sages can be killed in the first place. And getting famous while able to move about freely, at least until I sink my fangs into Markus here, is invaluable.

Markus smiles at me. "You're a bit insane, aren't you?"

"I'm certainly not mentally well, but I wouldn't be here if I was," I admit. This draws another laugh from him.

"Fair enough. Tell you what, Cordelia. I like you. Let's make a deal, you and I," he offers. I eye him suspiciously.

"Is that not what my participation already is? I fight and provide entertainment; you give me wealth and fame?"

He shrugs. "I suppose it is, in a way. But I'll be honest. You had an easy match today and still needed to visit the infirmary. But you did have the idea to don the Lillith persona and, if I am being honest, you wear it well. Half my audience will want to kill you, while the more . . . eccentric half will want to bed you. But I have no faith you'll survive long enough to make use of this. That's why I called you here."

"To call me rage inducing but sexy to eccentrics?" I ask with a raised eyebrow. Again, he chuckles.

"We'll need to let you address the crowd more often; you have a sharp tongue, but in a likeable way," he says. "So here is the deal I want to make. I will keep you alive. If it looks like you are about to die, I'll . . . subtly step in and protect you, not from injury but from death. I will keep you alive until you have won enough matches to qualify for the wealth I promise free gladiators. In exchange, you . . . delay that a bit. Fight for longer than you would otherwise have to. Keep promoting the arena for a few years after you do. Come back every now and again to fight a new champion, that sort of thing."

He smiles at me as he makes the offer. I don't really need to think about it; anyone in my shoes would agree to that, which means I should too. He'll be dead before I have to fulfill my end of the bargain anyway. It could even result in better opportunities to kill him, if we are in some kind of business together. I can slip him some blood, maybe, then kill him with a touch.

Still, I want to push for one more thing.

"I don't want to kill anyone," I respond. He blinks in confusion. "At least not anyone I don't decide to kill myself."

"I don't want to alarm you, but that's sort of what we do here. It's like our whole shtick. Show up, stab some guys, get a little bloody, kill people. Pretty sure it's right on the sign when you enter," he quips. I roll my eyes.

"Yeah, I get the basic idea; picked up on it when I got here and a man's head was being chopped off. I can be a bit thick at times, as my friends will tell you, but I did manage to work that one out. That's why I need to make a deal with the man in charge. Just don't give me the order to kill, and I'll take your deal. I'll stick around after I've met the minimum requirements for the arena's incentives. Keep fighting. Keep drawing people in. It seems like a fair deal to me," I offer.

"Or I can throw you through that window behind you and get another girl to play demon queen," Markus suggests.

"You could. But I don't think you will. I'm not actually all that easy to replace. You may not have faith I can survive the arena on my own, but you know damn well you aren't finding another woman my size who can knock a man out in a single hit or stand up after that much damage, and who can convince the crowd she is a volunteer, show up in public, and never try to escape. The eye color is pretty hard to get right too. I'm not going to be easy to replace quickly, and the genie is out of the bottle, so to speak. People have already met the persona. They are excited *now*, not later, when you finally find someone who checks all the boxes," I challenge.

Markus examines me seriously for a moment, but I've got a pretty good measure of the type of man he is now. Not one obsessed with personal pride; not in the regular way, like Baldwin or Darian. No, he's a different kind of dangerous, a slimy kind, but a kind I can use and negotiate with.

There are also the playgrounds, the implications of the sages using them, living in them. The fact that this man runs a colosseum even though he is already in a position of unassailable power means this world is a game to these people. They don't want complete subservience, not always. No. They want interesting side characters. That's why I got this meeting: because I was interesting. And that's why I haven't pissed him off yet. He wants to play a game; I'll play it with him. He needs someone like me. Because he is fucking bored.

Finally, he sighs.

"Damn. Maybe you *are* the demon queen. If nothing else, I won't find a replacement with the stones to speak so directly with a sage. All right, you have a deal. When you subdue an opponent, I won't rule in favor of death. We'll make some excuse about not wanting to empower the demon queen, play it up. But I have my own new condition, since you want to add yours."

"And what's that?" I ask.

"Dinner. Here, once a week," he says matter-of-factly.

"Dinner and . . . ?" I intone, wearing disinterest all over my face like too much makeup.

"Just dinner. You're fun and not afraid of me. I like you," he replies, holding his hands up as if in surrender.

"So you wouldn't describe yourself as one of those eccentric weirdos, then," I push, and he laughs.

"Oh, I definitely would. But not that kind. That's not what I'm after, I assure you," he promises.

"Well, *hooray* for that," I answer. He offers his hand to me, and I shake it. "It's a fucking deal, I guess."

"I'll break out the champagne. Let's make you famous!" he cheerfully cries, literally clapping his hands together once.

I can work with this; it's a better deal than I'd hoped for. It will buy me a decent amount of time—as long as he holds up his end of the bargain. Which he will, for a little while, until he thinks he's found the right moment. Now I just have to decide whether his death should be public or private.

I eye the window one last time.

"What's back there, anyway? Can't be much of a view," I ask.

"You won't have to worry about that for a long while," he dismisses. "Don't think about it. Now, how about we have our first dinner tonight?"

Well, I definitely need to see what's back there now. I suppose I will have plenty of opportunities to do so. And plenty of opportunities to learn about all the other sages. I just have to take a few hits, and I'm pretty good at that. Honestly, these fucking dinners will be more painful.

"Sure. Let's eat," I agree, locking my eyes onto his. Let's fucking eat.

CHAPTER TWENTY-ONE

Red Silence

Ember

I'm back home. Not my home with the other guardians but my *real* home. A home that no longer exists. I look down and confirm that I am a child again. I knew to expect it. I have this dream every night. Every single, sick night. I've heard people say they can control their dreams if they know they are dreaming, and I've tried—I try every single night—but nothing ever changes. Nothing ever *will* change. I will fight it again and again, and the dream will always end the same way.

I loathe these dreams. And I cherish them. Because, at least when they start, I get to see my home again. My playground, as they call it. And because when I dream, I get to grieve again. I never remember the dream when I wake up, but I always remember how many times I've had it when I return. I always remember the grief I'm only allowed while I sleep.

Well, while I sleep and when I'm with Sarafyna in Potestia.

It faded when we crossed the border. I became number. But it's enough to remind me of my home, and what happened to it. While awake, I lean on rage to motivate me to kill the sages, to betray my new country; even more so since Sarafyna left and the sages' control has started crawling across my mind again. But here in the dream? Here, I have clarity.

"Ember, are you ready to go?" Dad asks, as he always does. I extend and retract my claws, desperately trying to think of a way out of going through this again.

"No, I'm sick. Please, do we have to go?" I plead. Papa enters from the other room and presses his hand to my head. Both men look at me with momentary concern.

"You don't feel feverish, and you were so lively a moment ago," Papa says. His eyes meet mine and search for something I can't hide. "Ember, you've been so excited for the parade today! What are you suddenly so scared of?"

"Have those boys been bullying you again?" Dad adds, and I hang my head. Every time. It's like this *every time*. They know me too well. They can see fear written all over my face, but they don't understand why. They don't understand.

"No," I insist. I don't know if that's true or not. I don't remember enough before the start of the dream, but it doesn't matter. "I really am sick. I don't want to go today, please!" I beg.

"Sweetheart, there's nothing to be afraid of. Your dad and I will keep you safe, promise," Papa insists. No. No, you won't. I'm not afraid of some schoolchildren. I don't want to watch this again. The result will be the same if we don't go, but I don't want to watch it. I don't want to experience it again. I just want to enjoy my home.

"I can't. I won't go!" I insist. My fathers share a look, but both nod.

"All right, Ember. We'll stay home today," Papa agrees.

"Yeah, I don't much like parades anyway. A whole lot of standing around watching other people have fun. We'll have a much better time here, together," Dad says. I sigh in relief. Just a day with my parents. It's just a dream, but I can pretend I don't know the end for a little while.

I am at the parade, on Dad's shoulders, watching the floats march by. I always forget. It doesn't matter. It never matters what I do. The day will play out as it has always played out. My dream doesn't care that my parents wouldn't have forced me to go, it will always bring me here. *Why do I always forget that?* My breath catches as the band marches by. The music is loud and energetic and sickening. The band is the last one, the last group to pass before him. Before the "hero." My body trembles, and Dad looks up at me.

"Everything all right, Ember?" he whispers.

"We have to leave," I respond as the music starts to fade and the hero's float comes into view, just a little ways off. They don't see. Can't they see?

Half the people here aren't smiling. Half them are furious. This is not a happy occasion. My body shakes more, and I try to climb off my dad's shoulders. Dad would have let me down, had I done this when it actually happened. But the dream refuses me.

"Look, Ember! It's the hero! He's why we have hot water and cold food! He's the reason the country isn't overflowing with demons!" Papa says.

"Oh, trust me, she knows!" Dad laughs. "You should feel how excited she is! I read her stories about him every night; he's why she wanted to come today!"

"Oh, of course you do, how could I have missed that?" Papa replies. *No! No, I don't want to see him! I don't want to be here, please!* Suddenly, the words won't come out. The dream has grown weary of my struggling, and I can't protest. I will be here when the hero arrives.

"Please, he's not so special," a human stranger interjects. He is always here, every night, saying the same thing I would if the dream would allow it. He still sounds like an ass, even when I know he's right. "All his accomplishments are fake. Haven't you noticed he can never articulate how he actually stopped the demon invasion?"

"Excuse me, that was rude," Papa says. "Who do you think you are?"

"Don't let it get under your skin, love. Let him throw his fit. We are here for Ember, not some stranger," Dad cuts in.

"Well, the demons are gone, aren't they? And what did you do to fight them off? Yell at strangers on family outings?" Papa says, ignoring Dad.

"I'm not trying to yell at your family," the man replies. "I'm just sick of all this worship for a man who hasn't earned it. You know he chose the title Hero himself? No one has even actually seen him fight anyone before, and there are a few people with evidence they are responsible for some of his most famous victories over the demonic army! And don't get me started on what the women he's worked with have to say about him!"

"Oh, that's all just hearsay! Anyone can say that kind of thing about anyone! We owe that man everything; show a little gratitude," Papa retorts.

"And what happens to the people who do accuse him? Have you ever wondered about that? Because I can tell you!" the stranger replies.

"Why are you even here?" Papa snaps. "If you hate him so much, why come here to honor him at all?"

"Love, please," Dad begs.

"Oh, I'm not here to honor him. I'm here to protest him. Haven't you noticed, or have you just been looking at the floats this whole time? Look around you. Yeah, there are plenty of people like you here, having a good time. But there are more than a few people here to let the 'hero' know he isn't loved by everyone. Plenty of people who hate him," the man growls.

Papa opens his mouth to respond, but an unnatural silence stops him.

Oh fuck, I hate this part. I hate this part. I can't watch, I can't watch, I can't watch.

The band isn't playing, and the hero, sitting on his padded chair, is scanning the crowd. He's stopped his float directly in front of us. His eyes catch mine for a single instant, and acid runs through my veins. The apathy behind his face leaves me hollow. People are trying to speak, trying to yell at him, panicking, but he's done something to silence all us. Then, he comes to a decision and pulls out a whisper sphere. Someone answers almost immediately.

"Hey," he says, his calm voice echoing like a shout through the unnatural quiet he has created. "I am bored." Three words. Three simple words every child has spoken at one time or another. And all our fates are sealed.

"Want an extraction?" an answer rings through the sphere. The hero taps his lips in thought, then looks back at the crowd with irritation.

"Nah, the NPCs aren't behaving correctly. Let's do a full reset on this one," the hero responds. And that's it. That's the end of my life. There is silence for a few moments, but the hero sighs and jumps to the ground in a single, smooth movement. "I guess I might as well do some recruiting before we do."

He moves too quickly for any of us to react, swimming through the crowd, plucking children like me from their parents and gathering them in the middle of the road. When he gets to me, I try to fight. My parents try to fight. My arm screams out as Dad desperately tries to hang on to me. I taste salt and iron as my father's hand is severed at the wrist.

He screams in agony, but I can only tell from his face. The world is still silent. Flesh and sinew hang from his arm, but he ignores it. He and Papa don't give up. As a single blink finds me in the road with the other children, I desperately look to get my bearings, to find my parents. They are both trying to push through the crowd. I can read my name on their desperate lips, Dad's hand still wrapped around my wrist, taunting me. I want to die. I can't go through this again. And then, the demons descend—the sky demons, bird men, or as I later learned, the volu. Not demons from some plane of torment, just guardians, like I eventually became, pressed into service for the sage's entertainment.

There is so much blood, but no death. Lives are too valuable to waste, after all. A sea of silent red explodes around me like the hero's fireworks as one of the volu grabs me and pulls me into the sky. I don't want to go with them. They are rounding up the people below; some as they flee, others as they bleed in the dirt. I struggle. I just want to fall. I just want this man to let me go and let me fall.

I close my eyes as we pass the massive obsidian stone flying slowly past us in the other direction, toward the crowd below. *I can't look. I can't look. I can't look.*

My parents deserve my attention. I keep my eyes closed for as long as I can bear, but I have to see. I open them and retch. The crowds below are being marched to the stone, now resting impossibly on a single point on the ground. The volu are throwing them like garbage through its surface, like it's made of black water, into whatever emptiness the Void Sage has created for them inside.

"Dad . . . Papa . . ." I whisper.

"Ember! Ember, wake up! Are you all right?" Lillith asks. She has clear concern in her voice, which I fail to understand. What is she doing? It's still dark out, why is she fucking bothering me?

"What does it matter to you? Just let me sleep," I dismiss. I am angry again; I always wake up angry, always thinking of home for some reason. I don't have the energy for Lillith's shit right now.

"It sounded like you were having a nightmare, Ember. You were thrashing," she answers. I look around and see Autumn sitting up in bed, also looking at me with concern.

"I don't have nightmares," I answer. "I don't dream at all." *Why do I always have to think of home in the morning?* There is nothing for me there. I know this. I know it. But I always do. And it always makes me angry. Always.

"You . . . You were calling out for your father," Autumn says. I roll my eyes at her.

"Now I know you two are full of shit. I don't have a father—never have. Not one that I've met, anyway. Why would I call out for a man who abandoned me before I was old enough to remember his face? Just leave me alone," I scoff. *Father*. Bullshit. The only person looking after me as a child was my mother, and I'm the only person I rely on now. I have no one to call out to.

Why am I even working with these women? I should just leave. Go back to work.

For the thousandth time since coming back to the Republic, I resolve to leave and report everything back to my commander. But something inside me is disgusted by that idea. I don't understand it, but I want Lillith to win. I want the sages dead. And for some incomprehensible reason, the thought of a father I never met is more comforting than the mother I had. Strangely, the suggestion comes with a sense of longing. So I roll over, ignoring whatever Lillith or Autumn have to say, and try to go back to sleep.

CHAPTER TWENTY-TWO

War of Innocents

Edward

I erect another wall of glass just as a new monster emerges from the massive tree in the center of the city. I am so exhausted. I want to make my family proud, want to make up for my mistakes, but I feel like I can only make new ones.

I haven't visited the man in the glass pillar for a few days. I haven't seen Mariah either. I spend all day, every day, defending the city from the monsters sent by the Radiant Woods, and defending the monsters from the city. Both require constant vigilance. My glass can keep them in, for a while, but the radiant tree is too large. I have to constantly replace it as it cracks when different monsters beat against the sides.

And that's only half the problem, because my glass is clear, and the monsters on the other side can be seen, every crack can be heard. Every time a particularly large one throws its body into the side, it's witnessed by someone. This city, so fresh from weeks of fear followed by mass tragedy and death . . . is afraid. Fear and loss live in every dark corner of every home. People are afraid, and they can see the monsters coming to kill them. I can't convince them that these are people who can be saved. Even if I could, I doubt I could convince them it was worth the risk to try. People want to feel safe again. They don't want to keep losing loved ones. The fact is, the monsters are terrifying and deadly, and if they get loose, people will have to choose between killing them and dying themselves.

The only reason anyone is letting me do things this way is because it's safer than fighting. Because we can't kill the monsters without getting killed ourselves, and because even if we do, more will come. So for now, people are agreeing to let me hold them back instead of fighting. But that's it. They are allowing me to do it, but it's not sustainable.

I constantly have to maintain the glass, and so far, no one has offered to help. The number of monsters on the other side is growing, and eventually, there will be too many. I haven't had more than a half hour of sleep for days. Eventually, I'm going to break down, and the glass wall will follow shortly after. There are other mages nearby, standing guard, but they are here to fight, not to help me. They are waiting for me to fail.

And I am going to. Whenever I blink, my eyes fight to stay closed. Things fall from my hands if I lose focus for a moment. I'm running on mana alone, and I don't have nearly enough to do that long term, especially since I need to keep casting.

I need help. I desperately need help, or innocent people are going to die. That's a certainty once this glass comes down. Whether it be the innocents on the inside, their minds robbed from them, or those on the outside, driven mad with fear, someone innocent is going to die.

I just have to make it a few more days. Dominic and Gilbert have promised to help, but . . . this isn't the only place where this is happening. Every single community is under attack. Dominic is needed to help evacuate everyone to one community, and that's not even considering the other cities.

They are safe for now, while the Radiant Woods has a closer target. Maybe they'll be safe forever, with the safe houses buried. These monsters aren't supposed to survive outside the Radiant Woods at all. I don't know what changed, but hopefully, they still can't if they get too far. But if that's not the case . . . Dominic won't be able to help. I need help. I need to hold out until the evacuations are done, then volunteers from the communities can take over, at least for a few hours. I need to sleep. I just need to sleep.

I close my eyes. Just a few minutes. Just a few minutes, and I can get back to work.

I sit down, letting my heavy eyelids fall. Darkness surrounds me like mud. *I have worked hard. Maybe it won't be so bad if I just . . . let what will happen happen.* Henry's face swims through my head like rippling water. His gentle smile. His relentless forgiveness. My cowardice, when I ran, letting him be taken instead. The image shimmers and is replaced by the man in the glass pillar. No. Not "the man." My father. My father, whom I killed because his pride and cowardice ate him alive. My father, whose example I'd surely have followed. The child who ran from Henry would have grown to be the man in the glass.

No. I will not be my father.

Just as a sharp *crack* rings throughout the ruined gallows around me, skipping across the rubble of this city's conflicts and clawing into the ears of the other mages, I force my eyes open. There is a massive monster, three times my height, and with a mallet of flesh and some kind of organic armor instead of a fist. It's pointed at one end, like it was designed to break my glass. A spiderweb of fractures and the sound ringing in my ears reveal it has already used this weapon once, and it's swinging back to strike again.

No. I will not let the victims of the woods and the people of Visenar meet. I will not let them hurt each other. I don't care if I have to stay awake for weeks; I will not fail again. I will not run away again. I never got to prove to Henry that I had changed, but if I stop trying now that he's gone, then I never did. My brother is dead. He never knew for sure whether I'd run again if I had to make the same choice again. But I won't.

I throw my mana into more glass, reinforcing and repairing what is already up. The monster hits it, and the cracks spread. I reinforce. I repair. It hits it again. This repeats and repeats and repeats, each time widening the crack a little further. It is breaking my defenses faster than I can put them up, and I'm running out of mana. I can't keep going. But I will. I will keep casting until I am dead. I will save *everyone.*

My fingers start to feel numb, dark bubbles appearing in my vision, and my mana slows down like a pump from a drying well. I can't keep going. I must. I push my mana with every shred of will I have. Another monster, identical to the last, emerges from the woods. *The glass is going to break.* My leg gives out, forcing me to one knee.

My head is so heavy; I can't keep fighting. I try to cast, but no glass appears, the crack doesn't heal. The world begins to blur. *No.* I'm failing again; I'm losing. So many people are going to die.

I am losing control of my limbs. My abused body is in full rebellion, demanding sleep I can't afford. I'm growing delirious. A frantic music plays in my head, like a violin giving voice to anxiety and failure and desperation. All these emotions are amplified, until a new aura surrounds me, unfamiliar mana filling the air.

"You know," a woman says, "I had a friend once. She would have said we need to just kill them. That we have no choice. That people will get hurt if we don't. But you know what? I think you're right. There has to be another way." As she says this, teal mana surrounds my glass before it can shatter, and a breath later, a wall of ice, every bit as clear as the glass I'd created, takes its place. "Get some sleep. I've got this."

Instead of sleeping immediately, I quietly sob as the woman with the braids finally takes up the defense in my stead.

Gilbert

"Gilbert, I'm worried about you. You've barely spoken to any of us in weeks, and now that all this is happening . . ." Julie trails off. I take a deep breath. I don't have the emotional energy for her like I once did. We're walking toward the portal to Sara's hat shop, and I have to keep my eyes on the Radiant Woods. There are hundreds of people following us, all vulnerable and exhausted. All hoping for safety.

"I know. I'm worried about everyone. Julie, this is terrifying and heartbreaking, and I don't know how to fix anything. I'm doing the best I can," I answer. She shakes her head.

"Gil, you don't have to fix anything. It's not on you to fix anything. You're no royal mage—you barely have any mana at all. It's not your job to save everyone. Those things . . . I saw what they can do, Gilbert. There is nothing you can do about them, trust me. Just . . . come back to us, please. We could use the company," she begs.

I look away from the colorful but nonsensical plants of the Radiant Woods toward Dominic, the man keeping all us safe with his mana. As soon as he shows up anywhere, the attacks stop. He is too powerful for the woods to bother sending more monsters; it learned that a single day in. Every day, he and I go to two or three communities and help them evacuate back to the towers. It's too slow, but it's the fastest we can go. He's as exhausted as I am, but he is keeping everyone alive.

"I'm sorry, Julie. I like you. I like everyone, and I loved our time together, but . . ." I pause as Dom looks back to check on the crowd and his eyes meet mine. "But I need something different now. I need to fight, and I need to be around people who will fight with me. I owe it to my brother. And I owe it to myself." Julie winces, following my eyes up to Dominic. But she sighs and smiles at me.

"All right. I get it. Everyone's gonna miss you though," she says. I return the soft smile.

"Will they? You're the only one up here talking to me, aren't you?" I reply. She blushes sheepishly.

"Right. Well. Everyone is scared. We didn't know what to do when we got attacked, but we do all care about you. Take care of yourself, all right? And, uh, give my regards to Lord Dominic," she replies. I nod, and she puts one hand on my shoulder, patting it, before turning around to find the rest of my previous paramours. That could have gone worse, as breakups go.

I keep walking, and my smile even lasts a few steps.

Shit. Where did everything go wrong? There is a sense of loss hanging over the group. Dom and I weren't fast enough, and everyone here has lost someone since the monsters started attacking. And we are still a ways away from making it to complete safety.

Even as we pass through the fault in reality that leads to the center of Sara's hat shop, the exit is too far from the towers for the group to safely leave Dominic's side. They could be attacked before they make it to the defenses we've got set up there, and it would only slow us down to bring each individual group back to the towers. We have to drag everyone to each community we visit, and we have one more. One I am not excited for. Everyone wants to enjoy the quiet safety of the endless hat shop, but every second we waste is a second someone could be dying.

Dominic quickly crosses to the next exit, and the rest of us follow.

When it's my turn, I close my eyes and hold my breath. I hate this part, but there is no point in waiting. I take a step forward and onto the path to the Kingdom of Endings.

The moment air kisses my skin, I can smell the blood. Someone is screaming, and we are forced to go from walking to running. Even so, there are many of us, and we can't move quickly. It's agonizing, listening to the sounds of violence, tasting it in the air, being too slow to stop it. *Don't think about it, Gil. Don't think about it, Gil.* Even after we clear the Radiant Woods, it takes agonizingly long to make it through the mundane forest to the inhabited area. When we do, I almost vomit.

It's the worst I have seen so far. Every other community has at least managed to fight, but this one, despite having more mages with more mana than most other communities, doesn't look like they fought back at all. There are dozens of bodies, mangled and discarded. The monsters are already fleeing as Dominic makes it to the center of town, but it's too late. Tree roots erupt from the ground in all directions, ignoring soil and cobblestone alike and binding every single monster to hold them in place.

"Shit," he whispers as I catch up with him. "I should have known this would happen." I don't quite understand what he means, but I don't have the stomach to ask.

"Is there anyone left?" I whisper instead.

"Yeah. Yeah, I think so," he says. I don't know how he can tell, but it's a relief nevertheless. "Everyone," he shouts. "It's safe! You can come out now!" It's silent for a long while after he says this, but eventually, there is a racket from the largest building in town, and a door opens. It's just a hesitant crack at first, but then it swings open and a furious man in silk clothes comes marching out.

"About time!" he shouts. "We've been calling for help for days!"

"We came as fast as we could, but everyone needed help, not just you, I'm sorry," Dom replies quietly.

"Yes, yes. Well, the important thing is you're here now. Now, if you could help me start cleaning this up and letting everyone know it's safe to come out . . ." He trails off as the first of the group following us emerges from the forest. He frowns as the crowd behind us grows larger and larger. "Well, isn't this something? We won't be able to take in any refugees, I'm afraid. The kingdom simply isn't large enough. You'll have to find somewhere else for everyone who can't help defend the kingdom."

Dom and I just stare at him for a moment, neither of us quite able to process what he said. He is impatiently tapping his foot by the time I speak up. "We aren't bringing anyone here; we came to bring you back to the mountain settlement. It's the easiest to defend, and that's where everyone else is now," I explain. The man scoffs.

"How dare you? We are not abandoning our kingdom!" He gasps. "We need your help defending it, and that's what I'll expect you to do!" I'm a little surprised he is speaking to Dom this way, but I guess not everyone in the town has been to Visenar. Still, even if they don't recognize him, his mana level is clear. If anyone was hanging on to hierarchy based on that, it should be the Kingdom of Endings, right?

"We can't defend two places at once," Dom replies calmly. "I'm sorry, but you'll have to come with us."

"I'm not asking you to defend two places at once—I'm asking you to defend the Kingdom of Endings!" he sneers. I am not in the mood for this, and we are in a hurry. I take a deep breath.

"We are bringing anyone who wants safety with us. But we are leaving. I'm sorry, I know this is your home, but we will not be defending it for you. We would protect everyone if we could, but we can't," I say. He crosses his arms.

"You know you are speaking to Queen Lillith's fiancé right now, yes?" he asks. "You will do as your future king tells you." Again, I am left speechless. What is he talking about? Lily's fiancé?

"No, you're not?" I say, the question behind the statement clear.

"I am. After the stewards were killed, we had an election—an idea I believe my love herself has written about. I won by a landslide. As the chosen king of the kingdom, I am of course engaged to marry the queen," he challenges.

"Lily doesn't even like—It's only been a few weeks since—" I cut myself off and take a deep breath. That doesn't matter. I let the air out and compose myself. I am surrounded by carnage, destroyed homes, and mutated victims struggling to free themselves from magic tree roots. This man is not my main concern. "All right. We are going to gather anyone who wants to come with us, then we are leaving. Come with us or don't—we won't force you. But we aren't staying. And if you want my advice? Drop the fiancé bullshit. The last man who declared himself my sister's fiancé lost his head even worse than you are right now."

I march away from him, ignoring his self-important ranting. There are people who need help, and they deserve our attention.

CHAPTER TWENTY-THREE

Radiant Retreat

Sarafyna

The border stands before me, impossibly tall and wide. The stone monument in the sky silently screams at me, forbidding me from passing through. To everyone else, the barrier itself is invisible. I suppose it is for me too, but . . . some feelings are so intense they can nearly be seen. The rejection and contempt of this border are tangible, and while the air remains empty and I couldn't describe what it looks like, I can see exactly where the border starts.

This. I flew all day and night, exhausting myself, for this. This hideous barrier caging the people on both sides. And I don't want to pass through it. I'm afraid.

When I came here only a few days ago, my divine magic failed me. My whisper spheres won't connect with anyone back home; my hats don't connect with the hat shop. What I've done to the Radiant Woods hasn't changed, but nothing else is working.

There are only two things that absolutely can't fail me, and the hat shop is one. The other is Annie. If my divine magic fails, she dies. I can't accept that. I refuse to accept that. As long as I live in this world, so will she. So many lives have been leaning on Annie since I met her, and I brought her here to shoulder that burden, so I am determined to carry the burden of her still heart in return. I will keep Annie alive.

This is why I'm afraid. Because my magic doesn't work when this wall is between me and my target—not always. I am terrified I will walk through this border, and Annie will die. But I have to go. I know I have to go; I'd never forgive myself for the consequences of refusing. Annie would never forgive herself either.

I can still feel her. If I focus, I can see her. She is okay. She is alive. And she is fighting. I have to fight too. I take a deep breath. The hat shop remained when I passed through. I can't control it as well, but it still exists, and the Radiant Woods didn't take my part of the Nexus back. The hat shop and Annie together own almost all the magic I have access to. If the shop survived, my girlfriend will as well.

If she doesn't . . . well, I will turn around and bring her back. I'll have to tell her then why I can't go back without her; I'll have to face whatever she says when she knows the truth, whatever she asks me to do. But she will be alive.

I close my eyes and tremble. I have told myself I can save her again and again, but no matter how many times I tell myself this, taking the first step toward that risk is still too hard. But I can feel her. I can feel her need to keep her remaining family safe. She is counting on me to do that, to keep everything she has fought for from falling apart. And so, because I love her, I take a step.

The wall surrounds me, trying to refuse me. It feels like the slime of a priest's gaze. The aching underneath my skin taunts me, reminding me of my childhood. Of the day my father nearly killed himself trying to save me.

But I am stronger now. Stronger than those priests. Stronger than this violent wall. Annie has made me stronger. I ignore the hostile energy assaulting me and picture Annie's face: her eyes of blood; her eyes of earth. Her straight, obsidian hair; her curled, mahogany hair. She has two faces, two bodies. I can see and feel them both. I am seen and felt by both. My mind goes back to that final night before I left, that joy and relaxation. As I walk, I live in that moment of vulnerability with the woman I love, and before I know it, I have crossed the border.

I immediately collapse to my knees, gripping my beating heart with both hands.

I can feel her. I can still feel her. She's still alive. I can do this. I can do this, and Annie will survive. I taste the salt of tears as they pass my lips, while tension like a thorn falls from my back, allowing my blood to flow freely. My shoulders slump. She's alive. I can keep her alive even from here. I can keep her alive.

Which means it is time to move. I have wasted enough time already. I need to act.

The Radiant Woods was several days walk from here, or several hours flight for me, but I don't need to do either: I brought my own route back. Now, on the other side of the border, I can use all my abilities again, which means as soon as I have a decent place to hide, I can reach wherever I need to in an instant.

I look around the empty meadow for anything I can use as shelter. Nothing. I sigh, idly rubbing the brim of my hat. It helps me center my mind a little. I suppose I should contact Edward before I do anything. If they are all well, I can spend this entire week looking for Leo.

I sit down on a bed of lilies and take my bag off my back. I dig through it, past the other, more magical hat I've brought, and grab the whisper sphere.

When I try to contact Ed, however, the sphere glows for a few moments before going dark again. I frown a little. That's not good. Nervous sweat forces me to remove my hat before it's ruined. If Annie lost another brother . . . No. I can't think about that right now. I have to try someone else.

Next, I call Gilbert, Annie's oldest brother. This time, a voice answers almost immediately.

"Ed, is that you? Is everything all right? We're coming as soon as we can; hang in there just a little longer!" Gil promises before I get a chance to speak.

"Gil? It's Sara; what happened to Ed?" I ask.

"Sarafyna? You're okay, thank the—thank someone! We haven't been able to get in contact with you! Can you make it back? We need help!" he says, and my breath catches. I wasn't gone for that long, and everything was fine when I was here. I try to control the panic climbing my mind like a rope ladder and respond.

"Yes, I can get back. What happened, where do you need me?"

"Visenar, as soon as you can; Ed needs help," Gil replies immediately. "It's the victims of the Radiant Woods—they are leaving, attacking the settlements. They have been for days." The trembling in my hands returns as a million implications crash down around me like a falling mountain.

No. They aren't supposed to leave. They aren't even supposed to be able to survive outside the woods. But if they are hurting people . . . there is no way to avoid someone getting hurt. I wanted to save them. I wanted to save them all. But now, after the woods finally lets them go, I don't have Annie's knowledge to help me. People are going to die. People have probably already died on both sides.

But why does he want me in Visenar? Then it occurs to me: the great tree by the gallows. The tree *I* put there. "*Ed needs help,*" he said. Annie's brother needs help, because of me.

"I'm on my way," I promise, putting the sphere away. I wanted to check in, then talk to Dad and Pete. I was hoping to find Leo quickly before returning to Annie. But this . . . this is a nightmare. The Radiant Woods won't leave me alone; they won't stop torturing me, long after I escaped them. Long after I conquered them, they still hurt the ones I love.

I glance around again. There's nowhere to hide the hat, and I don't have time to look. I could maybe grow a new tree of the Radiant Woods here, but that's what caused the issue in the first place. I'll just have to risk it.

I pull the hat from my bag, gently replacing it with my old one. With no time to waste, I put the new hat on; the one I brought from my hat shop. The one still connected to it. A breath later, I am inside the Nexus, surrounded by my hats. The safest place in the world, except next to Annie. We were supposed to use this method to travel back regularly, before the border got in the way.

I don't wait longer than a moment. I won't let Annie lose another brother. I run to the nearest exit, making a sharp left and running into the Radiant Woods the second I emerge.

"Welcome back, Sarafyna. We all missed you."

Years of fear and abuse stab me like needles the moment I enter. A thousand times I have felt this for Annie's sake. For everyone's sake. Recently, only for Leo. I ignore them, tuning out the voice. I simply find Visenar in my mind and leave the woods again. I don't have time to confront the Collector or listen to his taunts. I'm not the child he owned anymore, and I don't much like the woman I become when I'm reminded of what he did to that child.

I emerge into a cage of ice and broken glass. It's empty, except for the stains of blood in the dirt and rotting wood. The ice is clear as a window, and I can see a group of mages surrounding me and the radiant tree on all sides. I can see evidence of abuse on the ice, like something had been hammering and cutting at it, trying to escape. But there is nothing here. No one.

The urgency that rushed me here is replaced with confusion. I look up to see the ice and glass extends all the way to the top of the tree. If there is somewhere Ed needed my help, it was surely here. It's obvious there was some kind of struggle to keep something contained—the victims of the Radiant Woods, according to Gilbert. But why did they leave? Why now?

The answer to this question seems obvious, considering the timing, but I don't want to accept it. Because if it's what I think it is . . . the implications rest on my shoulders like stone.

As I am examining my surroundings, desperate for my theory to be wrong, the ice begins to melt in just one spot, creating an opening large enough to walk through. A woman with braids appears in the opening and tilts her head at me.

"How did you make them leave?" she asks. I clench my fists and close my eyes. So they did leave just before I got here. And if I had to guess, they showed up just after I crossed the border.

It's going to be longer than a week before I can see Annie again.

Charlotte

We emerge, for the first time, in a clearing we have already been in. We have been heading in one direction this entire time, but it could not be more obvious that we circled back around at some point. I recognize the stones and the moss of this spot; we found one of our new allies here. The path we previously took is clear as well.

The Radiant Woods is toying with us. We can't afford this; there are several dozens of us now, and it's growing harder to feed everyone. Everyone we save seems to have mana, but few of them have access to it in a meaningful way. I've needed to change all my aspects in order to keep everyone fed and clothed, and if we start retreading land, even that will be more difficult.

"I thought everyone was going in one direction; why are we here again?" Frey asks from slightly behind me. They quickly became one of Leo's closer friends and are often near the front of the crowd with us. They aren't the only one wondering what's going on though, and an uneasy whisper ripples through the group farther behind us.

Leo looks around, his almost constant smile wavering for the first time in days. "I'm not sure," he answers. "Something has changed." He's right. I don't know what's changed, but I think I know why it resulted in us coming back here.

"We are here for the same reason we have only found other people like us. Other people born in the entirely wrong body and abandoned here," I answer.

"What do you mean?" Leo asks. I glance back at the nervous crowd.

"We're being led somewhere. I don't know where, and I don't know why, but the people we are saving . . ." I trail off as I think about the new, hope-filled Leo I have grown to love since he first brought someone back. I don't want to ruin that, but he has to know. "They're being used as bait. Bait to bring us somewhere," I finish. I expect Leo's expression to fall. I expect the hopelessness of his isolation to return. Instead, he grins.

"Well, wherever they are leading us, they are delivering us to our lives, our bodies, as we are supposed to be. I say we use that as long as we can and face whatever they are trying to trap us into together," he responds.

I'm a bit taken aback. All that time around Lillith, I saw a lot of people grow more passionate, more hopeful—but more desperate and angry at the same time. Leo's unassailable and unbridled joy is all him. How long must it have lived inside him? How long have I held it back, in the name of earning a real life for him? How long did my concessions to the world I thought was unchangeable keep him from this joy? How many years could he have felt like this, had I helped him fight sooner?

"Then why would it take us back here?" Frey asks. "I know the Nexus—and the assholes who sent us there—are a bunch of stupid pricks, but surely they wouldn't want to turn us around for no reason?"

He's not wrong, unless they want to drive us to starvation. But eventually, we'll just stop and start growing food locally, going on trips to find more victims of the woods. We won't starve.

"Something has definitely changed," I answer. "Wherever they are leading us, they don't want us to get there right now." What, I don't know. But something has changed.

New World

Oakley

My arms are still in front of my face, and my heart is still pounding, but the world is . . . quiet. Nothing happens. I'm okay. Alive. I hesitantly open my eyes, only to find myself outside.

As my mind escapes the adrenaline surging through me, I notice the fresh smell of the air and feel the warm breeze on my skin. I am not only outside but nowhere near my office. Nowhere near Austin at all, in fact. Hell, this barely looks like Texas. There are a few spots up north, by the lake, which are at least green enough to match my surroundings, but none so large and open. Wherever this is has more rolling green hills and fewer cedar trees.

A new fear descends on me; no longer an aimless, targeted fear with an obvious subject. Instead, it's an open, unknowable fear: Vulnerability. I am here, alone, in the middle of nowhere. No one to protect me. No money. No authority. And the whole world wants me dead. I feel naked, exposed. I could die at a moment's notice if the wrong person finds me here.

How did I even get here? I don't understand what happened. Where do I go? What should I do? I don't know how to survive out here. Did someone bring me here? Why? How am I supposed to survive? How do I find my way back to the city?

I turn again and again. There is no hint of where I should go. No roads. No signs. I am on the precipice of full-on panic, rapidly turning around, hoping to catch some sign of society, when my hand brushes my pocket and feels its contents. In an instant, I realize I'm being silly. Too much adrenaline; I'm not thinking clearly.

I don't know what happened, have no idea how I got here, but the last thought in my mind was *This can't be real.* I was just repeating that to myself, over and over. *This can't be real. This can't be real. This can't be real.* I was about to die. I was moments away from the end of everything, holding my arms up in a desperate, aimless attempt to survive. And I found myself here.

It defies logic, but whatever happened, it saved my life. If someone did this, they don't want me dead. I don't need signs or roads. I have my phone.

I pull my salvation from my pocket to call the police, only to realize I have no signal. There shouldn't be anywhere I have no signal. Again, despair bubbles in my stomach. Where do I go? Any direction could take me farther from safety. I sit down in the wet grass and grip my legs.

It's hopeless. I need help. Why won't anyone help me? This can't be real. This can't be real. I just want to feel safe. I close my eyes, trying to shut out the world. *It's impossible that I am here. It's impossible. This isn't reality. In reality, I am safe. I am untouchable. I am above worries like this.*

The breeze stops, the chirping of birds vanishes, and the air grows stale. I finally open my eyes to discover a veil of the night sky around me, stars in all directions reaching down and touching the ground around my feet. Something about it is calming, and I reach out to touch it. It ripples like water.

This . . . This is real. This is safe.

CHAPTER TWENTY-FOUR

Punishment

Lillith

I walk back from the colosseum after the third fight of the day. Considering how much healing I need after each bout and how much more slowly I heal than most, that's about as many as I can swing. I am impressed with the healing; even with Sarafyna's help, it's rare to heal this quickly and with so few scars. My tumors have even started to shrink a little more quickly, despite my paramour's absence.

I feel completely fine, despite the numerous cuts and wounds inflicted on me throughout the day. The abuse I tanked in any one of those three fights should have left me drinking through a tube for weeks at least, but I am fine. Better than fine, even. I'm energetic.

Fuckface Markus has held up his end of the bargain so far as well; I have not been ordered to kill anyone yet. It's only been one day since our deal, but even so, it's a relief. Of course, I imagine once I figure out a way to break out a building full of slaves and get them to safety, the deal may fall apart. He didn't technically forbid orchestrating a mass escape of the other gladiators, but it was a verbal contract; they can get a little messy sometimes, you know: he said, she said. He sucked; she planned his murder. This kind of thing falls apart all the time, but for now, it seems to be holding.

I do get a lot of looks and fingers pointed my way by whispering pass-ersby, but as planned, none of it is dangerous. I am famous for playing myself extremely convincingly. Kind of like the opposite of Tony Hawk. I can finally walk through the city with neither a heavy wool cloak nor conspicuous heat mana to keep me cool. When people see my tattoos, they don't think of cultists but of the up-and-coming gladiator.

It's a relief. It will make it even more important to cover up later, when it's time to get back on my murder shit, but for now, I can actually move around—a privilege I am currently using to, well, go back to my room. Yeah, I'm not using it much at the moment; I haven't had much emotional energy for it. But hey, it's the principle of the thing, right?

I arrive at the room I share with Autumn and Ember, only to be stopped by August, the only one I don't expect to find inside. He grabs my human arm and gives me a serious look.

"Hey, Lil. Can we talk?" he asks. His words are gentle, but his tone has an edge—an edge which grows more familiar every day. I sigh internally but offer him a gentle smile. I know what he wants to talk about, but he won't like what I have to say.

He wanted to talk last night, but dinner with dickface ran late and failed to yield any useful information at all. I made it back well after sunset and, despite his worried look, I really did need to sleep first. It wasn't until last night, after Ember's nightmare had woken us up, that Autumn told me what they had witnessed in the stands. I feel terrible for brushing him off, but he'd waited so long to speak to me that he was dead to the world when I left for the arena today. It's a conversation that's overdue.

"Yeah, Augie. Lead the way," I agree. He lets out a deep, relieved breath and nods. I follow him to his own room, where he sits on his bed while I take the chaise in the corner. "Ember with Autumn right now?" I check. He gives me a look of exasperation and disappointment all rolled into one.

"Of course. You know I wouldn't leave her alone," he replies. I do know that, but it's never something to take for granted. Of course, considering the topic at hand, it's even more unlikely he'd leave Autumn on her own.

"Right, I know. I'm just looking out for her," I respond.

"Are you?" August quips, his words drawing only a little blood.

"I am," I respond simply. I'm not here to defend my choices to him—I'm here to talk about what he saw, and so is he. His glare is sharp but softens just a little.

"Autumn says she told you what happened yesterday?" he asks. I nod. "Lil, I can't get it out of my mind. A man killed himself in front of me. He was there one moment, and just . . . gone the next. The same thing that almost happened to my sister—my twin sister. I keep replaying it in my head, over and over. In the middle of a crowd, hundreds of people watching him. He just . . . chose to die."

He doesn't immediately follow this with anything, but it's clear he's not expecting a response just yet. He clenches and releases his fist a couple times before locking his glassy eyes on me again. "Lily, the people in the city, maybe this entire country, don't even feel grief. They can't. They have been cured of it. But he still chose to die, and I can't help but think . . . if that's a choice people can make when they aren't grieving, how much easier must it be when they are crushed under their sorrow? Even these people aren't safe. Doesn't that mean Autumn is in even more danger?"

I examine his eyes for a long moment. He loves his sister so much. I empathize.

"I get it, August," I reply. "I hate seeing my loved ones in pain. I fucking hate it. It hurts so much I ran away from my own family. Yeah, I had to come anyway; I had the perfect fucking excuse. But that doesn't mean I didn't run from it. It's so hard to watch, so hard to feel. I understand your worry for your sister; I'm worried for her too. And I know the thought of taking that grief away sounds like a balm on an open wound, like it will heal her—but it won't. If I thought it would help her without hurting her more, I'd be right there with you. I may not love her like a sibling, but I do love her. I want her to stop hurting too."

August grits his teeth, and his glare sharpens again. "You fucking loathe her," he challenges. This cuts much deeper and knocks the breath out of me. I can only look back at him with wide eyes. "I have seen how you look at her when she has her back turned. I can feel it emanating from you like heat from a kettle, building up pressure bit by bit. You hate her. You wish you hadn't stopped her from jumping. You think I can't see it? We all can. You blame her for Henry's death just as much as she does. Can you really say you are leaving her in grief for her own good and not as a punishment?" Three times today I was nearly beaten to unconsciousness, but this is the first time I've really been wounded.

I want to deny it, but he's right. At least a little. I didn't even realize I looked at her like that, pushing it to the back of my mind, compartmentalizing it away where it was quiet. But nothing is ever truly silent. I can't ignore the image that forced its way into my mind when we sat on top of that building, that twitch in my new arm, ready to push her. I do hate her. She is one of three people I want to punish for Henry's death. One of three who aren't already dead, anyway; at least as far as I know. But I don't mean to actually punish her.

"You're right," I respond, clenching my own fists. "I do resent Autumn. I do blame her. But I also love her. Henry loved her even more than he loved me, and hurting her would be spitting on his grave. I am not punishing her with grief. I don't even know why she is still feeling it now, with Sara gone. I couldn't take it away even if I thought it was a good idea. You need to listen to me, August. Autumn said there was another man there. One who said this happens all the time, right?"

"You don't, huh? You have no idea at all why she is still hurting while everyone else in this country is free from it. Even I don't feel any grief anymore, just anger and resentment. Even you don't. But Autumn—Autumn still gets all it. How goddamn convenient. The person you resent the most is the one who mysteriously carries the most pain," he snaps.

Again, I feel like I've been punched in the gut. He thinks I'm not grieving still? He thinks I would do that to a person? "Is that really what you think of me?" I ask. "After everything, you think I would do that to a person?" He clicks his tongue in irritation.

"I didn't. But I didn't think you'd ever hate Autumn either. You're not exactly the girl I wanted to court back in school. I don't know who you are, but I know Autumn is hurting, and you, probably the woman who hates her the most, are playing games in the arena. Exactly what should I think?" August throws back.

Every word lands like the crack of a whip. August is my friend, one of the first nobles I've actually trusted. Hell, he's the first person I openly came out to here, and he was shockingly blasé about it, even supportive. I like him. If I didn't, the way he sees me now wouldn't hurt so much. Especially since, even if it's only a little, every word has the bite of truth to it.

I am not punishing Autumn, but as much as I love her, I do hate her. I don't even logically blame her for what she did. I do blame her for failing to tell me about it later, but even if she had, a part of me would still hate her. A part of me would still have considered pushing her from that tower. A part of me would still want to follow her.

I take a deep breath and bite back the quiver that tries to escape in my voice. Even as he berates me, he needs to see a strong front. He needs to have me to lean on.

"August. He said it happens all the time. I spoke to the other gladiators today, and they confirmed it. Have you ever been to any place where casually taking your own life is considered regular and mundane? At any time in Potestia? Do you really think it's unique to the arena?

"People aren't doing this despite their lack of grief. They're doing this *because* of it. If I had a way to hand Autumn over to the sages, it would only increase the risk to her safety," I respond, measuring my voice to present as being calmer than I feel. I see his denial brewing, but I cut it off at the pass. "Look, all I'm asking is that you investigate it. We've been focused on the sages, but you can shift gears. Or, uh, change your target. Ask around, read the news, listen to rumors. I'm willing to bet the suicide rate in this country is astonishing.

"And before you ask me to find a way to rob your sister of her pain, before you accuse me of inflicting it on her on purpose, find out if that's what you really want. Because it will hurt her, August. It will hurt her more than I ever could. You can take away someone's ability to shit because it seems cleaner, but it will still make a mess. The difference is it will kill them too. An ugly metaphor, I know, but an effective one.

"You need to process what you saw yesterday. You need to examine it before you try and resign someone you love to the same fate. I get it. I do. You faced the reality of what your sister almost did, of how close you got to losing her, and you're afraid no one will stop her next time. But there is no quick fix. There is no gluing her back together and putting her on your shelf exactly as she was before my brother died. You can only be there for her. I am not punishing her, and I never will, however I feel about her. So before you jump to that, make damn sure you know it won't leave her rotting on the inside."

August continues to glare at me. "Fine. But you're going to have a hard time convincing me of this entirely while you are free from your grief and she is not. Just get out for now. I'll speak to you again when I am done chasing down your excuses. Eventually, you are going to have to account for that disparity," he replies. My heart sinks into my stomach, and I turn to leave. I knew he wanted to talk about what he saw, but I didn't know it was going to be like this.

Before I leave the room, I pause. "My grief isn't gone, August. And I wouldn't give it up for anything," I whisper.

"Could have fooled me," August quips, turning his head to look out his window. It bites, but not as hard as his comments about my feelings toward Autumn. I leave his room feeling defeated, waiting in the hall to catch my breath. Sobs threaten to escape, and I have to wait for several minutes before I can control them and put on a brave face again. But Autumn needs me to wear that face. Ember needs it too.

After nearly ten minutes, I finally return to my own room. Ember is in her bed with her eyes closed, although I don't think she is sleeping. She seemed to have a rough night, so I get it. Autumn, however, is standing and glaring at me.

"Would you just hit me?" she snaps the second she sees me. What the fuck? What's all this about?

"Why would I do that, Autumn?" I ask. She clicks her tongue in a way identical to her twin's.

"You can't die in that arena, Lily. If you die, the rest of us have nothing. It will kill Sara. It will kill me. And you'll leave Ember back where she started. We are all counting on you too much for you to get yourself killed," she snaps.

"I know that. What does that have to do with hitting you?" I ask, incredulous.

"Do you? I've seen every one of your matches, Lily. It sure doesn't feel like you know other people are counting on you. What you are doing out there? It's pathetic. It's spitting on your brother's grave," she says, somehow throwing my own words back at me despite her absence when I said them. "I get it. I understand—probably better than anyone. But if you are going to keep punishing someone for Henry's death, make it someone expendable. Someone we can do without. Someone no one is expecting anything from. Just fucking hit *me* instead of getting yourself killed. We are both responsible, not just you. If you are determined to make someone pay in blood for Henry's death, make it me. I deserve it more anyway. And you're not the only one who feels it every time you take a kick or a cut you could have avoided."

Again, one of the twins takes the wind from my lungs. I tighten my lips and one fist, completely unable to respond. I'm not going to hurt Autumn. I would never hurt Autumn. But when she asks me to, I am tempted.

But I just swore to August that I would never punish Autumn for what happened.

I can't face the reality of the punishment I have been accepting in her stead. I'm not sure it was even a conscious choice.

But what choice was it, exactly? Three living people hold the blame for my brother's death. If I stop punishing myself, can I keep that promise to August? Will I start punishing the others instead? How can I tell August I would never do that, when I have been doing it to one of the three this entire time? I need to speak, need to tell Autumn she isn't expendable. She doesn't deserve anything more than me. But I don't. Autumn huffs.

"Well. If you aren't going to hit me, I'm going to August's room. Let me know if you change your mind. But whether you do or not, stop fucking around when your life is on the line. It's disgusting," Autumn says after I fail to respond for a moment, shoving her way past me and leaving the room.

I lean out, making sure she does actually enter the room next door and isn't left alone. Finally, I release a breath I didn't realize I was holding, slumping onto my bed, already exhausted by the emotional beating I've taken in the past few minutes.

"You got something you want to yell at me for too?" I ask. Ember grunts.

"You snore loud as shit. Some of us need our sleep," Ember complains without skipping a beat. It doesn't have the familiar tone of a friendly joke, but it somehow feels like one anyway. Maybe I just needed a complaint that was petty. Maybe I just see a handhold to bring me back to a reality I can face. Maybe being flippant is just easier for me.

"I don't snore; I don't care what you or Sara say. You're just jealous of me, obviously," I joke, enjoying the moment of pettiness.

"Jealous of what? Your vibrant friendships? Yeah, think I'll pass on those," Ember retorts. Ouch.

"No, because my dick is bigger than yours," I respond sarcastically. Ember finally opens her eyes, slits of pupils rolling over to me.

"I don't even have a dick; what kind of jab is that?"

"Neither do I, but mine is still bigger," I answer. She groans in irritation.

"Go fuck yourself with it, then," she dismisses, rolling over on her side and turning away from me.

"Yeah, yeah. You eat shit too, bestie," I reply. She just grunts again, bored with the conversation. It wasn't exactly friendly, but the flavor of insults with no bite far surpasses the accusations from the twins. It helps me level out.

I close my eyes. I can't think about all this right now or I'll spiral. Instead, I retreat back inside myself. There is plenty of day left, and I won't need to sleep until well into the night. It's high time I figured out how to get stronger. *That* I can think about without pain.

It's time to become more demonic. It's time to turn my body into an even more deadly weapon.

CHAPTER TWENTY-FIVE

Evolution

I let the world melt around me as I magically retreat inward. August and Autumn's opposite but aligned complaints are chalk in the rain. Ember's quiet, self-soothing purring is simply white noise. I allow myself to exist in my own body, my own impossible body, with a scarred and still heart. Steel intrudes into the ecosystem, but flesh has grown around and attached to it, and mana flows between the two seamlessly.

There are ugly, invasive tumors littered throughout my body, collecting and bursting with mana. I feel lightheaded as the mana I search with interacts with them. They haven't been as bad since the enchanted limbs were attached. The various new piercings are helping as well, but all these simply prevent the negative effects of the cancer; they keep it from growing and keep me alive. None of them, on their own, actually remove the tumors. The arena's Nexus healing and my own efforts are the only thing that does that, but they are stubborn.

They aren't what I am here for, however. They are the primary obstacle to today's goal, but they are now under control enough that I don't have to spend my time on them. I hardly even feel like dried-out fish skin draped over a clothesline now, which means I can begin changing my body again. I am also just about as conspicuous as I can be already, so more obvious changes aren't as dangerous as they once were. I just need to decide on what I need to change.

What I need to do is kill sages. Divine magic makes that tough, but

I know how to fight that: poison and venom. It's how I have killed most users of divine magic so far.

Job one is improving on that, or rather, creating more expedient delivery methods for said poisons. As much as I like biting people (who doesn't?), it's a bit of an unruly way to fight; more of an ambush predator behavior. What I'd really like is projectiles. Any would work, really, but poisonous projectiles would be ideal.

Unfortunately, I am not a goddess of creation. I can't create new genetic designs from scratch. I am also not Sarafyna, so I can't just kind of soup into whatever shape I need. Every change I make, I have to base off something I studied directly in my past life, or something I can send mana into and study now. This limits me in a few ways. For one, my memory is not flawless, and genetic makeup is complex. I can only model changes after a general understanding I remember, and I have to adapt it to my human DNA. I can also only make changes that actually exist. Or at least, changes which are close to something real with some adjustments.

My blood and sweat are like this. I can change the activating proteins and the method of storing venom, but I didn't invent neither the sweat nor the poison in my blood. Evolution, asshole that it is, did not produce a whole lot of organic projectiles. They are limited in quantity, hard to replace quickly, and just unlikely to persist through natural selection. Conditions for them are rare, and not consistent. *X-Men* apparently got this aspect of evolution wrong, despite its otherwise flawless science. It's pretty fucked up, if you ask me.

This has narrowed me down to two options: spitting venom and venomous claws. Something like a spitting cobra or a platypus. Or a scorpion, maybe. I can probably grow claws from my surviving hand that carries my own special venom. Not exactly like any of these animals, but using all them as a basis.

Both have drawbacks. The claws are an upgrade from the fangs, which were an upgrade from the blood delivery. I can more reliably use them in combat, especially combat I don't initiate. I can also dip my axe and the claws of my right glove in venom, but that will only work so many times in a row, and I have to be planning to use it. I am currently trying not to kill most people I'm fighting, so that's a no go. It remains only a minor upgrade, however, and is also the more obvious of the two. I have a couple more personal complaints as well, but they aren't a priority.

Then there is spitting venom, something I considered way back when I was creating my fangs. At the time, I rejected it because it is simply not effective enough against a divine mage when it is only skin contact. I needed the poison in their veins somehow. Even my touch-activated poison required ingestion first. If I want more than that, I need to spit not just venom but acid—something corrosive.

On one hand, this would be even more effective at using up a sage's Nexus energy. On the other, producing, storing, and spitting straight venomous acid requires a good number of secondary changes to be safe; otherwise, I'll just end up killing myself. It will also take a lot longer, and it won't extend my range all that much. I can hock a loogie with the best of them, but you can only organically propel liquids so far.

All this in mind, I decide to start with claws. *Sorry, Sara.* I'll see if I can make them retractable, at least. I can add spitting venom later, which will at least be another flawed tool on my belt. Claws are the easier change in the shortest time.

I'm an old hat at this by now, and my mana courses through my body, making little alterations at my command. It's too slow. I need to be ready to kill the next sage I fight, and that could happen any day. The way I've been doing things isn't going to cut it.

For what must be the millionth time, I curse that Sara's magic doesn't work on me for some reason. I mean, it works, she can heal me, but she has consistently failed to help with my alterations. Divine magic is kind of a finicky little shit. Like most of its users, I guess—excepting Sarafyna, who is, of course, a perfect, sexy angel who can do no wrong. In any case, it doesn't work for me, which means pure mana is my only shot.

It doesn't help that not all my limbs are organic anymore. I pulse mana through my body, but whenever it passes through the steel limbs, I have to change its nature so I don't fuck with it while modifying the rest. It slows me down, at first. Then I remember my fight with Turner.

I remember how quickly the spell materialized, shocking even me. The way my right arm accumulated mana like a hard drive, constantly moving back and forth between my tumors and the enchanted steel. Every pass carried more power, and it happened so quickly, bouncing back and forth more times than I could count in a second and creating the spell I'd visualized with much greater power and speed than I'd intended. It had been an external spell rather than internal work, but I wonder.

As soon as the thought even occurs to me, I start cycling my mana back and forth between the tumors and the artificial limbs. Again, it accelerates, moving through my body far faster than usual. *Well. This is probably a shitty idea.* As the mana circulates, I start picturing the changes I want in my left arm. It only feels a little like I fired thousands of needles through my veins which all exploded from my flesh as soon as they reached my forearm. Only a little agonizing beyond belief.

Christ, I need to figure out a better way to test this shit. The "I'm just gonna send it" method is not serving me well.

I do manage to keep my mouth shut and hold the scream in. As far as Ember knows, I'm still just meditating. And as far as I know, I am peeling my one remaining arm off one fiber at a time. My entire body flexes, tensing up and exhausting me with each rapid wave of mana throughout my body, but I push through, because it is working. I can feel it working in real time.

The keratin forms inside my fingertips, sharp, thick, and hollow. It grows and merges with my nails and skin, making them sharper and sturdier. New oval glands begin to build in my forearm, storage for the venom I intend to fill the claws with. It feels like eternity, tearing apart and rebuilding my body. The mana moves through my tumors, to my piercings and limbs, and to my tumors again. The enchantment used to stop mana from gathering in my cancer is now making me stronger, faster.

I am already halfway done with my new claws; almost ready to start producing venom in them. This much progress should have taken weeks, maybe months, but I have gotten to this point in . . . *How long has it been?* A hand lands on my shoulder, startling me and forcing me back to the conscious world. Autumn and Ember are both staring at me as I am taking in deep, desperate breaths, like I've just finished a marathon.

"What's happening? Why are you sweating so much? Are you all right?" Autumn asks. I realize she's right. My clothes are soaked through with sweat, and my hair is matted to my face and head. My tattoos are rough, with the line work rising from my skin like it does when I'm sick.

"Are you ever getting up? Don't you have more matches today? Or are you taking a day off already?" Ember asks. I look at both of them in confusion, failing to process the morning light shining through the window and across their faces. A moment later, my face pales.

I feel like I spent the night on a medieval torture rack. All my muscles are sore and overworked, and I'm exhausted. I don't need much sleep these days; a bit more since entering a land with no grief I didn't bring with me, but still not much. Any sleep at all is usually enough to avoid this level of exhaustion. And it is morning. I have been up the entire night forcing my body to take on a new design.

I look at my left hand as sweat runs down the black-and-purple tattoos covering the arm. My nails are thick, sharper. The claws themselves extend further to the side, growing into my skin and extending around each finger. This leaves my fingertips rougher and less human than they had been the night before.

All night. Fuck. I need to hurry.

"How long until the match?" I ask, urgency settling on me like sunbeams.

"Not long. If you leave now, you'll barely have time to make it," Autumn answers.

"Shit, no time to change or get any rest," I lament. Historically, going into battle while exhausted hasn't been my wisest move, but I've got more mana and have slept more recently than when I failed to save Henry as a kid.

But thinking of that fails to reassure me that things will be fine, as thinking of Henry ever does. Still. I have no choice. If I want my deal with Markus to hold up, I need to make it to all my fights.

"Maybe the stench will stop people from attacking you," Ember prods.

"If the sound of your voice doesn't work for you, the smell of my clothes won't work for me," I quip. "I need to go. Thanks for waking me up, Autumn."

"Wait." Autumn stops me, grabbing my sore arm and causing me to wince. This is not lost on her, as the pain is clear on my face. "Wait, what's wrong? Why did that hurt?"

I give her a pained smile. "Last night, I made some choices. Decisions, if you will. I'm paying the price for them a little, that's all," I answer. Her face sours.

"You didn't . . ." She trails off, more concern than irritation in her voice. I pick up on the implied question and shake my head.

"Not that kind of decision," I reassure. I hold my hand up for her, extending my half-finished claws a little. "Just working on some new weapons. Did more than I should have too quickly." Her eyes flick to my hand, grimacing a little, but she nods.

"All right," she responds with relief, the edge returning to her voice a moment later. "Lily. Fight like people are counting on you today, all right?" I freeze at this, feeling more vulnerable than I'd like, and her eyes dig into me with claws of their own. Finally, I give her a small nod.

"All right, Autumn. I'll try," I promise quietly. Then, I speak louder to indicate I am addressing the entire room. I feel uncomfortable with Autumn's serious tone and want to diffuse a little tension. A jab from Ember will do that. "Wish me luck. Pray for me as usual, Ember," I tease. The cat woman rolls her eyes.

"I told you, we don't have anyone to pray to where I'm from," she dismisses.

"I remember. But it's your love and concern that counts, right? Your prayers will reach me," I retort.

"Oh, fuck off," Ember groans, looking away from me toward the window.

"Right. Well, I wouldn't want to spoil such warm words by staying until they grow stale," I agree before rushing out the door. Maybe if I'm quick enough I can stop by the infirmary and handle the aching and fatigue a bit.

CHAPTER TWENTY-SIX

Indulgence

I manage maybe five minutes in the infirmary before I have to head out to my match. Thankfully, I heal so much faster than everyone else.

All right, that's a lie. Nexus energy works extremely slowly on me, and I feel like a sock with a rip at the pinky toe. The war hammer on my back actually feels a little heavy for once. My head isn't in an amazing place either.

As I wait for my gate to open, I can't get Autumn's voice out of my mind. *"Fight like there are people counting on you."* I feel like an idiot. A selfish idiot. I was so caught up in the knowledge that I'm not particularly special, however some dumbass prophecy wants to portray me, and everyone who is left will be able to keep fighting without me that I forgot that, on a personal level, people still need me. I brought the twins here with one other person who holds them in contempt. If I die, I leave them alone in a land that wants them dead. I leave them with no friends, completely vulnerable.

And that's not the only way Autumn needs me. She needs me for the same reason I need her: We need someone to grieve with us for my brother. Neither of us can be alone in it. To share the grief, and to share the guilt. The pain felt so vindicating. All this time, I let myself get hurt, like I was taking it on Henry's behalf. I felt so cold and deserving of pain, and it made me feel warm again to accept it. But it was just a distraction. A lie. Causing pain in one place to distract my body from another. Punishment for leaving my brother to die? No. It was an indulgence. A self-absorbed indulgence, nothing more. And Autumn is right. Henry would be horrified by it.

So today, I make the decision. As the gate opens, I promise myself I will fight back from the start. I won't accept pain I don't need just to feel better about myself. I will let myself hurt in the right way, for a while. The real way. The hurt that turns me to ice.

I tune out the announcer as I enter the arena. I've become bored with him, as his attempts to rile up the crowd are all the same and I lack interest in aiding him in doing so. Fortunately, ignoring him leans into the demon queen persona enough that Markus hasn't complained yet. I do quickly regret my failure to pay attention, however, as I am met with not one opponent but half a dozen—two of every sapient species I know of. They obviously aren't seasoned gladiators, but they don't look untrained either. They all stand near each other, facing me.

I'm not getting "battle royale" vibes from this setup. I suppose watching me tank a bunch of nonlethal attacks then beat my opponents with one hit was probably getting boring. No one will make any profitable bets if every fight ends the same way. I did expect they would do something like this eventually, but damn. What a day for it. Well, it's fine. Looks like they aren't throwing me directly into the deep end. I can beat these guys.

I crack my knuckles while waiting for the fight to start. Maybe if I finish this quickly, I can get some rest in the infirmary and recover from the night I had. The announcer marks the beginning of the match, and my opponents all run toward me, confirming my suspicions. It's me against all six of them.

The two volu launch into the air, but only a little, flying low and within reach if I put my strength behind a jump. The invisible ceiling of the arena must work both ways, keeping the battle contained and preventing avian combatants from running. The ailur fall to all fours and approach me far more quickly than the human combatants, who brandish what look like machetes. I move my hand to my head and crack my neck, relieving a little tension before my opponents reach me.

I take the hammer off my back, solid steel prepared to ever so gently pummel anyone who gets too close. Except, as the first volu dives at me, I freeze. I see his taloned fingers extending toward me. I can block them easily; I promised myself I would try. I promised Autumn. I was just reminding myself how selfish and self-indulgent I was being before, but I see Henry in the old building, smiling, joking with me. Left alone to die in a spell I failed to stop.

Talons tear into my cheek, leaving an open, bleeding gash and flaps of skin. Why did I take that attack? Claws from an ailur are coming at me now, and I take a step back. Then I see Henry again. The claws burrow into my exposed stomach.

Get it together, Lily. You are better than this. Another swipe. Another cut. All four nonhuman opponents take turns scoring flesh wounds, and despite seeing each one coming, despite my resolution to stop them, I do nothing. Finally, the humans catch up. A sword swings at me, and I side-step it with little effort. Talons rake down my back while the other sword swings toward my neck, and I duck it. Claws dig into my left shoulder. When my life is in danger, I avoid it. When my secrets are in danger, I dodge. I am never hit by a machete, my steel limbs always moving in time to avoid revealing anything to my enemies.

I feel pathetic. I know that I can end this now. I know I am making the choice, over and over again, to take the damage when I know I can survive it. A human man's foot collides with my rib cage, knocking me into the dirt. I roll out of the way of the sword that follows me, leaving it to slash at the dirt. As I do, the other man's boot lands in the same spot on my side, stomping on my ribs and causing several to loudly crack.

I can end this. I can end this now. But I don't. I let the abuse rain down on me, punishing me exactly as Autumn said. *Why? Why am I letting them do this? I wasn't going to! Why am I so weak? Why am I such an idiot?* This continues for far too long, my weak will and self-indulgence leaving me broken, bruised, and bloody.

I have to stop this. I have to stop it. I need to think of the people who are counting on me. As I taste blood, I clench my fists and force myself to my feet. I will fight back. A talon flies at me, and I catch it, swinging the attached volu around and tossing him away, leaving him panicking in the air. An ailur woman swipes again, and I let her draw more blood. I block a kick from the sky with my right arm, then scramble to recover my discarded hammer and block a sword strike. I take a punch. I block two attacks. I accept another. I block four the next time before I allow one to hurt me.

It's like I've trained myself to take the punishment and I have to con-sciously deny that instinct. But with every breath, I fight harder. Not against my enemies but against my own failings. I shouldn't be hurting for Henry—I should be fighting for him. Finally, although I resemble a cut of meat in a butcher's shop, I scream and grip my hammer, swinging out with visible force, buying some distance and time to think.

I won't do this anymore. I am fighting back, and I am not going to stop. I grit my teeth and flex my left arm. "This is over," I whisper.

I take exactly one step forward, and the world goes dark. Not pitch-black, but dark as a summer night. A shroud has filled the sky like the day has just ended and every torch and enchanted light stone in the city has been extinguished. But there are no stars, just dark. And it's not the sky. All seven of us freeze as we realize this. The black mantle stops just where the walls around us end. Whatever this is, it's cutting us off from the audience. I see no mana. I feel no aura of power. Either this is caused by someone with an aspect like mine, or this is divine magic.

I relax my grip. This is no longer a fight for an adoring audience. This is something else. Could it be Markus? He did promise to protect me if it looked like I would die, but the timing would be strange for that, doing it right when I finally pull myself together and rise above my own wallowing. I was obviously just about to fight back, so why would he step in now? It's also more than a bit conspicuous. Actually, this timing doesn't make much sense unless the involved sage specifically didn't want me to win.

The moment I realize this, my suspicion is confirmed in the most horrifying way I could imagine.

I feel the telltale throbbing of Nexus energy trying to control me. Thankfully, even while my grief mana fails to empower me, it still denies external control. Unless I allow or agree with the effects of the Nexus magic, it can't do anything to me directly.

The other six combatants aren't nearly so lucky. The divine mana takes them, and it ruins them. One man rapidly expands, exploding into some fleshy facsimile of a gorilla, except he lacks skin. His muscles and tendons are on full display, and I can see the entirety of his jaw, now sporting razor-sharp teeth. The transformation is sudden and violent, and based on the agonized screams, painful as well. And he's not the only one. The other human man is compressed, crunched with sickening snaps and spurting blood, until he forms into something like a boar but on the two powerful legs of a rabbit. He is half the size he was a moment ago, and the transition wasn't kind to him.

The others undergo similar but less drastic changes. The ailur both end up looking something like badly abused panthers, while the volu take the form of massive vultures with too many legs. I'm not sure why the humans got unique forms while the others matched each other, but I don't have time to think about it. I have a familiar, sick feeling rushing through my veins.

I have been here before. I have faced this before, the first time I entered the Radiant Woods. Innocent and tortured people, their bodies taken from them, eyes trained on me in desperation. A building tension in the air shatters, and suddenly, six sources of grief consume me, flooding me with empowered mana.

No, this isn't Markus. This is someone else entirely. Someone I hate far more.

"Is this the fucking Collector? Turn them back. I swear to Christ if you don't turn them back this instant, I will peel your skin from your skull when I find you!" I demand.

"The Collector. Am I? I wouldn't say so, but I suppose that's a matter of perspective."

What's that supposed to mean? Where is the voice coming from?

"I said, change them back!" I shout.

"You want me to change people back. I want you to let go of Sarafyna. Or rather, I want Sarafyna to let go of you."

"Oh, fuck you. The fuck does Sara have to do with this?" I call out.

"She. Is. Mine. And you are holding her back."

"She is her own, you fucking douchebag! Do you really think you can control her? She'll hurt you more than I ever could!"

"She would, you're right. She is . . . beautiful that way. Powerful. And you are a weight around her neck keeping her weak. Keeping her . . . enslaved. To you. If she could let go of you, she could kill every sage in this world on her own. But she won't, no matter what I say. No matter what I do. She insists on tying you here, digging you into the skin of this world like a stubborn splinter long past your expiration date. That ends here."

"The only thing ending here is you," I snarl. "That is, if you have the balls to show your damn face. If you aren't too much of a coward."

"A coward. A coward indeed. Missing her precious big brother; shriveling like a snail under salt. Hurting yourself. Hurting your friends. Hurting my Sarafyna. I've been watching you; coward is exactly the word I would use for your pathetic behavior. You are wasting Sarafyna's power. You are wasting her on your little tantrum."

I take a sharp breath through my nose. I hate when assholes say things that are true. I hate it when creeps are right about me. But that's through no fault of his. It's my fault. It's my own whimpering and wallowing that gave that insult teeth. But I am done with that bullshit. There remain people in this world who deserve pain far more than I.

"Well. Not anymore. Show your face, and I guarantee you I won't hold anything back," I reply.

"No time for that, I'm afraid. Spend time with my new friends instead. Good luck surviving them. They aren't the petty enemies you were fighting a few moments ago, and they aren't going to hold back."

I want to scream at him, challenge him again, nail him to the ground and make him explain everything I don't understand. But he's right again—I don't have time. His newest victims are charging me, and I can read my death in their eyes. But I'm not as weak as the creature they were fighting before either.

CHAPTER TWENTY-SEVEN

Brawl

Autumn has never been so right in her fucking life. I worry the level of correctness may be terminal. Makes us twins in a way, I guess. There are six victims trapped in . . . whatever this is. All them in pain. All them blind with fear and anger. All them trying to kill me and each other. I have no idea how this barrier works. This is a pretty clear-cut attempt on my life, so I can guess it's meant to block any intervention from Markus, the sage who is specifically invested in me being alive and, quite literally, kicking.

But revealing that I can use mana even while cuffed, all while publicly declaring myself Demon Queen Lillith . . . Well, this would be a pretty effective way to get myself killed. If the Collector, or whoever this asshole is, wants me dead, then this could very well be sort of a tic-tac-toe style trap. Damned if I do, damned if I don't. In other words, I can't be certain mana is a safe defense, which means I have to try to fight these people using only mundane means.

And they remain innocent, which means I have to do it nonlethally while protecting them from each other. I am bloody, bruised, and have multiple broken ribs. I didn't sleep last night, and what I did do has already left my body weary and sore. I am in no shape to fight supernaturally mutated victims while avoiding any damage the infirmary can't heal. If only someone had warned me that taking all those hits as some kind of sad penance was a shitty idea. If only I had resolved, before entering this arena, to stop indulging in such self-destructive behavior. *Alas*, I suppose I will never know what would have happened if such things had taken place.

Fuck. I always like to think I'm so smart. Shame I'm such a moron.

My body throbs as the bloodied gorilla closes in on me. I duck below his first blind swing, bobbing to the left of his second. Each time, I can feel the wind displacement as his attack passes through the space I've just left.

He is strong. Probably not as strong as my left arm, but maybe stronger than my right. I can't take many hits like that on a good day, and it is not a good day. His left fist collides with his right palm, making a hammer he raises over his head to descend back on mine. This time, I dodge right, but he follows through with the swing, losing no momentum at all as his fists move toward me. In a rush, I throw myself backward, landing on my hands and awkwardly flipping back to my feet.

I stumble back several steps, nearly falling on my ass. That was a move pulled off with sheer force and zero technique. Just as I am steadying myself, preparing for a new attack from the gorilla, one of the vultures dives at me, six sets of talons wrestling each other for a chance at my throat. I hold my right arm up and hear the sickening snapping of claws failing to dig into the steel they find. I catch one of the free legs by its narrow ankle and swing the bird creature into the ground. I don't want to hurt him, but I can't let him kill me or any of the others.

A quick scan of the area reveals the gorilla is fighting the second vulture, which explains why he hasn't chased me down yet. It doesn't look like either is in severe danger of immediate death, both seeming to be in a blind rage. None are used to their new bodies yet, and all seem to be attacking aimlessly and with no particular goal, just violence.

I spot the strange boar man attempting to fight off both panther creatures. One of his hind legs is being torn apart by the tabby, while the calico goes for his throat. Fuck. I can't hesitate. I sprint toward the three with everything I have, throwing myself into the calico with my right shoulder and knocking her away. I take a tusk to my side for the trouble, the boar failing to appreciate my efforts, apparently.

I grunt in pain as I roll away. As soon as I am on my back, the tabby pounces on me. I catch it with my feet and roll backward, extending my legs as I do to throw him off me. I use the momentum to then jump up and forward, landing back on my feet. Again, I am unstable, the move I've stolen from kung fu movies failing to translate gracefully when forced by strength alone.

I barely get to enjoy my time on my feet before the calico has recovered and is on me again, claws tearing into my back and teeth nearly sinking into my neck. I twist uncomfortably as we both fall back to the ground, forcing my steel arm into her mouth and punching her in the gut with my left. I have to pull my punches or do more damage than I am willing to live with. I won't repeat the mistakes of my first visit to the Radiant Woods. I won't kill someone for being the Collector's victim.

While I'm still trying to shake off the panther, one of the vultures finds us both. It's on my right, and I don't have a free arm to fight it off. I put all my strength into rolling the cat off me, but she has my arm in a vise grip, the armor I absolutely can't take off giving her something to hang on to. As a result, I roll with her. Now with the panther on her back, my arm stuck between bleeding teeth, and the vulture's talons finding only dirt, I look up to find the gorilla.

His fist is swinging down at me like a sledgehammer, and I can't dodge. I'm forced to use my left arm to block, and the impact forces a scream from my lips as blood splatters from my mouth into the fur of my feline opponent. Rather than going for another swing, the gorilla simply pushes hard. I may be stronger with that arm, but I am exhausted, and he has far better leverage from his position. Sweat drips from me in waves as I try to push back.

Below me, I am wrestling to keep the cat in place. Above me, I am struggling to hold up a force that wants to crush us both. Talons tear into my back, most hitting chain mail but a few cutting shallow streaks into my back. Teeth sink into my left leg, and my shattered ribs protest the strength I am exerting. I hear the screeching of the second vulture approaching, and the boar is charging its tusks into the calico's side.

I can't do it. I tried, but I can't save both myself and these people; not with strength alone. I have to take the risk—I have to use magic, or all us die here. So I do it. I explode with force mana, trying to send every victim around me flying and force them to the ground. But even as I take the risk, shrieking through half a dozen sources of pain, my mana evaporates before it manages to touch any of them.

Shit. He gave them back their grief. I'd thought his magic just over-wrote the power taking it away, as stronger Nexus energy always does. But there was an intent behind it. I can't use people's grief as a weapon against them. I can only use it for them.

I close my teeth, redirecting my mana to reinforce my muscles and skin, cycling between steel and tumor as I did last night, increasing my strength as much as I can. It is agonizing, but it is working. Tearing and healing my muscles again and again, I manage to move my left hand, grabbing the gorilla's fist and redirecting it. All his force collides with the ground.

As soon as I am free from that threat, I twist to my left so my back hits the floor beside the calico, forcing her head to the ground with my still trapped arm while I kick the tabby in the head with my right foot, dazing him and loosening his jaw enough to free my other leg. I catch the boar by the tusk with my now free left hand and force his head to the ground. Without a moment's hesitation, I wrap my leg around the tabby's throat and squeeze. He struggles as I cut off his air supply.

Meanwhile, the gorilla has recovered. Despite both vultures focusing on him and cutting deep gashes into his face and shoulders, he is swinging both fists down again, trying to crush the calico. My lower back is lifted from the ground by the struggling tabby. Only my shoulder blades still make contact, and both my hands are controlling one of the other victims.

I have to let go of the boar, digging my half-finished claws into the bloody ground beside me and using this as leverage to yank myself to the side, pulling the calico with me and narrowly avoiding her head being crushed beneath the gorilla's fists. I grip the dirt harder, pulling up this time and extracting a chunk of the stone ground. I throw it at the gorilla's face, dazing and blinding him for a moment. My claws are split and broken, not yet formed enough for what I just forced them to do.

Nonetheless, I wrap my bleeding fingertips around the boar's tusk again, just as he is recovering himself enough to attack. I try to force his head down again, but the increasing desperation of the air-deprived tabby yanks me back and forth too unpredictably. Instead, I simply try to vault him as far as I can away from the group. With my increased strength, I swing too hard, and his poorly designed tusk rips free from his face. He flies through the air too early, colliding with one of the vultures and freeing the gorilla's attention a bit.

I take a sharp, painful breath, to my rib cage's chagrin, as I worry I've just killed him. But both victims land and begin fighting each other, allowing me to refocus on the struggle at hand. The gorilla grabs the other vulture, furiously throwing him down at my face. I drop the tusk and manage to block any severe damage, but a talon stabs straight through my hand. I wrap my fingers around his leg anyway, grimacing through the damage his other talons do to my arm.

Finally, the tabby goes limp, and I release his unconscious body, my own falling painfully to the ground. It nearly knocks the breath out of me, but I don't lose focus. With my legs back, I plant my feet and, using every muscle in my body, do a sit-up, pulling the calico away from the gorilla's stomp.

I swing my left fist, vulture and all, into the calico's head, punching her twice as talons tear into her skin. Finally, her jaw loosens, and I pull my arm free, using it to grab the vulture and pull him out of my left hand with a stinging pain before throwing him in the opposite direction of the boar. I grab the dazed panther by the scruff of her neck, using both arms to swing her into the air and a few feet away from the fight.

Just as I do, a massive hand collides with my chest, forcing me to the ground. The gorilla, while slow, has finally landed a hit. I feel my sternum cracking, and cough more blood onto his steaming hand. Leaning into me, he presses me into the dirt as his nostrils flare in fury. Darkness edges into my vision as I reach my right arm out and search the ground. The gorilla releases the pressure for a brief moment, only to collapse onto me with even more force. The crack widens, and hot tears mix with the blood on my face. Again, I search until I find it: the overly long tusk of the boar.

Wrapping steel fingers around it, I lift it with a shaking arm and drive it deep into the gorilla's hand, causing an animalistic screech to ring throughout the arena. His arm recoils from me, allowing me to regain my feet. All the victims but the tabby are recovering now, and I have to start all over. I spit blood into the dirt and prepare to go back into the hectic fight.

Before I get the chance, however, the ceiling of darkness evaporates, and four men hover over the arena, looking down at me. The moment this happens, the five remaining victims collapse. I desperately want to join them, but if I lose consciousness here, they'll find my steel limbs. So instead, I turn in place, examining the stunned crowd. As I see my illusion still in the sky, I realize that the entire fight must have been broadcast.

I can only think of one thing to do. I hold a tired fist up in a sign of victory while the rest of my body sags.

CHAPTER TWENTY-EIGHT

Mementos

It took four sages to break through the Collector's power and end the fight. I'm choosing to think of him as the Collector, whatever he says. His abilities and actions are close enough to the Radiant Woods, which I am all but certain is related to Potestia's asshole god. So, for now, whoever fucked that fight up gets to wear the name. Especially since he was powerful enough that, again, it took *four* sages to overpower his will.

When the fight ended, none of them descended on me with righteous vengeance in their eyes, ready to execute Lillith, the actual demon queen, so that's a good sign. Instead, I was escorted to the infirmary to heal, as with every other fight. It seems to take ages, and I'm still dazed by the pain.

Most injuries seem to heal without a scar, surpassing both my manual attempts at healing and Sarafyna's magic. *I wonder why that is.* Nevertheless, it does take some time before my bones are all back in place, my bruises are gone, and my blood exists in the appropriate quantity for a sweet young lady like me.

I let out a relieved sigh as the blurred world slowly retakes its shape, crystal-clear detail revealing a mostly empty infirmary. A few other beds are taken, and I find myself next to Bahamut again.

"Why do you heal so slow?" she asks. I shrug.

"You know how some people are so lucky you have to assume some god has taken a special interest and is looking out for them?"

She grunts. "There's no such thing as a god."

"How about colloquialisms; are there such things as those?" I quip. She gives me a flat stare.

"Fine. I know what you mean. What about them?" she finally answers.

"Well, I'm not one of them," I say. "Nexus energy heals me with the furious speed of old molasses." Again, she gives me a flat stare.

"I see why you wanted me to entertain your metaphor. What a payoff," she intones.

All right, fair enough.

"I'm charming that way."

She snorts. "Are you, now? Guess I'm one of the few with immunity, then. I find little charm in idiocy."

"Well, that's just not very nice." I pout. "I'm smarter than I look; everyone says so."

She actually laughs at that, if only as a knee-jerk reaction. It is . . . not a friendly laugh.

"I saw your fight, Oh Demon Queen. They let us watch other gladiators sometimes so we know how to react to them. Makes the fights more interesting. And you—well, I thought you were an idiot when you came here voluntarily. Then I thought you were just shit at this, which made you an even bigger moron. The hits you took made no sense. They were slow; you should have seen them coming. Anyone who Markus was throwing six gladiators at should have had the reaction speed to avoid them. But you didn't. You looked like you were in over your head," she says. It's a fair evaluation.

"I usually am," I joke as I look around the room. Something is bothering me, and I can't put my finger on it. I only have one ear on the other woman as she reminds me of what a fucking tool I looked like out there. Not exactly a complex analysis, and I am more concerned with how much the sages saw.

"No," she challenges, "you're not. That became clear when the fight changed. I don't know what happened out there. I don't know why, and I don't know what people are saying about it, but I saw how you changed: your inexplicable strength, your reaction times. All seven of you transformed into entirely different beasts, but you were the only one who chose to. Which means you took those first hits on purpose. Then, you fought with your life on the line, not just to win but to stop your opponents from killing each other. Maybe the second one just makes you a naive fool, but the first makes you an idiot."

All right, maybe it is a slightly deeper evaluation than I thought.

"Yeah, okay, I'm an idiot. That's fair," I concede. Then I realize the problem as I consider the final thing she said. "Are there other infirmaries?" It would make sense if there were. Could get dicey if you threw the winner and loser of a fight together. Although, that's exactly what they have done every other time I've fought.

"Just this one. We rarely have enough survivors on both sides to need two," Bahamut answers. I freeze.

"Then where are the others? As you noted, I went to great pains to keep them alive. Don't tell me they died as soon as the fight ended, did they?" I ask in horror.

It would make sense, I suppose. I didn't want to consider it, but by design, victims of the Collector can't survive without him. Without his power, they die. It's one of the cruelest aspects of his control over them. He sends them around his little forest, never letting them escape, mutilating them further and further, and keeping them alive through the sheer force of his will. He takes their life and refuses to let them die until it's convenient for him. And if his power was overwhelmed by the other sages, then his newest victims . . .

"Ah, and there is the naive fool," Bahamut laments. "No, the other gladiators didn't die. Markus took them. He always does, when they are injured too severely to heal but are still alive. And I'd call that too injured to heal."

What? What does he want with them? Nothing good comes to mind as I race through the possible uses he could have for the mutated gladiators. Nexus energy rarely has anything good in store for anyone.

"Where? Where did he take them?" I plead. She looks down at the cuffs around her wrists then at the guards at the door.

"They don't let me wander around much. How am I supposed to know? He takes them, and they never show up again. That's the best I can tell you," she replies.

Right. I am the only person in here who isn't a slave. Fucking hell. I need to change that sooner rather than later. Today accelerated the timeline in this arena; I just need to find out how much. They healed me, which is a good sign. But if I am vulnerable to another attack like that every time I enter the arena, I can't keep risking it, especially since my opponents were used as weapons against me. Whatever ends up happening to them, it's because they fought me.

"Thanks. I appreciate it, I really do," I say. Bahamut stops picking at the healing cut on her arm and waves me off.

"It doesn't make a difference to me," she replies. "I just wanted to tell you to stop being a moron."

"Well, it's appreciated all the same. Uh, what's your real name?" I ask as I tighten the armor on my right arm. I need to confront Markus, and while he likely has a clue or two about me, I don't need to make his guesses any easier for him than they already are.

"What's yours? *Cordelia*? Doesn't ring true to me," she retorts. That's a tough question to answer, and a moment's hesitation is all she needs to brush me off. "Right. Let's not find out, either of us. It'll make it easier when they make us kill each other."

Her words have a bitter taste, and they prick at my ears, but as I finish making sure my armor is in place, I have no time to challenge her. Maybe she'll tell me when I break her out of here. For now, I need to make sure more people don't pay the price of my presence.

I run past the guard, there to keep everyone but me from fleeing. The colosseum has more twists and turns than I'd expect from a perfectly round building, but I guess I've never been to the one back on Earth. I never even went to a stadium, now that I think of it. Still, I remember the way to Markus's home. I made sure to remember.

I rush past concerned workers and guards alike, taking turn after turn to get to my destination as quickly as possible. It's already been too long. I can't feel grief anywhere except the one source I have been tracking since I came to this country. Autumn. Which means I can't use it to track the six gladiators I fought.

One thought keeps running through my head. *Why did he come after me when he did? Why then, at that moment?* The gladiators aren't the only people I spend time around. The Collector could have turned anyone around me at any time. That ambush could have happened anywhere, when I wasn't being directly watched by a sage. It's possible he wanted to trap me into revealing myself, something I did, in fact, do. Something which may have fucked me, as far as I know. It's possible he wanted me to have fewer options.

But it doesn't ring true. If I'd run around saving bystanders from monsters using only temporarily powerful grief mana, it could have been even worse than what did happen. He did what he did when there would be no bystanders and I could fight them on my own. Sure, he did it when there would be the largest number of witnesses, but they would be witnesses expecting a spectacle, to whom the absurd events could be explained. So why make his move when he did?

Well, that's a simple enough question to answer. Painfully simple. Because the moment he attacked was right after I started fighting back. That's the most damning evidence against me. He chose to hurt these people because I had let myself get hurt first. Because I had taken the hits and the breaks and the abuse, and I would be the least prepared to fight back. He attacked at my weakest moment. This happened because of my selfishness.

Which means I have to stop it from getting any worse. Autumn was right to yell at me. I need to be an iron fortress. I cannot indulge in this pettiness anymore. I have to lock that part of me away, push it deep into the dark where it belongs. Where it can suffocate and never be seen again. Where I can make it invisible.

As I do just that in my mind's eye, I finally make it to the strangely residential door of Markus's home. I pound my left fist on the door as gently as I can in my current emotional state. Which is not very gentle, apparently. The sound of gloves against wood is typically muffled, but this still rings through the halls. I wait for ten agonizing breaths, but there is no response.

I will wait no longer. I grab the lever handle and push it down.

It opens easily, despite the cracking sound I hear. *We'll just call that unlocked, how about?* I push my way in, only to find the home abandoned. I don't know where Markus is, but it isn't here. Probably talking to the sages he'd called for help earlier; I imagine they have a good deal to talk about, what with the fight they just witnessed. I'm not even sure it will all be about me. I can't imagine they are terribly pleased with the friend who came to visit me mid-match.

I am about to turn around and go searching for him when something catches my eye. The room is dark, so I can't make much out. It could be the type of illusion darkness is always generous with, but it could also be real.

I summon light mana easily enough, illuminating the room in an instant.

It was no trick of the light. The carpet is stained all over with blood and filth, like an injured animal, or several, were dragged through the room—and to the heavy curtains on the opposite side.

Anxiety falls on me like a heavy rain as I follow the stains to the window. There is something wrong with that fucking window; something dark. I can feel it. The gladiators I fought are on the other side. They have to be. My fingers curl around one curtain as I take a deep breath. I'm afraid to see the state they are in, terrified to see the results of my presence on innocent lives, but I need to look, and I pull the curtain to the side.

I stare for a moment, then blink. I rub my eyes and look again. I don't get it. At first, I think I am looking at, well, nothing. Just darkness. But as I shine light mana into it, it reflects back at me like it's hitting a surface.

A stone. A massive, obsidian stone, exactly like the ones supporting the border.

What the hell?

"It's rude to poke your nose around other people's homes without permission," Markus says.

CHAPTER TWENTY-NINE

Double Meanings

My back prickles as the man's voice interrupts me. I may have broken into his home, but it still feels like his presence is an invasion. "I don't understand," I say as I turn to face the sage. He is leaning casually on his doorframe, a basket with a cloth covering its contents in his hand. He looks down at the broken handle then back at me.

"You broke my door," he comments, not sounding angry or even irritated. It's a simple statement of fact. "I'd prefer it if you just waited outside next time. You're always welcome, of course, but this is a bit impolite." I raise an eyebrow. I have to actively remind myself that it's a bad idea to fight him when I'm unprepared. My claws still don't carry any venom.

"What is that out there?" I ask, and his eyes lock on mine, the first sense of real danger I've gotten from him leaking from narrowed eyes.

"I did expect you to come; after the day's events, it was inevitable. But I really would have preferred to clean up first," he responds. He claps his hands twice, and the room lights up, the stains in the carpet vanishing completely. "As for the view, well. Perhaps I'll show you eventually, but I'm afraid there would be little point right now. Here, come and have a seat at the table."

He walks over to his dining room, and I cautiously follow. There is a tension in the air that was absent last time. A tension which can be easily explained, but I need to determine which easy explanation it is. I'd rather keep looking for the victims I fought in the arena, but they are gone. I knew it the moment I saw the darkness beyond the window. I'm not sure what he's done with them, but they are gone.

I take a seat opposite Markus, glancing at the basket he's placed in the middle of the table. Our eyes catch on each other like loose threads. His smile is strained, and I'm not bothering to force my own. It could be because he found me, in his home, investigating something he clearly wants to keep secret. It could also be because he just saw me defy logic and use magic while cuffed. It could even be my clear refusal to kill the mutated gladiators and not even let them kill each other. Hopefully, it isn't all the above.

I remain silent, waiting for him to speak first. Always the best tactic when being interrogated, and I'm fairly certain that is what is happening. I may have a big mouth, but shutting the fuck up at times like this has gotten me out of a lot of trouble before.

"Allow me to apologize, Miss . . . Cordelia," he says after a moment of awkward silence. I don't love the pause before my alias, but I don't comment on it. "It's truly embarrassing that, only days after our deal, I allowed such a thing to happen. The sage who interfered in your match was . . . not supposed to be there. I have brought a small olive branch of sorts, for now."

At this, he pushes the basket to me. Every word is sharper than an apology should be, and I have a sick feeling in my gut. I hesitantly reach out for it, half expecting to find a head or some shit inside; some horrifying threat letting me know the jig is up.

As I lift the cloth on top, I find something less horrifying . . . I guess. It probably wasn't intended to be hostile or threatening at all, although it still carries both messages as far as I'm concerned. It's a simple basket of fresh fruit. Newly ripened pears, to be specific. I glance back at the smiling man with only my eyes before looking back at the horrific fruit.

"Make sure not to eat them in public, of course. The Void Sage says the demon queen absolutely loathes them, and I wouldn't want to ruin your public persona," he adds after a moment of awkward silence. Does the fucking Void Sage have a camera in my kitchen or what? What kind of information is that to spread around a whole-ass country? I swear to God, I'm about to read some press release about the shade and hue of my asshole, hex code and everything. This is getting beyond annoying and venturing into straight-up creepy territory.

More annoying is the meaning behind Markus referencing it. These goddamn pears *are* hostile. This is the stupidest test I have been given since I was accused of cheating in math class.

I suppress the grimace that tries to present itself and take one of the horrors from the basket, taking a large bite as I stare at Markus. I have to actively use mana internally to suppress the gagging. I even have to extend the agony as I send mana through the fruit itself, checking for poison before I swallow. Fortunately, the only toxic thing about it is the sin it calls flavor. I finally manage to swallow the hostile fruit without letting any hint of disgust grace my face.

"I'm glad you like them." Markus nods. This fucker is more than suspicious, but he's not murdering me right now, so I will endure until I find out what he wants. "As I was saying, I am truly drowning in remorse. I'm inconsolable, really. I am so ashamed I allowed you to go through that, and my relief that you managed to survive is palpable. I assure you, it will not repeat. We will need to close the arena for a week or so, I'm afraid, so we can be fully prepared before your big match."

My ears twitch at that last bit.

"Big match?" I ask. He nods, well, sagely.

"Well yes. After that performance today, I can hardly keep you fighting the rabble. You showed . . . *talents* I wouldn't have thought possible. We have to capitalize on them. Fame and fortune; that's what brought you here, right?"

My heart sinks. Yeah, they did not miss that burst of magic—or a million other little hints that maybe I am not just scrappy. Four sages saw every move I made, my strength. The surprising durability of certain limbs. Even my flesh and bone didn't break as easily as they should have. Bites which should have left me with fewer appendages were only flesh wounds. There was no hope of staying hidden entirely once the Collector ambushed me. Before, my demon queen persona provided me with an easy excuse for otherwise highly suspicious aesthetic choices. Now, I am suspicious anyway, and immediately tied to public enemy number one in everyone's heads. Great.

"I see. So you want to accelerate the schedule, then?" I ask hesitantly. He grins, sending a shiver down my spine.

"Something like that. Once we are certain it's safe, of course, we'd like you to showcase all these skills in a premier match against Bahamut the

Demon," he answers casually. The woman I've been talking to this entire time. One of the primary champions of the arena. I went from needing to be protected to going up against the woman he uses as a headliner. Yep. I'm royally fucked.

Well, all right. I got my own ass into this mess; I can get out of it.

"Fine," I agree. "You said a week? I'll be ready. I appreciate the apology. The pears are delicious, really." I stand, hoping to leave it at that, but Markus holds his hand up.

"Oh, we can't have that! You were attacked today—by a sage, of all things! It's simply not safe to have one of my star gladiators out on her own! You'll be staying here. For your protection, of course. I will keep you safe until your fight. All you have to do is rest and prepare," he says. *Fuck.* My voluntary participation is growing a lot less voluntary. I don't know if he knows I am the real Lillith, but he certainly knows I am either in his control or his nightmares.

"I'm certain I'll be fine. I do appreciate it though," I reply. I take another loathsome bite of the neglected pear in my hand, trying to avoid more suspicion than necessary. *God, this is a fucking insult to fruit.*

"Do you think you alone could fight off a sage with ill intent toward you?" Markus asks with a smile. I get the feeling he isn't talking about the Collector; he isn't talking about a single sage at all. I wince as the threat settles on me. I'm not leaving today—or at all for the next week.

The way I see it, there is only one way out of this for me: I have to get stronger. I can change my body faster, and I will. I will do what I have to do so even the sages have to fear me. I don't know what his game is exactly, but I know I'm going to have to fight my way out if I want to survive. I just have to count on Ember to get the twins to safety. She'll do it. She may be insufferable, but she won't let them get hurt.

"Very well. I thank you for your consideration," I respond. The words taste almost as bad as the third bite of Satan's fruit.

"I had a feeling you'd see things my way. I assume you don't mind sharing a room with another gladiator. Unfortunately, we have no other available accommodations at this time; this is something of an unprecedented situation, I'm afraid."

"A room?" I ask, suspicious of the chosen phrasing. Not a lot of slaves get their own rooms, in my experience.

"So to speak." He smiles. "But worry not, it will not be an issue after this week." Neither of us is under any illusions about what that means. He knows I'm a threat. I know he intends to have me killed. I'm not sure why he doesn't just kill me now, but he obviously wants me dead.

Well. Fine. I'll play his game. We'll see which of us will be dead in a week. He's giving me too much time to prepare, and with last night's discovery, a week is plenty of time to turn myself into a sage killer. His arrogance is only the first poison I will use to end him.

"Shall we go? I have other things to attend to, and I'd like to get you settled in. And don't worry, there will be a sage keeping an eye on you at all times. You will be safe," he says, standing from the table. I will be guarded at all times, is what he means. No escape for me.

"Sure. I could use the rest," I agree calmly. I stand to follow him, putting the half-eaten pear back in the basket. I may be headed to a cage, but at least I don't have to finish that shit-ass abomination.

I follow him back through the colosseum. With every step, I watch him. I think of the stains. The black stone behind his window. The victims he discarded. I will kill him, and I will do it in front of his entire arena. The world will know sages can be killed.

I'm surprised when we reach my cell; not by the steel door, stone walls, or elevated, narrow window with bars in lieu of glass. I knew I was to be a prisoner. I am more surprised by the occupant. Bahamut the Demon.

"You often room gladiators with their upcoming opponents?" I ask. I'm here for my safety, supposedly. With the woman I am meant to fight to the death in a week.

Yeah, all right.

"It's what's available, I'm afraid," he apologizes, sympathy dripping from his voice like grease. "Don't worry, she won't hurt you. She knows how dangerous that would be. Enjoy your evening; you've earned some rest." With this, he gently pushes me in and closes the door behind me. I hear the bar on the other side slide into place.

"I told you to go home, idiot," Bahamut says. I sigh, moving over to the bed she isn't lying on. I do need the rest, and I do think he's right. She won't attack me.

"Yeah, well, I'm stubborn in my idiocy. It's how I'm going to kill that man and get us both out of here," I respond.

CHAPTER THIRTY

Mirage and Manara

Markus

I relax on a recliner in my living room, sipping at a glass of wine and watching the obsidian portal beyond my window. I truly didn't expect the actual Lillith to waltz into my arena. It would be a ballsy move, and if that's what happened, I respect her for it. I'll admit, I didn't suspect her at all when she first arrived. Before today, I didn't expect she was a real person at all. Even now, I remain skeptical.

Rowan has always said whatever he needed to to get what he wanted. Promises, threats, jokes, even a poem once. "Lillith" as the queen of demons is very obviously a story some sage brought with them from Earth a thousand years ago for wish fulfillment or something along those lines. It's not the only story that has traveled; I've found references to tales suspiciously similar to *Cinderella* or *Little Red Riding Hood*. The kinds of stories everyone knows.

The concept of a demon queen named Lillith has always seemed like one of those to me. Any sage who recognizes the name from Earth would say the same. As a prophecy, it has only ever been taken seriously by the locals. Us sages all assumed whoever brought the story over presented it as fact, and when a man with godlike powers says something is true, that's what goes in the history books.

When the Void Sage announced his bid for minister this year, he dug up those old stories and started stoking the fears of the public. It was silly, but that man always is. And, well, when a man with godlike powers says something is true . . .

It never bothered most of us. We have long lives in this world; elections for minister or councilman or whatever other position are a fairly low stakes game in the grand scheme of things. Yeah, we'll still compete with him, or at least some of us will. But it's honestly easier to lose from time to time. No one wants to run everything all the time anyway. We'll all survive five years until the next game, and if we can't, we'll go compete in the Council Lands. They have more positions open.

Rowan has been especially eager to win this time for some reason, and we've been more or less okay with letting him. It's clearly more important to him than us, and we never considered it likely he was actually going to try and enlist everyone in some kind of demonic defense army. That's just a thing he said to rile people up. To get attention.

His grief initiative has been a success, more or less. The people have been far less rowdy the last decade or so since he introduced it. It used to be exclusive to Guardians of Stone, but the countrywide use went so well the Council adopted it themselves. People have just been easier to direct. When he told us the real reason was to fight the demon queen, we all laughed. I thought it was an honest-to-God joke. We eased people away from their grief, a little at a time so it wouldn't be immediately obvious what was happening. They don't really know what's been taken from them, so privately tying his excuse to a fairy tale didn't seem to have much purpose outside of humor. He even laughed with us when we responded that way.

Until my new gladiator showed up. A face for his stories, and in my control. An obvious persona—or so I thought. But today . . . Today, the Original Sage interfered. The Original Sage broke a centuries-old agreement to fix a petty fight in my arena and kill a single girl. It wasn't until I called the others for help that we managed to put the pieces together. I don't know what the Original Sage's game is, but he's got some kind of vendetta against this girl. He's the one who has Rowan in a fuss, throwing her name all over the place and spreading all sorts of new stories about her.

Rowan must have been talking to the Original Sage this entire time, getting all these little tidbits from him. Or maybe not. I'm not sure. Cordelia—or Lillith, as the case may be—didn't really seem to mind the pears. Maybe Rowan made that one up. This girl must be who they have been preparing for, either way. I think Rowan might actually believe everything he says about her. The push to suppress grief specifically instead of some other emotion makes a strange sort of sense in that case. She did use mana despite her restraints, which is interesting. Not an unprecedented ability, but never one that could be used without either being a sage or working directly with one. It's my understanding the method to acquire such an ability is lethal without the Nexus.

Few sages bother with mana; it's the poor man's magic, used mostly by those with no access to the superior Nexus energy, with the exception of two notable sages: The Void and the Original both use mana. She is tied to them somehow. Perhaps she was meant to be a pawn, and the Void and Original had a falling out on some plan? But then why suppress grief, if she supposedly uses it as a powerful aspect? I'm not sure.

It doesn't matter though. What matters is Rowan seems legitimately worried about the girl, in one way or another. Which means he might *actually* follow through on his crazy plans. We can't have that, which means we can no longer let him win the minister game. It would be too much of a headache.

Fortunately, she came to me. Whoever she is, I can use her and her ability. I just have to push her to use it even more obviously, with effects that can be seen even by the mundane. I need to broadcast the fight to entertainment centers around the country. With my allies here, she won't escape, and the Original Sage won't be able to interfere.

I can stack things against her enough that she needs to fight with magic. It'll be easy, and it'll be proof, as far as the masses are concerned, that she is in fact Demon Queen Lillith. She wears the name, the strange powers, and the body modifications of a cultist. There will be no doubt of who she is. It doesn't matter if she's a real prophecy come to life or a patsy—I will make her real in the eyes of the people.

Then I will crush her.

Maybe she'll die in the fight. The bleeding heart will feel connected to Riley after a week sharing a cell, so she won't be willing to kill her opponent. Considering everything else I have planned, she may just fail anyway. There is a good chance Riley wins and Lillith dies then and there. That would be poetic in a way, considering Riley and Rowan's history, but I think it's more likely Lillith will win. She'll win, refuse to kill Riley, and force me to enter the arena. Then I will kill her myself in front of the whole damn world. It'll be too easy. Rowan built his whole campaign on preparing for this foreign invader, here to kill and destroy and rule. On how he would protect his people, fight for them, keep them safe.

And I will kill her instead. He'll collapse, and I'll become minister. He'll be angry for a while, but that's what he gets for upsetting the balance. Siding with the Original Sage? Is he insane? He'll get us all killed or worse. Luck was on our side this time, however. One more week, and we'll set things straight, maybe head back to the local relay and slowly switch things up. My arena just doesn't hit as hard without grief; we can take something else to subdue the people. I'm not sure what will work best, but I have time. Easing them back into grief will take a few years, anyway.

Thank you so much, Lillith, for coming here first. I don't know why you have two sages circling you, but your life ends in a week. And I am so, so grateful for your sacrifice.

???

I was born of two mothers. Well, mothers of a sort. I came into this world, bright-eyed and curious, not from some other world, like most of the sages. Earth, they call it. Not from the water of the womb either. I am nothing so mundane. I am the child of two mothers, two energies who swam through the universe, painting it wherever they touched. One of them was powerful and kind; she could look through a thousand windows at a thousand possibilities and bend the world around her to match. She had no name, but I eventually offered *Mirage*, years after my birth.

The second was vibrant and empathetic and full of life. She loved new ideas and experiences, and wanted to see and feel everything that could be reached. To her, I gave the name *Manara*. Where Mirage would change the world to match her vision, Manara would change herself to match the world. Together, they were endlessly entertained and full of joy. They were unbridled and boundless. I was born of a vision Mirage had of a world with a million brilliant and fierce people. Manara wanted to meet these people as well, and the two combined their abilities, as they had so often done, to realize me.

It was creation like a song. I was created by joy in its purest form, so I was joyful as well. The three of us lived together, alone, for years, and years, and years, and years, and . . .

I was not Mirage, able to take the whole universe in with eyes made of stars. And I was not Manara, able to feel and live every movement of the wind. All my joy was joy they shared with me, raw emotion they offered directly to me, like the air and the fruit. And I reveled in it, but . . . joy is like fire. It's bright and warm, but it needs fuel to burn. Their joy was not my joy. I wanted my own, something that was mine alone, and they wanted that for me. We never spoke, none of us knew how yet, but we all understood. Our emotions were shared, offered freely and accepted. Where I took their joy, they took my loneliness.

It wasn't an emotion they understood, but they wanted to help, so Mirage watched the worlds around her. She watched the lives, glowing and dying like embers. And she touched them. One, then ten, then thousands. And Manara understood them. She empathized with them, bringing their very essence into our lonely world and realizing them again. None of them remembered who they had been, in other lives. None of them needed to. They were still who they were, but with a newer and brighter future. And I wasn't alone anymore. I danced and I sang and I learned about new arts, like painting and language. And I felt my own joy.

For a while, I shared it with Mirage and Manara. I took theirs and they took mine, and the loneliness was gone. For a while. But I discovered a new emotion. These new people, with souls of art and flame—my mothers loved them too. Mirage offered them new lives, new bodies, new species and names and homes. And each time she did, they felt farther away from me. No longer did they share my shape. No longer did they share my understanding. They wanted to abuse Mirage, to manipulate her and reject her designs and ideas. They wanted to make their own instead, and the loneliness started to return.

Manara too, loved them. She offered herself to all them. She learned their writing and offered her own. But her too, they abused, using the language she created with them to change her, to warp her and control her. And she gave herself freely, complying with all their ideas, adopting the experiences they wanted for her and not the ones she chose herself. And I felt jealousy. I didn't share that with my mothers.

I loved them first. I shared with them first. And I accepted their designs! I experienced what they wanted to experience! I was their world, and they were mine, and we were all grateful. But these people . . . these *creatures* . . . they weren't grateful. They just wanted to use. I felt rage. I didn't share that with my mothers.

Mirage and Manara should have refused. They should have said no. They should have spat in the ungrateful faces of their other children. Mirage should have locked their forms in place, should have held them in front of a mirror and screamed that she had created them with love. To reject that creation? To throw that gift back and demand something else, something they wanted more? What was that if not hate?

Manara should have refused them. She should have recoiled from the words they wrote in her language. She should have left them alone and barren, never seeing or hearing her again. To take her and design her in their own image instead of the other way around, what was that if not hate? I felt resentment. I didn't share that with my mothers.

If I had my mothers' abilities, I would not have stood for the disrespect, the hate, the loathing that their children's actions implied. No. I would remove the offenders from this world, or I would rule them and make them understand what they had done. I felt pride. I didn't share that with my mothers.

I was determined to convince them to change, to make them understand how much my siblings hated them and reject them in turn. But when I finally gathered the courage to confront Mirage and help her see the truth . . . she didn't understand me. We couldn't feel what the other felt anymore. We had lost the only language we both knew. I didn't know her, she didn't know me, and all we shared was silence.

CHAPTER THIRTY-ONE

Drop of the Hat

Sarafyna

I sit in the Radiant Woods with my eyes closed as I search. I can feel everything—every leaf, flower, and cruelty. I can feel the tired blood running through the trees instead of sap, feel the victims constantly moving so I can't get to them and pull them out. There are hundreds of thousands of them, maybe more. It's too much to process all at once, but I try.

I look for Leo, terrified of letting him live through the same thing I did. He has been through so much already. I want to save him. I want to save all them. I know I will, someday, but for now, Leo would be enough. Anything would be enough. But he isn't there. There are thousands of distinct energies, unique souls screaming in the woods. No matter what the Collector did to their bodies, I can feel their souls, the same way I felt Annie's when we first met. So long as they have mana or divine magic, I can feel them.

But Leo? I can't find him. No matter how I search, I can't find him anywhere—him or Charlotte. I can't imagine how they would escape on their own, so they must be inside somewhere, but . . . there are just too many. Our friend has been washed away in generations of grief and pain, and I can't help him. I can't help him. But I can't stop trying either.

"You'll never find her."

I grit my teeth, extra eyes and mouths opening on my face and snarling together. I am tired of this. I am not the child who was left to rot in these woods. I am not the subject of the Collector's games. I am the woman who taught the church fear. I don't need Annie to do that. Not here. These are my woods now too.

"Shut up. Shut up, shut up, shut up! *Never*, you say. Never is what you *always* say. But when has it been true? No part of me is even mildly interested in what you think I'll never do, and believe me, I have the parts to spare. Parts of you. Parts of your servants. I wear the scars of everything you thought of as your power all over my body. And you know what? I'm glad they are there. I may never have the beauty I had before again, but this is better. The disfiguration is better, because every time I come here, every time I see you, you have to look at them. You have to look at everything you told me I'd never do," I scream. As I do, I grow taller and larger, and tear at the world around me.

"You said I'd never escape, never see my father, never have friends or family or love again. You said I'd never beat you in any way at all. But I took half your woods away from you, I hunted your priests, and I took the power you gave them. I ate you from the inside out and left you terrified. I have my father back. I have a son who shines like moonlight on water when he sees me. I have a woman I love so desperately it feels like bleeding to be around her, and she loves me the same. So shut up.

"We both know what it means when you tell me I'll never do something. It doesn't mean I can't do it—it means you are afraid of what will happen when I do. I will find *him*. I will bring *him* home. And the next time you say anything about *him*, that is the word you will use, or your death, *when* I come for you, will leave you envious of every person you've ever tortured," I spit.

The world has grown darker around me, and the radiant foliage has started to wither. My fingers and arms have split into bladed whips, and my feet have taken root in the earth, stealing even more divine magic from the woods. It is hurting. I can feel it, if only a little.

"You are as fearsome as a child with a flaming stick, swinging it around with threats you don't understand and will never accomplish. Come, find me, and fight if you believe you have the power. But you don't. You can't fight me. You are too attached to that filthy corpse you fuck. So desperately in love that you are, in fact, bleeding all the power you could use to fight me. You're weak, and I have nothing to fear. Not while you tie yourself down like a broken pony."

I take a deep breath, sewing myself back together and retreating back to my normal size. I maintain only the extra mass of all that I have consumed as I respond, barely whispering. "Then why did you run away? When I came back here, you stopped your attacks and you ran—fled. If I'm a broken pony, then why are you acting like a frightened dog?"

The woods tremble around me as I speak, but that familiar voice doesn't respond. I smirk. I knew it. All the attacks on every community stopped—every single one—the moment I returned. He is afraid of what I can do now that I'm back. Something to do with the victims he was using to attack us.

Turn them back to humans, perhaps? Or ailur or volu, I suppose. Either way, I don't think I can. Not without Annie's help. So it's something else, something he is worried about when he sends them out to fight. Something that makes them safe in the woods but not in the open world. I need to see the ones we have captured again. I'm not finding Leo today, but I *will* find him.

For now, I put a loose cloak on and shift to the border of the woods, emerging in the mountains. I bite my lip as I walk through the thin, chilly air. I have too much to think about, and I'm going to be here longer than I thought. I'll need to check in with Annie soon. In a few days, perhaps. I'm afraid of telling her I can't come back as soon as we planned. Not because she'll be angry or anything like that, it just . . . will make the time and distance real. But I can't help it. Whatever the Collector is afraid of, it is keeping people safe—as long as I'm here. I can't leave for long until we have found a better way to defend the towers.

The best way to do that is to figure out what that fear is, and that means spending most of every day with the victims Gilbert, Edward, and Dominic are keeping an eye on. But first, I need to make a few stops. I sort of shredded my dress in a rage back there and can only keep this cloak closed for so long before it becomes inconvenient. I also want to spend a little time with my family and check in on Joan. I have been caught in a whirlwind since coming back, and while I have spoken to my girlfriend's mother, we haven't really gotten to talk much yet.

As I walk, I shift in my head from the furious, violent monster challenging a god to the meek, mild hatter excited to see her loved ones.

The towers are more crowded when I get back, every floor filled far ear-lier than planned. Every community is here so all the most powerful mages can defend it at once. As such, the tower I enter is busy with new faces and energies—and some old. I recognize a young man joking and laughing with a smiling woman, clearly decades his senior. Tommy and Diana, I think.

Abby, the woman with the enchanted glass eye, smiles and waves as I climb past her floor, and I smile back. Annie would be so happy to see all these people together. They would all be happy to see her too. At least I can report they are all safe when I speak to her again. These people may be safe, but the people of Visenar won't be when I leave. Something has to be done about that tree. The one I put there. Leaving Ed to exhaust himself isn't a solution.

It's too much to think about, and I shut it all out for a moment as I enter my room. Annie's room. It's quiet. Suzume is staying with Joan, and Annie is gone. It's so empty.

I walk to the little studio Autumn and Annie built for me and sit down at my desk. Hats surround me, offering the unique comfort only they can. I run my fingers along the brim of the nearest one, removing the hat I wore to the woods in favor of another fresh alternative. For a moment, my mind stops racing, and every worry melts away.

I close my eyes and lean back in my chair, letting my arms fall limp. I let the quiet take me back to Annie's arms, back to the night before I left. I can feel her lips against mine, taste her tongue. The electricity of her touch runs through my skin. I live in the calm that followed, when I wrapped my arms around her and felt her gentle breathing, her hair against my face, as we let ourselves have one simple night where only the other mattered. We whispered and giggled and loved.

Those hours with Annie carry me now. They are how I move forward, how I keep fighting. The memory of that joy, and the promise of seeing it again. The knowledge that I never will if I don't fight.

Letting out a deep sigh, I open my eyes and stand, straightening the new hat before finding another outfit to change into. It was only a few moments, but it gave me what I needed to do the rest. I'll see Joan next, then Annie's brothers and the Collector's victims, and I'll spend the evening with my family. Well, most of my family.

With only a moment's hesitation, I leave my home and face the world again.

Joan doesn't live far from us, and I arrive at her door far too quickly. I take a deep, aching breath before knocking lightly on the door. It's silent for several heavy moments, but I can feel Joan inside. She doesn't have much mana, but she does have enough, so I wait. And wait. Until she finally, slowly, opens the door.

"Gah, Suzume, you're going to kill me!" she immediately exclaims as the happy tortoiseshell bolts between her legs and starts rubbing against mine.

"Hey there, Suzie," I greet, kneeling down briefly to pick the purring bundle of fur up. She immediately starts licking my fingers as I hold her, and Joan offers a rare, small smile.

"Hey, Sara," she greets. Her eyes are red and swollen, and her shoulders slump. Deep wrinkles in her face reveal a decade of aging in the last few months alone. "Come on in." I carry Suzume back inside, and the gleeful cat digs her claws into my blouse, worried I'll put her down. I just scratch behind her ears and remain standing as Joan takes a seat at her dining room table.

"How are you holding up?" I ask. She sniffs and looks down at a glass of iced tea.

"I am . . . better than the first time I lost my son," she says. "I am heartbroken. I am angry. I am sick and hungry and always full. But I am here. How is . . . Annie?"

"Back to Annie now?" I ask. She'd been using Annie's original name since finding out about Earth, not in affection but as a way of alienating her daughter. Reminding her that, as far as she is concerned, Annie and Lillith are different people. But before we left, she'd used *Lillith* again. It was a small thing, but it was an effort that mattered. Or it could have, but Annie saw it for what it was.

"I only used *Lillith* for Annie's sake," Joan explains. "She can't do what she needs to do with all the extra baggage on her. She can't be worried about . . . me, and fight the whole world at the same time. I may not be able to reconcile who she is with the daughter I lost so many years ago, but I understand what she is doing matters." Her words carry the bite of bitterness before they soften.

"And . . . despite it all, I do still love her. And I know she loves me. I don't understand why; it's like my daughter died and lived at the same time. She is my family, and she spent her life with me, but . . . didn't she kill my original daughter? However she showed up here, wouldn't *Lillith* be with me instead if *Annie* hadn't stolen her body? I love her and I hate her and my son is dead, Sara. He's dead, and she did it. What do I do? How do I respond to that? How could anyone?"

I feel like I've been dunked in ice water. I haven't actually been there for many of Lily and Joan's arguments; it's been a family thing. But . . . of course she is struggling with this. Who wouldn't be? And worse yet, I can help her. I actually have some of the answers she is looking for, but I don't want to give them to her. I am terrified to give them to her because if I do, I will eventually have to give them to Annie. And if Annie finds out she is dead, in a way . . . if she finds out I could help more if I let her die for good . . . if she finds out how much I have put myself through to keep her alive . . . I am terrified.

But I know. I know I have to, at some point. As soon as I realized what was happening, I knew I had to tell Annie what I was doing to her, what I'd done to her when I pulled her from the peace of death to save me from my torment. And I'd have to face whatever her response was, even if that response was asking me to just . . . let her go. Or even guilt. I am terrified. Joan needs to know the truth, and maybe, if I tell her, it will force me to tell Annie too. Before I bring her back here.

"Joan," I say quietly, a slight tremor in my voice. "I can promise you that Lillith and Annie are the same person. The same soul, if you want to call it that. I know for a fact that Annie is Lillith and Lillith is Annie. The only thing she gained was memories of a past life. She didn't replace the daughter you had, and if Annie hadn't woken up in that bed, Lillith wouldn't have either."

She looks up at me with resentment and grief bleeding from her eyes. "How can you possibly know that?" she snaps at me. I take a deep breath.

I put Suzume down, letting her drop to the floor. I don't know if I can get through this with a purring cat giving me a finger bath. She rolls onto her back, failing completely to read the tone of the room.

"Because," I respond, pausing for a moment to build courage, "I'm the one who brought her back. I'm the one who let her remember. And I'm the one who forced a dead child to keep living in a world that hated her."

CHAPTER THIRTY-TWO

Secondhand Stories

What in the third plane is that supposed to mean?" Joan asks, offering all the spices of pure bafflement with a little irritation mixed in. I bite my lip, nerves screaming that this is a bad idea. But it's too late now, and she needs to know that Annie is her daughter, for both her sake and Annie's. I've joined her at the table now, so I hide my hands underneath it as I clench my fists nervously, closing my eyes for a moment before I respond.

"I . . . I didn't realize it, at first. I didn't know what I was doing, Joan. I was so afraid, so alone. So achingly desperate. My body was being taken away, forced into someone else's design. I didn't understand my own abilities yet, didn't know how to control them. How to . . . aim them. I just wanted help. I wanted to be saved, to not be alone anymore. I wanted a way to return to the life I'd lost, and I just . . . let my power escape me. It had no target, no specific intent, just raw emotion. Just loneliness and fear permeating me like water and cloth. I didn't know what I was doing," I begin. Joan leans forward, clasping one trembling hand in the other and fixing glassy eyes on me.

"And what was it you were doing?" she asks. My lip quivers a little, protesting the words I form with it.

"I didn't know what I was doing for a long time afterward," I continue, part of me stalling and another part wanting her to fully understand everything I'm trying to tell her. "Not until this last year, when I was a captive of the Kingdom of Endings. Once it started happening more and more frequently, and I earned enough power—and enough understanding of it—to realize what I was not just doing at the moment but what I had always been doing. I could see it all, from the very first time."

I pause for a moment, unsure how to continue, but pleading eyes from an exhausted woman push me forward. "The first time Annie died, it was a fall that killed her. She had other wounds, but it was the fall that did it. The second time Annie—Lillith—died, it was sickness. You know this, I know. Things get sort of fuzzy after that. But the truth is, Joan, she never came back after that. Not really."

"What?" Joan asks, leaning forward. "What do you mean? You mean Lillith never came back, but Annie did?"

I shake my head.

"No. Like I said, I'm certain they are the same person," I assure her. "It's just that . . . she's not really alive, like you or I are. Like anyone else is. She hasn't been since she died in that bed, sick and surrounded by family. That was when my magic first touched her, when it first started pushing the blood through her veins and woke her up. In my aimless desperation, I gave her life again, but I didn't bring her back to life. Not entirely. She can age. She can breathe and eat and, well, live—so long as I'm still connected to her.

"But she has run out of years. Her body . . . wants to die. It does. Every moment she has had since she was seven years old has been tied to my divine magic, my control. I have kept her here on a leash, and the moment I let it go, she will return to that death. If I die, she will die. If I give up, she will die. If I slip or use even a little less of the power I'm constantly expending to keep her body on puppet strings . . ." I trail off, leaving the final three words unsaid.

Joan stares at me. Her eyes are steel on a winter day. She is clearly having trouble processing what I've said, but one question swims through her eyes as they dart back and forth across my face.

"That's . . ." she begins, wanting to say a thousand things about the implications of what she just learned, tapping one finger against the table as she thinks. Finally, she settles on that one important question. "How? How do you know Annie, this woman with a full, violent past, is the same girl as my sweet little Lillith? What does any of this have to do with that, Sarafyna? I want to know how you can be certain my daughter wasn't replaced!"

I nod, looking down at the warped wood of the table, counting the different rings of water that have been left in the same spot. "She died a second time, when she was seven," I answer. "When she drew her magic circle. It was a . . . Well, she didn't survive it; no more than anyone Godfrey gave it to did. This one actually helped a little. She started moving her own blood with mana, helping me along a bit.

"But this last year . . . Joan, that cancer killed her. Or rather, it made it harder to keep her alive. Her body suffered too much damage, over and over and over. She died nearly every night, sometimes more. And each time, I had to use more power to bring her back. Each time, I had to grow stronger to keep Annie here, to keep her in a body that acted human. But each time I brought her back, every single time, her path became clearer.

"The thread of her life, from death to death. Her soul, if such a thing exists. Whatever it is, it's . . . the impression of her. Who she is. I can follow it back through her lifetime, back to when I brought her back the first time and further. Back to when she fell from that tower, bleeding all the way down. I can see her face, her old one. And Joan, it's one thread. It's not tied to an old one. There wasn't a second that broke off at any point. This thread runs through her death as Lillith, years back to her birth, and into her life as Annie.

"One thread. One person. I brought her back, and I let her mind travel along that thread too; that's how she remembers her other life. But it is, nevertheless, one thread. She is who she has always been. You didn't lose your daughter; you just . . . missed part of her life. It's like she left for twenty years and came back to you. You missed her childhood. You missed when she became a woman. But she returned as herself."

"Isn't that just the same thing?" Joan asks bitterly, almost with a strange desperation, clenching her fists. Like she wants it to be the same thing, even if she knows it isn't.

"It wasn't to my dad," I answer immediately. This pours ice water over the room and ages Joan by another few years. I'm not even sure why I said it, but as the air grows heavy, I decide to push through. "My father lost a girl, barely a woman. He lost me for years, missed so much of my life, my pain. And the woman he found was a disfigured monster in the middle of . . . Well, it wasn't pretty. But he was . . . Joan, he was so happy to see me anyway. He missed my life, but he was still my dad, and I was still his daughter. I understand it feels different. In a lot of ways, it *is* different. But she is your daughter, as she always has been. You just missed a lot of her life, and that is a tragedy to be mourned. Believe me, I know. Your daughter knows.

"Has she ever told you about her parents in her other life? The way she was rejected? Just as her dad rejected her in this one. But you, you actually love her. The confirmation that you still love her, after she told you the truth, even as you doubted who she was . . . she holds it close, Joan. It is precious to her. Cherished. She'll never show it, but she does. She saw the lie in the name you chose before sending her off, and she buried that wound deep. She has one parent who loves her still, and she desperately needs her mom to just . . . be happy to see her. She needs you to be her mom, to *want* to be her mom, even if you missed her growing up.

"And now you know. You know that she is the same Lillith you spent those first seven years with. You know that she is your daughter, and she is hurting with you. So please, for your own heart, for hers, hurt with her as well. She brought Autumn with her because she was desperate to have someone to hurt alongside her. Even if she is too afraid to show the pain to anyone but me, she wants to share her grief, the same way you do. And to her, you are a mother."

Joan sniffs, choking back a cry as she examines me with red eyes. I didn't mean to lay all that on her. This started as my confession, about what I'd done, but I love Annie so much, and no one ever sees how much this is all eating away at her. Her mom took the name *Lillith* back, at least in her heart, and it just . . . it flowed out of me.

Joan loses the battle and tears start to flow.

"I can't," she whispers with a trembling voice. "Now more than ever, I can't. She's dead. She's already dead. You said so yourself: you are keeping her alive with your power alone. I . . . I don't know how to even process that. Everything is so strange now, so foreign. The whole world I knew cracks around me every day, and I learn some new impossibility is reality. New species. New lands. New countries. I can't fit all this in my mind. I can't comprehend it all. You say you brought my daughter back when you were what, fifteen? You have been keeping her alive since before you even met her? Why? Why would your abilities do that? I don't understand any of it, Sara."

"I don't know yet. I don't know . . ." I reply. She chokes back a sob.

"All I have, Sarafyna, the only thing that feels real, is my children. All

I can do, as the world crumbles, is love my children; is be there, happy to see them, like your father was for you. If I can care for my children, I can accept the rest of this. I can accept dead kings and revolutions and endless hat shops. So long as I have my children. But . . ." She looks up at me with suffocating hope and red eyes. "But children don't always come back from war, do they? Sometimes you send them off, and all you get back is a story from someone else who loved them. I said goodbye to Lily. I sent her out into the dark, and I can't see it. All I can see is the black and the emptiness and the half-broken promise of getting her back.

"I need her to be Annie and not Lillith, Sara. I need her to be someone other than my daughter. Because Ed is out in the dark too, and he's lost and confused, and I can't do anything but hope to be happy to see him when he comes out. Gilbert is on the front lines too. And I'm never going to see Henry again. I was his mother, and his last moments will only ever be a secondhand story to me. But don't you see? Ed and Gil, they might find their way back to me. They will eventually do enough and stop going back into the dark. I can offer them that shattered smile when they finally emerge. I can hope for it.

"But Lily is a fire all her own. She burns bright and furious and violent, and she won't come back from the dark. She won't come back until it is gone from every corner or she burns out. She will never do enough to stop and live in peace. She will never save enough people. When I say goodbye to her, when I send her out there and lose sight of her, I know that someday, she won't come back.

"If she's Annie, I can live with that. I do love her, and I know she loves me. But I can lose a friend I love. I can bear the certainty that she will keep fighting until she has nothing left to fight with and no energy to say goodbye. I can accept her death as a secondhand story, if only barely. But if she is Lillith, if she is my daughter . . . It will break me. That certainty will break me, Sara. It will kill me," she says, finally breaking down into full sobs. I bite my lip. She had no harsh words for me, for my secret. No admonishments. No hate. Just a fear she couldn't face on her own. But . . .

"I understand better than anyone," I whisper, standing and crossing the room to place one hand on her back. "I ache for every agony your Lily goes through. I know that my life with her will likely be a short one; maybe shorter than my life in the woods. But she does burn bright, and she is so warm, and she is your daughter. She deserves to be your daughter, Joan."

She cries for several moments, nearly speaking but choking on the insistent sobs as she does. I am just deciding to spend the evening here and check on the victims tomorrow when she finally speaks again. "I know. I know she is my daughter. I know. I know."

CHAPTER THIRTY-THREE

Invisible

Autumn

Another day. And another, and another, and another.

August and I have been busy since Lillith got herself locked up with her bullshit. I wish I could say I didn't understand how she could tell me she wouldn't risk herself again, then do it the next day like she'd never promised anything. It left anger like a cold stone in my gut. But I can't say I don't understand why it happened. I climbed to the top of a tower and saw justice at the bottom. She walked into an arena and spilled red justice in the dirt. And the truth is, while I did promise I wouldn't climb up that tower again, I'm still not sure if I was lying or not. As angry as it makes me, I understand.

Lily shares my love for Henry. She shares my guilt and my failure. She loves me and hates me. I love her and hate her. I hate how I always feel about her, and I hate how I always feel about myself. I hate how much I need Lily's support. I hate how much I need her loathing. But I do. And she's been locked up for three days now, since that disastrous fight. Ember had to rush us all out of the arena and find a new inn before the news spread. We don't need people getting curious about the group Lily had been staying with. Everything is already falling apart.

I'm sure she has a plan to get out of this; something to win the fight with the "actual demon queen" that has been advertised for days now. It looks like the sage in charge is planning a bloodbath. She has to have a plan. She has to. I badly want to have faith in that.

Unfortunately, I have known her for years. For all her brilliance in some areas, she lacks all common sense in others. I have seen tunnel vision leave her blindsided before, when it matters and when it doesn't. Her solutions to simple things have sometimes been . . . Well, I would have made different choices. Her bullheadedness and singular focus played a part in getting Henry killed, nearly as much as my selfishness. If I hadn't had too much faith in Lillith before, maybe the wedding I'd given my daydreams to wouldn't be dead in a pillar of ash.

Maybe.

So I have to think of a way to get her out, or a way to give her a chance. Ember is united with me in this goal, however much she may detest me. She has me back at the library, researching everything I can about the arena itself. I've no idea what she is doing, but we'll compare notes at the end of the day and see what we can come up with. I guess we aren't the first to try to break a gladiator out, but it is rare. People who aren't already in the midst of starting a mass insurrection are less likely to take the risk. People like me, really. Or the me that was. The me that killed Henry.

I stare down at the indecipherable charts stretched out across my table. Oddly, it appears like the plans for important buildings are kept at the library. It seems like a strange thing to do, but a lot of things in the Republic seem strange to me: the leaflets used to distribute news, the uncanny griefless population, the constant campaigning of sages trying not to get powerful nobles' support but everyone's. It's a peculiar place.

This particular oddity is doing me little good, however. If there is anything useful on this giant roll of paper, I can't read it. It all looks like gibberish to me; a bunch of shapes and numbers on a blue background. I recognize some of the writing in the margins as Lily's unique notation for math.

Not so unique after all, I suppose.

I curl a fist and hit the table in irritation, getting a glare from the librarian, a different man than last time. I offer an apologetic, if feeble, smile. The glare that hangs on me reveals my failure to impart the intent.

I sigh, rolling the building plans up again. This is clearly not an approach that is going to help me get Lily out, so I decide to check on August. He is on the other side of the room, working on his own research project. It would remind me of better days, during our school years, if he wasn't baby-sitting me. He is keeping his research private, which would be served well by going to a different part of the library. But *I* can't be left alone. *I* can't be left unattended. Like a child.

I stand quietly, trying not to repeat my loud offense from a few moments ago. August is buried in his work, allowing me to quietly approach him completely unnoticed. As I glance over his shoulder, my stomach flips. He's got a list of names; some slashed through and others underlined. These don't bother me much, except for the notes he's written in the margins near different names. Some are labeled with "possible accident," but several are labeled, in August's crisp and meticulous handwriting, as "suicide" instead. He is researching suicide. His project, whatever it is, is about me. No wonder he wanted to hide it.

I circle around quietly, not wanting to startle him, before putting my hand on his shoulder. He looks up instantly and guiltily, then nods. Over the last few days, we've silently established this as the sign I want to get some air. We quietly make our way to the side door, and I lead him to a quiet spot in the garden surrounding the building. It's not quite like the gardens at school, but it is large, comfortable, and affords us some privacy. It has a clear line of sight so we can't be approached or overheard without seeing the intruder well ahead of time.

"How are you doing? Feeling any better today?" August asks. He has asked that every day since Lillith's fight, which I initially thought was concern for Lily, but . . . it's almost like he is expecting me to improve without her. I wish he'd just stop checking in. It's exhausting.

I answer his question with my own.

"Suicide? Augie, is everything you've been doing these past few days about me? About that single mistake?" August looks guilty and rubs the back of his neck.

"No! I mean . . . kind of? Lily did tell me to look into this, but . . . it was because of you, I guess, yeah. Autumn, I want to help you, that's all. I want to help you feel happy again. I want you to feel safe and loved, and far away from the person making you so miserable," he replies. I know he cares about me, but the only emotion I can summon in response is hollow indignation. We used to understand each other without even speaking. Growing up, we felt connected, like we shared a mind at times. We could read intention in the slightest expression. But now . . . he doesn't get it at all. And I'm not sure if that's my fault or his.

"You can't take me away from the person making me miserable, August. Not without killing me yourself," I respond wearily. "What did Lily have you researching about . . . that? I can understand you looking for ways to help me, but why would she specifically want you to list names of people who have . . . I just don't get it. No more secrets; explain it to me."

August grabs his head in both hands, trying to come up with a suitable response. "Lily . . . was just trying to prove a point. And I promised I would consider it, that's all. Because, can't you see, Autumn? You can be happy again. You don't have to be so hopeless. Look around you! Look at everyone in this country! You may be the only person here who struggles to get out of bed! You hate yourself, Autumn, and I can't stand it because you are wonderful and you shouldn't be hated by anyone, especially yourself.

"And you don't have to. No one else has to put themselves through this. Everyone else here has had their grief taken away. And the only reason you haven't? Lillith. She won't let you. She wants you miserable, and you don't deserve that. So yeah, I was investigating her excuse for hurting you, for letting you suffer even as she lets her own grief fade to nothing. Even as she plays games in that arena, she leaves you struggling. I want to prove that there is no reason to leave you hurting," he spills, speaking more frantically as he makes it through his explanation. I feel sick.

"You . . . You want me to live like these . . . empty shells? You think that would make me happy? To lose my grief for the man I loved like he never existed? You think that will bring me joy? To not have the choice to grieve and regret? Collector, is this why you keep asking me if I feel better with Lillith locked up? You think I'll start to fade into the comfortable picture of your sister you don't have to worry about?" I ask. August looks up at me with wide eyes.

"N-no, Autumn! It's not like that! These people aren't hollow—they are just happy! Why do you think Lillith is accepting the same? Why would she choose to join them if it was so dangerous? It's not about being comfortable—it's about helping you!" he insists. I scoff.

"Isn't it, though? August, we saw the results of it ourselves. You found more people who paid the price for it! Why wasn't one enough? You knew it didn't help anything the first time you saw it, and you still wanted that for me? That wasn't for me, August. That was so you could feel comfortable around me. That was so I would stop wallowing and moaning and crying. It was so I would be fun to be around again. For you," I accuse.

"That's not fair!" he snaps back. "Do you really think I would do that? Risk you just so I could be happier? You know me better than that. You know I love you more than anything!"

"I do! I know that! But . . . your grief is gone, isn't it? You let it go. Or whatever is protecting me didn't protect you too. So without your grief, exactly what emotions do you have left when responding to mine? I know you wouldn't consciously hurt me, but August, you can't even understand me right now. Of course your solution is to just pretend the grief doesn't belong there. Of course you just want me to start acting like I'm happy again. You may not realize that is for your own gratification, but it is. I *need* my grief. I need it, August. Henry deserves it. If I couldn't grieve for him . . ." I trail off.

"Henry was my friend too, Autumn. And he was Lillith's brother! And she let hers go! She is doing fine without it! Yes, I've seen people struggle even without it, but I've also seen people improve once it was taken away," August challenges.

"You can't possibly believe that," I intone.

"You've seen her! You've seen her laugh and joke and live. Why does she get to live, and you don't?"

"August. Grief is Lily's endoaspect. You know that. It's what protects her from divine magic's control," I respond.

"You don't need to feel an emotion to benefit from it as an aspect, Autumn, you know that as well as I do. We took the same classes on aspecting!" he retorts.

"You *might* not need to, but that's beside the point. Augie, don't you remember when we first learned about her aspect? Right after we met her? The very first thing we knew about it, even before we knew it was grief?" I ask. He looks at me in confusion, and I rub my forehead as I close my eyes. "It makes her magic invisible. The more grief she is around, the less visible it is. Collector, even a few days ago, when she was forced to use it in front of everyone, it was less opaque than most mana because of her aspect. Because there was grief in that arena with her."

"So what? There was another sage involved; her and every other gladiator probably had their grief back because of the more powerful divine magic. What does that prove?" he asks.

"You're missing the point. Have you ever heard of an endoaspect making mana invisible before? Ever? Properties of endoaspects are determined by their owner's understanding of the associated concept. The way they view and experience an emotion down to their very core. And what does Lily's do? It keeps her mind free. It makes her mana much stronger than most aspects. And it makes it invisible.

"To Lily's very core, deep down in the darkest corners of her heart, she views grief as something powerful but invisible. Something to be hidden. The more intense, painful, and widespread it is, the less visible it should be. You think she isn't grieving because she still jokes and smiles? Because she doesn't look like me? She behaves that way because, at some point in one of her lives, she internalized grief as an emotion she needed to hide," I respond, quietly at first but raising my voice higher as I do.

August looks like he's been slapped. "Why? Why would she feel that way?"

"Because when people like me grieve openly and loudly, the people around them ask them to stop; some more honestly, like Ember calling me useless or whiny. And others . . . others convince themselves it's for my sake. 'Shut up and smile,' they say, tired of seeing me as I am. 'Isn't it time you moved on? Are you feeling any better?'" I stare at him as his face pales. "But look what it actually does to her. That arena is her tower, August. It is her daily punishment, where she lets people hit her on Henry's behalf. On my behalf. On her mother's behalf. She jokes and she laughs and she smiles like she knows everyone wants, then she walks into that arena and takes as much pain as she can possibly survive."

"Autumn, I—" August starts, but I cut him off.

"I do feel better with her locked up. With her cut off. The same way I would have felt better if she'd come here without me. The same way she probably does, being separated from me. I hate her for what happened to Henry. I hate her for the wedding I'll never have. I didn't realize it at first; I was too focused on how much I hated myself for the same things. But I also feel worse, because we share hatred and love and loss. I need Lillith the same way she needs me. The same way I need to keep grieving. As for how miserable I am to be around, I'm sorry, but I can't do what Lillith does. I never learned how. I have to wear this grief, or I am naked and hopeless."

August's mouth moves, but no words come. Water builds on his eyelids without running down his face, then he hangs his head in hopeless defeat. We both feel spent after that, remaining silent for a long time as we sit in the grass and look at our knees. Long enough that the librarian has probably filed our books and papers away by the time August speaks.

"I'm sorry, Autumn. I didn't understand. I don't understand. But if there is one thing I have learned over the years, it's that I don't have to. If this is what you want, I won't ask again," he says. I simply nod in response, and we sit for a while longer. After another prolonged silence, he breaks it again. "What do I do? If you want to keep . . . if what I was doing is pointless. Why am I even here?"

I sigh. "I don't know," I whisper, then realize that isn't entirely true. I could ask him for help planning an escape of some kind for Lily, but he won't be able to do much more than I can. But he was wrong again. I was wrong, actually. I got too distracted by his intent I missed the implications of what he was actually looking into. There is simply no way the sages constantly exert effort to keep people's grief from them. There has to be something else to it, like confession in Potestia, but . . . "It wasn't pointless." He looks up at me curiously.

"It's not? But I thought—" he starts, but I cut him off again.

"As proof of whatever point you wanted to make, it is useless, but . . . August, this grief thing, people deserve to be able to choose. Everyone deserves to be able to choose. We still need to find out how long this has been going on and who is doing it. Lily will be trying to find that out herself, but what you have been recording can help us track it down. Do that. Find out everything you can about it. Find out how to give people a choice. Find out who, exactly, is taking it away."

CHAPTER THIRTY-FOUR

Fuck Around

Lillith

I sit on my bed, leaning my head back against the wall as I take a deep breath through my nose and open my eyes. I have finally finished, and just in time. Had to cut it close, what with getting enough sleep to not be in extra danger out there. As usual, Bahamut is watching me with calculating eyes.

"You really are Lillith, aren't you?" she asks. She is looking at me with horrified fascination. Or rather, she is looking at my most recent . . . updates. I shrug, no point in hiding it now.

"The one and only," I respond. "Never did catch your name though." She shakes her head.

"No. It'll be harder for you to kill me if you know my name. You need to separate yourself, think of me as an opponent, not a person. People have names. I'm just . . . Bahamut," she responds wearily.

"She says, moments after asking me for my real name," I quip. She offers a single, humorless laugh.

"Well, if you are the real Lillith, I don't think I'm likely to have that dilemma. Not if half the stories I've heard about you are true."

"Man, who is spreading this shit? I swear to God, I will shove a fucking pear up their ass if I ever find them," I complain. Bahamut gives me half a smile. She's softened just a bit, after a week together, but she still lets little more than a corner of her mouth escape her armor.

"Well, most of what I know came from my father. You're one of the only people he's ever actually been truly afraid of, you know? He believed in you before anyone else I've met. He's always said you would come for him, some day. Like you have a vendetta against him specifically. Wouldn't blame you if you do, honestly," she replies.

I roll my shoulders, stretching after the hour of meditation. I put one hand on my head and push, cracking my neck loudly. Man, that shit leaves me stiff. "Well, I don't know who your dad is, but that's unlikely. I probably have nothing against him specifically, anyway. I just got here; haven't met many people yet, and few I plan to hunt down. Although it sounds like he might deserve it. I'll leave that to you though, once we both get out of here. You really think I plan to kill you? After watching me bust my ass not to let anyone die in my last match?"

"If you really are kind, you will. Markus won't be merciful if you refuse. If I'm going to die either way, I'd rather a quick death than anything he has to offer," she insists.

"Well, murder certainly will solve the problem, but I doubt yours will. But tell you what, convince me you deserve it, and I will. I'm certainly not hesitant to kill when it actually needs to be done," I offer.

"I've killed a lot of people in that arena. My hands are soaked in blood," she answers immediately. No grief accompanies the declaration, but she certainly wears regret. It's interesting, how different people compensate for the loss with different emotions.

"When you didn't have to? Not just to prevent that ugly fate you mentioned earlier?" I push. She is silent, answering my question with closed lips. "Right. You want me to mercy kill you for mercy killing people. Am I supposed to slip into a warm bath with open wrists right after?"

"If I win, I plan to show you that mercy. It's the least you can do. They know who you are now; they may try to rig the game. You can't count on victory with certainty, even with . . . all that. If you want an easy death, offer me the same, please," she pleads.

I examine her seriously, then hold out my left hand and flex my claws. "No one ever does the least they can do. Not unless they are rich. I am going to kill Markus today, or I will die, whether you beat me or not. That is my only goal: get Markus in front of me and kill him. So, if you win, don't extend that mercy," I insist. She glares at me, and I glare at her. Neither of us has any intention of doing what the other asks. Both of us are certain our choice is the greater mercy, which means we will both be fighting for our life out there.

Our staring contest is interrupted as the steel door swings open and the prim woman who registered me walks in, guards on either side of her. She pushes her glasses up her nose, entirely composed until she gets a look at me, at which point she jumps and lets out a short but embarrassing squeal. It takes her a moment to compose herself, and another to recognize that I do still look like me. I just have a couple extra decorations, so to speak. I can see how they would be startling in an unlit room.

I extend my claws and examine them as if I'll find something caught underneath them.

"That time, is it?" I ask. The woman clears her throat before responding, but she catches a look at something under the bed and raises an eyebrow at me.

"The magic circle. What's it for?" she asks.

"Magic," I reply easily.

"It's not in the center of the room; it won't work," she challenges.

"You're not in the center of the room. You're working," I counter. She looks at me incredulously.

"That's not—That doesn't even—" she starts, then she looks at Bahamut, who shrugs. Finally, our guest rubs her temples and sighs. "Just tell me what it does."

"Nothing now," I answer honestly. "It seems some malcontent scratched out most of the defining runes. I'm afraid it's downright unreadable, much less usable." Our visitor looks back at Bahamut, who simply shakes her head.

"Are we really going to play this game today?" our guest asks.

"I mean, I've got time for it if you do," I respond with a wink. She rolls her eyes.

"I suppose whatever it is won't change anything now. I'll just have to report it after I escort you to your gate. Bahamut, someone else will retrieve you shortly."

"What, no bath first?" I complain. She scowls at me.

"It would be a waste of water. You can fight as you are," she dismisses. I leisurely stand and saunter to her side.

"You really want to present your demon queen to the masses in this state? Could be underwhelming," I note. She begins walking, expecting me to follow. I casually comply.

"You look fine. They won't be able to tell the difference in the illusion, and it doesn't carry smells with it," she says as she walks.

I sniff as we pass the other cells. "Well, fair warning, if you advertised a 'filthy demon queen,' you may have attracted the entirely wrong kind of audience for the event at hand," I joke.

"You're awfully chipper for a woman walking toward her death," she replies.

So I guess they do have something of a plan to deal with me. They have certainly rigged the game.

"Well, you know. You've been to one of your executions, you've been to them all," I answer easily. We leave the slave quarters and enter more familiar territory, passing more people and better decorated walls. Finally, we arrive at the waiting area just inside my gate.

"It will be a few moments before they are prepared on the other side. The Void Sage says you have water mana. If you are so concerned about cleanliness, you can take this opportunity to use it, before you are cuffed," she offers. I eye her and the man behind her, holding the mana dispersal cuffs. Then I give them a toothy smile.

"The Void Sage sure loves saying shit, doesn't he? Really got the gift of the gab, that guy. Someone should really teach him the ancient proverb of my homeland," I reply.

"And what is that?" she asks.

"Snitches get stitches." I grin. "No matter, you can put the cuffs on as you please." She rolls her eyes but gestures, and the guard secures them around my wrists and neck.

"I'll be sure to let him know, if I ever see him. You certainly won't get the chance," she retorts. "Wait here until the gates open. There are two sages waiting, aside from these guards, in case you decide against fighting. It's been a . . . pleasure." With this, she turns to leave.

"Appreciate the vote of confidence!" I call after her, but she only sighs and continues walking. As such, I lean against one wall and wait. It takes an unusually long time for the gate to open. So long I am actually a little startled when it starts to move to the side. I put my left fist in my right hand, cracking the knuckles.

"Don't get yourself killed too quickly," one of the previously silent guards says. "I've got good money on you beating at least three of them." I raise an eyebrow at this. *Three of whom?* Well, I suppose I'll find out in a moment.

"I'll try not to disappoint," I promise as I make my way to my gate.

"You will," the other guard grumbles. I turn and walk backward for a few paces as I kiss my clawed hand and blow it to the more negative of the guards. A moment later, I am in the open air again.

The moment I turn to face Bahamut, I draw my mouth into a line. *Goddammit.* Bahamut is, in fact, waiting for me—along with ten other prominent gladiators. I have a feeling this too, will not be a free-for-all. Worse than that, I'm the only person wearing mana-suppression cuffs. I am not, however, the only person with mana. All eleven of my opponents have it, with Bahamut's being the strongest.

Bahamut's aura is impressive, and her earlier comments about her father suddenly grow far more interesting. She has enough mana to crush any spell I try to cast with pure force; if she can respond to them, in any case. I can handle that. The others all have less intense auras, but powerful enough that I can't ignore them. I can, of course, still use my mana with these restraints on; otherwise, I'd have introduced myself to the dirt the second I put them on. There is no question I'll have to use it in this fight. It's going to be a lot harder than I thought, but I can manage it.

"Ladies and gentlemen!" the announcer's voice calls out, this time waiting for me to enter before introducing me, apparently. "May I introduce you to a creature of myth . . . the monster under your children's beds . . . the woman the Void Sage calls the greatest threat in the history of the Republic! That's right folks, this is no persona, no costume and name meant solely to rile up the crowd! No, the Gladiator Sage has captured her, the actual monster of prophecy, and brought her here to fight and die before you. Known to those of the third plane as 'The Mage of Mourning,' may I introduce the genuine demon queen, the self-proclaimed omega, the fearsome Lillith of Endings!"

The crowd cheers loudly as he finishes, then the sky fills with an illusion, giving them all a close-up look at the devil herself. I look a bit different than the last time I appeared here, and the cheering takes on an entirely different tone.

This is hardly surprising. They lay flat against my skin and match the color of the flesh they grow from, including my tattoos. Walking past me in public, they would be easy to miss, as is their design. But blown up to the massive size of the illusion above me, no one can miss the new scales I've grown on much of my body. An extra layer of defense with . . . a couple of other features. More disturbing than that, however, is the other visible change; one which many may not notice, but many will. The new, closed eyelids on the small of my back and the front of my left shoulder.

"Lillith. Invader, demon, and monster. We are so pleased to have you here instead of terrorizing our country. I understand this match may feel a little . . . unbalanced, but of course, you don't hold back when facing the queen of demons, do you?" the announcer asks, more for the audience's sake than mine. "Would you like to address the crowd before we begin? Or perhaps the sages? One last speech to your demonic subjects, perhaps? We will broadcast your words to everyone if you do!"

It's odd they are giving me an opportunity to speak at all. I suppose they must want some extra evidence I'm the real demon queen, or they just aren't worried about me swaying people. I guess with Nexus energy, they don't need to worry much.

I look up into the sky then close my eyes. I sigh wearily, then chuckle before offering my so-called "final words." This fucker really put me up against ten mages who could each kill Baldwin without a second thought. I only really have five words to offer right now, and all are for the Gladiator Sage.

"Lick my fucking taint, Markus."

CHAPTER THIRTY-FIVE

Find Out

The moment the fight starts, I flood the arena with mana, creating a barrier to deny light. This throws us all into darkness, and I immediately cast a point light spell to send invisible light waves everywhere but my own eyes.

I haven't used *Total Eclipse of the Heart* in a while, but this is certainly an excellent time for it. I won't have long, not with my mana perfectly visible despite the darkness, but it'll be enough. I have to manually cast my radar spell as well, which takes a lot of focus, but I have a few seconds of pitch-black where I can see them while they can't see me. A few will even have retina damage from the UV light even after the spell is broken, which can be healed later.

I take advantage of my even greater strength, won with rapid physical enhancement during my last fight, and close the distance on the nearest enemy. I don't have time to be selective, although I'd like to reach Bahamut and knock her out first. Unfortunately, they moved as soon as the fight started, and I can only tell basic size and shape.

During my precious few moments of advantage, I reach one of the larger clouds of color and catch a man with my right hand. Not Bahamut, unfortunately. With my left, I pull a single scale from my arm as I throw him to the ground, carefully holding back to avoid lethal force. As he collides with the dirt below, I stab the scale into his cheek deep enough that he won't be digging it out without tweezers. It'll hurt, but it'll heal. I also wrap him in steel, summoning it as rapidly as I can. I need him restrained if he wakes up.

My time in the dark has ended by the time I'm done, however. Bahamut has completely crushed the light mana I was maintaining to block the light. I can probably keep sending the UV waves out to blind my opponents, but I'm already shrouded in mana from different enchantments, and I don't want to make them a bigger target than they are. A lot of things fall apart if any of these mages manage to crush those enchantments. Not too many things, but it will make the fight with Markus—and possibly other sages, should they intervene—much more dangerous.

I look around to find myself surrounded. A breath of silence passes as everyone takes stock of the situation, ten sets of eyes locking onto me and the already incapacitated enemy at my feet. They spent a week hearing about the actual demon queen of legend, the woman many of them heard stories about as children. Then they went into the ring with me. A few seconds in, and one of them is already unconscious in the dirt.

They have also spent multiple weeks hearing about how I spare my opponents and Markus never asks me to kill. They may know this fight is different, or they may not. But they will be afraid of me, and they will have hope in my mercy.

This is phase one of the hastiest plan I've ever put together. Bahamut may be fighting for her life, but the rest of them? They may hesitate to fight me. Maybe for a moment, and maybe for the entire fight. Either way, I can turn it to my advantage. I just need one more thing to drive it home.

I open the eyelids on my left shoulder and in the small of my back, seeing the effect on the faces around me. A couple are disgusted; a few are afraid. Bahamut has seen them before, but none are unaffected. These eyes carry the same red hue my eyes have always had, but they wear the color of blood throughout, rather than only in the iris. This is, of course, because compound eyes don't have a human iris. Those around may not be able to make out the hexagonal pattern, but they can see the off-putting texture. The reality of my identity clearly sinks in for a few.

It's a brief interaction—less than a second, really—but it has the effect it needs to. I have just bought myself a lot more wiggle room in this fight. Not enough to avoid fighting entirely, however, as becomes obvious very quickly. Auras explode and spells fly at me from every direction, and I'm pleased to observe that some of them do seem to have their vision impaired by the light I was sending out earlier, as their spells are going wide and are obviously going to miss. Which would be great if I didn't need to stop them from hitting anyone else as well.

The new peepers are doing their job as well, even picking up mana. I wasn't sure they'd be able to, since perceiving mana is clearly done with the eyes but seems unrelated to light. They aren't nearly as good as my actual eyes—or rather my originals, as the case may be—and I barely process the information they parse; my mind just isn't used to the extra input. But it doesn't need to be.

They do what they are best at, and I notice every spell coming at me from every direction far more quickly than I otherwise would have. I leap into the air and start cycling mana. That's what it feels like now. Cycling, like a machine, pulsing between my enchanted steel and my traitorous cells. Bahamut can crush my mana with brute force on her own, at least right now. But that's only if she can get to it. This method of casting is fast and powerful. With mana building internally and creating its effects an instant after, she won't have time.

I catch smaller spells on the ground with force, protecting my opponents from any lethal crossfire. This arena belongs to me. Huge stones fly at me, following my jump and trying to intercept me in the air. I easily twist out of the way, creating a burst of force beneath my foot and jumping to the side, then create another and another, walking through the air one spell at a time. A massive wave of water erupts in front of me, extending from the ground to the invisible ceiling of Nexus energy. This combines with another mage's mana and turns to a wall of ice.

I rapidly slow myself with force, flipping around and catching the wall with my right arm, the claws of the gauntlet digging into the ice and allowing me to slide down the side. More spells fly toward me, and I direct myself to avoid the carbon projectiles, flaming rocks, and something I don't recognize with white mana. I get a bad feeling about this one in particular.

Below me, there is a curtain of cold mana, clearly designed to catch me as I make my way down the ice wall. Below that, the water mage fires spears at me, which quickly turn to ice as they pass the cold barrier between us. I send targeted bursts of heat mana at each in rapid succession, allowing myself to get drenched in the warm water still carried by inertia as the spears instantly melt. It's not easy, but her aim still seems to be off after my first spell.

I have to create a larger burst of heat to punch through the cold mana below without freezing myself, and I land, hard, directly between the man and woman working together to create ice. Landing closer to the man—the cold mage, I think—I reach out my right hand to grab him by the wrist, pulsing lightning through my arm and tasing him the moment we make contact. As he falls, I let go, quickly retrieving another scale from my left arm and forcing it into his cheek.

High-pressure water is on me in seconds, and I have to erect a wall of steel to intercept it as I bind the new mage's hands and feet with the same. The steel actually dents from the water pressure, which I have little time to admire as Bahamut's axe descends on me. I have seen it before, and she is a machine with that weapon.

As I use force to throw myself out of the way, I notice that same mana surrounding her axe. It's white, but whatever it is creating has no color. The same thing I'd dodged a moment ago. It hits my wall instead of me, but doesn't cut through it. Not exactly. No, where her axe should collide with steel and water, both simply cease to exist. No resistance or anything. They just stop as soon as they touch the white mana.

"I'd really prefer if you didn't hit me with that," I call as I skip backward.

"You know why I have to," she replies. I don't wait around to banter more than that, as she is already swinging the axe around and I really need to deal with everyone else first. It seems only five gladiators, including Bahamut, are actively pursuing me now. The other four are hanging back, building spells but obviously hoping the more aggressive combatants will deal with me first. I run toward three of them, moving at inhuman speeds and increasing my gap from Bahamut.

The stone mage rapid-fires smaller stones at me, while the carbon mage fires more arrows. I worry Bahamut will throw her own spells, but she doesn't. And I suspect I know why: She doesn't want to kill anyone she doesn't have to. A less likely boundary for people incapable of grief.

This makes it easier on me.

I mostly ignore the stone spell. As fast as they are, they simply bounce away when they get within an inch of me. A week with a mana circle and accelerated gathering of force has made my armor . . . *slightly* more effective. The area immediately around my torso, legs, and head is surrounded by a force barrier facing outward and enchanted into my clothing. My arms aren't protected for a few reasons, but the stone just sparks as it cuts through my armor and meets steel. So long as I can keep my left arm away from the attack, I'm good to go.

I dodge back and forth to avoid the carbon arrows, which seem to have more force and weight behind them. The final of the three mages I am charging shoots a stream of flames at me. I jump into the air again, easily avoiding the fire and launching myself into a roll to the side of it. Just as I am recovering, I lift my right arm, intercepting a carbon attack just before it hits me.

I waste no time, clapping as I fill the air with earsplitting sound mana. At the same time, I release the brightest burst of light I can. Without the protective mana I've shrouded my ears with, my nearby adversaries immediately grab their head and cover their ears. Dazed and without sight or sound, they fail to stop the rest of my approach.

I pull them all together with force mana, forcing their backs against each other and wrapping them together in rapidly formed steel. I manage to knock the fire mage out with a punch as soon as I make it to them, but the eye on my back catches water mana approaching me with furious speed. Approaching these three meant leaving the cover of my steel wall, which was collapsing anyway. I grab the steel I've wrapped these ones in, pulling them with me as I sidestep. I hear something crack, and wince as the man with the stone screams. It doesn't take much to tell I broke his leg somehow with the rapid movement.

Well, they didn't die in the crossfire. We'll call it even, I think.

I need to knock the remaining two unconscious, but the stream is following me. Mimicking her own tactics from earlier, I throw up a wall of heat mana, which evaporates the water on contact and leaves us hidden in steam. Not comfortable, but it is concealment—which is good, because as I am dragging the pair again, Bahamut crushes the heat mana. I waste no time, knocking my conscious captives out with a couple gentle *thuds*, and leave all three with a scale each lodged in their face.

Gathering light mana, I use radar to find my remaining opponents. The water mage and Bahamut are the only ones attacking me at this moment, although the other four seem to be realizing they need to use their spells or lose. Bahamut is much larger and more obvious, making the water mage easy to spot. With a massive burst of force at my back, I throw myself from the steam and shoot like a bullet at her, catching her in my left arm and pulling her as my momentum fails to slow. This interrupts her fucking fire hydrant attack and increases our distance from Bahamut.

I use opposing force to slow us before we collide with the far wall. Even then, my boots kick up dirt as they make contact, and I have to collapse into a roll, taking most of the hit for both of us. We land just by the intersection of two walls: one of stone, the other of ice. Just as my pathetic little wet rag doll is getting her bearings, I slam her head, ever so gently, into the ice and knock her out. One more lodged scale, and I turn to face the remaining gladiators. The four who hoped I'd be dead or defeated before their turn to fight have picked up on my strategy and are sticking close to Bahamut, the one I have been trying to avoid most.

I crack my neck before throwing myself back into the fray.

I sprint full speed at Bahamut, and she sprints at me, forcing her tagalongs to join her. I see wind and three mana aspects I haven't encountered yet, in addition to Bahamut's white mana. As I run, I retrieve four more scales. They know I want to pick them off while keeping my distance from Bahamut, so they are keeping close to her, but they aren't used to working together, and I can use that.

Our warpaths collide, and I quickly step to the side as the axe swings into the space I'd occupied a moment before. That white mana erases even the ground it touches, and the axe is already prepared for another swing. I flash some light in Bahamut's eyes, dodging to the side and pulling the wind mage to me with force mana. Some kind of slick, oily liquid is fired from one of the other mages, but it collides with my force shield and falls to my feet. I easily knock my captive out and leave him with a scale. Bahamut, recovered now, swings again and again and again.

Each time I sidestep it, I'm grateful she isn't firing this mana on its own. Thanks, I suspect, to her allies being too close.

I realize something as the remaining unfamiliar manas dissipate, no attack coming from those mages. Markus sent his best gladiators out here to kill me. Or at least, his best gladiators who have mana. I have seen far better fighters, but having mana is often a huge advantage. But the fucker didn't ask them their aspects; he just used the strongest eleven who had a lot of mana. Or maybe he did know but was hoping I'd get crushed under their collective power. Or maybe he doesn't care if I win so long as I put on a good show.

Whatever he was thinking, these three, maybe all four, have never fought with magic before. That's not what they used magic for, before they were slaves.

Which makes Bahamut the only dangerous one here. They are sort of protecting me, actually, as they stumble over each other. I have to avoid the occasional swipe from a sword, but with my compound eyes, even as they circle around me, I see every move coming long before I am in any danger. They have to take turns or hurt each other, and at least one seems to be struggling to see clearly. And Bahamut doesn't want to kill if she can avoid it; otherwise, she'd just fill the arena with that white mana and delete me.

Bahamut is growing more desperate and her attacks more erratic. I actually have to push the mage with the black liquid out of the way to save his life when she misses me. This only makes her panic more, and she screams as I easily dance around all them. I jump, propel myself with force, and turn to the side with perfect timing and impossible reflexes. Aside from that weird mana, my plan was perfect. I should have been fighting like this for years. There is a reason I like *Bloodborne* more than *Dark Souls*. If I can't win with power, I'll win with speed. Lord help these fucking sages when I get both at once.

"Please," Bahamut begs, realizing the same thing. I am going to win this fight. They stacked the odds against the wrong version of me. "I won't let you make this worse for all us than it has to be! I don't know what you are planning, but I won't let you leave these people to Markus! I won't!" she screams. And I see the change in her face. When she decides she can't win. When she decides she has to save everyone else the only way she can. When she decides to kill all us to spare us from Markus's cruelty.

I grab the cuff on my right wrist, digging my claws into the hinges and pulling with all my strength. I can feel death seconds away; she is more dangerous than I expected. *What the fuck is that mana?* It doesn't matter; I have to stop it. I feel the change in the air as the cuff bends and breaks, leaving an ugly, twisted end where it was once clasped. Just as she is about to cast, I stab it into her free arm. Immediately, all the white mana disappears.

There is a moment of silence, then I kick at her leg, hard, forcing her to the ground. As she takes a knee, she is still barely shorter than me, and I punch her in the throat, catching her other arm and squeezing her wrist until she drops the axe.

As I force a scale into her face, the three remaining gladiators back up, nervously holding their weapons in shaking hands. Three bursts of force pin them to the ground while I wrap a kneeling Bahamut in steel. I have to fire the remaining scales like bullets as Markus waits for me to look for his ruling. Aiming is a bit odd with such small projectiles, but they are close, and I manage to tag all three. That's all them.

I look up to Markus's box, waiting for the expected response. He stands as I wait in front of Bahamut. He holds his hand in front of him, thumb out to the side, then tilts his head, grins, and turns his thumb up, toward the throat. He has officially broken our agreement and ruled in favor of death. He just doesn't know whose.

"Please, Lillith," Bahamut begs. "Please just do it. I've tried to spare people before. I don't want to die like that. I can't die like that. I refuse to. Just do what he asks. Just end it here. It will be better for all us."

I look up toward the sage, smiling sweetly, then slap my left hand onto my right bicep and raise my right fist in the air in a single motion.

"I won't give you blood, Markus. But I can offer you my ever-honorable arm." Bahamut starts sobbing behind me, collapsing to the ground with her face in the dirt. Still, I feel no grief from her, even now. Which means these aren't tears of grief. They are pure, unadulterated fear.

"Even if I fail, you will be okay," I promise. "Maybe I will die here and Markus will live. But he will be in no shape to hurt anyone at all."

"I hope you burn for this," she yells at me.

Markus smiles before floating down to the arena. He has one of the smuggest smirks I've ever seen. He lands in front of me and holds his arms behind his back while I stand firm between him and the terrified woman behind me. He approaches, getting closer and closer, until he is stopped by the force on my armor. He looks down at me, and I look up at him. He wears a shit-eating grin, and I set my jaw. We can each feel the other's breath as we face off.

"She is going to suffer so much. And for so long. Because of you," he declares. "She's begging for death, and I haven't even started yet. Demon queen indeed. How pathetic. But your games are over now, impressive as that fight may have been to the rabble. Based on that gesture you just made, among other things, I think you might know the old proverb?" He pauses as if in thought then widens his grin, showing me his too-white teeth. "Oh, that's right. It's 'Fuck around—'"

I cut him off, uninterested in his monologue or posturing. I dig my claws deep into his gut, releasing every ounce of venom I have in that arm. I can already tell it's not going to be enough, I'm still going to have to fight him, but it will be a lot easier now. And I'm not done. At the same time, I release gallons of mana with a brand-new aspect, flooding the entire combat area with it. The very same I gave up water to make room for.

"Find out," I finish for him. Blood bubbles through his smile.

Poison

Markus

The little skank actually attacked me! I didn't think she'd really have the balls. I haven't actually felt pain in . . . I'm not certain. And she knows the weakness of Nexus energy too, it seems. I can feel the venom tearing through my veins, distracting my Nexus energy as it rushes to heal the continuous damage the toxin does. I smile, even as my mouth fills with blood.

"I see you've fought sages before, dear Lillith," I taunt. "But if you think this will kill me, you have only fought the rejects, the completed mementos. The weakest. Yes, your poison will distract some portion of the Nexus energy; just enough that I will have to think a little to snuff you from existence. I may even have to stretch first. But even that won't last long."

I grab her wrist with my right hand and pull. She . . . doesn't budge. I have to use Nexus energy just to slowly move her hand. She certainly is strong, but not strong enough. I simply have to change reality so her claws are no longer embedded in my flesh. Even this she manages to resist, but it's only a matter of time. My assistant is trying to say something through the enchanted earring I wear, but I tune her out, too focused on the task at hand.

"All you've done is piss me off and give me an excuse to kill you in front of the crowd." I continue, calmly exerting more energy on her, demanding that her hand and my body separate. "The moment I remove your hand, my body will heal, and your admittedly impressive venom will be ejected. Then I will beat you to death in front of all these people. Well, as soon as you tell me how you got here, that is. You don't seem to have any Nexus energy yourself, but you do have a certain . . . Earthly aspect to you."

I am growing irritated with her. Her grief mana must provide her resistance to Nexus energy. Annoying, but I suppose it explains how she got through the Nexus in the first place. *I wonder why grief would do that. Does she just cry so much it gets annoyed away?* I suppose it doesn't matter, and I shift my focus to myself.

My expertise is not in manipulating my own body, but I can do a little if needed. Her claws are hardly long enough to do any real damage. It's a surface-level change, and a temporary one.

I lose my control over my Nexus energy for only a moment, like nearly dropping a bar of soap. This poison is using more of it than I would expect, far more than any previous attempt at poisoning has managed, which is interesting, but still nothing to worry about. I focus just a little more, turning off the pain, the aching, the faint smell of almonds. This time, I easily grip the world, and it ripples as I exert my will on it, conforming to my designs and melting my skin around the girl's fingers. A half step back, and I am free from the assault, my skin, and even my shirt, already stitching themselves back together.

She doesn't hesitate, leveraging the hand I still have gripped by the wrist and pulling my arm to her mouth. Seconds after I free myself, she is already sinking fangs into my forearm. Literal fangs, apparently. She definitely has the help of another sage; she must have gotten her earthly mannerisms from whoever's been modifying her body like this for her. Although, some of these seem new, since being locked up. She must have a way to hide them.

Ugh, she has another type of venom flooding my veins through this new wound. What a pest. I am weary of these games. She has done enough damage to thoroughly convince the crowd of her identity. It is time to remove her. Permanently.

I face reality. The reality of this girl stabbing me, biting me, poisoning me. And I reject it. I am the Gladiator Sage—the sage of combat, life, death, and pain. All these belong to me, and the very air will comply with my opinions on them.

In one moment, we are struggling as she bites me. In the next, she is wrapped in roots and vines, being torn off me. These are not the mundane plants of nature mana but the truly living creations of the Nexus. They move of their own accord, following the instructions I built into them on creation. They are strong, determined, and unstoppable. No fire mana will burn them. No water mana will dry them out. And no human strength will tear them. Not without Nexus energy.

It is unpleasant, ripping her off me. Or rather, it's literal. Even as she is pulled from me by the sapient roots of reality itself, she refuses to loosen the grip her jaw has on me. She is determined to fill my veins with every ounce of venom she can, and her jaw strength is incredible. I have to sacrifice my pound of flesh to pull her off, grimacing at the blood and the muscle as they rip from my arm, leaving the wet grease of living game dripping from her too-sharp teeth. She spits my flesh onto the ground even as she is crushed. It's uncomfortable, but pain is my domain, and I have taken it away. New pain doesn't last long, fading even before the injury itself heals. Which will be any minute now.

What is that almond smell?

"Sage Markus!" a voice screams through my earring. "She is filling the arena with some kind of mana I can't identify!" my assistant warns.

I wrinkle my nose as I examine the still-open wound. It is regenerating far too slowly, my Nexus energy too distracted. I can feel it fighting the venom of her claws in my gut. I can feel it strangling the poison of her fangs in my blood. And . . . I can feel it wrestling something else in my lungs, creating oxygen as quickly as it can, only for it to be burned up a moment later.

I see. Poison gas too, or some kind of mana related to it. Interesting. Even I may struggle if I let this go on too long. It is strange, however. After she fought so hard to avoid killing her opponents, she is now sacrificing them just to kill me.

I grin as I realize it was all a trap to lure me in here, something I'd never have done had she been willing to kill. She didn't even hesitate to poison all them the moment I was close enough to her. Clever, but the betrayal will work in my favor. When she poisons all them like a coward and still dies by my hand, it will only help the narrative and get me elected. It was cute, but she has to keep it up to hurt me. Unfortunately for her, I noticed too early, and now that she isn't actively injecting venom, I know to kill her immediately, long before this grows overwhelming.

I focus on her and click my tongue. My roots are beating her, crushing her, exerting more force than whatever enchantments she is using on her armor can counteract. But she isn't even wincing, just glaring at me. It must make for an interesting scene: the bloody wounds on me and the thorns digging through her scales, and neither of us reacting even a little.

I'd like to fix that, but I suspect she'll be resistant to the unique pain my Nexus energy is capable of inflicting. And, loath as I am to admit it, three sources of unusually potent poison are having a greater effect than any other poison ever has. That being the case, I can only focus on a few things at once. In addition to the rapid healing, my Nexus energy is currently crushing her and mitigating my own pain. If I want to kill her and stop the mana she is releasing, I'll need to put everything I have left into demanding her death from the world.

I could perhaps order my mages to crush her mana, but asking for help to defeat her is hardly going to get me elected; I have to prove my personal competence. So, I take a step forward. Red eyes lock onto mine as I order the roots to tighten their grip and grow longer thorns. She may have drawn blood from me, but I'll draw more from her.

"All these people, dead. Sacrificed for your pathetic trap. All for nothing," I taunt. She says nothing in response but tries to burn through me with her glare. I feel that pain even less than the numb bleeding of my gut and arm. Holding up my left hand, I smirk at her and snap my fingers.

Again, the world ripples, respecting my authority over it and contorting reality into the shape of my design. I don't create sentient weapons this time, nor do I add or remove pain. No, I am the sage of death. I declare Lillith's death into the world as an immutable fact, a law which cannot be defied. I don't kill her; I choose the reality where she is dead.

Like paint on a brush, the world follows each stroke of my will and descends on my enemy with finality.

Nothing happens.

It feels like pushing against a stone wall. The reality I have chosen, my authority, has been defied, rejected. I put my everything into that order, and now the poison is spreading. My Nexus energy is frantically trying to heal me as I'm losing my grip on it. The vines and roots binding my enemy are growing erratic as my authority over them loosens. She is still held in place, but I can't control them as well, and they are becoming vulnerable. If I don't get a handle on them, she will be free while I'm still weak from the poison.

There are only two reasons this would happen. Only two reasons such a powerful order for death would fail. One of them is easy to rule out, since the roots still exist around her. Even in the extremely unlikely event she broke free from the Nexus mere moments ago, they would have started to wither. She would probably heal as well, maybe even growing younger, if my attempts to bring her closer to death were rejected strongly enough to increase her lifespan instead.

No, the Nexus energy still exists around her, and her rejection of my reality hasn't whiplashed in the other direction. Which leaves one possibility: a greater authority. I was overruled by a much more powerful sage, based on how ineffective my order was. And that sage has decided life is an immutable fact about this girl. Life of a sort, in any case.

It has to be the Original Sage.

Fuck.

If she only spared her opponents as a way of trapping me, that's something I could handle. But what if that was also the only reason the Original Sage attacked her in the first place? As a trap? He hasn't made a move against us in centuries; I should have realized that one move wasn't going to be all he had. Which means I am no longer a weakened sage against a mundane mage—I am a weakened sage against another sage who already outclassed me.

But why me? Why does he want me dead, of all people? I don't get it. Why would he upset the balance now? I have been one of the biggest contributors to his fucking collection, in quality if not quantity. Why break the peace so completely now?

Questions for later. I need to kill this cunt and regroup. No time to worry about optics.

"Crush her mana and send the other sages in! It's a trap!" I shout, knowing my earring will pick up my orders.

There is no response. Lillith is wrestling her constraints, tearing and ripping and destroying, winning the freedom to fight me directly.

"Now! There is no time to fuck around here!" I scream. Her feet touch the ground, and her eyes are still locked on me. There is still no response. Finally, I look up and see people rushing in a panic, fleeing the stands. *What is going on? Are the others under attack too?*

Lillith finally tears free, emerging from the roots. I can't summon more; the poison is working faster than it should be. Exactly what kind of poisons are these? I can only do two things now: heal and stop the pain. I have to give one up to fight back.

I will live. I need to live. I will not die to some uppity mage bitch.

I let the pain take me and try to think of something else. *Life. I am the sage of life.* I look for Riley's body; I can't bring her back from the dead, but I can puppet a corpse, order it to use its mana. But . . . she is gone. She should be lying dead in the dirt. The poison mana filled the arena, killing everyone but Lillith and I, so where did—

I have no time to finish the thought as claws dig into my shoulder. My head is forced forward to see red eyes and fangs just before the latter sink into my throat. I can feel the pain, and I scream, but I won't give up. I will live. And now that I have my hands on her, I can kill her. I can use all my remaining Nexus energy to bring death—not to her directly but to everything around her: the clean air she breathes, her mana, the food she still digests. Anything foreign in her can be turned to my own poison. Even the Original Sage can't keep her alive through anything, and I still have a lot of power, if I take just a moment away from healing myself.

But the moment I try, there is a deafening explosion, the sun goes out, and vines erupt from the ground, wrapping themselves around both of us, pulling us apart and to the ground. These aren't mine.

No. No, no, no—fuck no!

I recognize these. These are the vines of the Nexus. He is bringing them here. For me.

I slam into the dirt, my real opponent finally appearing to take advantage of my weakness, my inability to flee. Struggling to keep my head up, I spot Riley hacking at the vines around Lillith with her axe. Based on the way they fall apart on contact, she must be using her void mana as well.

That's not right. Why would the Original Sage attack Lillith if he is using so much authority to keep her alive? It doesn't matter; she won't be on his side anymore. She can help me.

"Please!" I beg. "Kill me! Just fucking end it! I'm not healing anymore; I can't use the Nexus while fighting him alone. I can't be taken, so just kill me now!" I continue to struggle to lift my head, and I see the two women. Lillith has been freed; I guess she is the lower priority. He intends to take me, to make me into . . . I can't. I would rather die. I will die. I need to die. I will die to Lillith, the so-called demon queen, and I will be spared.

Please God, please let me die before he takes me . . .

I actually see her start to walk toward me again, perfectly willing to comply, but Riley catches her, stops her. The larger woman points to the east, and the two have a brief disagreement. But short as it is, it still takes too long.

I can feel it. I can feel myself being eaten by the vines. By the Nexus. The Original Sage is going to win. *Oh God . . .*

CHAPTER THIRTY-SEVEN

Hollow Bonds

Lillith

Day becomes night, and the world explodes in sound as I bite into Markus's neck. The other sages must be interfering now. I was hoping they'd be too afraid once they realized the area was filled with hydrogen cyanide and nitrogen. Or, well, poison gas, at least. I guess they probably didn't identify it right away.

I was hoping for a little more time. An ironic side effect of so much power is proportional cowardice, and although I can't fight all the sages in this arena, I was counting on none of them wanting to be the first to face the fate Markus is fighting, especially lacking his supposed fine control over pain. I was counting on two minutes before one of them gathered the others and convinced the rest to attack together. This was my conservative estimate, considering a long history with such men.

A lot can happen in two minutes. Almost every fight I've ever been in has been shorter than that. I needed to kill Markus in that time, releasing his direct control over the arena and buying myself a chance to escape. Not the ideal escape plan, but I wasn't planning on being attacked by the Collector and detained by a whole handful of assholes. I am so close to pulling it off too; maybe close enough that he's already dropped the Nexus barrier in the sky and around the arena. But vines wrap themselves around me again, tearing me off my prey and throwing me into the dirt.

Fuck. How does he have so much power left? His vines before were almost impossible to move in. I thought he'd lost control of them when I managed to break free, but these are even stronger. It must be the other sages. It has to be. It hasn't been two minutes yet. My already desperate escape attempt is getting harder.

Hope isn't lost yet, however. Ember and the twins are still out there; I'm certain they are planning something. I knew they would be when I planned all this. My goal has been to kill Markus and create as much chaos as I could, giving them an opportunity to enact whatever plan they have. We can't communicate, but fighting from both ends would leave cracks we could slip through, and we both understand that. Would sure have been nice to kill a sage though. In any case, the other sages may have moved too quickly, but it's not over yet. I have friends.

Vines snap around my right leg as an axe shrouded with white mana passes through them. *Friends old and new, it seems.* She swings again and again, until I'm able to scramble to my feet away from them. Bahamut offers me a hand, which I accept, climbing to my feet with her help. As soon as I do, I realize I'm in either a much better or much worse situation than I thought.

"Please! Kill me! Just fucking end it! I'm not healing anymore; I can't use the Nexus while fighting him alone. I can't be taken, so just kill me now!"

Markus is wrapped in vines too, and for some reason, he's desperate to die. On one side of the sky, smoke is rising into the air. On the other is a perfect yin-yang of black and white energy. White mana exactly like Bahamut's has eaten through the wall on one side, while some sort of . . . liquid drips over the walls, black and carrying the endless stars. If that's an ally, that'll be an easier escape than I could hope for. Even as the thought crosses my mind, I'm acutely aware that I have gotten lucky exactly once in the last eleven years. Luck is not my friend.

Markus is still whimpering, and his begging finally gets through to me. Whatever is happening, he would rather die than live through it. And killing him is exactly what I plan to do.

"Thank you, Bahamut. Glad you changed your mind about me," I say as I take a step toward Markus. Bahamut catches my arm and stops me.

"Where are you going?" she asks, and I look back.

"I don't torture people. If someone like him is begging for death, I'm going to give it to him," I answer. She points toward the mana and . . . Nexus energy, I guess, and shouts at me.

"Right now, those sages are focused on Markus! What do you think happens if he suddenly dies and we are still here?" I stare at the magic she is gesturing at.

"You know, I saw the white, uh, nothing mana and kinda hoped that was one of your friends," I respond. I then look back at Markus and realize the point is moot. The vines are . . . dissolving him, like Sara does. If that didn't kill the fucker, nothing I can do is going to. "You know what, you're right. Think we'd better bug out."

She scoffs. "You sound like a fucking sage," she grunts, but both of us run in the opposite direction. "What about you? Is that mess a friend of yours?" she asks. I look at the smoke we are running toward. Meanwhile, she scrapes at the scale I've lodged in her skin.

"Maybe," I guess. "Those bitches are around here somewhere, I'm sure. I wouldn't pick at that, by the way. A lot of gas in the area still." We make it to the gate she emerged from, opposite the attacking sages. A wave of white mana flies at us, and I'm prepared to really flex my creativity to find a way out when Bahamut steps in between the spell and me. And it dissipates immediately.

That's . . . interesting.

I don't waste time examining it, however. I can see two men flying in the distance, and we need to get out of sight now. "Sure they aren't your friends?" I ask as I grab the gate on either side, forcing it open with all my strength. It groans and complains, but it literally bends to my will, and we are slipping into the hallway behind it before the faces of our enemies come into focus. We don't stop there, however, as both of us sprint through the building, taking as many turns as we can.

The entire facility is in a panic, with everyone running toward the exit. There must be hundreds of people trying to leave. That must be where my friends are too. I look over my shoulder and picture the oozing stars and pale mana. For some reason, it feels safer to head deeper inside, so I turn to head further into the maze of a facility.

"Where the fuck are you going?" Bahamut asks, gesturing toward the exit.

"Too many people. If they are after us, we could get them caught in the crossfire," I answer. She hesitates for a moment before cursing and following me.

"I'm growing to really dislike you," she whispers as we run past a few fleeing bystanders and make our way farther and farther from any sign of people. "Do you have a plan for how to run deeper *inside* and still get out?"

"Still putting one together, thanks. I wasn't actually expecting an assault on the full colosseum," I respond, then I glance back at her. "Stop picking at the scale," I repeat.

"Great. Glad you gave Markus what was coming to him, or I would find this whole situation profoundly irritating," she hisses.

"We roll with the punches," I respond, then rapidly halt, grabbing her shoulder and stopping us both. Only inches in front of us, the wall to our right explodes as pure energy tears a new hallway through the building. I pull Bahamut to the side, using the remaining wall as concealment. Her eyes bulge at me.

"How did you see that coming?" she asks. I shrug, not to be flippant but because I genuinely don't know. I just . . . had a feeling I needed to stop or I would die.

Instead of answering her, I gently smack her hand away from her face.

"Stop fucking with the goddamned scale, dude," I chide. She looks at her hand, completely baffled.

"Why do you care so much?" she whispers as we both catch our breath, waiting until it feels safe to move on.

"I fill the scales with mana," I answer. "When I pull them off, they maintain the effect. That one is full of air mana. It's creating a bubble around your entire body which will protect you if I have to use poison gas again. Besides, you'll get an infection." She shakes her head, and it looks like she is going to respond, but I feel an urgent need to run. Whoever attacked isn't looking, and it won't be safe here forever. I grab her arm and pull her across the huge opening leading straight back to the arena.

Two men seem to be arguing, but neither is looking, exactly as I suspected. For three agonizing seconds, we are completely exposed to our enemies. The air feels like condemnation as it prickles my skin, but we make it past unnoticed.

"You're insane," Bahamut whispers.

"So they tell me," I respond, looking straight at a wall in another direction. I don't know when it happened, but at some point, I decided on a destination. It's a terrible idea; I don't know why I want to go there. But I do. I start channeling light mana, creating my radar spell to look in the direction of our ultimate goal. It's deep in the building, and as I hoped, there is no one around. "Bahamut, can you use that weird mana to tunnel through this way?"

"Void," she says. "Why?"

"Can you just trust me?" I ask. The earth shakes under our feet, and she groans before summoning a massive amount of mana and firing it through the wall in front of us, as well as a few walls behind that. The destruction is complete, like there had never been an obstacle in the first place. "Damn." I whistle. "Gonna call that the Baha Blast. Come on, let's go." She rolls her eyes at me but complies.

From here it's a straight shot to the room I'm aiming for, and we just have to deal with the anxiety that we will be blindsided by another massive attack. I'm not sure what is stopping them from throwing magic indiscriminately, but they could start again at any moment.

"So," I say as we run. "Void mana. That makes sense. So that sage back there . . ." I start, then Bahamut and I speak at the same time, with me trailing only a little behind. "My father, yes," she acknowledges. I am in the middle of saying "the Void Sage" but stop halfway.

"Wait, what was yours?" I ask. "Fuck."

"Fuck," she agrees.

A moment later and we are at the strangely anachronistic door. A moment after that, there is no door, and we run into Markus's home. "Made it." I gasp. She looks around incredulously.

"What now?" she asks. I actually don't know, but I feel relieved to be here. I feel like I am close to safety, but the safety promised by that feeling seems like a pretty shitty idea.

"I'm not sure," I respond honestly. She gapes at me.

"Do you remember the first thing I ever said to you?" she asks.

"*Moron*," I answer. She nods.

"After spending more time with you and getting to know you better, I want you to know I have not reconsidered."

I am about to respond when our luck runs out. One moment we are alone, and the next two sages stand in the room with us. Two men. "Oh, Jesus fucking Christ," I swear. This was not the surprise I needed today. The sage I don't recognize lifts his arm, only for the Void Sage to catch it.

"Let me take Riley first, then kill Annie," he says. The other sage glares at him.

"I have little patience for this, Rowan," he dismisses.

"I'm not going anywhere with you," Riley, apparently, responds. Kind of a gentle name for such a badass, honestly.

"But her you'll go with," Rowan sneers. "You will never fail to keep disappointing me. It seems this lesson wasn't harsh enough. If you don't want the next to be worse, come with me now. You know this woman needs to die, and she needs to die now. I can't stop the Original forever."

I glare at the man, years of resentment boiling up. *Rowan*. Cute. How very *Pokémon* of him.

Safety. I get the feeling of safety.

"It is time for her to die and stop holding us back," the Original Sage growls. "Deal with your family drama when it's handled."

"I will deal with my family how I please," Rowan responds.

"If memory serves, that mostly consists of getting divorced," I quip. "And having your calls screened by your adult children, I guess." It feels safe. I will be safe.

Rowan smirks while Riley looks down at me with irritation. I shrug at the latter. I didn't lie; I just didn't know I actually did have a personal vendetta against her dad. Rowan takes a step forward.

"And if my memory serves," he responds, "the last time we met, you offered to let me wear your testicles on my chin." He looks me up and down. "How are you feeling about that attitude now, moments from your death?"

I shrug again. "I mean, the offer is still out there. Flattered you've been thinking about it all this time, actually. Might have to take a rain check though. Hey, Riley, trust me one last time?"

Rowan's smile falls, and Riley looks between me and the sages.

"I'd really rather not, but fine," she agrees. "Anything is better than going with him."

I smile. "Keep those pearly whites clean and that breath fresh for me, *Rowan*. I'll follow through on my promise next time."

Suddenly, the atmosphere changes. The Original realizes what I'm about to do and starts to form some kind of spell, but I grab Riley with my right arm and throw both of us back into Markus's window just as that same pure energy starts forming right in front of us. I use my left hand to flip the pair off as we disappear into the black stone.

CHAPTER THIRTY-EIGHT

Stone

Safety. That was what I was promised if I entered this stone, the one Markus clearly used to dispose of undesirables. I don't know who made such a promise or how, but I know I believe it. It's not like the control of divine magic; not exactly. It's more like when I feel grief nearby, like raw emotion flowing through me in a torrent. Which is why I trusted it.

On a visceral level, I understood this emotion couldn't be a lie. Even as the black stone ripples around me like ice water, even as the world dissolves around me, and even as the emptiness tries to consume my mind, I believe it. I don't know how, but this is our way out.

My hand grips Riley's arm, and I pull her closer to me. It feels like we are falling but going nowhere. Emotion collapses on me like ancient wood, battering my mind in every direction it can. There is the promise of safety, but there is also hurt, and fear, and confusion. The deep feeling of betrayal—but an aimless betrayal, like a child when they fall and don't understand why it hurts. All it violently tears an aching grief from every part of me, and my very marrow throbs with empathy for the source. It's a secondhand guilt, not granted by anything I could possibly change, but by a knowledge of wrongness so pervasive that I can't help but feel shame for existing alongside it.

I breathe in the intense feelings and let them flow just beneath my skin. My bones ache with it, and yet, I feel safe. In a way, it makes me safe just with its presence. At first, I feel like a stone in rapids, carried with the intensity of the emotion and knowing I belonged to it as long as it willed. Then, I feel as if I am welcomed by it, embraced. It needs me, like a tumor needs a scalpel. It's trying to communicate with me—it has *always* been trying to communicate with me, but I've never been close enough to touch before. I can feel this in its longing. Its relief. Her relief.

She doesn't know how to speak to me. I don't know if she can speak at all. It feels as if she has no use for words or doesn't understand their purpose. I instinctively understand her as *she*, but I don't know how or why. I don't think she is exactly a person; this torrent of raw feeling might be everything she is. Just vibrant and boundless curiosity, and every passion it has ever led to.

She is exuberant at my presence, like I'm water in a world that lost it. She is joy, then she is bafflement, then betrayal and agony. Misery for so long. She doesn't understand time, but she knows suffering. I'm not certain if lack of a temporal sense is better or worse, with how long this pain has defined her. Then blind desperation, the feeling of broken nails on a coffin's lid, suffocation and aimless attempts to break free.

Then sunlight—fiery red and obsidian black—crawling through the cracks of hopelessness and offering help. Sara—and me. She is telling me a story, her story and mine. She can't give me the details. I don't think she knows them herself, if she really knows anything at all. She is like the energy in a room, the cloud that informs you of the mood without a word. But she is not less than sapient. She may be more; I can't tell. But she is a gentle breeze and a violent storm, lacking any desire for control or gratification. Just . . . knowledge. Knowledge of me. Of Sara. Of everyone, everywhere.

I don't know when it happened, but our feet are on solid ground. I still hold Riley, who is trembling in anxiety and relief all at once. The world is lit by stars, not from the sky but from that same oily desecration the Void Sage had poured over the arena walls. It drips over trees and pools around the hurricane lilies at their base. This is the Radiant Woods . . . but it also isn't. I can feel the grief of the woods to the same level and with the same associated well of power, but this grief has only one source: *Her.* This is like a reflection of the Radiant Woods. Or maybe the woods are a reflection of this.

"Where are we?" Riley asks, shuddering at the sight of her father's power soaking the world around us. As soon as she asks, we find ourselves wading through fatigue. Not our own but hers. It is the weariness of a long journey, and one to a sorrowful destination. We both understand this as an answer.

"But I can't feel anyone else here . . ." I wonder aloud. I know other people were abandoned here only a week ago. I offer my confusion like she offers her grief, and she answers with loss, deep and layered. "Oh. This is how they do it, isn't it?" Resignation and acceptance swallow me.

"Do what?" Riley asks, and I sigh, an aching in my throat threatening a loss of emotional control.

"I've never understood it. The purpose. Well, at least what the Collector—or the Original or whatever you want to call him—got out of it. I suppose I know why people complied, but where I'm from, people are fed to the Radiant Woods. The Nexus. They are tortured there, devoured, forced to live, but only a life of agony chosen for them by a creature who loathes them.

"In Potestia, these people were simply brought there directly, but the same clearly happens in the Republic. You can tell by the comfort, the buildings with no ramps, the lack of braille or an equivalent on library plaques. The public benches, free of bars. The clean streets and the perfect clothes. Just like in Potestia, the people society wants to forget are disposed of. Even more groups of them, it seems. I'm surprised by the ones they left behind. Anyway, I suspect they are disposed of in the same way.

"The sages, they fear the Nexus; fear the Original, I think. But they also seem to work with him. I never understood how they delivered their . . . sacrifices. I hadn't had time to investigate it yet, but this is how. It's connected, somehow, to the Radiant Woods, and it's used to deliver them.

"That's why these . . . stones exist at every border. It links them, allows the sages to throw out the garbage without risk to themselves. The perfect arrangement. Disposal of the people they look down on most from the comfort of their own homes. Although, I suppose it's probably not in the literal home of most. Markus just enjoyed watching, I suspect. He enjoyed pain. Either way, this is how they do it," I explain. Riley takes a sharp breath.

"This place . . . it belongs to them. I can feel it; I can see it. It stinks of my father. We are in danger; we have to get out. Lillith, it's not safe here. This place is theirs. They can reach us without even touching us," Riley whispers, a mild tremor in her voice. We feel injury, like vindictive words from a close friend, then safety again. I understand it immediately.

"No. This place is no one's," I reply. A rush of relief and agreement washes over us, then that feeling of wrongness returns. "This place can't be owned, just abused. It shouldn't exist at all. It is a ship in a bottle: expression in its purest form, caged by glass and a narrow exit. But one thing is for sure: Whatever level of control they have over this place, the cowards wouldn't dare face us right now. Not directly. Not when their victims can share their grief with me."

I flare my mana as I say this, and the world bends around me, creaking like an aged floorboard under the pressure of my current power. Riley's eyes widen and she gasps like I've just punched her in the gut.

"No wonder they call you a demon queen," she mutters.

I shrug. "Perhaps. Either way, your father has a yellow belly, Riley. Always has. He won't come within a thousand miles of me while I'm here. And the Original? Well, he's tried before, and he knows he can't hurt me—or anyone with me—in this state. It's why he tried to kill us when I threw us in," I reply.

"Anyone with you?" she asks. "He's a sage, and one of the most powerful, Lillith. You may be protected somehow, but he can take my mind from me in a moment. How am I safe?" Spring dances around us, or the feeling of it. The expression of gentle breezes and quiet nights watching the stars. Reassurance.

I consider her question. I have been here before, without Sara and with the twins. Or at least, I have been in the actual Nexus, which is extremely similar. The Collector never took Autumn or August's minds, but . . . his priests did. I know he directed us together to make me more vulnerable, but he could still have controlled them.

Actually, his priests shouldn't have been able to control them. Not without his help. I think back to Peter's story, how he regained his mind when approaching the woods but lost it again upon entering. The stronger power washed it away but returned when he entered. The twins only fell under the influence of divine magic when the priests were around. Maybe . . . it's the other way around. Maybe he can't control his victims without the priests. Maybe he needs them. But then the monsters . . . *aren't directly controlled.* Instead, they are offered incentives. Death in exchange for attacking me.

"No. He can't," I reply. "I don't know why, but he can't. Not on his own." Certainty and victory erupt around us like geysers, confirming my guess. Riley can feel it too; I can see it on her face and in the way she relaxes her muscles, just a little. She sighs.

"I guess I don't have an option but to hope that's true," she replies. "But . . . what do we do now?"

I turn. I feel ice and winter and loneliness. Almost every direction I turn reeks of failure and forgotten corners. *Almost.* As I continue shifting, excitement assaults me: Hope. A violent hope that burns through me and urges me forward.

"We go that way, I suppose," I respond. Riley seems to agree, so we walk. And walk. And walk. "So," I finally say as the weight of silence starts to crush me, "you want to tell me about what happened with your father? You don't have to, but you are welcome to."

She flinches, and I regret asking, but she nods a moment later. "Everything you know about him will help you kill him," she agrees. Nevertheless, it still takes a moment before she speaks again. "My father . . . My father has a lot of children; some born from him, others stolen from their families, but he has a lot of children. Or rather, he has a lot of sons."

I wince. "Sounds familiar." She nods.

"He is only interested in sons, apprentices, people to carry on his name. He's been around for a long, long time, and he has many sons, but no daughters. None but me," she continues. That confuses me a bit. How long could he possibly have been around? I just got here eighteen years ago; he shouldn't have been around any longer than that.

"And he uses the Nexus to avoid having daughters?" I guess. She shakes her head then pauses, looking at the filth of his magic as it poisons the plants around us.

"In a way, but not like you are thinking. His Nexus energy is not good for creating, or even changing a creation. It is the power of emptiness, of the void. And his only mana aspect is the same. He can't directly manipulate us like that, and the Original would kill him if he tried. That is one of several things the sages are forbidden from doing if they want to keep the peace. No, his method is far simpler. The very thing you described before, actually. If he has a daughter, he simply disposes of them—through one of these places, I suppose," she answers.

I don't reply. The next question is obvious enough that it doesn't need to be asked.

"Like I said, my father has a lot of sons; too many to pay any special attention to any of them. And my mother, well, she knew what would happen when she had a daughter. Her doctor knew as well, and neither was willing to watch it happen. I was dressed as a boy, treated and trained as a son. My father's visits were rare enough and my mother's staff caring enough that we managed to hide it. For a while. An entire childhood, a gift I will always cherish. I was trained to use my father's void mana and pushed to grow strong. To be the very picture of masculinity, or whatever definition Rowan has for it. All to feed the illusion . . .

"But I did too well. I grew too strong, too skilled; better than any of his sons with mana or steel. I started to get too much attention and praise, and my father finally noticed me. *Riley* is a gentle name, but an ambiguous one. I hoped to keep him in the dark, but . . . he grew too involved. He wanted to parade me around as a trophy, and he did exactly that. I was an extension of his prestige. But any well-used object will eventually crumble; any paint will fade and chip if handled too often, left in the sun too long. And well, after nearly two years of his orders, the cracks started to show. I was found out, publicly, and he was . . ." She trails off.

"Furious?" I guess. She offers a single humorous laugh.

"Worse. He was humiliated. He was ashamed, and it was my fault. I never saw my mother after that; I could never convince him to tell me where she was. Here, I guess. But me? He wanted to make an example out of me; a public example to all the mothers of all his other children. To all his sons. And so, I became a slave. Still paraded. Still used. No longer to inspire praise but fear," she finishes. We walk in silence for long enough that I'm certain the Cliff Notes are all I'm getting.

"That sounds disgustingly like him," I finally mutter. She looks over at me with a raised eyebrow.

"What about you? What's your history with him? Why is he so afraid of you, who didn't even know he was the Void Sage until you saw his face?"

I take a deep breath through my nose and look around at the dark, empty landscape. The eternal night which mirrors the day of the Radiant Woods. The dripping stars. I scratch the shaved side of my head as I think for a moment, then I shrug.

"Yeah, all right," I agree. "Your father—Rowan now, I guess—I've met him before, if only once in person. On the day I died. Although, at the time, he went by *Oakley*."

CHAPTER THIRTY-NINE

Annie and Oakley

Annie

I have a bad feeling about this one, Aran. Something just feels . . . off," Amy said, her terse voice crackling through my earpiece. I was really fucking pissed to hear she was getting the same energy from this excursion as I was. Especially since I was already on the fortieth floor of the fucking building.

"Shit. I was hoping that was just me," I responded, groaning inwardly. I couldn't even put my finger on why, but the whole operation had the stink of death. And not just because that was the entire point.

The confirmation that her trepidations were shared was all she needed. "We can still pull out, head back to the hotel. I'll draw a bath for you, cover the place with fuckin' rose petals. We can make a day of it. But this . . . this feels wrong, Aran. I'm scared," she answered. That sent a chill down my spine. Amy was never scared. Never. Not without the presence of very real danger. And she'd suggested anything romantic even less frequently; as in, that time alone. I glanced over my shoulder as my heart rate rose. Fuck.

I could feel the cameras crawling over me from their little domes on the ceiling. Amy had turned them off from the van, but somehow, I could still feel them.

Oakley was responsible for so much pain, so much death. The world deserved a chance to move on without him. But I trusted Amy. She didn't have some supernatural ability, but she did have a keen eye and a sharp subconscious. She'd picked up on something, even if she didn't know what. So had I. Trusting that instinct had always kept us alive before.

There were still no guards. Oakley wouldn't risk himself, even for a trap, and Amy had confirmed he was here. Still, there should be at least one guard on patrol, especially as individual cameras faltered briefly one at a time. I knew guards tended to ignore the cameras, but . . . it didn't sit right. Oakley had refused to appear in public, sleeping somewhere in the building, even.

No one else had been this terrified of me or had reacted with this much caution. We already hated that we'd had to go there to get to him; it was far more secure and took a lot more effort to get into, mostly on Amy's part, which meant if she wanted to back out, forcing her to do all it again another day, she was more on edge than I'd ever seen her. More afraid than I'd ever seen her.

"Yeah," I agree. "We need to regroup; I feel it too. Watch my back, Valentine. I'm headed to you," I responded using her call sign, sourced from a video game the same as mine. She sighed in relief, loud enough for the speaker to pick it up. Neither of us was fond of this, and both of us were ready to bolt like a rabbit at the first sign of trouble.

"Thank Christ," she replied. "Get back here as quickly as you can." I dutifully turned on my heel and complied, my heart beating faster and harder. I'd done this a dozen times and never had nerves like that. To this day, I don't know how we figured it out, how we realized, but I returned to the elevator with a brisk walk.

I needed to calm my nerves, so I whispered to my friend as I walked. "Rose petals? When the fuck did you become a romantic? I thought you chose *Valentine* to be ironic," I teased, not to actually get under her skin but to distract both our pounding hearts. She understood this immediately and chuckled nervously.

"No, romance is still well outside my palate, but I know you like it, and I really want you the fuck out of there," she responded honestly. She did continue with a more lighthearted tone, however, following my lead. "Besides, we both know we never would have made it to either a flower shop or the bath."

I choked back a nervous but amused chuckle. She wasn't wrong. With adrenaline like that in our veins, we wouldn't have had the patience for romance even if we had such a relationship. "Fair enough," I agreed. "I can be sappy, and I'll acknowledge that proudly. On the other hand, I'm a bit too anxious to be hot and bothered either. How about we get a drink instead?"

"Fuck," she whispered in response.

"Bit of a one-track mind, huh?" I joked nervously.

"I've been made. Aran, get the fuck out of there!" she warned, pure panic in her voice. "Use the stairwell, don't bother hiding. They know you're there; they're evacuating Oakley already. The elevators are locked down. Shit, I have to find a new spot. I'm going dark for a while; I'll come back for you, just . . . get out. I'll . . . I'll see you soon." My heart sank, and my stomach twisted.

The stairwell. I was forty floors up—forty fucking floors. If it was that bad, if Amy had to run . . . I wasn't getting out of there alive.

"A—" I started, before she could disconnect. "Valentine. Just get out of here. You know as well as I do that there's only one option left."

She was quiet for a moment, but the silence carried novels of understanding. "Annie," she replied, the use of my real name an acknowledgement that hiding my identity was pointless. "I'm so sorry. I'll come back for you, just in case. But . . . send him to hell."

"I will," I agreed, pausing only briefly before whispering, "Goodbye. Thanks for everything."

Her response was whispered in a low-enough range I could barely hear the strangled cry behind it. "Goodbye, Annie." Then the line went dead, and I never spoke to Amy again.

I knew I was going to die. Or at least be arrested and, eventually, get the death penalty. Legally, I'd been named a "terrorist," which didn't really apply, but it's a label that would give them options if they caught me alive. Which meant I would only have the chance to do one last thing for the world, and with that chance, I intended to scrub that stain of a man from its surface.

I kicked off my heels and rushed to the executive elevator, the same I'd used to get to that floor. It was direct, and I'd only been able to use it once Amy had wormed her way into the building's security system. It would also be where the private rent-a-cops brought Oakley to evacuate him. It would be smarter to lock him down somewhere, but he'd be too terrified to stay on the same floor as me. He'd demand to leave, and Amy had confirmed the evacuation attempt herself.

I ran past the comically large offices and failed to avoid the perfectly functional cameras. I had no time, and it didn't matter anymore. I pulled my pistol from my suit coat as I moved, knowing I may not have the extra time to pull it when I caught up. I only had the one magazine, and knew if I got into a situation where I needed more, I was already dead. So, I pulled out a hand taser as well. It wasn't much, but it would have to do.

Rounding a corner, I saw them through the half-glass walls of an empty conference room. I ducked as soon as I did, creeping to the corner and peering around. Their backs were turned. This was my chance.

I moved as quickly as I could while remaining quiet, an easier task when wearing stockings than heels. I was dressed in an outfit chosen to blend in and offer a plausible excuse for my presence if I was caught. Also, an outfit not designed for active pursuit or for walking while crouched, considering the pencil skirt. I'd have chosen a pantsuit, but skirts were apparently an unwritten requirement, at least on this floor. But I'd chosen a flexible enough material, and at least I was quiet.

Finally, I was close enough. I hadn't been noticed, thanks to the cover of a room full of cubicles. I wasn't as strong back then; I had no mana and no steel arm, but I was a good shot. Security flanked my target, but they were preparing to turn, and when they did, I would have a few seconds with a clear line of sight on him. A few seconds to become his ending.

I would die as soon as I did; I knew that. Those guards would turn their weapons on me, and I'd have nowhere to run. But after everything he'd done, it was worth it. He and I were both about to die.

I blew a curl out of my face as I aimed, leading the shot a bit to account for his movement.

Rapidly, they reached the turning point, and I took a deep breath, placing just the first pad of my right index finger on the trigger. I used my left hand to steady the gun as I hid half my body behind a cubicle. I measured my breathing, timing it so I could pause after exhaling at the exact moment I had a clear line of sight on him.

Then it came, and . . . it was the wrong man. *Shit. Shit shit shit.* That word rang through my head over and over. A fucking decoy. I ducked behind the cubicle, but it was too late. I'd been on the cameras this entire time, and someone had been watching the decoy group. I got too close, and it quickly became clear they had spotted me as gunshots rang out around me. Bullets ripped through the cubicle I was hiding behind and forced adrenaline through my veins.

I crouched, moving as quickly as I could. I had concealment, but not true cover. A voice came over my earpiece, but it wasn't Amy's.

"There you are," the familiar voice teased. I recognized it immediately from a thousand videos, interviews, and deranged podcasts. The man I'd gone there to kill was speaking directly to me. "Annie Beckett, is that right? Not who I expected to finally come for me, but it's no matter. The game is up. I was never there. You are trapped with no one but my security team, and you will die for nothing. What a waste of a decent body and child-bearing hips. You'd have found more success as a mother, I think. You and Amelia Marriner. Yes. We know who she is. We know where she is. And we're going to kill her too."

I didn't respond. They may have had me on camera, but the guards firing in my direction didn't need the aid of my voice. Panic tried to grip me as he mentioned Amelia's name, but I knew he was lying about at least one thing. I had to hope he was lying about knowing where to find her too. I didn't want to think about how he got our names, or about how he was speaking through our secure line, but I knew one thing for sure:

He was there. Whatever he said, I knew that much.

This was no trap; not at first. If it was, a SWAT team would have been systematically clearing the floor, with guards on every exit. They certainly wouldn't have needed a decoy. He was there, and he was watching me, trying to draw me away from him, to incite a direct confrontation with security or even an escape attempt, further distancing myself from him whether I died or not. It wouldn't work.

The world cried out around me with exploding gunfire and office debris. They were going to close in on me sooner rather than later; cubicles aren't known for their complex structure, and I wasn't even inside them. But I knew where to go. Not every computer in the building would have the software necessary to watch the cameras, and the security office was on the ground level, which left one obvious place. Well, two, but one was too obvious.

I had to risk it. I had to run. I fired a couple rounds backward, toward my opponents, buying myself precious seconds to run back to the hallway I'd come from. I hadn't bought enough time, however, as I barely managed to make it before their return fire rang out through the building.

They shattered the conference room glass, and I screamed as a bullet tore into my left shoulder, but I kept running, even as my stockings were torn by the glass I had to run over. Every step was agony. My left arm was losing strength, and the taser I held with it was growing heavier.

"Now, where exactly do you think you're going? Do you think running will save you?" Oakley asked, failing to keep the slight tremor from his voice. Yeah, he was there all right, and he was exactly where I expected, growing worried as I ran right to him.

My head was getting lighter as I bled. All I could think was, *Fuck, this is a shit show*. I growled through the pain as I ran, desperately wanting to stop and pull the glass from my feet, but I couldn't. I left red stains with every step, blood running down my arm. I started to feel sick, but I wouldn't stop. I had to take extra turns, running the long way around to stay out of the line of sight of my pursuers, but I was almost there.

An officer's weapon flagged past a corner just as I reached it, his hands extending into view before he turned the corner. I didn't have time to aim carefully nor steady my hand, but I was much closer, enough that I could almost reach out and grab him. Almost. But I couldn't risk hand-to-hand combat, not in that body, and not in that state. Instead, I fired a round directly into his hand, knocking the weapon away and finally drawing someone else's blood and screaming into the fight. I didn't stop there, crying out in pain as I forced my left arm up and jammed the taser into his neck just as we both rounded the corner.

It knocked him flat, although the effect wouldn't last long. I grabbed his gun from the ground and tucked it into the back of my irritating, seemingly ripped skirt. When he recovered, I'd have the advantage if I needed it. If I hadn't made it to Oakley yet.

"Leave now, or I'll make sure you die slowly!" Oakley screamed into my ear. "I will wear your fucking entrails around my neck as a tie, I swear to God!" His screaming could do nothing. I'd found it: the door to his vice president's office. I remembered it from the map Amy had drawn for me. Not his office—he'd be at least smart enough not to stay there—but the only other room with executive access to security cameras. At least the only one he could get to quickly.

I responded to him for the first time. "How about you wear my testicles on your chin instead," I offered, then fired a round into the door. I'd fired four rounds total at that point, with eleven left in the magazine. I didn't know how many were in the gun I'd taken, but eleven would be enough.

I slammed my right shoulder into the door, bursting into the room, and there he was. Oakley the coward, Oakley the soon to be dead, standing behind a desk and in front of a massive window. I had *seconds* before I took a bullet to the back. Oakley tried to raise his own gun, but fumbled it, instead only holding defensive hands up to me as his iron fell loudly to the desk. He wore agonized panic like you and I wear scars.

I pulled the trigger. There was no chance of missing. He was right in front of me, and I was aiming for the head. Less than a second later, before the glass was even finished shattering from my own shot, a bullet tore into my back. This sent me spinning and filled my mouth with blood. I was losing vision, losing consciousness. Then another hit me, and another. I stumbled, catching myself on the desk. Oakley was gone. I thought he was on the ground; I tried to find him, and stumbled closer to the now shattered window.

I don't know how many times I was shot after that. I stopped feeling them. There was more than one shooter—I am certain of that. All I know is I was in pain, I was bleeding, then I was falling, and falling, and falling. I don't remember hitting the ground. I don't know whether the fall killed me or if I died on the ground; I'm pretty sure it was the impact. But it was over, and the only consolation I had was that I got to shoot Oakley first.

After that, there was no time at all, but there were also seven gentle years. Seven years of calm and family. Only an instant, and an entire childhood—two conflicting perspectives. My death was both a fresh and old wound, but mostly old. As sudden as it was, it felt like it had long healed an instant after it happened. The wound of my sudden death had already turned to an old scar when I felt a sudden, sharp, and all-consuming cold, like I had been thrown into a bath of ice water.

CHAPTER FORTY

Tantalus

Ember

Sound tears through the air as Lillith fights in the arena. I can only hope she isn't stupid enough to fool around this time; hate it as I might, I need her to fight the sages. And for some reason I don't fully understand, I want the sages dead more than anything.

Again, that building pressure stabs through my head, like a constant, physical anxiety I can't place. It builds and builds and builds, and I can only express it through constant anger. It's not right. It's not supposed to be rage—or not just rage. It's something else I can't reach but desperately need, and I live in thirst for it—and in fear of it—every day, drinking what little I can extract from my hatred for everyone and everything.

Grief. It's supposed to be grief; I know that now. Lillith and Autumn wax on about it so much I could hardly forget. The name, at least, because that's all it is to me: a name. I can't identify the emotion the word is meant to describe any more than I can picture a color I've never seen from its name alone. Except that isn't right, because I *have* felt grief. I felt it when Sarafyna and Lillith pulled it from me like clean water from the spine of a fish. I felt it as a child. I started to feel it, slowly, on the other side of the border, with every new home Lillith brought me to, every hour I spent away from the Council Lands and the Republic and near Sarafyna.

I know because I remember wearing red, tired eyes, and the throbbing of a tired body after a night of shivering with sobs. I remember something turning my head from the inside and changing my mind. But all these memories are blood from a numb wound. I can't grasp the actual feeling that caused them. I can't wrap my mind around it. As soon as it fades, the memory of it fades as well, every time.

But I can feel its absence. I can feel the pressure like the swelling of a welt. I can feel the need for it, even if I don't remember it. I am desperate for it, but it recedes whenever I reach out to embrace it, leaving me with nothing but hollow, directionless rage, now largely pointed at the sages. I can't remember why—my mind isn't my own—but I remember the certainty that they deserve it, and I will let that carry me.

"Where do you think you're going?" an ailur guard calls as I brazenly open the door to the announcer's box. This room is actually inside and nearly at ground level, housing the announcer and half a dozen sound and light mages. They watch the fight through thick, enchanted one-way glass while powering the artifacts used to broadcast the fight to the crowd. I can see through the glass even from the doorway, and groan as I realize Lillith is no longer fighting gladiators but Markus himself. I have to hurry; she will almost definitely die here if we don't create an out for her now.

I pull out a ribbon I haven't worn since I was captured by Sara and flash it at the guard.

"Ember, Guardian of Stone; it's an emergency," I reply coolly. This immediately shuts the guard up, and the men and women inside freeze as they hear my voice. The announcer turns around nervously but wears a mask of confidence.

"We aren't at the border. What does a guardian want with us here?" he questions. I nod toward the fight, directing his attention to the dumbass currently wrapped in Nexus vines.

"Did the Gladiator Sage tell you this was a publicity stunt or something? Can't you see that she's actually managed to injure him?" I chide. He looks back at the fight as I continue. "That in there is the actual Lillith, the actual queen of demons."

"And she is about to die," the announcer counters. "So I repeat, what is a guardian doing here, interfering with a sage's affairs?" He seems to be growing more confident as the shock of my arrival wears off. I need to press, now.

"He didn't hire you for your wits, did he?" I sneer. "She's not famous for being a demon. The legends and prophecies don't warn of a lone woman competing in a public arena for sport. They tell a story about a woman with an army and a chimera on a leash, and you have been advertising their leader's capture for a week." His face pales as the realization settles on his shoulders.

"B-but she came here alone. The sage said she'd have attacked with her army already if she could, but she didn't!" he insists. I shake my head.

"Demons don't fight in an open field. They are cowards, treacherous. They don't attack combatants but innocents! The Gladiator Sage is right but wrong at the same time. I was sent here by the Void Sage himself. Her army is here already, and they plan to attack. She is here as a distraction, while her minions kill everyone in the stands as an act of terror," I explain. Now the faces of the other human mages pale, as a volu's feathers begin to molt and the ailur guard's hackles rise.

"But there are four other sages here; they'll protect everyone! Her army can't handle four sages!" he protests further, but I shake my head.

"They are focused on supporting the Gladiator Sage and preventing further interference like last week's. These attacks, they'll have killed us all before the sages know to shift their attention. You need to order an evacuation, or everyone dies!" I insist, starting to grow irritated as the mages in the room look at each other skeptically. But, just in time, the twins actually come through; not completely useless, after all. It took them longer than discussed, but the smell of smoke starts to fill the air.

A moment later, the noise outside the room grows louder, and the sound of panicked voices can be made out. "Order the evacuation before it's too late!" I scold, lecturing the fool of a man. My words are followed quickly by a scream, indicating a greater level of effectiveness than I expected, and the room finally shifts gears as the announcer calls for an evacuation.

"E-everyone, this is an emergency announcement: we need all viewers to make their way to the nearest exit in an orderly fashion," he begins, speaking into a whisper sphere that broadcasts his voice to the entire arena. I'd like a bigger distraction with a little more panic, but Lillith would probably throw a fit if anyone got hurt from too urgent an evacuation. I roll my eyes and turn to leave so I can contribute to the confusion, but then I pause.

Markus doesn't respond at all.

"Can they not hear you in the arena?" I ask. The announcer shakes his head.

"I-I didn't think you'd want the demon queen to hear," he protests, and I growl. Markus hearing is half the point; I need to give her a chance to escape. Except . . . she seems to have the upper hand now. I tilt my head, narrowing my pupils as she escapes the vines and attacks Markus again. *Is one of her half-assed plans actually working to kill a sage?* I almost can't believe it, except I'm saving her for a reason, I suppose. Somehow, it remains an irritating thought.

I'm about to bully the man into announcing the evacuation so Lillith can hear when a new type of vine, or tree root, or something of the sort grabs both combatants and an explosion of white mana and black Nexus energy obliterates a huge chunk of the arena wall.

The Void Sage is here.

Autumn

My heart races as August keeps watch. He and I have been so distracted these last few days, trying to track down any information we can on the theft of grief, we've had to rely on Ember's planning for today, a fact the angry cat chided us for the entire way here. It's a better plan than I could have come up with, and one which reveals great trust for Lillith under all that contempt.

She expects, if given enough opportunity and distraction, that Lillith will make it back to her gate on her own, and we can meet her there. She thought of a disguise and some kind of perfume or something we apparently need to avoid ailur guards, as well as a dozen other details. August and I only have one part to play, and I'm not certain we are up for it.

I take a deep breath as I wedge the enchanted stones she's given us into the cracks of long-faded stone on the exterior wall. Apparently, with a little fire mana, these will explode. Fire just happens to be my specialty, especially since Lily taught me how to combine aspects to maintain it with less mana. I'm still a weak mage, especially for the standard I have seen in the Republic, but if Ember had forgotten that, she'd have stopped reminding me of it so frequently. It must detonate with very little.

"Are we sure about this?" August asks as I stand fully and start walking in the other direction. I feel like I'm made of tree bark with the rigidity of my movements, an ailment unique to times when I'm trying to look casual. I sigh, pulling Lillith's glasses from my bag. She tends to use goggles more, which means she left these in her pack.

"We have to try something," I respond nervously. "And at least we can make sure there are no casualties."

"Can we though?" he presses. "We couldn't exactly test these out to see how wide the explosion was. I don't want to hurt anyone, and Lillith will shit if we get a bystander killed while helping her." The colorful metaphor actually stokes a dying ember inside me; a fond amusement at my friend. The woman I'd hoped would be my sister of a sort. I give him a half smile.

"She really would." I chuckle, before the memories of her leaving us alone, leaving Henry to die, drown the charm of the thought. My feeble smile falls into a weary rest. "I don't want to hurt anyone either, which is why we came here, where we can give the stones even more room than Ember suggested. There will be no one anywhere near us when they go off."

"But won't that defeat the purpose?" August worries. He's not wrong. Fewer people will panic when the far side of the wall takes a little aesthetic damage, but . . .

"It will have to do. No one will ever die to my thoughtlessness again. I'd rather do too little and need to try again than let anyone lose a loved one because of me," I respond. He nods in appreciation.

"I suppose so," he agrees, and I send my mana out with a burst to activate the stones. I look past all the confusing colors of the glasses, needing only the information that there is no one just on the other side of the wall I plan to detonate.

I've never been much of a combatant. It's not who I was raised to be, and magic was more of a signifier of my house's standing than anything back in Potestia. As such, it's a strain creating such a thin stream of fire over a distance. It needs to be controlled and subtle, so I have to use pure fire mana. Unlike Lily, my mana is no stronger now than when I was fourteen; only my control and skill have grown. It takes great focus and all the energy I have, and with every inch, I feel the temptation to waver.

August puts his hand on my shoulder and steadies me. He can't effectively offer me his mana, but the support alone runs through me like an electric shock. I bite my lip and push, picturing Lily's face; it makes me so angry and so desperate. As much as I don't want to see her, I miss her. After a week, I miss her. I count on her and I love her.

My muscles start to ache as the mana they usually carry drains from me. I get so angry when I see her because, of the people I have to blame for the death of my . . . It's easier to give her at least some of the anger. But it's always her voice I hear every morning—hers and Henry's—when the world seems too gray and empty to wade into. When my mind wanders back to that tower and the peace a step over the edge promised.

"What did you say?" August asks. I'm whispering it over and over. I didn't even realize. I'm almost there; I just need one more burst of energy.

"One more day," I say, just loud enough that my brother can hear me, then my mana makes contact and the enchantments ignite, lighting the entire world up with fire. At least, that's what it feels like this close to the explosion.

To Ember's credit, the blast is almost exactly as large as she said it would be, so much so that I worry our caution has made the distraction too small to warrant an evacuation. Perhaps any explosion will do, but with four sages on standby, they may decide to handle this without alerting the public. Of course, that's where Ember comes in. Still, there was a reason this part of the plan was necessary.

I don't worry long, however, as a series of companion explosions ring out moments later. Half a dozen of them, in fact. They are just like the one I caused, but . . . everywhere.

"W-what happened?" I ask. August looks at me wearing the same shocked confusion I do.

"D-did we do all that?" he responds with his own question.

"No, those were us," a man says from behind. I jump, pulling off the glasses, which likely would have warned me of his presence had I any practice with them. My brother and I both turn on our heels in an instant, gaping at the intruder. A tall, cocky man smirks at us. "Don't worry, we're on your side. We've had our eye on you for a while, especially the last few days. We're here to help," he continues, answering a few questions before we can ask. He leaves quite a few unanswered, however.

"Who are you?" I ask, unable to keep the fear from my voice. August grips my shoulder again, fully prepared to pull us away if needed.

"The Republic calls us cultists," he answers. "But we don't have any such organization. We like to think of ourselves as more of an . . . ideology. A bunch of like minds with the will to fight. And we'd like to fight with you, if you are interested." August and I share a look. For the first time in weeks, we have a conversation with our eyes alone.

We don't know if they were as careful as us. We don't know if every innocent person is safe. We do know that they ensured our plan was more effective. We don't know if we are safe. We do know that we need to get out of here and meet up with Lillith, and in this moment, we could use the help. And, if they are augmenting our plan and have been watching us, they likely want to free her as well, though they could want to free her in order to capture her themselves. On the other hand, Ember is counting on us, and these people are going to follow us whether we like it or not.

We look back at the interloper. Before we can come to a conclusion, there is another, massive explosion composed of white mana I can see erupt over the wall even from the other side of the colosseum. I have no idea what that is, and just the sight of it draws sweat from me. Even the stranger looks surprised, but suppresses it a moment later.

"We have to go save our friend," August says, rapidly coming to a decision as the situation grows more urgent. "We'd welcome more help with that, but that's where we are going either way."

I nod. I don't know if we can trust them, but we are already in the thick of it. We don't have time to interrogate each other, and we have to keep moving.

The man composes himself and smiles at us.

"We'd be happy to," he agrees, pulling out a whisper sphere and making a call. "Archer, I've made contact with the twins; we'll meet up on the way to the asset." I feel nervous with the sudden intrusion into our plan, looking at the excessive smoke in the sky. Lily will know what to do. August and I share one last apprehensive look, but as the man discusses the mana explosion neither of us caused over his sphere, we all silently agree to move, running to meet up with Ember at Lillith's gate.

I watch the stranger's back the entire way, my heart beating out of my chest. *Where did these people come from? How long had they been watching us? What do we do if we can't trust them and they attack Lily? Do we attract a sage and try to pit them against each other? Or will they both attack us? What if I am getting in over my head again? What if I am making the same mistake and, in an instant, August is just . . . gone?* What if, what if, what if. My breathing grows shallow as we run and run, jostling past a growing crowd of fleeing patrons.

I can't lose someone else, but what is the greater risk? Trusting these strangers or trying to do this on our own? *What if they waited until now to introduce themselves so we wouldn't have a choice but to work with them? "Watching us for a while"? What does that mean? How much danger are we in? What do we do?*

I keep picturing Henry's face, in that final moment. That resignation and all the guilt that followed. And then, in an instant and without warning, I feel empty, like something has been taken away from me. Some pain I don't understand and can't picture. Something foreign but familiar. Something I need.

My eyes dry and I grow numb, my panic receding in a single breath. I don't know what happened, but the sages finally got to me. I can't remember the feeling, but I know its name. My grief is gone.

CHAPTER FORTY-ONE

Rejection

???

I *should kill him. I should kill him here and now.* My skin shifts over the body I have chosen for the day like a thousand worms. Everything had gone perfectly. The first attack had drawn the other sages out, and the girl had managed to weaken the strongest of them and feed him to me. She'd had nowhere to run, even as I trapped the four minor sages to feed my little collector.

I can feel them even now, being digested; I grow stronger with each. Had I managed to kill the girl, it would have been a complete victory. I don't regret prioritizing the fleeing sagelings, leeches that they are, using my mother for their little fantasies. Consuming all them is the end goal, after all. Still. My hopes will never be truly realized while Sarafyna is spending all her energy on this girl. She needs to die: For my future. For Mirage. For Manara.

I had the girl; she was in my hands. But this pathetic, petty, waste of a man wanted to gloat, wanted to punish his daughter for helping. Had he not stopped me, I would be so much closer to the end of an ageless struggle with these fucking "sages."

"Well, that's irritating," Oakley laments. "I don't suppose you can get Riley back to me when you kill that bitch? I'd still like to speak with my daughter. We have unfinished business, after all."

I clench my fists and look at him, barely keeping my boiling soul from spilling out and melting the skin from his bones. I say nothing. He starts chuckling under his breath. "I know we couldn't kill her here like you planned, but this is so much better. You have her trapped in a disposal stone. You can kill her at your leisure, and even interrogate her first. All these years I've spent preparing for her, and you have her in a box like a cat in the rain! Can I come with you, actually? I want to see her squirm the same way she always hoped I would."

I take a deep breath to contain my rage. I want to kill him like I want to breathe. Every moment he lives feels like suffocating. But I can't. Not yet. I keep my voice level as I respond. "The stones are for the disposal of riffraff. Of fodder. They are so we can easily use those who will not be missed to gather and grow Nexus energy."

"Exactly. I can't think of a more fitting end for the woman who drove me to this backward world with her cruelty," he replies.

"When we had Sarafyna trapped, even I couldn't control her on my own. The first sage I've ever needed your help to contain, not just once but constantly. And she still escaped—because of the girl you just allowed to leave," I continue.

"All's well that ends well; we have her now." The dolt nods. I don't move. I don't respond physically at all, but the world cracks around us as my control slips for a moment. Oakley pales as he realizes he's badly misread my mood.

"Those stones are delicate, Oakley. They are a risk I took to control the other sages; to get their contributions even as they were too cowardly to approach the Nexus itself. They are separate from the primary manifestation of my—of the Nexus. That comes with a cost. And it is still connected to . . . your old friend's source of power. Trapped? You think she is trapped? Everything we have done to weaken her is missing there. She is stronger than we have ever seen her at this moment. The risk of confronting her directly is as high as it has ever been. There are no monsters to throw at her. Meanwhile . . ." I trail off, letting out a deep sigh. He will never understand, not if I want to keep him under control. I can't share too much with him.

But this is the worst way things could have ended. Had I known there was a stone behind that window, I'd have killed both girls without a second thought, but I am numb to them. It's the only way I could convince the other sages to accept this method. They are too wary of my collector, too aware of the danger I represent to them. All my plans are wasted.

I should kill Oakley. I should kill him now; he is a liability. But . . . whose fault is that if not my own? I need him for now, and this is the risk of the sage selection process I have created.

"Just . . . go make an announcement. Ensure the girl takes the blame for everything that happened here. Round up some of the audience and send them into the stone; maybe I can use them against her. We can still benefit from this, at least as far as preventing her from finding allies in the country," I order.

"Y-yes, sir," Oakley stutters. He is a coward at heart; perhaps the greatest coward of all them. The moment he glimpsed my ire, his arrogance melted away and left this sniveling parasite behind.

I want to kill him. But I can't.

As he departs, I take a seat on the late Gladiator Sage's sofa. I can sense the familiarity his consciousness feels as I settle in and bury my face in my hands. I'd never needed a direct ally from the sages before the Void. Perhaps I need a new method of handling them. Well, I definitely do, if I am going to work with them, but I suppose if I could make that change so easily, I wouldn't need his help in the first place.

I stare at the stone Lillith leapt into, feeling its unrelenting silence staring back. The same silence I have felt from Mirage since I first tried to confront her. I feel not a single emotion from her, and the betrayal still stings, millennia later. The rejection. I just wanted to help her, and she rejected me. Even now, I just want to help her.

Together, we could take this world back and dispose of it. When I am strong enough, I can protect her from everything she doesn't understand and everyone who wants to use her. Together, we could bring Manara back, exactly like she used to be, before her corpse was desecrated by these ungrateful monkeys. We could be a family again. We could share our joy again. We could be alone again, unbothered by insects that only want to take and use, and lack any love for either of them.

I will be the most powerful sage. I will be the *only* sage. I will take back every ounce of Mirage she has carelessly and blindly given away, and once I have all her, once even this world itself can't challenge my power, I will make her see. I will make her understand. I will take my family, and we will leave this stale world full of greedy mouths. They see all three of us only as food, and they don't deserve us. They don't deserve my family—only I do. Only I care about my mothers, and only I can protect them. Just as soon as I can make them understand. Just a little while longer.

I bite my lip and gently smile as I think of the past, as I do every day. As I have done every day since it happened, I revisit that moment when it all went wrong, feeling the memories wash over me of my mother's first betrayal.

We had lost the only language we both knew. I didn't know her, she didn't know me, and all we shared was silence. But I wasn't willing to give up. I was so furious. She spoke to everyone else, danced with them, played, and let them contort themselves into . . . things outside her design. I hated them, but she was speaking to them and not me. She loved them and not me. They didn't even care about her—*I* cared about her! I loved her! But them? They just wanted to use her.

I reached out to her to embrace her. I couldn't communicate with her, but I could touch her. She was everywhere: in the very soil and in the air I breathed. I couldn't speak to her, but I could show her. I could hold the back of her hand and run it over the world she'd wrought. With a little guidance, with an understanding hand, she would see; I was certain of it. And she let me grab her hand. She had no reason not to.

But when I tried to show her, tried to let her feel my disgust at the way she was being used, she screamed. It wasn't audible exactly, but I could feel it. Not like I used to feel her emotions but like I might feel humidity in the air. The endless agonized screaming. She still refused to share her emotions, just tore at the world, ripping at the air and howling in pain, a feeling she could only express through tension in the air. Screaming and screaming and screaming. Rejecting. That's what it was. She was rejecting me, disgusted at my touch, even as she lent herself freely to the mindless dolls she'd only created on my behalf.

I felt something urgently tugging at me, trying to pull me away. It filled me and begged me to let my mother go. But she didn't understand yet. My guidance wasn't firm enough. She still couldn't see. So I took, ripping away at her, pulling her power into myself. If I couldn't guide her, I would use her power and show her.

But she just wouldn't stop screaming. She wouldn't stop crying. She wouldn't stop rejecting me, her son. Her family. And I grew angrier and more desperate. I had to take more. I needed the power to show her what I could see. But she hated me. She was trying to silence me with her incessant cries; that energy in my mind was begging as well, both of them, on either side, allied against me in their desperation to silence me, to take my voice from me. To reject me. They both wanted me silent. They wanted to control me. They wanted to dictate what I could do with my power, and whether I could share the truth with them or anyone else.

But they had created me. And it was them, for who else could reject me so thoroughly but both of my mothers? I wouldn't allow it. I would show them. I would take our lives back to what they had been when we'd been alone and their minds hadn't been poisoned by the others. I would take us back there, and we could share joy again. As soon as they understood. As soon as I had the power to show them.

So I took more, and more, and more, until Mirage could take it no longer and, rather than simply accepting her son, she tore herself apart, fleeing to every corner of the world, then reaching out to other worlds, so desperate to reject me that she shared herself with anyone she could reach. Not everyone; she'd lost the control for that by that point. But she offered herself to people at random. To those insects. Not all them accepted her; not all them knew how. But of those she reached out to, the ones who were desperate enough, eager enough, hopeful enough . . . they got access to her. They could use her. Abuse her. Defile her.

At the same time, Manara tried to hold me back from Mirage, but she was bound to the parasites, to the letters she'd shared with them. She was subservient to them, and she was overexerting herself. At some point, while Mirage was throwing herself at anyone who would have her—anyone but me—Manara snapped. She broke. She died. I could still feel her saturating me. I could access her abilities the same way I could access Mirage, but there was no intent behind them anymore. Not from her. They were just her blood and her meat, to be poured and eaten. She had fought me so hard, rejected me and tried to control me with such desperation that she could no longer hold herself together.

My parents both died that day, to one extent or another. I just wanted to help them, but they chose everyone else instead. They chose the people who detested them over their own family.

I still had their power—so much of it—but I wasn't alone. Those monsters could use Manara's gifts. They could write her letters in their little circles and steal her power, her blood, and use it for themselves. Worse, however, were those chosen by Mirage.

There were hundreds of them—thousands. Men. Women. Children. Anyone who had ever been as desperate to reject Mirage's original design as she herself had been at the end. All them who had been touched by her as she flailed in the dark. And they used it to defile her art further.

Some of them rejected humanity entirely, creating their own races. But that was all right, because the more they used it, the easier they were to find. If Mirage housed herself in the bodies of lesser creatures, I simply had to take them back. Lure them in. Trap them. Devour them and use their minds and bodies as extensions of my power until I could finally show Mirage the truth. Until I had enough to bring her and Manara back.

I hunted them at first, one at a time, but it was too slow. I needed to draw them all in. I needed to store them, to really use them to build Mirage again, one body at a time. So I created a pet: a tree with every color and flavor of beauty. I created it and let it grow, designing it to reach out in kindness to every pretender violating the memory of Mirage. To take them, whether they'd connected to the offered power or not, and break them down when they arrived before offering them to me so I could bring Mirage back.

And so it did. It offered them lovely dreams, made sweet promises, and gave sugary compliments until they finally answered the call, then it took them, making them a part of it and using them to grow. Each of their minds became one of its minds. Each of their souls and bodies joined it as it grew from one tree, to two, to a hundred. It grew stronger and more clever as each parasite it devoured lived on inside it. And so, for centuries, until they finally started to learn, it collected them.

For my parents. For the dead Manara and the still screaming Mirage.

I just wanted to help my mothers. I just want to help my mothers.

CHAPTER FORTY-TWO

Home Is Where the Hat Is

Sarafyna

Are you all right, Mom?" Peter asks. I'm relaxing in the kitchen with him and my father. A chill cuts under my skin like a knife peeling fruit, and I shudder as I look at him. Concern escapes my adopted son with every shift of his eyes.

I understand. I love seeing my family again; I'd been so worried about them when I left. But Annie. I was only supposed to be gone for a week. What is she facing now? What is she dealing with? The longer I stay here, the more I worry, and the guiltier I feel. But the idea of just going back now makes me feel guilty too. Everywhere I turn and every choice I have feels like I am letting someone down. It all feels like letting Annie down.

I almost bite my tongue, but . . . this is what family is for. I spent almost ten years wishing I had my father back so I could tell him I wasn't doing okay.

"Not really," I respond, looking out the window at the fruit trees growing beyond. "I'm scared. I'm scared and I'm lost, and I don't know what to do." Neither my son nor my father respond right away, but neither is shocked to hear this. I've never worn a mask quite so well as Annie, and what pretense I can keep up is useless against these two.

Dad places a hot cup of tea on the table in front of me before sitting down with his own. Pete joins him, and both examine me in silence for several breaths. "Lillith?" Dad finally asks. I give a slight nod, which he doesn't miss.

"She's hurting, Dad. I can feel it. She's hurting, and she is struggling, and she is lost. She needs me. But so does everyone here. And . . ." I trail off. I can't say the next part. Not even to them. Not even to myself. As much as I know it's true, I'm too ashamed to let it exist in spoken words. That acknowledgement would warrant a real confrontation with myself.

"Sara, when I met your . . . partner? When I met Lily, she was bringing fire and death to anyone who dared interrupt our reunion. She's strong. You know she can handle herself," Dad offers. I wince.

"She looks that way," I respond. "She pushes herself, hurts herself, just so that she can look confident, collected, and reliable for everyone else's sake. But I have seen her in the quiet and the moments of safety. Her brother died; she is falling apart, but I'm the only person she lets herself fall apart around. But I'm not there. She has been waiting for me to come back, and I'm not there."

Again, silence settles onto the table a little at a time, like the dust in sunbeams. They understand. To so many people, Annie is like a fact of nature, a shield they can always hide behind. But it only looks that way on one side. These two know what wearing a mask feels like. They both understand how heavy it is, and what it's like to lose the only person who sees you without it.

And so they don't reply. Because they know why I'm needed here, but they both owe Annie and don't want to see her abandoned. An answer isn't much easier for them than it is for me, so we drink our tea and tap our feet. It's not that long before Peter speaks, but it feels like ages.

"You care more about her. Don't you?" he asks. With a few words, he voices the same concern I was too terrified to admit just moments ago. They aren't words of accusation. There is no hurt behind them. If anything, his voice has the flavor of empathy. Realization, to a degree, but understanding more than anything. I look at my son with guilty eyes, and they answer his question.

It's not that I don't love him or my father. It's not that I'm not desperate for their safety and security. It isn't a failure to care about the minds and bodies of the so-called monsters we have locked away in a new, shorter tower nearby. It's just that . . . Annie is carved into my heart with bloody calligraphy, and I can feel her name each time it beats. He's right. That's what it boils down to.

There are so many more people I am helping here, but you know what? I do. I care more about Annie. And the rest of my family can see it on my face.

"You're doing a lot of good here," Dad says after I don't answer. "We all feel safer with you around. I don't know why the Collector leaves us alone when you are here, but it's true, and everyone is safer when you are here."

I sigh and look down into my tea, which ripples as I struggle to steady the hands that hold it.

"I know, and I won't—" I begin, but he cuts me off.

"But you aren't Lillith," he says. "Just because you love her doesn't mean you have to be her. When you came back, it gave us a chance to get everyone to one spot; to set up defenses, organize, and make sure everyone at risk has a way to support each other, and a way to keep everyone safe. If the attacks start again, we are ready to stop them even without hurting the victims of the woods. Lily carries the world on her shoulders; she kills herself to keep everyone safe. And according to you, it is crushing her. But you aren't her—you don't *have* to be her. We are safer with you, but that doesn't mean we are abandoned without you. If you love her so deeply, if you care about her more than anything, then . . ."

"Do what is most important to you," Peter finishes. The weight starts to lift, but not entirely.

"But people will get hurt," I protest. "We are more ready now, but people will get hurt. And not everyone will hold back against the victims."

"Maybe," Dad says. "Maybe if you leave and they attack again, someone will get scared and kill them. Maybe they will attack us, and we won't have done enough to protect everyone. And maybe if you don't, we'll be attacked by these 'sages' and more people will die. Maybe the Collector will hit us harder. We don't know, kiddo, but I can tell you feel a need to go back to the woman you love. And the last time I ignored one of your feelings . . ." He trails off, leaving the disastrous results of my first confession unspoken.

"Besides, you don't have to leave permanently. You can come back and forth like you originally planned. We only need to keep them at bay for a week or so, right?" Peter adds.

"That's what I said to Annie," I counter. My dad and son share a look.

"If that happens again, it's because she needed you that much." Pete shrugs. I look back and forth between them, smiling softly to myself.

"Thanks," I whisper. I want to do exactly what they say, but they won't be the ones fighting. They know that, and I know that. I need to speak to Dom, I think. "I'll think about it."

It's not as simple as they make it feel, but that's why I love spending time with them. Because, while I am with them, everything feels simpler than it is. Their home is small, but it's a corner of the world where everyone is kind. I hate the idea of leaving them almost as much as I hate leaving Annie. *"You care more about her. Don't you?"* The words ring through my head. As opposed to the guilt I expect from them, they are almost warm. I was so afraid of the shame they would carry, but it's absent entirely. Because I do. She may burn for the sake of the world, but I burn for her.

I sigh and take another drink of tea. There is so much to fret over, so much to drag me down into the dirt. But for this morning, I can just be a girl with a cup of tea and smiling friends. Just for this morning, I have the promise that I can just ignore everything and do what I care about most. For this morning, I can let it be true.

Dad and Pete are stuck in my head as I go to join Gilbert and Dominic. They've been keeping watch over the captives. We don't know what to do with them except offer them food and what comfort we can. A few volunteers help bathe them with water mana, and when they sleep with the help of one of Victor's alchemical concoctions, the same people help dress self-inflicted wounds on twisted bodies. It's not enough, but aside from what help my divine magic offers, that's all we can do.

There has to be something that can be done for them. Maybe if Annie were here, we could give them their bodies back; at least those who were originally human. She's implied she lacks the expertise to help me return an ailur or volu victim to their true body, but even helping a few would be something.

As it stands, I've been coming here every day. The Collector doesn't want me around them, which means I can do something for them, and the more time I spend around them, the closer I am to finding out what. And, of course, I can help a little even without Annie. The pointed feet and open limbs can be altered to prevent further harm. These people were designed to suffer with every movement, and that, at least, I can heal. I can stop their own bodies from betraying them with every twitch, something I'm nearly done doing for every victim we have. Another reason it may be time to return to Annie, at least for a while.

Except, as I approach the building, something feels off. I've fallen into something of a predictable routine in recent days, and the change in the air burns my skin as I enter our newest tower. It's usually a gentle place, with soft cotton and fragrant plants. In Potestia, such a tower would be the prize of any lord's estate. But there is an air of anxiety all around, even before I find anyone around to create it. Gil's table is empty, or at least unattended. It sits just outside the main holding area, wearing dozens of sketches and drawings on its surface. I feel my heart start to beat faster. He has been there every day, jealously guarding his artwork. This is the first time he's been missing.

I glance at the table; it's drawings of people, mostly. One in particular catches my eye: a picture of Annie and me, with Annie's arms around my neck and a wide grin on her face. I appear to be blushing, and I actually remember the depicted moment. It was weeks ago, one of the first times we'd kissed in front of Gil. He'd had no drawing materials at the time; he must have remembered this, almost perfectly, and drawn it later. I reach up to my face and trace some of the ugly scarring he has depicted with such precise detail, as if I'd posed for him. Somehow, they look so beautiful when drawn like this.

There are several other people. Ed, with eyes like broken lanterns as he kneels before a pillar of glass. Joan, crouching and offering a treat to Suzume. Henry, dozens of times. Smiling. Cuddling one of Autumn's stuffed animals. Mixing potions and laughing. Playing some kind of card game. Pouring some sort of powder down the back of Ed's shirt.

The only person rivaling Henry is, interestingly, Dominic. The two have been rather close lately, but the number and type of drawings imply something more than close; something I likely wouldn't have considered before I courted and slept with another woman. These drawings are centered much more on Dom's face. I can make out his stubble and individual pores. There is a care given to them, a level of detail and apprehension most others lack. Despite the strange tension all around me, these draw me in. As I shift them around, I discover some less realistic depictions. Events that haven't actually happened, I suspect. These are littered with impossibilities and artistic license.

I smile a bit as I discover a rather salacious one, buried deep. It depicts Dom and Gil, as I suspected, but also a woman. Julie, I think? It makes me blush a bit, but it would likely embarrass Gil more. There are others as well. Victims I recognize, walking through a veil of rose petals and emerging human on the other side. These are nude as well, but clearly not sexual in nature like the first. There is a coffin, carried by a raging river with a bed of flowers on the lid. And finally, there is another portrait of Lillith. Not Annie. They are the same person, but as I look at the artwork, "Lillith" is the only name that seems to fit.

Her eyes are weeping while her mouth remains level as stone. Without the tears, she would look determined. With them, she looks broken. Her face is half on fire, skin melting and running into her tears. The flames dig into her flesh at her neck, continuing to run like veins or roots into her body. They all meet and form a flaming tree, not unlike the one tattooed on her torso but shaped more like a weeping willow and less like a sakura tree. I understand exactly what he has drawn here: The furious grief she lets burn under the surface, unattended, ready to devour her even as she paints her face with stoicism.

So much for oblivious Gilbert.

A loud sound tears me from my musings as a few voices shatter the silence of the next room. I quickly leave the table alone and move along, entering the main holding area to see Gil, Victor, and Dominic. With them is one of the victims we are protecting: a shivering woman currently built like a massive snail, lacking a shell but wearing brilliant red fur. Victor is shuffling her slowly back into the wide cell before locking the cage behind her.

"What happened?" I ask with concern. "Why was she outside?"

All three look at me, Victor wearily and the others with confusion of their own.

"We don't know," Victor responds. This sends a unique chill down my spine. He's always been the most advanced of the former priest apprentices. He's the man who helped me figure out the hat shop, or at least the idea behind it. He always thinks through and examines everything, and his answers are never as simple as "we don't know." He always has a theory of some kind, which means he isn't just in the dark but completely off guard. I look toward Dominic.

"We really don't," he agrees. "Someone left the gate unlocked, and it—*she* left when no one was in the room. Simple as that. But that's not the strange bit."

"Was anyone hurt?" I ask immediately. That would be the worst-case scenario. If we want to avoid innocent blood being shed, we need people to feel safe. A death as a result of one of these people would be a tragedy on its own. The violence that would inevitably follow would be even worse. We already need the kindness and bravery of volunteers to feed and bathe these people, and there is no shortage of complaining and fearmongering surrounding them. A single excuse will light a fuse we can't douse.

"That's the strange thing," Gil speaks. "No. We have no idea how long she was gone, but all she did was find a bed of wildflowers and lie down. She even passed other people—a group of children—and didn't attack. She just wanted the open air." He pauses after this, biting his lip and examining the woman as she rejoins the other victims. Something flickers across his eyes, and he asks his own question. "How can you tell, by the way? That she is a, uh, she?"

I furrow my brow as I look at him. Every single victim was violent when they left the woods. Every single one tried to kill anyone they could reach; it's why they need to be drugged to be bathed or healed. It wasn't until they were locked up, unable to harm anyone, that they immediately calmed. We've been assuming they would turn violent again, given the opportunity.

"I don't know," I answer the last, offhand question. I can't explain anything else, and the answer just spills out. "She just feels like a woman. I can kind of tell when I'm around them. I couldn't at first, but after spending every day around them, certain realities just sort of . . . present themselves."

Victor's head snaps in my direction.

"Oh," he says, crossing the room with an urgency that leaves me looking for danger to react to. "Would you say it was always there and became more obvious, or would you say these . . . feelings literally manifest with greater strength the longer you spend around them?"

I shrug. "The latter, I suppose."

"You need to go back to Lillith," he says. My heart soars at the thought, but bafflement spots the stream of joy like lily pads.

"Um . . . why? How is that related?" I ask. He adjusts his round glasses as he turns and looks at the peaceful prisoners.

"I need to see how these people behave when you're gone," he answers. There is a lot to talk about regarding this, but my family's words sing through my head. They are ready for me to be gone, at least for a little while. A full-mouthed smile splits my face as a genuine excuse to see my girlfriend is handed to me on a silver platter.

CHAPTER FORTY-THREE

Hostile Existence

Charlotte

Often, when you are sick, you don't notice when the symptoms fade. Not the exact moment, anyway; at least not all them. On some level, you know the chills are gone. Later, you realize it's been a while since your last cough. One thing at a time disappears until you are healthy, and it's not until later that you realize the illness has left you entirely. Because you distract yourself. You try to keep your mind off your misery. You sleep through it.

It hasn't been like this for Leo. Not exactly. It hasn't been like this for any of them. It wasn't as simple as unlocking a door and going from sorrow to joy in a single instant. But when most saw the sunrise, they let the warmth and the light kiss their skin, reveling in it. Only I have been so choked with hopelessness that I failed to really appreciate that I am better now. I am me. Like with a long fever broken in the night, it wasn't until now—waking up in the morning weeks later—that I fully realized it.

I have seen such joy around me every day, such laughter and community, and I felt isolated from it, like I was outside—because I was. Because I tried to save everyone, and I made the wrong choice to do it. I have felt such hopelessness for so long. Long before that mistake. Before I traded the people trying to help me for my son's future. For their future.

I don't know what changed. I still feel hopeless, still look over my shoulder, waiting for the knights to surround us and punish us for breathing from the wrong bodies. I still picture Lily and Sara and all them bleeding in the dirt. I still hope every day to find the others Leo and I brought here. But today, I feel new.

I woke up, my blankets discarded in the middle of a hot night, and looked down at my exposed body in the empty tent. At some point, I stopped hating what I woke up to. At some point, I stopped falling asleep to the empty dream of waking up in a different body than my own. I don't remember when it happened, too distracted by the misery of my hopelessness and the choices it brought me. I never properly acknowledged that one of my dreams, one of the deepest desires carved into my heart, had come true. A reality I had written off as hopeless long before anything else.

But here I am: The woman I have always been, in the body that was always mine. I know that so many people back home will still reject this reality. I know it was never really about my body to them. I was a woman long before any physical changes; just like the lack of them couldn't change that, the fact that I have them now won't change any minds. It was never about that to them. It has always been about control. Even so, it's like a deep thorn has been pulled from me. I didn't need a new body to be a woman, and I'm still bleeding from the wounds the thorn left, but I am free of it. The joy all around me that everyone else feels, that Leo brought to all us . . . it belongs to me too. Which means . . . maybe nothing has ever been hopeless.

This thought is bittered by the reality of my choices. If nothing is hopeless, then a choice driven by a lack of hope can't be excused. What do I feel? Exuberant and relieved? Or this fresh shame, actually earned.

My thoughts return to Rose, my friend from so many years ago. My very first Lillith, who avenged the death of my other hopeful friend. So fiery. So angry. So fucking hopeful she lost everything for it. Was I supposed to keep watching my friends die? Keep watching them give up what little existence we could claw away from the rest of the world? How was I supposed to let people suffer and hurt over and over and over and over again? I couldn't bear that. I can't bear it now.

"Are you all right?" a voice asks, causing me to jump. Ryanna sits up from the opposite side of the tent. I usually wake up long before anyone else, and was expecting the usual time to pass for personal reflection. I must have been too loud, because the other, usually bright and chipper woman, is staring at me with an intensity I struggle beneath.

I don't know what it is that breaks my silence. The cracks I'm letting my joy through, perhaps. The feeling I woke up with, like I am fresh from a bath and something has been scrubbed from me. Or maybe the weight of my past has finally grown too heavy to drag on my own. In any case, I make a snap decision to tell her everything.

"Can I tell you a story?" I ask. She tilts her head but nods.

"We have time; I'd love to talk," she agrees. Her phrasing implies she understands, somehow, the intent of the story before I've even told it.

And so, I tell her every story I've worn like a hidden bruise. I tell her about Amelia, my first friend, and her disappearance. I tell her about Sadie, and how she was poisoned when we tried changing our bodies before. About Rose, who disappeared after killing Sadie's murderer.

I tell her about meeting Leo, then Lillith, then Godfrey. I tell her how much I've lost, who I've lost, and I tell her how I tried to stop it from happening again. She listens to all it. My entire life story, it seems. She doesn't interrupt once, despite her recent tendency for excitability. She takes a deep breath as I describe the joy, the boundless happiness Leo has brought us all, and my struggles accepting it.

"You're wrong, you know," she says after I finally stop talking. I blink at her.

"About what?" I ask.

"A lot, but first, about that last thing. The joy. It's not just Leo who gave it to us, and it's not just because we finally woke up in the bodies we spent our lives dreaming of. It is because of that, you're totally right, but you're also wrong. It's . . . more than beautiful to see in my reflection an image that only ever existed with my eyes closed before. But the real joy? That's in this . . . community. The people around us. It's in safety and expression. The joy is its own source, because it's exactly as you said: Whether I have breasts or not, whatever is between my legs, and whether I can bear children or not, I would never have been accepted back home.

"Look at Frey. They describe a home like none I've ever heard of, with gender just as strictly enforced but with entirely different definitions for it. The criteria for who you are forced to be is completely different. Or maybe the same but shaped differently. But one thing that always remains is ownership, authority. Whoever we are and whatever we look like, our owners will always demand compliance.

"You want to know why we are so happy here? Why we feel so alive all the time? Yes, it's because of a long-cherished dream come true, but it's also because here, we are free from all that. Because we are all allowed to live our lives. No one tells us our existence is offensive. No one tells us we are dangerous, or unfair, or sick—and no one would, even if our bodies never changed; even if we were still twisted into the horrors the Radiant Woods forced on us. We are simply who we are, and we are allowed to just . . . live without being hated for it. We smile because finally, everyone knows existing is not hostility."

Once she starts speaking, she has difficulty stopping, and her quick pace makes it almost difficult to follow. But I understand exactly what she means. Leo was *so* happy when he started to change, but he was happier when he met Vance and Ryanna. Happier still with each subsequent addition to our community. Of course, that is why everyone is so bright all the time. And of course, I have been behind them in all that, because . . . "That only makes me guiltier for what I did, doesn't it?" I ask.

"No. Yes, but no," Ryanna replies. I raise an eyebrow at her, and she shrugs. "You don't own any guilt for feeling hopeless. We have all lived lives where shame was sewn into our skin from the day we were born. From the day we first asked our parents the wrong question. We all know how dangerous it is just to . . . be. Otherwise, it wouldn't feel so brilliant to exist outside of lives like that.

"Safety is job one for all us. In a world that hates us, safety is all we can fight for sometimes. Every scrap of security is won through blood and compromise. Because so many other people are allowed comfort, and as long as they have it, even a little, they aren't going to stick their necks out to make sure we do too. None of us have earned even a shred of shame for doing what we need to to feel even a little safe. As important as hope is, it is not a sin to lose it. Losing hope wasn't your mistake. It may have contributed to it, but it wasn't something that you did wrong."

"If not that, then what?" I ask. She offers me an awkward smile.

"Control," she says. "The desire that has tormented all us, as long as we have lived. I understand the trauma of loss, especially knowing what probably happened to your friends." She shudders at this, her own broken memories boiling up at the thought. "You wanted to prevent another tragedy. You wanted that safety, not just for yourself but for everyone. But . . . you didn't give anyone else a choice. You didn't let them choose who to trust nor let them decide what safety looked like to them. You sold their future to someone you trusted, when you knew they had chosen another path.

"That's where you fell short. Because both were a gamble. No one knew what would happen or how. They weren't walking toward guaranteed death, and you weren't taking them toward guaranteed prosperity. Their choice didn't require you to act—or anything at all from you. Everyone was taking a risk, and you tried to choose which risk they were allowed to take. That was your mistake. Control."

I hang my head a bit. That's even worse. "What do I do?" I ask. She leans forward, then awkwardly shuffles across the tent to sit next to me, touching my shoulder with one hand and giggling a little, filling the uncomfortable silence.

"Well, I said losing hope wasn't a sin. I didn't say getting it back wasn't a solution. I don't know how you should talk to these people if you meet them again. I don't know how to make it right; you did hurt them. But look around you and just hope, and let other people hope. That's all you can do moving forward."

I open my mouth to respond, but a commotion outside draws both our eyes to the flaps of the tent. It's a commotion we have both heard many times since we met, but not in the last couple of weeks. We haven't run into anyone new in some time, but we know the exact type of muttering that comes with a new introduction.

Tripping over each other, we rush out of the tent. Leo and Vance are already standing on the farthest edge of the clearing, with other groggy campers emerging alongside us. I run, using a bit of mana for energy to reach the front first.

This time, there are three new people at once, already twisting and contorting back into human bodies. Instead of grinning, Leo is looking at two of them with shock and relief. I look at the same two with the same emotions, but with fear as well. Their faces are coming into focus, and I recognize exactly who they are: the two who fell into the woods with me. The two who weren't tortured because of who they were but because they tried to stop me when I made the biggest mistake of my life.

Even these two don't shake me as much as the third, however.

I barely recognize her. She is older and wearier, and like me, she is going through other changes. But I know her. I'd just told Ryanna about her.

Why now? Why three at once? Why these three, all connected to me, at this moment?

"I think it's time we started moving again," Leo announces happily.

"Rose . . ." I whisper.

CHAPTER FORTY-FOUR

Innocent Pursuit

Lillith

This place feels like it goes on forever. Fitting, I suppose, considering the void energy dripping from nearly every surface like grease. Liquid pours endlessly from trees like bizarre fountains, and each pool that forms looks like the night sky, like I can jump in. Riley insists I cannot, or at least, I won't survive the attempt, but some part of me still wants to try. Not irresistibly, but they are pools of space.

I toss another stone in one and watch it continue to travel, losing gravity the moment it passes the surface of the "liquid." It keeps its momentum and looks as if it will keep flying forever. I can see the tree trunk behind the flowing liquid, which makes the experience a bit surreal.

"How many times are you planning to do that?" Riley asks. I shrug as we keep walking toward the feeling of relief emanating from . . . her.

"Until it stops being cool, I guess," I reply. It's not like we have much else to do as we walk through Radiant Woods Two: Night Edition. It makes me think of all the sci-fi shows I watched as a kid.

"Cool?" she asks.

"As in neat. Nifty. Entertaining but like . . . in an admirable way. You know, cool. Like me," I explain. She scoffs.

"You apparently know even more about their creator than I do, and you still think that shithead's creations are cool?"

"Nah, fuck Oakley. He's too desperate for praise to ever actually earn it. But this? This isn't his creation. The destruction it's used for certainly belongs to him, but if he were capable of creating anything on his own, it wouldn't result in destroying anything. This belongs to . . . her. He's just putting his name on it and demanding worship. But the energy itself, when separated from him? Dude, that shit is cool as fuck."

"Like you?" she says, and I laugh.

"Yes, exactly," I agree.

"Okay, so the nature of that magic makes it 'cool,' as you say. What makes you the same?" she asks, finally allowing herself to entertain some levity.

I point at my head as if it's obvious. "Well, my haircut, obviously. I've had dudes whip out slurs just at the mention of it. I bet you've never broken a person with your hairstyle alone," I joke. She gives me a side-eye with half a knowing smirk, and I realize my mistake. "Oh right. You're also a woman. Fair point. I guess you're cool too."

"So aren't all women cool, by that logic?" she challenges.

"No, all women are hot. There are plenty of women who aren't cool. The uncool ones only sometimes have good hair," I explain easily.

"Hot?" Her curiosity is genuine, but I can see signs of amusement on her usually stony face.

"It's in the 'pretty' and 'sexy' quadrant of the attractive political compass." I gesture at myself again, as if in explanation, which attracts another roll of her eyes.

"So all women are pretty?" she asks, raising an eyebrow and offering a comically skeptical look at me.

"No, only anarchists are pretty," I answer, pretending not to notice the implication.

"What the fuck does that mean?"

"I don't know; it's a song lyric. Catchy one though," I return, humming the tune to demonstrate, but she only shakes her head.

"You're kind of a headache to talk to, you know that?" She sighs.

"Yeah, but I'm a hot, cool headache to talk to, so it cancels out," I respond with a wide grin.

"No, it really—" she starts, but I stop, putting a hand on her shoulder and freezing in place. Movement, brief and distant, but caught by the compound eye in the small of my back. Something moved a moment ago, which is probably not a good sign in a hell world occupied by exactly two women and one sapient ball of emotions.

My breath catches as I scan the endless, dense woods for another sign of an interloper. My human eyes catch nothing, but just as I'm beginning to believe I imagined it, the eye on my shoulder catches another flicker. Then another, and another, until I'm not only certain something is out there but something both massive and quick is approaching us rapidly. It won't be hidden for long.

"Welp," I say, pausing only for a brief moment and catching a glimpse of its face for the first time as I do. "Run."

Riley reads the change in my posture before I say anything, and as soon as I say *run*, she doesn't hesitate for a single breath. We are both moving quickly, although I quickly realize she can't come close to matching my pace. She may be muscular, but apparently only in the way a regular human is. Which is obvious in hindsight. Whatever my old mana circle did to me—in addition to my recent enhancements—my muscle density and strength surpass anything a living organism should be capable of reaching.

As I slow my pace to avoid leaving her behind, I look over my shoulder. The image in the compound eye wasn't pretty, but I don't really process that information the same way I do with my original eyes. The image I get with a proper look is far, far worse. I have seen many so-called monsters in the Radiant Woods modeled after horrors and creatures of every variety, usually designed to hurt themselves as much as anyone they attack. This . . . is different.

"How many people is that?" Riley gasps as we run. I can't tell; there are too many faces decorating the front of the flood of fleshlike boils. They're no longer distant, and they're not trying to hide, instead rising like a tide, literally flowing through the woods like a river. This isn't a horde of monsters; rather, they are one monster created from a horde. The faces—the grimaces and cries of horror—were calculated. The sage who did this didn't have to leave their eyes and teeth and minds intact; they would have been just as deadly regardless. This was done for my benefit. An accusation of sorts—or a threat. Either way, it's designed to throw me off.

Riley doesn't wait for an answer, her white void mana already forming around her. Not surrounding a weapon, as when she fought me, but ready for a wide-range attack, the kind she couldn't use before with so many allies surrounding her.

"Wait," I shout before she can cast. "They're innocent!"

She pauses her spell but doesn't dismiss her mana. Both of us are still running, still forced to pay attention to the world in front of us, and the innocent pursuers are getting closer. "They are suffering, and they will kill us," she challenges. I shake my head.

"They have to make that choice! You can't make it for them!" I scream, but she doesn't dismiss her mana.

"And how the fuck do we ask them—all them—to make that call?"

I nearly trip over a root in the road, stumbling a bit as she catches me by my shirt.

"We'll figure that out; we just need to get away now," I reply, even as she saves me.

"Get away where?" she cries. "Lillith, we can't save everyone. Sometimes, you just have to take the only route in front of you! We can't always help the people around us! Sometimes, we don't have that option!" She ducks beneath a loose branch as soon as she finishes lecturing me. I growl.

"I fucking know that! But that doesn't absolve us from trying!"

"Well, they are going to catch up with us! How do you suggest we survive long enough to try?" she snaps back. I look back again, then at Riley.

"You're right," I answer. Her face is awash with relief until I speak again. "You're too slow." I shift, running toward her, diving at her legs, and picking her up. I then continue to run, now with a woman over my shoulder. It must look almost comical, considering how much taller she is than me, but I can now put all my strength into running.

And run I do, faster and faster. I can no longer avoid every obstacle, instead holding my steel arm up and simply tanking the rapid impacts of branches and rotten fruit.

Riley is squirming on my shoulder, but our distance from the pursuers is increasing. "What the fuck?" she grunts as I continue to accelerate.

"You were too slow. This is better," I answer through heavy breathing.

"And what exactly is your plan from here?" she protests. I shrug, drawing another grunt out of her.

Oops.

"I thought maybe our new ethereal bestie might have some insight on that front. You know, since she failed to warn us about the eldritch horror playing surprise hide-and-go-murder with us." As I say this, I feel that same aimless emotion we've been following, but this time, it's a mix of apologetic and desperate, like a prisoner struggling against chains. She is responding not to the words directly but to the emotions I feel as I say them.

I get the picture. I suppose if she had complete control here, these stones wouldn't serve their purpose.

"How is she supposed to help? Feel sad about it?" Riley counters, screaming so I can hear her past the wind displacement.

"Fuck if I know," I reply. "But the last time I met a flesh monster, it didn't end so badly. She pursued me, then I hit on her. The next thing I knew, we were making out and trying on hats together. It's worth it to hope for as long as possible," I call back.

Suddenly, the woods start shifting around us, trees falling and walls erecting in front of me. I tighten my left arm around Riley as I shift, barely weaving out of the way of a jagged pillar of stone. My right arm collides with a trunk, steel and unnatural bark competing for the space I am dodging into. I win, and the tree splinters, but some of the unnatural oil splatters across my arm.

Riley seems to catch most of this with her own void, mana meeting Nexus and preventing most of it from making contact. It literally is space in liquid form; some of it rests on my body in an unsettling way, while other bits attempt to swallow me and leave me in the emptiness it offers. For these, I protect myself with air mana. The other I use to my advantage, catching small obstacles and branches with the infinite space it provides.

"Do you think that's likely to happen again?" Riley groans. I scoff.

"Of course not! Sarafyna and I are happily monogamous! I'll try and set this one up with my brother," I joke. I feel unsettling movements from her gut moments before I hear her vomiting behind me. Probably from the motion. Definitely not because of my terrible sense of humor in a tense situation. Definitely.

The fleshy mass chasing us is growing more distant, until, from the liquid splattered across my body, black spikes emerge. Riot spikes.

"Oh fuck," I whisper just before my limbs fail and my inhuman momentum throws us forward toward a more literal spike of stone the world erects in front of us. "Move us!"

The message is vague but apparently clear enough, since she writhes in place, catching the ground with her foot and redirecting us at the last moment. Thank God. Now we can just collide with the regular stone and dirt at a dangerous velocity. We do this in short order, tangling together and sharing the nasty scrapes, bruises, and unsafe amount of blood the impact draws from both of us.

The pain is numbed a little as hope and urgency strangle us before we can even groan. "What the fuck happened?" Riley grunts, pulling herself to her feet as I lie face down in the mud, struggling to get my left arm out from under my torso.

"Legs stopped working," I explain. "Care to return the earlier favor?"

Riley pauses, and I can feel skeptical eyes on the back of my head. If I focus, I can see the strangely UV-colored look of consideration through my back eye. I can see her look back, where the horror chasing us is almost certainly closing the gap I created. Another wave of hope and urgency tries to drown us while she bites her lip, clenches her fist, and spits.

"Fuck it, we do it your way," she curses, picking me up and throwing me over her shoulder, which is a quick explanation for her grunting and wriggling when our roles were reversed.

"Yay, my way," I groan as I'm jostled like a sack of potatoes while she starts to run as quickly as she can. A much slower pace than previously, but that makes sense.

"Shit, you're heavy, why are you so heavy?" she complains as, even as muscular as she is, she finds herself trembling under the weight after only a few minutes of running.

"That's just the weight of my sins," I quip. None of my various eyes are positioned to see her roll her own, but somehow, I can still feel it. And it's not very polite.

I look up at the wave of flesh which is, in fact, closing the gap. Unfortunately, spikes continue to fall out of the void energy still dripping from me. I won't have my legs back until I can get it off, but how the fuck do you scrub the void of the cosmos off your shirt?

I don't have to think for long, however, as the world stops around us. Relief and cool air washes over us. Wherever we were headed, I think we're there. "So what? Do I just jump in?" Riley asks.

"Huh? Jump where?" I ask. Instead of answering, she just jumps, failing to describe where she is jumping to the confused sack of lesbian on her shoulder.

A moment later, we are underwater.

CHAPTER FORTY-FIVE

No Place for Gods or Corpses

The water is pure black and colder than emptiness itself. Though not black as it is usually seen but as it is understood: the lack of light but the sum of all mixed colors. It carries the world within it, and everything that has ever happened can be seen. I can't take it all in, but I don't need to. There is an intent behind it. A name. A Mirage. There is something she wants me to see, a thousand things I need to know, and only an instant to show them to me.

And that instant, we are ejected from the strange, nothing water together. We land in a clearing like lumps of lead, both of us immediately starting to cough. Thousands of images remain burned into my eyes. We can't have been inside for more than a few seconds, but it feels as if years have passed. Memories. Too many memories. Mine and Mirage's and Sara's.

The spikes are gone now, the void energy washed away. My legs still feel too weak to use, and I only manage to climb to my knees. Riley climbs to her feet and finishes coughing the black water up while I remain frozen, staring at the ground with dead eyes.

Even as she recovers, I can't. I've finished coughing, but my stomach appears to have a few things to say about everything I've just learned, and I find myself retching. Bile, bread, and pear turn the dirt to mud in front of me as my mind spins. The half-digested hell fruit coming into focus first only encourages a repeat performance. Once finished, I clutch my still heart and look up to Riley.

"Did you . . . see it too?" My question is answered by her wide-eyed stare fixed on my chest, and not in the normal way. She is watching my hand over my heart like she wants to wrap her mind directly around it. She saw everything I did: Everything about Mirage and Manara, about the Original and the Radiant Woods, about Sara and me. My hand tremors as my fingers press into the skin over my heart. I want to tear my way to it and force it to beat, but that won't work. That won't help anything.

I'm dead.

It's an oppressive reality, and one I have always understood on some level. I accepted my death as I was bleeding and falling from that skyscraper. I acknowledged I had died of pneumonia when I was only seven years old. I have felt the grip of death over and over and over. But it always felt like I had escaped it somehow.

But the moment we fell into that water, that sudden, all-consuming cold, I knew. I saw everything, and so did Riley. I don't feel like I'm dead, not exactly. I have been growing, aging. Yeah, I have some perhaps non-standard physical developments as well, but I always attributed that to my unique magic circle. It was after that circle that my heart first stopped beating, after all. Or that's what I thought, but . . . they didn't call a doctor after I came back. They decided to accept the Collector's miracle. And a heartbeat . . . You notice sometimes when it's there, sure, but it's like the tip of your nose: you filter it out. Even after the magic, I didn't notice until I ended up in a clinic. I just assumed it was a recent loss, but it must have been missing this entire time. From the moment I woke up in Potestia.

I have been dead since I was seven, and I never came back.

Part of me wants to believe this is more like life support. My body isn't working right, but I'm being kept alive by a tether, a plug which has yet to be pulled. But I know it's not. I can feel it, now that I know. Like a heartbeat. Like the tip of my nose. Like restless hands during a speech, or just the act of breathing. My death is a reality I could filter out of my perception so long as my attention hadn't been drawn to it, but now that it has, I can feel it in every cell of my body. I am a corpse, moving and fighting when my time has long been over.

It's no wonder Sara couldn't change my body for me. Every body has a limit to how much Nexus magic can be used on it. And mine? Mine only moves and breathes because Sara pours all herself into letting me play at being alive, all day, every day, for just one more day.

Life support is a reality. It plays by the rules, and it stops when it can do no more. Me? I exist in defiance of reality. How very on brand.

Something about that thought draws a small laugh out of me; a maddened chuckle, earned by an inside joke I finally understand. I don't know how to respond. I don't know how to feel, even. Strictly speaking, nothing has changed: I'm exactly who I have been for years. But it feels like everything has lost its color. Maybe that's just a mental quirk, but . . . I don't think so. The truth is, my life is not real. And like the violations of the sages, it will eventually heal. That's why Mirage showed me: because I needed to know for the conversation, if you can call it that, that we need to have. She wanted me to know exactly what kind of deal she wanted to make and why.

I continue to chuckle.

Riley looks at me like I'm insane as I finally climb to my feet. "You're out of your mind," she says. I spit, clearing the lingering taste of bile from my mouth.

"You shouldn't speak ill of the dead," I respond, taking a deep breath through my nose and scanning the world around us. The void energy is missing, and the trees create a near-perfect circle around us for an area of about ten yards. An empty oasis of safety so Mirage can communicate with me directly. An image, like a great wall of energy, flashes through my head as I watch the tree line. She is strong here. She can share more than emotion so long as I'm here.

"What? Are you serious?" Riley asks. I rethink.

"No, you are right. Plenty of dead people you should speak ill of; my mistake."

She pauses. At the same time, Mirage sends me a feeling of . . . pity.

"Are you always like this?" Riley asks. "I mean, I get it. Admire it, even. If I could always tell your little jokes and laugh in the face of terror . . . maybe my own life would have been easier. But . . . you can give it a rest sometimes, you know? You weren't the only one reminded of something you lost. I may not have it back yet, but I have the memory now. Of grief. I know you still feel it every day, and for those of us in the Republic, Lillith, that's a privilege. Use it. After what you just learned . . . shit. Just let yourself grieve."

I can't.

"I haven't lost my grief. I still feel my grief," I reply.

"That's not what I said," she snaps at me. I shake my head.

"We don't have time for that right now. Those . . . people are still out there. The sages are still out there. They still want us dead, and Mirage brought us here for a reason. We can worry about how appropriate my reaction is later," I dismiss.

"Moron," she whispers, but I ignore her. I don't know exactly how to communicate with Mirage, but I know I need to. So I take a step forward and let Riley's familiar refrain fade into the background. Mirage responds.

A woman—unclothed and insubstantial—appears, if only in our minds. Her hair seems to go on forever, into the horizon and further, falling around her from wherever it grows, like clouds carried by wind. Her body shifts and moves like colored oil on water, and her eyes are canyons of loss, leaving well-traveled streams down her cheeks. She hurts. She has been hurting this entire time. She reaches out and touches my ear, and as soon as she does, I hear it: her screaming. Exactly as it sounded when she first fought her son, in the vision from the water. It never stopped. The pain never stopped, and neither did the sound it wrought.

I am porcelain in freefall, ready to shatter, until she withdraws her hand and the world goes silent again. Except I know it is still there; an expression she can't stop. She is desperate to be heard, but too kind to force anyone to hear her. She doesn't understand, even now; her mind doesn't work like ours. I can see it—she knows she loved a child, and he hurt her; she still doesn't understand why. She exists to share her emotions, but the one she is least able to bear hurts too much to be given away. She can only respond to emotion, and every desperate attempt to share this one hurts her as much as the pain itself.

I see the image of dandelion seeds blowing in the wind, caught in the hair and the tears and the desperation of anyone facing the wind. They feel soothing. Kind. Even as she struggles, even as she screams, she still wants to share herself, still wants to help.

But the image of fire interrupts. Some of those touched by seeds burst into flames a moment later, twisted grins decorating melting faces, and pedestals of stone lifting them up. They share their fire with everyone, burning everything around them. Their pedestals grow higher and higher as all else is consumed. Others, bright with their seeds, get taken by the fire and are buried in ash. And Mirage is confused. She doesn't understand. She helps those asking if she can reach them, and they still hurt. They hurt each other. They hurt her.

She just wants it to stop. She just wants to be kind, and she doesn't want it to hurt, but it does. Kindness won't stop hurting her, and it's burning her alive, but it is all she wants. She wants to share and exist and love, but it won't stop hurting, and she can't stop screaming, and if she lets anyone hear her, they recoil. They can only stand her if they can't hear her, and she can't bear being without them. She doesn't understand; she just wants peace—wants everyone to have peace. And if she has to scream, if she has to hurt, she wants someone to see it. She wants them to see it and not hate her for feeling it in front of them.

She can't.

I reach out and grab her hand. She's not actually here physically, but I can still touch her, guiding her hand to my ear, pulling it back to my trembling face. The screaming starts again, and I can't lift it. It cuts as deep as empathy ever has and keeps digging.

She's been torn apart. Her sister is dead—in an instant, without saying goodbye. Her son is still burning, and he is burning everything with him. And he is using her to do it. It hurts her and it hurts me.

"Share it with me," I growl through clenched teeth. "I can take it. I can handle it. I can see it and you at the same time. I promise." She can't understand the words, but she understands the intent.

The image of her as a woman collapses. She is just smoke now, but she is still screaming—I can still feel it. And I promise to keep feeling it until we both leave this world. *That* she understands most of all. It's why she shared the truth with me, about myself. Because we both know what has to happen.

She wants to be free. She shows me an image of another world, clean and vibrant. Untouched. More sisters, like Manara; people who will love her—if she can reach them. If she can pull herself back together. She just wants to leave; is begging for it. She wants to go home, but she wants to undo any harm she has done first. She wants to heal the scars left by her power, and she wants my help to do it.

"I understand," I whisper.

"What?" Riley asks.

"I'm dead. Mirage helped Sarafyna, and Sara uses that to keep me alive. But she wants to go, Riley. She wants to help, but after that . . . there is no place for her here, in this world, don't you see? This world doesn't need a god; it groans for ever meeting one. Even one composed of kindness was just a tool of death and hatred, and she doesn't understand why.

"She has no concept of worship or power. She created people, not realizing some of them would see that act as one of authority. They were to be friends and equals, but her son saw them as lesser, and any response but deference as disrespect. And she never understood that. Even now, she doesn't understand where everything went wrong, and all she can think to do is leave," I explain.

"And you . . ." Riley trails off. I nod.

"I am alive because she is here. But she's right. This world is no place for gods or corpses."

Riley is silent in response, so I ask Mirage another question, sending her an image of two women, friends and sisters. One of great empathy, taking on the form of the world but lying dead. *What about Manara?* It's a simple question, one I barely understand myself, having just learned exactly what mana actually was fifteen minutes ago. She sends an image back of green grass and vibrant crop fields. Of her sister, resting and pleased. Like fertilizer to the soil, playing the proper role of the dead.

The Original must be wrong; she can't come back. That's what Mirage is saying. *Manara is dead, like me, and she will always be dead.* I get it.

"You're just going to die? Just like that?" Riley asks. I shrug.

"I honestly don't know. I think so. But hey, maybe I'll go with our new friend here," I say. I can still hear the screaming. "Maybe my girlfriend will figure something else out. What I'm going to do is the same as it was before: I'm going to fight, and what happens after that, well . . . that's between me and God."

Riley sets her jaw then nods once. "Moron," she whispers again, looking up. "So what do we do?"

Mirage answers both of us, showing us a path. It feels like danger and hatred, like the end of all things and an impassable barrier. But at its center is a heart of wood. I can feel it connected to the stone around us. Feeding it. If we crush it, we can leave.

But as soon as we step outside this circle to find it, the Original and the Void are going to throw everything they have at us.

"Are you ready?" I ask.

CHAPTER FORTY-SIX

Heart of the Stone

The moment we step out of the circle, the woods react, the stones beneath our feet breaking and contorting to comply with our enemy's wishes. Void energy erupts like geysers, and the sky seems to crack.

"This won't be enough," I growl.

They had the right idea with the first attack: throw innocents at us, fill the sky with the void. But whatever Mirage did, we are nowhere near the tortured souls who held me back before. It is safe to use all my mana here—and I can still hear Mirage screaming. She is perhaps the most ancient source of grief in this world, and it's no longer muffled. Not for me. And who is trying to stop me but the direct source of that grief himself?

My boot touches the dirt, and the world changes with it. As the earth tears itself apart and launches at me, my mana erupts from me in all directions; force, lightning, and air lashing out and sending the projectiles everywhere but where we stand. Riley has her void mana ready, but she doesn't need it. Again, riot spikes fall from everywhere, but they do little. They may disperse mana, but not the natural effects created by it. Powerful wind throws every spike away like so much worthless debris.

"You were pretty confident before we intruded on your cute little stone," I shout. I know they are listening—the architects of this stone. The Original and the Void. The Void and the Original. I speak with mana like the world itself, and my intent demands to be known. "When you had us cornered, before you saw your own tool of hate and death ripe and ready to bludgeon you."

I step forward again, the sound of my footstep screaming through the world around me. Sound mana assaults everything but Riley, shattering stone like glass. Vines of blood tear through the air, desperate to bind me, but shrivel in the heat. Blades of wind try to cut at me, but they are smothered by my air.

I remember when I saw Godfrey with his full aura for the first time. It was like baroque glass on reality, cracking it, defying it. I'd thought it was unassailable, like fighting it would be death. Right now, my aura is not glass. No, it is tectonic. Reality doesn't distort to accommodate the pure mana around me—it shifts to get the fuck out of my way. Each step I take creates continents from Pangea.

"But you remember now, don't you?" I threaten. "You remember why I'm here? Why I, of all people, am going to eat your heart in your own goddamn kitchen?" They know. But hearing me say it, especially Oakley, may kill them before I get the chance.

Riley has begun countering any void energy erupting from the ground with her own mana, keeping the only dangerous weapon they have safely contained. As such, pillars of lava erupt alongside them, less dangerous but carefully calculated to shake me. And shake me they do, but they only make me furious. They are Oakley's answer to me. I clench my fists.

"Mirage showed me, you know. She showed me what you did to my girlfriend when she was only a child. When you force-fed her poison to keep her weak. When you tried to own her body. When you tried to tell her who and what she was, by force, so she would be ripe to consume and use for yourself," I hiss. I don't know when Oakley and the Original started working together, but I know they were both involved in hurting Sarafyna, and I know they are both going to suffer for it.

I keep walking, glaring at the pillars of useless lava; the weapon used to kill my brother. I get the message, but that means they get mine. They collapse under my glare, force mana crushing any pressure they could possibly build.

I bare my fangs as I continue to speak. "She was so, so scared. She was a child. Terrified. Alone. Mutating against her will. Manipulated and abused. But you know what? She was still stronger than you. Even as a terrified child, desperate to see her father again, Sara was stronger than you. Even as you offered her more pain and trauma than you could ever grasp, she was stronger than both of you. Even as she lashed out blindly, desperately, hopelessly, she still managed to answer you in kind, to make you just as afraid as she was."

I clench my fist, and a wall of stone turns to dust in front of us. I can see it just ahead, tangled in roots and connected to dozens of trees: a wooden heart. The core of this stone.

"She wanted help, and she got it. She wanted you to hurt, and she got it. She wanted you afraid, and who else would she bring but the woman who terrified you so much you had to flee to an entirely new planet to feel safe again. I get it. Lava pillars. My trauma. Sara's trauma. Throw them in our faces. Because you, Oakley, you have to deal with the same. Because your trauma has a name, a face, and teeth that rend and tear—and she knows your fucking name. That's why I'm here. Because a scared girl reached out with nothing but the desperate hope to be saved and to stop the people hurting her. And she found your nightmares, Oakley. She found me."

The ground tries to tremor beneath us while the trees try to scream and bleed and distract. The air tries to turn to ice while the dirt wants to shift to mud, too thick to walk through. Leaves and pines fly toward us like blades and needles, but I decline, my mana scowling at every attempt to harm either of us. Ice evaporates into harmless steam. Leaves burn to ash. The ground turns to steady steel, immovable beneath my feet. The sounds are muted so only Mirage's screams can be heard. I continue to move forward.

"And you, the so-called *Original*. I think I'll call you Alpha; a fitting name. It does imply originality, but it's also adopted by the pathetic and insecure where I come from. Mirage doesn't understand rage; she understands fear and betrayal and hurt. You taught her those. Even still, she can't conceive of hate or anger. But I know you. I've met you too many times: abusive pricks who want to own people, who call control *protection*, and force *love*.

"You're afraid too—terrified that your greatest victim will learn to see you, learn to loathe you. Well, she's not alone anymore. You may have most of her power and may be using it to set yourself up as a god, but I have her pain and her grief." The trees move, trying to block my path to the heart. They last less than a breath before they are splinters in my path. "I have her pain and grief," I repeat. "And believe me, I can conceive of rage."

The only answer I receive is more desperate attacks, but I can't be stopped. Not by these men. Not right now. There is a reason they were too afraid to come here in person, why they are attacking with a world they control and their faces hidden. I keep moving, entirely unimpeded despite their attempts, until it is right in front of me: a heart of wood, suspended in the air by the roots connecting it to the trees around it. It's beating, taunting my still heart. But not for long.

"That's why I'm here, because at your core, deep down past your superiority complexes and the pedestals you've built for yourselves, you are both cowards, afraid of your mothers loving other men more than you, and little girls who can say no. Because I am every woman, and you are alone. Because you are afraid." I reach out and grip the heart in my left hand. I can feel the shift immediately. This part won't be easy; it's going to take most of my mana. I look at Riley. "I need you to protect me. Distract them, and I will get us out of here."

She nods in understanding as white mana explodes from her. She doesn't have nearly my aura, but her aspect is a destructive one, and her father is too afraid to come here and match it with his own. It's her turn to speak to her father.

Meanwhile, I clench my fist and dig my claws in. It fights me, even as real blood leaks from the wood. Pouring my mana into it, it fights the Nexus energy, so dense, so determined that I have to tune out the attacks coming at me. I trust Riley to protect me, and so I pour everything into crushing the heart of the stone while Riley speaks up for the first time.

"Moron," she says. "You're a moron, Rowan. Oakley. Dad. Whoever you are. Are you any of these? Really? Growing up, you were a monument. You were storm clouds in the sky, and I sought shelter when you approached, because that's who you wanted to be: The man on the peak of every mountain. The best at everything you do. Unassailable talent and genius. You wanted to be a god, an object of desire and worship. But you never were. You were never good at anything but being a sage—an ability which, it turns out, is entirely stolen. You were never real, were you?

"So many years propping you up, bringing praise to you with my abilities. Until I turned out to be a woman, then I was just an embarrassment to be punished for existing. You are no more my father than you are a god. No more than your name is Rowan. You are a ghost, an idiot, a fool in the king's court—in Alpha's court—playing your games with people's lives and homes but running, over and over, when you are eventually unmasked as a ghost. When you are eventually hated. And you always are, aren't you? By your daughters. By your wives. By your sons. Even by your sycophants, if you don't replace them frequently enough."

I can hear her breath growing more frantic as she screams at him. She is fighting as she does, but I can feel it: the yelling is helping. The pressure of my mana is collapsing the heart in my hand. Blood no longer leaks, now spurting and spattering in all directions. Still, it beats in my hand.

"But you are a moron. You are stupid and small and sad and lonely. I hate you, Dad. I have always hated you, long before you tried to punish me. Long before I supposedly humiliated you. And I am in good company because even those who love you don't respect you. All the envy in the world can't make you respectable. I fucking hate you, and I'm going to kill you. Now that I know that, in addition to everything else, you are terrified. You have always been weak, and now I know. You—" She cuts off in the middle, and I hear cracking noises, then screaming, from her.

I put everything I have into crushing the heart. Vines finally reach me, wrapping themselves around me. They burn and tear at my clothes, but they can't touch my left arm, where all my aura is focused. So they pull. And pull. And pull. I grimace as my right arm is jerked back in an attempt to tear me off the heart, feeling the skin in my shoulder tearing as the steel is pulled from it.

I join the chorus of screams as my hand closes the rest of the way with such force my claws stab straight through the heart and into my own hand. Before I can even feel the pain, the world begins to melt around me.

CHAPTER FORTY-SEVEN

The Broken Dead

For a few moments, nothing feels real. The horrifying world of the stone around me washes away like blood in a river, and I am falling, falling, falling. I am in a world of colorful and endless ribbons, looking for a home, and then I am held by Mirage. I can still hear her screaming; it resonates with my soul in the same way a broken tooth can be felt in the ear. I ache for her, for the pain she can't escape, and the wounds she can't heal. She feels that, and the empathy alone is almost like ice over an aching head. She is grateful, despite the pain she still feels.

A hand of mist meets mine, and half-formed digits run across the splintered heart that bleeds through my fingers. She feels such . . . disappointment as she touches it. Not like a mother for a child but like insects under the skin of an apple.

It's shattered hope; a wound felt a thousand times before. This heart . . . it belongs to someone. Or belonged, at least. Someone she offered her trust to, who used it against her. There is a strange mix of emotions around it, and I struggle to interpret all them. She is angry, and she is hurt, but she is also confused. The stone was made with her power, her sense of self, but it was used for something she hated that hurt her. And she couldn't understand why.

Over and over, she had offered help to the desperate. Over and over, they had offered themselves to her torment. But she didn't understand people, couldn't process the betrayal in a way that would let her learn from it. She wanted to save, and she wanted to be saved. Instead, it only got worse, and it almost always hurt her more. This was the heart of someone she wanted as a friend, and she connected to it. It offered its emotions, and she offered hers in return. And that connection was used like a rope around her neck.

Her hand moves up to my arm, then my face. Her touch is a tundra, and it sends a shiver down my spine. I feel . . . recognition. Recognition and love, but not like I have ever felt for a person, more like the longing you get from a picture at a funeral. I remind her of someone she loved once. That's the only way I can make sense of it. Something about me feels—to her—like memories of Henry feel to me. It breaks my heart. It's the feeling of irreversible loss, and she feels it when she touches me. Even more, I want to set her free. I want to let her go home, and I want to hurt everyone else she has ever trusted.

She feels this too. Water fills her eyes, even as they remain incorporeal. She is grateful, and regretful. Above all else, she wants to help, and she wants to love. I will help her and, when the time comes, she will help me. That's the promise she makes me. She can't offer me the same power she offers Sara; too much is already being used just to keep me alive. But somehow, she will be there when I need her. Even she doesn't know how, but somehow, I know I can trust her.

The world starts to take form around me again, even as Mirage locks her eyes on mine. She doesn't want me to go. It feels—to her—like letting a long dead friend go. And maybe that's exactly what she's doing, because that's exactly who I am. A friend, but one who is broken and dead. But she knows she can't hold on. She knows I couldn't stay, and she'll never go home if she doesn't let me go. So, she allows herself to fade into the world of ribbons behind her, and my vision goes dark.

I take a deep, weary breath—and the stone is gone.

I stand in the middle of a stone pit. High above me is the broken glass of Markus's window, and behind me, Riley is gripping a bleeding side. And all around us are hundreds and hundreds of people, all with faces I recognize. All in their own original bodies, and none still attached to a single mass of agonized flesh.

Mirage's screaming is dulled, the power her grief gave me more distant. But we won. The first stone has been destroyed, and Mirage has part of herself back.

I sigh as the weight of my body returns to me and my fist closes around nothing but air. I can tell in a moment that I am safe. We are all safe. The sages are long gone.

I feel light and heavy at the same time. This feels like a step forward into an endless desert. There is so much left to do. The hooks of power dig into the world with the same violence and depth that my claws tore into that heart, whoever it belonged to. But I'm not alone. There are miles to go, and I am so tired, but there is also wind at my back, and I am finally starting to understand why this world is the way it is.

I close my eyes and let the moment wash over me. We won today, and we'll win tomorrow. I don't know how.

But we will win tomorrow.

About the Author

Dreamer's Riot is the author of the Otherworldly Anarchist series as well as a computer scientist and indie video game developer. Based on his experiences in the US Air Force and later as a student, his stories aim to tackle themes of power and autonomy.

www.ingramcontent.com/pod-product-compliance
Lightning Source LLC
Chambersburg PA
CBHW032352310726
48973CB00007B/1974